*D*IANA'S MOUTH DROPPED OPEN AND A WILD ENERGY played in her chest. He was darker than when she'd last seen him, and his skin looked especially tawny against the collar of his white linen shirt. The bridge of his nose was a color that suggested he had been out in the sun that day, and the expression disappearing from his face indicated that moments ago he had been having a careless good time.

"Hello, soldier," she managed at last.

"Diana?" Henry said, as though the sound of her name might confirm her unlikely presence in front of him. "How—" he stammered, "how did you come here?"

"I was looking for you." All the sentences she'd imagined saying to him escaped her. The only sentence she could think of was the one she'd just uttered, and it seemed to her, at that moment, to contain the only relevant information.

ALSO BY ANNA GODBERSEN

Splendor

A *Luxe* NOVEL

ANNA GODBERSEN

HARPER

An Imprint of HarperCollinsPublishers

alloyentertainment
Produced by Alloy Entertainment
151 West 26th Street, New York, NY 10001

ON THE COVER: Dress by Maggie Sottero

Library of Congress Cataloging-in-Publication Data
Godbersen, Anna.
    Splendor : a Luxe novel / Anna Godbersen. — 1st ed.
        p.   cm.
    Summary: In 1900 New York City, fashionable debutante Diana Holland and
married soldier Henry Schoonmaker risk their place in society to be with one another.
    ISBN 978-0-06-162633-3
    [1. Social classes—Fiction.   2. Wealth—Fiction.   3. Love—Fiction.   4. Conduct
of life—Fiction.   5. New York (N.Y.)—History—1898–1951—Fiction.]   I. Title.
PZ7.G53887Sp   2009   2009035009
[Fic]—dc22   CIP
                                                                                        AC

Design by Andrea C. Uva

10 11 12 13 14   CG/RRDH   10 9 8 7 6 5 4 3 2 1
❖
First paperback edition, 2010

For Sara

FIFTY YEARS AGO, EVERY AMERICAN GIRL WANTED to be a European princess. One could detect it in her gowns and gestures, for they all tried to dress as European ladies did and to imitate the manners of Parisian salons. But now they come from the old world to see how we behave and decorate ourselves here in the United States. They stand on the decks of steamers, gloved hands gripping the guardrail as they catch their first glimpse of Manhattan, that island of towering buildings and smothering secrets, brimming with its millions of lives celebrated or forgotten in almost equal measure. What a narrow strip of land, those sea voyagers inevitably remark in surprise as they begin to take in the new world, for so *very* much to happen upon.

Of course, roughly as many ships go out of the harbor as come into it. Even those whose names are regularly cast in the smudgy glory of gossip columns, and followed in every detail by an eager public, must sometimes leave. How many top-drawer souls were entrusted to the hands of the Cunard

Company, whose twelve o'clock steamer was already drawing resolutely away from land, en route from New York to France? The crowd on the worn wood planks of the dock was growing smaller, as was the city that cropped up behind it. A gentleman or lady leaning against the rail could not even make out the handkerchiefs waving at them anymore, although they knew that fine examples of embroidery were still being held aloft in the thick summer air. Did they regard their hometown with love or nostalgia or resentment? Were they glad to see it slip by, block by block, or did they already miss its drawing rooms and shady clubs, the verdant park at its center, and the blocks of mansions lining its borders?

There, those fine New Yorkers looking back at their city might think, *if I followed that street I would arrive at Mamie Fish's house. Or I could take that one to where the William Schoonmakers live, or to the Buck mansion, or to any number of Astor holdings.* They might reflect, thinking of those landmarks, that it has always been a world that holds its children tight to its breast, or else sends them away to wander like exiles. What slights and embarrassments, what suffocating marriages and unforgivable deeds, what grand social missteps might the voyagers under that cloudless July sky be trying to escape?

For any bright sets of eyes gazing a last time at the island of their birth, there will be a certain glow of longing for what was left behind. But the anguish of leaving will dim with every passing second as the excitement of what they are yet to see grows. Especially for a girl who, say, has only recently come to understand what hearts are capable of, or where love and a healthy sense of curiosity can take her; or a fellow who has just experienced the thrill of truly cutting ties for the first time, and of stepping out as his own man. After all, it takes only a few seasons to learn how everything changes, and how quickly; to realize that the glorious and grotesque lives lived at the currently fashionable addresses will soon seem quaint and outdated. New York will always be there, but it grows stranger every day, and staying put will not make it stay the same.

And in the end it doesn't matter, because these eyes had to go, and the distance from shore has rapidly become too great to swim. There is no going back now.

One

With the younger Miss Holland, Diana, away in Paris for a finishing season, it is a most lonely social era, and we have all had to content ourselves with lesser beauties. There are those of us who remember those chocolate eyes and glossy curls and sulk in the corners at gatherings awaiting her return.

—FROM THE "GAMESOME GALLANT" COLUMN IN THE *NEW YORK IMPERIAL*, FRIDAY, JULY 6, 1900

$\mathcal{I}$N THE MORNINGS, SHE LIKED TO WALK ALONG THE seawall. She went by herself and usually only passed one or two gentlemen, canes ticking against the stone, for the locals preferred to stroll later in the day, after siesta. Lately the weather had grown extreme, and there were occasions when the ocean would sweep over her path; at first this frightened her, but by a humid Friday in early July, she had come to view it as a kind of baptism. The force of the sea—as she had written in her notebook the night before, just before falling asleep—stirred her, and soothed her, and made her feel reborn.

Once she had crossed the Paseo del Prado, she turned and headed into the old town, with its shadowy arcades and glimpses of tiled and verdant patios just beyond the crooked streets. There were more people there, lingering in arched doorways or around tables in the squares. She wore a wide, drooping straw hat, and her short brown curls were pinned up at the nape to disguise the peculiar length. Not that it mattered—she was a foreigner, and all of her peculiarities were obscured by that one vast difference. No one recognized her here; it did not matter to any of the Habaneros passing in the street that she was Diana Holland.

That was in fact her name, and in other parts of the world it carried certain implications. For instance, that she had been taught from a young age never to show the naked skin of her hands outside of her family home, nor to walk on the streets of her own city unchaperoned. And although she had routinely flaunted these restrictions, she had never known what it was to be so thoroughly free of the rules of her hometown until she had arrived in Cuba. In her light-colored, loose-fitting dress, on the streets of a very foreign capital, she was both quite noticeable and, in a manner, invisible. She was anonymous, and, like the sea, this state of being made her feel all new and clear-eyed.

The ocean was behind her now, as well as the slate gray clouds that were massing over the bay and beginning to crowd out the blue sky. The green of the palm trees appeared extreme in contrast. The air was thick and moody with the possibility of rain, and the weather looked bad, but for her there was something satisfying in such a landscape. The shades of dark, the looming quality, all seemed to her a kind of expression of what was in her soul. Sooner or later the downpour would begin, first in big drops, then in heavy sheets that would soak the striped awnings and flood the gutters. It was not long ago—a matter of weeks, although sometimes it felt like forever—that she had arrived in Havana, but she was a quick study of atmospheric disturbances. This one had the color of suffering, and she would know.

She was alone and thousands of miles from home, but of course it wasn't *all* suffering. If Diana had been pressed, she would have had to admit that there was only one thing she really wanted for. Even the loss of her curly mane of hair had not been truly bitter. She had cut it because of Henry Schoonmaker—she'd foolishly tried to enlist in the army to follow him, even though he was her sister Elizabeth's former fiancé, and currently married to a rather terrifying girl, who as a maiden had gone by the name Penelope Hayes. A thing Diana wouldn't do in pursuit of Henry had yet to present itself. Before this she had been a barmaid on a luxury liner, and before that she had hustled her way to Chicago on trains. That was when she still believed that Henry was in a regiment headed for the Pacific by way of San Francisco.

She had gotten used to the short hair, which had been a self-inflicted wound in the first place, and anyway there was nothing chopped tresses could do to contradict the rosy femininity of Diana's petite body. In the previous months she had found herself capable in ways she could not possibly have imagined back in the cozy rooms of the townhouses of old New York. She had never, during her adventures,

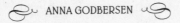

gone without food or slept out of doors. But, oh, the lack of
Henry—how that wrung her delicate heart.

Diana had been all manner of places since her boy-short
hair had failed to convince the United States Army that she
was ready for basic training back in March, but none of them
had looked remotely like this. As she walked, she couldn't
shake the sensation of being in a very old city—New York
wasn't so much younger, she knew, but somehow it effaced its
history more effectively. She liked the idea that the cathedrals
she passed, the façades with their wrought iron detailing and
the red roofs above them, might still shelter aging conquista-
dors.

Officially she was in Paris. That was what the papers
were reporting, with a little help from her friend Davis
Barnard, who wrote the "Gamesome Gallant" column in the
New York Imperial. He was also the reason she knew Henry
wasn't where he was supposed to be, either—apparently old
William Schoonmaker held such sway that he had not only
secured a safer post for his son in Cuba, but had managed
to bully all the New York newspapermen into keeping mum
about the transfer. Diana liked the idea that neither of them
was where they were supposed to be. They each had a decoy
self, out there in the world, and meanwhile their real selves
were moving stealthily, ever closer to one another.

Presently she passed through a square where dogs lay

languidly in the shadows and men lingered over their coffees in outdoor cafés. She had never been to Europe and so she couldn't say for sure, but it seemed to her there was something Continental about the city, with its long memory and crumbling buildings, the ghosts in its alleys and the warbling of its Catholic bells, its slow and pleasant traditions. There was that smell in the air that always comes just before it rains, when the dry dirtiness of a city rises up a final time before it is washed away, and Diana began to hurry a little in anticipation of an onslaught. She wanted to arrive home, to her little rented rooms, and hopefully avoid being drenched.

She had reached the edge of the square, and was moving quickly enough that she found it prudent to put her hand up to better secure her hat. Ahead of her were two American soldiers wearing fitted dark blue jackets and stone-colored slacks, and Diana's eye was inexorably drawn to the easy gait of the taller one with the jauntily cocked hat. It was magnetic, his stride, and familiar, and for a moment she swore the sun must have broken through the clouds to cast the skin at the back of his neck a golden shade she knew well.

"Henry!" she gasped out loud. It was characteristic of Diana that she spoke before she thought.

The tall soldier turned first, slowly. For a moment her lungs had ceased to function; her feet felt like unwieldy hooves and wouldn't move forward, no matter what urging she gave them. She forced oxygen in through her nostrils, but by then the man's face was disappointingly visible, and she saw that the features were too soft and boyish, the chin too covered by reddish beard, to belong to Henry. His face was confused, devoid of recognition, but he went on staring at her. His mouth hung open a few seconds before breaking into a grin.

"My name ain't Henry," he drawled. "But you, little lady, you can call me by whatever name you like."

His eyes went on gazing at her until they seemed a little fevered, and she couldn't help but return his smile faintly. She liked being appreciated, but she did not want to be stalled. She had made the mistake of straying from Henry when he had not seemed to be hers before, and the recollection still horrified her. There were American troops all over the city, and someday soon she would run into the right one. She was as sure of it, as of something fated.

In the meantime, she gave the tall soldier a wink—though not a very special one—and then hurried on, toward the Calle Obrapia, where she would ready herself for evening. The day was young, and everything in the city was bright, and Henry was out there somewhere, and she wanted to prepare for the day when the stars arranged themselves auspiciously, and long-lost lovers came face-to-face.

Two

. . . Of course no one has seen Miss Diana's older sister, the former Miss Elizabeth Holland, as of late, either. She has happily wed her late father's business partner, Snowden Trapp Cairns, and if rumors are to be believed, there will be a new member of the family by fall. We congratulate the Cairnses; the lovely Mrs. deserves nothing less after her harrowing experience of last winter, when she was kidnapped by a love-crazed former Holland family employee and barely escaped with her life after a violent scene in Grand Central Station. . . .

—FROM THE "GAMESOME GALLANT" COLUMN IN THE *NEW YORK IMPERIAL*, FRIDAY, JULY 6, 1900

*T*HE BRANCHES OF THE TREES WERE SO THICK AND verdant over the pathways of Central Park that Elizabeth Holland Cairns—perched on the velvet seat of a phaeton, under the partially opened black leather roof—felt almost as though she had entered into the shade of a grotto. It was summer and the air was dense with moisture, and no one could blame the horses for moving slowly. She had not been out much since the day in late winter that had quietly changed her surname; a lady in her condition was not supposed to be seen. But the heat was so severe that even the walls of her apartment had seemed to sweat, and eventually her husband had convinced her that a drive in the park would do her good. She stared at the dappled light on the dusty path ahead and let her hand rest on the round belly that protruded from her petite frame.

The pleasant sound of plodding hooves was interrupted by the voice of her husband, Snowden. "We don't want you out in this heat *too* much," he said, before adding a gentle "my dear."

For as long as anybody could remember, Elizabeth had been the kind of young lady who did not merely heed propriety but experienced the upholding of gentle traditions with genuine pleasure. When they were transgressed, she felt a corollary deep shame, but she was currently protected from voyeurs not only by the folding leather roof, but also by a broad straw hat. Her spirit sagged a little at his suggestion, for she was enjoying the leafy smell and the occasional sight of a long skirt swishing back and forth as a girl strolled with her fellow.

Elizabeth disguised her disappointment with a docile smile and inclined her heart-shaped face and brown eyes in Snowden's direction. He wasn't handsome, but he did have a neat, not unpleasant appearance, with his preternaturally blond hair worn close to his head and his blocklike features unimpeded by beard.

"You know best," she added, perhaps as a small consolation, a show of respect to make up for the secret act of equivocation that she committed every time she uttered the word *husband*. For husband to her was the late Will Keller, while the man everyone erroneously assumed was the father of her child was no more than a kind of shield to protect her from society's censure. Romance had never been a factor in what only a few people knew to be her second marriage.

The balance of the phaeton shifted as Snowden leaned forward to give instructions to their coachman, but Elizabeth scarcely heard him. The carriage was turning; the horses were pulling them in another direction, but none of it mattered to her particularly. When she closed her eyes, she was with Will again, walking across the warm brown hills of California, planning out a life together. She had loved Will from the time he came to work for her family—he was just a child then, and he had been orphaned by one of those fires that swept through tenements entrapping the poor souls who lived there in a final earthly conflagration. Neither of them could ever remember when their camaraderie became romantic love, but once it had, that love dictated a whole new way of life. They had been trying to return to California, where they had been happy—they had almost boarded their train—when they were spotted by a group of policemen who shot Will down.

Elizabeth's eyes opened suddenly; she was a little startled by where her thoughts had taken her. This mixture of bitter memory, current contentment, and ever-present guilt brewed under the former Miss Holland's straw hat as their carriage drew out of the park and into an unexpected intersection. They were on the southern tip of the park, traveling past the Plaza and New Netherland hotels and across Fifth Avenue. Their home, a modest eight-room apartment in the Dover, was on the park in the Seventies, but she now saw that their driver was acting on instructions to go downtown. Her lips parted and her irises drifted in her husband's direction. But he did not turn toward her, and she was not the kind of woman to question.

They headed down Madison, a fact Elizabeth apprehended with relief. She was less likely to be recognized here, and if she was, then she felt sure that it would be by someone with enough manners not to mention seeing the former virgin princess of elite Manhattan in a public place in her swollen condition. Fifth was where showy people built houses that looked like monuments to worldly accomplishment, so that they could be spied upon and spy back in equal measure. It was the place for people like the Hayeses, whose only daughter, Penelope, was her sometime friend, and who, given the choice, would always pick the dress most likely to draw attention to her person. Now Penelope was said to be such good friends with Carolina Broad, the heiress who in her previous life had been Elizabeth's own lady's maid. She was having a party tonight, which everyone had clambered to get invited to as though her pedigree were not make-believe, and which they were all probably getting gaudy for right now, back on that more strutting avenue and everywhere else. The cast members were all different from a year and a half ago, when Elizabeth was the debutante everyone wanted to know. It was dizzying, she reflected, how quickly the sets changed. But she was on Madison now, where the old families lived in handsomer, quieter houses, according to hallowed traditions and without such an appetite for exhibition. Elizabeth was relieved to have no parties to go to that evening, and felt at peace thinking what the plain brownstone faces of those houses signified.

"Isn't that where the Harman Livingstons live?" Snowden asked her, after a prolonged silence, gesturing at a stone mansion on a corner. She smiled and nodded, for though she was sure her husband knew the answer, he was allowing her to play tour guide in her native city, and she was happy for the opportunity to accommodate.

"And there the Whitehall Vanderbilts?"

Elizabeth nodded again, and as they went farther she answered similar questions and even suggested a few points of interest on her own. It pleased her to be giving Snowden something, even if it was just little parcels of information, and her sense of enjoyment suffered only when she heard him say, "And there the Cuttings?"

"Oh, yes." Elizabeth's voice fell to a whisper, and she turned so abruptly to look that, for the first time that afternoon, enough light fell on her delicate features that she might have made herself recognizable.

For the only male heir of the Cutting shipping fortune was a boy named Teddy, who'd proposed marriage to her twice, when Will was still alive, without her or anybody else taking him very seriously. He was Teddy, after all, this friend who sat by her at her father's funeral, and was of such a quiet, subtle nature that he was almost invisible to her when her head was so full of the strapping boy who'd lived in her family's carriage house. That past winter, when she'd traveled to Florida with her old friend Penelope, Teddy had hinted at the feelings he still harbored for her, and she had hoped, during a brief window between the day she realized she was carrying a child and his enlisting in the army, that he might propose to her again. She had even, if she was being honest, yearned for a kiss or a little tenderness from him, but that was a desire she had since buried rather deep, and now had difficulty looking at straight on. After all, such longing meant the betrayal of not one but two husbands. Even if it hadn't, Teddy was now stationed far away in the Philippines, and Gemma Newbold was said to be expecting a proposal from him upon his return.

"And that house . . . ?"

Elizabeth blinked and tried to shake off the disorienting guilt. The house Snowden indicated was a well-appointed brownstone, three high windows across and four stories tall. It was elegant and understated and stood in the middle of the block on the west side of the street. Over the front door, there was a handsome fanlight of white and gold stained glass. They were in the low Thirties, not altogether far from the house on Gramercy Park where she had grown up and where her family still lived. She should know this house, and yet she didn't.

"I'm not sure that I recognize . . ." Her brow furrowed, she turned toward him.

"I believe," Snowden began, a smile creeping onto his face and his gaze now holding hers, "that is where the Snowden Cairnses live."

"Pardon?" Elizabeth's fingers rose involuntarily to cover her heart. Already she could feel gratitude spreading across her chest and edging out the dismay she'd so recently experienced. It was just the sort of house she would choose for herself: large but not ostentatious, serious and well built according to the old New York idea of gentility.

"The baby will be here soon," Snowden said simply, "and I thought it was time my wife had a proper home."

Elizabeth stared at the house where she would raise her child, becoming surer with each passing second that it was the perfect place. "Oh, thank you, Mr. Cairns, thank you so much," she gushed when she was able. She blinked at him, still a little light-headed with incredulity. She was terribly lucky, she reminded herself, and should be more vigilant to not forget the fact. The sounds of traffic were growing louder in the late afternoon, and all around them the buildings took on a golden hue from the ripening sun. The very natural smile that the sight of this house had brought to Elizabeth's face held. Then Snowden leaned forward and committed an act without precedent. He put his mouth against Elizabeth's and kissed her.

There had never been any suggestion of romance between them, and the shock of the gesture changed the temperature inside of her all over again. Perhaps she looked as scandalized as she felt, because Snowden then patted her on the knee the way a grandfather might if she were a young girl up past her bedtime.

"We can move in as soon as you like," he told her in a formal voice, before inclining forward and instructing the driver to take them back up to the Dover so that they could begin packing. He did not so much as look at her during the entire ride uptown, and by the time they arrived she was convinced that, if there *had* been anything lustful in that kiss, it was nothing more than her guilty, overactive imagination.

Three

The situation in the Pacific is a stark one, for though the Spanish have been properly licked, the American commanders, before they attempted to hold provinces of 200,000 or 300,000 hostile inhabitants, had scarcely any idea of the size of the Philippine Islands. According to some experts, the American presence there is slightly over half the size it need be to secure the region. In light of this, it is especially heroic for blue bloods of our own city to be serving there, among them Mr. Teddy Cutting and Mr. Henry Schoonmaker, whose exact locations or regiments are naturally not disclosed for safety's sake. . . .

——FROM THE *NEW YORK IMPERIAL* EDITORIAL PAGE,
FRIDAY, JULY 6, 1900

"THEY SAY THEY'LL BE CALLING TROOPS HOME SOON," Colonel Copper said, leaning forward to refresh his drink from a wicker basket stocked with rum, mint leaves, and sugar. The basket sat on the polished blond planks of a large sailboat, a sailboat that Henry Schoonmaker was steering across Havana Bay. Henry was wearing a white linen shirt, unbuttoned to the sternum, and light-colored army-issue slacks; beads of sweat lazed on his skin. Stubble shaded the aristocratic line of his jaw, and his dark hair was pomaded into sections. When he had first volunteered, he'd been careful to always keep his face neatly shaven, but there didn't seem to be much point anymore. "Home, and then on to the Philippines where they are really needed."

Though the word *home* had piqued his interest, Henry's black gaze shifted from the mountainous clouds collecting over the gray-blue water, where vessels of all kinds drifted in the afternoon breeze, and across the length of the boat, where a few army men who far outranked him whispered to pretty local girls poorly disguising their boredom. The ivory sails bloomed overhead; the weather had not yet become anything to worry about, although there was less sun than before and a storm was coming, tonight or tomorrow. The boat, which had been commandeered from a fleeing Spanish naval officer, was as well appointed as some of those the Schoonmaker family maintained, and although Henry felt comfortable at its helm, he was having trouble deriving any pleasure from sailing that day. It had always been one of his diversions, but New York and the person he had been there seemed strange to him now.

"They'll be sending us on to the Philippines, then?" he asked, keeping one hand on the polished oak tiller and the other on his drink. His old friend Teddy Cutting was stationed in the Pacific—they had enlisted at the same time, and yet their careers as soldiers could not have been more dissimilar. It was the place where Henry had once imagined he might die, and if not die, experience real danger and then discover what it was to be a man.

The colonel glanced up, and his drooping mustache rose with the corners of his smile. "Some troops will go, but don't worry, you won't be among them, my boy." As he settled himself back against the pillows that lined the deck, the leather flask on his belt made a swishing noise; it was, like all the colonel's affectations, suggestive of an expensive sportsmanlike masculinity. Henry had, on occasion, accused Teddy of being too serious, but he heartily wished he could be with him now and escape the idiot company in which he currently found himself. "You are too important to me here."

This was not intended as a mockery, but Henry couldn't hear it as anything else. His great importance was his ability to sail small boats in the bay for the little races that the colonel liked to entertain himself with, ever since the June elections and the peaceful period they had ushered in. He knew he was ridiculous for feeling disappointment at the colonel's assurance, but he was having difficulty viewing the man, and life under his command, as anything but a joke. Henry brought his glass up to his lips and sipped before looking away across the seascape to the inlet where the ships came into harbor. The *Morro* glowered from atop the hill, fearsome and war-like, on the opposite side of the bay from the tiled roofs and arcade-lined squares of the old town.

"No, I wouldn't let you leave Havana now. Not when the race against Lieutenant Colonel Harvey is in a few days!" Colonel Copper chuckled. Lieutenant Colonel Harvey responded in kind. Henry glanced at them, seeing only the popped red blood vessels on their broad noses, and then away. They said it was only ninety miles between Cuba and Florida, and sometimes in his dreams he swam it. He had been to Florida once, as a civilian, last winter. He had made a terrible mistake there and given into the desires of his duplicitous wife, but he could also remember those warm days before his error, when he still had a chance at something true. "You know, señoritas, Henry here comes from a very old, very prestigious family. The Schoonmakers are said to be one of the ten richest . . ."

Henry blinked into the breeze and almost pitied Colonel Copper. After all, he was only guilty of the same delusion that plagued most people: He believed that he wanted to be like the Schoonmakers, to own yachts and Fifth Avenue mansions and be written about in the papers, and he could not comprehend what Henry had only recently begun to understand, that all of that only meant that it was rather difficult to do what one actually wanted to do, or love the woman one was actually in love with. Henry hadn't even been capable of enlisting right, for God's sake. Colonel Copper had assessed Henry, determined that he was one of *the* Schoonmakers, and more or less relieved him of any kind of active duty. Thus had Henry's vision of patriotic service and experience ended; that was back in April. Most of his days since then had begun with sailing and ended in the humid barracks whispering the name Diana Holland while he tried, in vain, to sleep.

For a brief moment, Diana Holland's love had been a possibility for him, the shimmering, pure goal that would give all his shiftless years meaning. But then he'd behaved execrably, and brought a horrid cynicism into that sweet girl's life. If he was lucky, his dreams about her were from the period when she still had cause to believe in him, but as often as not they were nightmares of the evening when he walked into a room and saw her caught up in the arms of his wife's brother. There she had been, his girl, in the shadows, against a wall, in the grip of that inveterate gambler. It was a scene that still sickened Henry, but one he knew he well deserved. The memory of it made him want to die, but there was no chance of dying here, except by drink, which he went on downing at more or less the same rate as he had in New York. The only change in him was the color of his skin, which had grown brown in the sun.

"Aren't the ladies here lovely and compliant?" he heard the colonel saying behind him, and though Henry did not turn to look, he felt it was safe to assume that he was making awful leering faces at the girls under his arms. "Don't they wink and flirt as girls back home never let themselves do?"

Henry was overtaken by the sudden desire either to throw himself overboard or be very, very drunk already. The former seemed the more heroic choice, but upon reflection he realized that the fall would not kill him, it would only get him wet, and already he was sweating in irritation at all the colonel's inane chatter.

"Come, Schoonmaker, stop staring out to sea! Let's get you a girl."

An angry light darted through Henry's black eyes, and his fingers gripped at the tiller. He knew that the colonel was now standing up, because the balance of the hull shifted below him. Still he refused to look. All of a sudden he was furious, for reasons he could not begin to understand. He only knew he was tired of Cuba, and of himself, and of all the places he'd ever been and all the things he'd ever wanted, save one.

"Oh, Lord have mercy, Schoonmaker, your wife won't find out! Live a little, while you can! She can't be *that* lovely."

"It's not my wife I'm worried about." Henry stood and spun around so that he was facing his commanding officer, unbalancing the hull again and causing the ladies closer to the bow to cry out in fright. He remembered one of them saying that she couldn't swim as she'd stepped nervously from the pier, and though in some corner of his mind he worried for her safety, his thoughts were elsewhere. "But, yes—the woman I am faithful to *is* that lovely."

"Henry," Colonel Copper went on, growing faux-serious, "I am your superior, and I *insist* that you have a good time!"

The two men faced off by the stern. Soon a cloud would pass, and the situation would come to seem absurd. But the colonel was several drinks into his leisurely afternoon, and the righteousness was heady in Henry's veins. He stared back at the older man with all the rage and confusion he felt toward a life that kept bringing him back, despite all his best efforts, to afternoons of cocktails and boats drifting in no particular direction. Neither said anything, and perhaps in a moment the silence would have reduced them both to laughter. But then a passing cargo ship caused a wave, which rocked their vessel, and the girl who couldn't swim grabbed clumsily for a rope to hang on to. Her flailing set the mechanics of the boat in motion: The boom swung across the deck, narrowly missing Henry; he was relieved to find himself still safely on board. In the next moment he heard splashing and sputtering, and realized that while he'd been spared, the colonel had been knocked forward into the water.

For the first time all afternoon, Henry cracked a smile. The sight of the colonel floundering in the tranquil, opaque water was too comical to inspire any other reaction. The girls all shrieked and crawled forward to look at the foolish American whose fancy uniform, like the rest of him, was now submerged in the bay. They shrieked again when Henry undid the remaining buttons of his shirt, threw it on the deck, and dove in. He plunged deep into the cool silence; for that one moment of immersion it seemed to him that Florida was not, after all, too far to swim. The water, however murky, had a transformative effect. By the time Henry had gotten his arms around the colonel, gasped for breath at the surface, and pushed him back onto the deck of the boat, his anger had dissipated.

"Are you all right, sir?" he asked, hoisting the colonel on

the deck. The resentful lethargy he'd been feeling was washed away.

"Yes, my boy," he replied, clapping Henry on the wet back. There was something stunned in his appearance, but there was nothing really wrong with him. "All in good fun. I won't harangue you about girls anymore, so long as you pour yourself a drink and at least pretend to relax a little."

"Yes, sir." The air felt cooler now, and Henry pulled the sleeves of his shirt back over his slick arms. When he was finished with the buttons, he accepted the fresh glass of rum that Harvey's girl had poured for him. Drinks were being passed all around.

"To Cuba," the girl said, raising her glass, "*y Los Estados Unidos.*"

They all drank to a long friendship between their countries, and Henry, in his own mind, said his usual private toast: To Diana, whatever she might be doing these days, and to the grain of a chance that she might one day forgive him.

Four

The party that everyone wants to attend this evening is being hosted by Miss Carolina Broad, at her new townhouse on East Sixty-third off the park, and will be attended by such luminaries as the Prince of Bavaria, Mr. Reginald Newbold and his new bride, Adelaide, and Mrs. Henry Schoonmaker, the former Miss Penelope Hayes, who has been convalescing since a small family tragedy of early spring, and who may cause something of a scandal by going out so soon when her husband is still serving his country abroad. One invitee sure to be absent is Miss Broad's new neighbor, Leland Bouchard, whose European tour was extended several times, and whose Atlantic voyage back to New York has been delayed by bad weather....

—FROM THE SOCIETY PAGE OF THE *NEW-YORK NEWS OF THE WORLD GAZETTE*, FRIDAY, JULY 6, 1900

*T*HE HEAT WAS STIFLING, AND EVERY CONCEIVABLE inch of floor—from the shiny granite of the foyer, up the polished oak of the spiral staircase, to the herringbone parquet on the parlor level—was obscured by black dress shoes or sweeping skirts. Perfume and innuendo filled the air, although one could scarcely hear the voice of one's neighbor, if that lady or gentleman were speaking at anything like an appropriate level. Music played, but only the best dancers kept going, for space was at a premium and everyone would have thought poorly of a less talented couple throwing their limbs about at a time like this. The throng pressed against the ivory-and-rose-flocked wallpaper of the first three stories, and although the windows had been left open, the air inside remained stagnant. Of course, no one dreamed of leaving. On that Friday evening, there was no place any of them would have rather been.

Through the crush and up and down the stairs darted the hostess, Carolina Broad. She caused a little stir wherever she went, and not only because of the lavender silk dress that revealed her shoulders, hugged her hips, and trailed behind her like a bridal train. The beadwork on her bodice was so minute, it might have escaped the attention of her guests, had it not been for the incandescence those beads created in the chandelier light. There had been a time when she would have hidden her shoulders—they were big and bony, and in the summer they were darkened by freckles the same way her nose was—but she had learned not a few things since inheriting the mighty fortune of her late benefactor, Mr. Carey Lewis Long-horn, and among them was that a girl, if she is clever, owns what she already has. She had come from a Western family, a copper-smelting fortune, which was somewhat modest compared to her current holdings. That was the official story, at any rate, and her big, bare shoulders, their pale skin adorned with auburn flecks, the teeth that were slightly oversized for her mouth, confirmed it. Now, if she seemed a little large or coarse in places, it only enhanced her aura.

The evening was a triumph, but she could not begin to enjoy it. The one person whose presence she cared about was somewhere out on the Atlantic.

Perhaps to distract herself from disappointment, she moved hurriedly, setting off little currents and eddies among the guests who filled the halls and galleries of her new townhouse—No. 15, with a redbrick façade and tall, narrow layout. She had wanted one of those grandly squatting mono-liths that they built on Fifth Avenue nowadays, but she had been very specific about wanting a home on this particular block, and number fifteen had been the only one available. To her surprise, this choice had proved advantageous to her. Everybody knew that she could afford someplace grander, but they applauded her in the press, and over decadently laid din-ner tables, for choosing something elegant and appropriate to a young heiress without a family.

These days, and especially tonight, everyone wanted to whisper in her ear. Carolina smiled and posed, and when her cheeks grew a little red from the warmth, that only served to make her green eyes look especially so in contrast. She exchanged coiffure compliments with Mrs. Reginald Newbold, née Adelaide Wetmore, who was stationed with her new husband under the life-size portrait of Carolina as a horsewoman that hung over the mantel in the third-floor library. It was the largest of the late Longhorn's collection of portraits of society beauties, and his final commission. Half-way down the stairs she exchanged cordial hellos with Agnes Jones, who had at one time been a charity case of Carolina's childhood friend Elizabeth Holland. Agnes was not in and of herself an interesting person, but she did—Carolina had recently discovered—feed bits of gossip to the *New-York News of the World Gazette* society columnist, and so if one was kind to her, one could count on that kindness being returned in print. Carolina flirted casually with Amos Vreewold at the entryway of the second-story rosewood-paneled drawing room, and his reputation for rather familiar compliments did not disappoint.

When she couldn't stand it any longer she broke from the throng and stepped toward the south-facing windows. The fragrant summer city smelled of heat and leaves and vaguely, not entirely unpleasantly, of animal. There were horses below, beside her guests' drivers, who waited, and would wait some more, probably until the very advanced hour of the morning when the party, to everybody's disappointment, ended. Carolina took what seemed her first breath in a long while, and then she did something she did almost every day, and some days every hour: She permitted her eyes to drift down the block, to a limestone mansion with the number 18 carved into its impressive face. That was where Leland Bouchard lived—at least, when he was in town, which had not been the case for several months.

For a moment she'd let herself hope that he had finally returned, but now she saw the windows were just as dark and inscrutable as they had been for months. She swallowed dejectedly, and her shoulders slumped. Leland was supposed to have arrived from Europe two days before—Carolina knew because his departure from Paris had been announced in the society column. It was the whole reason she had decided to have her party that evening; it was the whole reason she had chosen this particular house on this particular block in the first place. But then stormy seas had delayed his ship, and he had not returned in time to attend the opening of her house after all.

They had shared a few perfect days together in Florida— all swooning and dancing—but that was back in February. Once or twice she had imagined the words *Marry me* on his lips, although of course that would have been very quick indeed. When she last saw him, it was in New York and the winter had still been bitter, and she'd believed herself a ruined girl. Since then she had become very rich, truly rich—all her greatest fears had blown over. Now she dreamed every night of the moment when he'd finally walk through her doors and witness her in all her glory. Waiting was painful, and the only thing to assuage it was to look dolefully from her south-facing windows at his house, willing the lights to flicker on.

"Why, Miss Broad, whatever are you staring at?"

Carolina turned too quickly to disguise the blush on her cheeks. Penelope Schoonmaker was approaching, long and shimmering and bedecked in her old vermilion glory, which had not been on such generous display since her little "illness" of late spring. Miss Broad blinked and kissed Mrs. Schoonmaker on either cheek. Although Carolina's presence in Penelope's bridal party that past New Year's Eve had announced the former as a young lady of sound importance, they were not the kind of friends who liked to show one another their vulnerabilities. The only person who knew the depth of Carolina's feelings for Leland was her older sister, Claire, who still worked as a maid for the Hollands and who savored any small tidbit of her younger sister's life among the fashionable people. But of course life was very busy, for an heiress anyway, and the sisters hadn't been able to have one of their secret meetings in some weeks. Or was it months?

"Your house is exceptionally good," Mrs. Schoonmaker remarked after a moment. The two regarded each other like wary allies. Carolina was gratified to see that Penelope's best diamonds dripped from her slender neck and across her alabaster décolletage, and that her oval face had been made up with prodigious care. It was obvious, to the hostess and everybody else, that she had not taken the evening casually.

"You must come see it again soon, at a quieter moment, when we can talk more intimately," Carolina replied, in a studiously refined voice. "Now that you are going out again."

"I would enjoy that." Penelope smiled crisply. A sharp quality came into her round blue eyes; when she spoke again, it was with counterfeit concern. "But now tell me—whatever is it you're gazing at? You can't afford to grow distracted during your first big party."

"No." There was irony in Carolina's tone, even though on the surface she pretended to agree. Still she itched to swivel and glance again at Leland's empty house. "I cannot."

"I myself would not have invited Agnes Jones," Penelope went on, turning to assess the other wealthy New Yorkers who packed the corners of the rooms and jammed the doorframe. "Although I was relieved not to see that divorcée Lucy Carr in attendance. Pity Leland Bouchard was not returned in time. . . . " She paused portentously. "But, oh, look, the lights have just gone on in his house."

Now Carolina felt her mouth grow dry and her lips part. For a moment she insisted to herself that she would not be obvious, and so continued to meet her friend's archly knowing gaze. But the desire was too great. She turned her whole body and looked across the street. This scene, which she had seen so many times since moving into No. 15, had suddenly undergone a transformation. The lights were now on, and the windows had been thrust open. Many pieces of luggage were being carried from a motorcar, up the steps and into what appeared all of a sudden to be a very warm place.

"Excuse me," she whispered. She did not pause to gauge Penelope's reaction. She did not care what it was. She had to find her butler, immediately, and send him to summon Leland.

Now, hurrying back across the floor, her body had become

unusually light. The humid air was nothing to her, nor was the weight of her skirts. She was stopped only once en route to the second-floor landing, by a garish face she recognized a few seconds later as belonging to Mrs. Portia Tilt. That lady was wearing acres of green satin and sticking out among members of Manhattan's best families like a fly on fondant; she had been the hostess's employer for a few days during late winter, and had dismissed her then-social secretary after an episode of unforgivable insubordination. Of course, since then, Carolina had come into more money than the Tilts could ever dream of, and had been seen out with all the people Mrs. Tilt had hoped to get in with. Carolina stared at her for a moment, and then smiled in a partial way that did not really communicate hospitality—the invitation had served its purpose, and Mrs. Tilt now knew which of the two was the more consequential lady.

They exchanged careful smiles, and by the time Mrs. Tilt's began to fade Carolina was already moving past her, onto the crowded staircase landing. She felt a surging agitation, because she feared the butler would be impossible to find just now, when she needed him so. The din was too loud for her to call for him, and meanwhile he was probably on some useless errand, trying to replace the melted ice under the oysters long after everyone had stopped caring about food. But in the next moment it became clear that she wasn't going to need him at all. There, below her, Leland Bouchard stood in front of the door, glancing about him at the giddily shrieking partygoers, with their lit cigarettes and drained champagne flutes, looking adorably just a touch out of place.

"Mr. Bouchard!" she called, before pushing past the bodies crowding the stairs. None of the subtly dishonest ladylike quality that she had mastered over the previous season had been evident in her voice.

The lavender silk and chiffon of her dress fit her tightly in some places, holding her upright and imperious; in others it bloomed, as though all of her were some fragrant and enticing bouquet. She blinked and took in his height; his light brown hair, which was overgrown and tucked behind his ears; the pale, plainspoken blue of his eyes; the gorgeous width of his shoulders. All of these qualities contributed to the sense that her cool exterior was about to crack again.

Men in black jackets and women in sweet silks were still all around, but they no longer mattered. Carolina's smile overtook her face before she could help it, and then Leland smiled back in a way that caused her chest to swell pleasurably with air. She took the final step down and joined him on the shiny granite. In her fantasies of their reunion, she began by offering him a tour of the house or a glass of Scotch, but neither of these seemed worthy of the moment. She was now close enough to grip his upper arm in welcome. What she most wanted to do was not very ladylike at all—but then, she was from a western state, and maybe he would assume that what was appropriate for girls was different out there.

When she next spoke, her voice had fallen to a near mumble: "How did Paris suit you?"

"Oh . . . wonderfully. I saw all variety of new automobiles and traveled a great deal. I . . ." He paused and shook his head, as though his travels had lost all importance. "I thought of you so frequently—it quite surprised me."

For a moment the elegant Manhattanites leaning against the second-story railing, or pressed up against the cloakroom, or smoking on the landing, ceased to exist. It was late, anyway, and quite a few cases of champagne had been drunk already. She turned her face up toward Leland invitingly, and found that he scarcely hesitated before putting his lips discreetly against hers. When he pulled away, his eyes shimmered with silver and his voice had deepened.

"Carolina—you aren't like the rest of them."

Everyone on the second and third floors had concluded, several hours ago, that the hostess was a success. But now she saw that, for entirely different reasons, she was a success in the foyer, in a private scene that could not have been more perfect if she had scripted it herself in advance. Every inch of her skin radiated with the pleasure of Leland's words. A

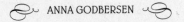

confession played, briefly, on her tongue, and she considered telling her handsome neighbor exactly why she wasn't like the rest of them. But then she didn't want to ruin anything, and so went on beaming at him as the night lengthened and the party went on upstairs without them.

Five

When a lady takes a less established girl under her wing, she always runs the risk that she will someday be outshone, which is why she must do so only sparingly and with the greatest care.

—MAEVE DE JONG, *LOVE AND OTHER FOLLIES OF THE GREAT FAMILIES OF OLD NEW YORK*

"THEY'VE ALL GROWN SO SMALL," PENELOPE SCHOON-maker announced, several hours after arriving at the party, but when no one had yet asked her to dance. She had always been said to have dramatic features, but her eyes were especially wide now, in disbelief. The feel of the flocked wallpaper at Miss Broad's had become hatefully familiar to her; she had never been the kind of girl content to go unnoticed. Three months of convalescing were behind her and she was dying for a little fun, but she was finding that not so easy to come by as before. "Buck, don't they look small?" she repeated insistently

"Not me," replied her friend Isaac Phillips Buck with a little self-effacing laugh. His tone indicated he was joking, but what he had said was perfectly true, for Buck stood a full head taller than Penelope, and was several times her girth. Buck liked to give the impression of being from the august Buck clan, but this lineage was dubious at best, and his prestige was almost entirely based on his reputation for being indispensable when one was throwing a party. It was a reputation that had been fanned in no small part by the former Miss Hayes. But that he was not a small man was indeed true, although it was only one of the reasons his longtime patron found him irritating at that particular moment.

"They must be small-minded at least if they actually believe Carolina Broad is as fine as they pretend to think she is," Penelope snapped. Fashion was vicious; it moved quickly, she knew, but she had not been in bed so long, and she was still better looking than any of them. She remembered when Carolina was just another disgruntled maid, let go by the Hollands—but that was before she had befriended the old bachelor Carey Lewis Longhorn and somehow or other persuaded him to leave her his vast fortune. She had been playing heiress at first, but now she really was one, and the evidence was above them in coffered ceilings as well as on the handsome façade that boasted her new address. It was stomach-turning how formal she had been with Penelope—who had done so much for her—and how quickly she had excused herself to chase after Leland Bouchard.

For Penelope, the agony of having stood so long in a room while being paid so little attention was far greater than any that could have resulted from a physical blow. She was dressed in eye-catching vermilion that enveloped her like plumage, and the lace that sheathed her arms and the suede that circled her waist revealed how dainty she had become since she last had been seen out. Her dark hair was up above her face like a cloud at midnight; her eyes looked acutely blue lined in black, as they were now.

"I never knew how unkind New York could be until today," she concluded bitterly. For although it was not the kind of thing that was printed in society pages, the reason Penelope had been confined to her bedroom for so long was that she had lost what would have been her and Henry Schoonmaker's first child. And to make it all the more pitiable, the whole unfortunate episode had occurred while her dashing husband was away at war.

Or not really at war, because Henry's father, William, had arranged for him to be sent to Cuba, where the danger had mostly passed. And no baby had truly been lost, because she had never *actually* been with child. That had been a story she cooked up to bind Henry to her and punish the irritating girl he persisted in believing himself in love with. She could not really have been with child, because she and Henry did not really act like man and wife in that sense, except on one occasion, in Florida, when he had been very drunk. For a moment the muscles of Penelope's face relaxed and her blood warmed at the thought of the summer when Henry and she had been intimate in every back corner of their families' homes they could manage . . . but she stopped herself. She was in a room of people incapable of sympathy, but apparently quite capable of delighting in her downfall, and she could not afford to grow wistful.

"Look!" Buck was laboring for a cheerful tone.

After a stubborn pause, she did turn her gaze in the direction Buck had indicated. There, through the crowd of red-faced people shrieking in delight at whatever inanity, moving about the dance floor gracelessly—or, she supposed, with what had come to pass for grace in Mrs. Schoonmaker's absence—stood a tall, broad fellow in shiny black garb with eyes almost as strikingly blue as her own. There was something wholesome, but also exotic, about his chestnut hair and the sparkle of his smile.

"At what exactly?" Penelope replied in the well-practiced voice that implied she was not impressed.

"It's the prince of Bavaria." Buck inclined himself toward his old friend and continued in a confidential tone: "He's been touring the New World for some time. They say he is soon to be engaged to that little slip of a thing at his side—French, can't be more than sixteen—but her mama, the countess, was made nervous by all his roving, and has followed along in his footsteps."

Penelope had to press up on the toes of her satin heels, which were adorned with pearls, and crane her neck to glimpse this creature. Through the crush of evening garb and sweating faces she caught sight of not one Frenchwoman but two, neither particularly tall. The elder fanned herself indifferently, and the younger, who wore a pearl-and-diamond choker, gazed up at the fine shoulders of her escort in dewy adoration. There was something about her untouched skin and wide dark eyes that put Diana Holland back in Penelope's head, along with a twist of rage.

"He was in Florida when we were there, but I never saw him."

"You can tell how beautiful the countess once was."

"Yes," Penelope agreed, but only after privately noting that lady's sunken cheeks and rather overdone makeup. The prince was smiling at some sycophant or other with an air of patient disdain, which Penelope recognized from her own repertoire of facial expressions. She felt a touch of sympathy toward him for being so obviously, so painfully superior to those around him, just as she always was. Then he glanced up so that his eyes settled on her and caught the light. She had become tough in the previous months, but she softened at the sight of a man who was clearly of her caliber.

"Oh . . . Mrs. Schoonmaker."

Penelope turned, distracted, in the direction of her name, and saw Adelaide Newbold, whose maiden name had been Wetmore. The new bride smiled tightly as she passed, and then swept onward in an insignificant wave of mauve.

"What was that?" Penelope managed to keep her voice quiet, but was unable to wring it of the fury she felt. The ignominy of being cut by a girl who had married at a more advanced age than she, to a man of far less means than Penelope's husband, was almost too outrageous to believe.

"It is perverse how they all think Miss Broad is so high and fine, all the while giving *me* nasty faces. Does that make any kind of sense to you?"

Buck's silence continued as she turned her gaze, slowly, in his direction.

"Does it?"

"Perhaps . . ." Buck pressed his fat lips together. The plentiful flesh of his cheeks threatened to obscure his eyes. "Perhaps it is that they think—erroneously, of course—that you are out a little soon after your . . . illness. When your husband is away, that is, and in harm's way."

A collection of words have never been more carefully strung together, and yet they could not have sounded more cloddish, stupid, ill-informed to Penelope's ears. "I'm thirsty," she snapped. "Get me a drink."

She did not watch Buck go. Already she was crossing the large parlor on the second floor of Carolina Broad's new house with proud purpose. The panels of her red silk dress caught the chandelier light, as the lace of the underskirt frothed up around her feet. The elegant people all around her must have

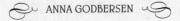

suddenly come into some reserves of reason, for they moved aside for her with a suggestion of deference. She stalked to the middle of the room where the girl with the petite stature and Holland-esque face was standing, and promptly looked away from her.

"Would you believe that no one has asked me to dance all night?" she demanded of the prince of Bavaria, allowing the absurdity of the statement to bear up in her voice, along with the flat American vowels.

The prince—he was unusually tall, she realized when she was beside him, and his skin had the glow of all things very rare and expensive to maintain—assessed her with amused, appreciative eyes. His jaw shifted. "No," he said after a minute.

Penelope cocked an eyebrow and let her chin rise just a little, the better to display the long, pale symmetry of her neck. The countess and her daughter were watching this American girl in her unseemly red gown with an air of European haughtiness, no doubt, but their expressions were irrelevant just then. As she waited, her confidence, as well as the excitement of being in the middle of a room, at the center of attention, of having done something slightly irregular, grew. Then the prince reached for her hand and planted his lips on the other side of the gaudy engagement ring that she had had to buy herself.

"Allow me the pleasure of being the first," he replied in English just slightly inflected with a foreign sophistication.

Neither she nor the prince glanced at the Frenchwomen as he lifted his arm so that her hand could remain rested against his and aloft while he led her into the adjoining room. Several of Miss Broad's guests were still dancing, but they parted for them with reverent interest. A hush fell over the couples. They were all watching her now, Penelope realized, and she smirked a little to think how easy it was to win their attention, even after everything.

The prince's eyes darted once more to her hand before he circled her firmly with his other arm, and moved her backward into a waltz.

"What a pity you're married," he said, in a voice that implied a greater familiarity than could possibly have been justified by their few minutes of acquaintance. He was dancing very close to her, closer than an American boy would have—but then she was not shy of holding his gaze.

"Well, you see, my husband is at war," she replied with a broad flash of smile. "In such situations, you never know who will be coming back, and who is gone forever, and a lady must always be hedging her bets."

For a moment she feared that she had gone too far, that the prince would find her cavalier assessment of Henry's soldiering and possible death unseemly and leave her standing alone on the dance floor. But then he tossed his head back and laughed heartily, until she too laughed, emitting a twinkling bell-like noise in the direction of the coffered ceiling. Then he moved closer and went on dancing her across the floor in a way that made all those people who had so recently snubbed her stop what they were doing and stare at her gape-mouthed. The prince of Bavaria was still laughing, a little smugly now, and this indicated to Penelope that he had a rather perverse sense of humor and also that, over the course of the evening, they were going to have a very good time.

The skirts of the women all around them brushed up against one another to form a solid wall of fine pastels; their mouths, and whatever they were whispering, disappeared behind their fans. Light twinkled from the jewels that sat on Penelope's wrists and neck and waist and hair. The fearsome Mrs. Schoonmaker had been away for some months, but it had only taken a few hours, and not especially much of her patience, to once again captivate an entire room.

Six

A gentleman travels to become hale and experienced; a lady travels to complete her hat collection, and must be mindful she does not rub up against too much of the world.

——MRS. L. A. M. BRECKINRIDGE, *THE LAWS OF BEING IN WELL-MANNERED CIRCLES*

"DRINK UP NOW, BOYS!" CRIED DIANA HOLLAND, IN a brassy tone that would have made her mother shudder, from a location that would have made the old lady weep. "Because it might be a hurricane tomorrow. . . ."

Out of doors the winds were loud and full of bluster, but there was no rain yet. The air inside Señora Conrad's was hot and festive, and the barmaid with the curly wisps of short brown hair pinned away from her face could hardly see through the crowd of soldiers, from her post behind the long wooden bar, to the open shutters of the saloon and whatever weather lay beyond. The fabric of the white button-down shirt she wore fell away from her lightly sweating skin. The sleeves were pushed up to her elbows and tucked into the long, plain black skirt that was secured with a wide, brown leather belt. Her pretty skin had grown rosy with exertion, and her lashes formed black, pointed coronas around shiny eyes. A mad piano played in the corner, encouraging the droves to drink faster and laugh louder—an imperative they merrily obeyed.

"The rain will begin soon," Señora Conrad said from her perch at the end of the bar.

"But," Diana returned gaily as she poured glasses of straight rum for the gentlemen who watched her from the other side, "it is not raining *now*."

Señora Conrad's was off the Plaza de Armas, and the bottles shone with reflected light from the candles lining the elaborately carved wooden shelves. Mostly men came there—Cuban businessmen as well as hordes of the American servicemen who had been stationed on the island since the conclusion of the war. The proprietor was the first wife of an American whose interests in Cuba had dried up. She decorated her generous figure in black as though she were a widow, although in fact Señor Conrad had simply returned to Chicago, where he began trading commodities again and started a second family with his third cousin. But he had loved his Gertrudis, and had left her with a business of her own to live on. There were plenty of gold flourishes in the place, just as there would have been in any of the gentlemen's watering holes in New York, although the effect was shaded with a heady dose of Spanish gloom. On a Friday night, all the little round tables were circled by men in uniform, who stretched their long legs across the old stone floors and toasted to being far from home.

A thunderclap close by shook the bottles and rattled

the windows. The saloon customers quieted momentarily and turned toward the street. Although a distinct wetness hung in the air, still nothing fell from the sky. Señora Conrad made a low, whistling noise; a moment later, the din rose again. Then everyone moved toward the bar, rowdily calling out that they would have another. As the crowd began to roar, the old gentleman bartender, who worked in front of the large oval mirror to Diana's right, removed his bow tie as if to say that now, finally, he was ready to get down to business. Beads of sweat clung to his forehead—even they were too lazy to move—and though Diana thought it might be interesting to go on observing him, voices all around her were demanding one more. She bent forward, shoveling ice into glasses, setting up another row of drinks.

Working made her arms weary, but it was a kind of fatigue that she'd grown to like. It wasn't that she needed the money so much anymore—she had saved what she'd earned on the luxury liner, not to mention what she made selling pieces of gossip about the top-drawer people on board to Barnard back in New York, as well as a few little local color sketches, which he had complimented excessively. She was beginning to see that stories were not only to be overheard on the plush settees of drawing rooms at teatime, but might also be observed when one is out, at night, where people congregate.

"What's a pretty American like you doing in a place like

this?" called a man with a wide bushy mustache as she pushed a full glass in his direction. Diana, who was used to such questions, and the rather forward flattery that followed, took his money with an evasive smile. At first it had surprised her how differently men behaved toward her here, uttering phrases or asking favors as they never would have dared in New York. But she quickly came to see that they were a long way from home, and from the women and children they were bound to there, and that distance as well as drink had a way of lowering men's inhibitions.

A fresh-faced soldier appeared behind the mustachioed man, who was still leering at Diana with rummy eyes, and called out for a beer in a timid voice. He seemed as young as she was, and apparently all his politeness had not yet been rubbed off by his colleagues, because he could scarcely look her in the eye. She gave the boy an appreciative wink before turning to fetch a bottle from the icebox. Winking had become a kind of flirtatious compulsion with her, and as she reached into the cool darkness, she decided she was going to have to cure herself of it before she found Henry. When she turned back around, the boy was gone—as far as she was concerned, anyway. He had become as invisible to her as the rest of the bar.

Diana's mouth dropped open and a wild energy played in her chest. She had forgotten all the tasks that constituted her job, or how to perform them. The only man in the entire bar that she could now make out was darker than when she'd last seen him, and his skin looked especially tawny against the collar of his white linen shirt. The bridge of his nose was a color that suggested he had been out in the sun that day, and the expression disappearing from his face indicated that moments ago he had been having a careless good time.

"Hello, soldier," she managed at last, with what she could gather of her breath.

"Diana?" Henry said, as though the sound of her name might confirm her unlikely presence in front of him. "How—" he stammered, "how did you come here?"

"I was looking for you." All the sentences she'd imagined saying to him since that day at the end of February, when he'd entered a doorway and seen her wrapped up in another man, had escaped her. The only sentence she could think of was the one she'd just uttered, and it seemed to her, at that moment, to contain the only relevant information.

"You were?"

"Yes."

"I mean—you got my letter?"

Diana nodded. She had received it indeed. The pages were sewn into her suitcase; she had read them a hundred times.

"You don't hate me?"

There was no gesture that could have communicated how far her feelings were from hatred, but she shook her head in a kind of attempt anyway. Whatever emotion she was experiencing—was it shyness, or trepidation?—was new for her, and she was a little surprised at herself for being unsure in front of Henry after everything that had happened between them, and all she had done to bring this moment about. He was staring at her with those inscrutable black eyes. Her heart had begun to tick with the fear that their meeting was almost over, that her quest would end here with both of them tongue-tied. After all, he was older than she, and more experienced, and perhaps now that he was a soldier, and not just a rich playboy with nothing else to do, he no longer had time for little girls.

The touch of Señora Conrad's thick fingertips on her shoulder shocked Diana back to the present. The room was still full of people, noisily talking up the working girls or clambering toward the bar and banging their glasses against its worn surface. She glanced at them, at the row of faces red with joy, and then back at Diana. A surprised and knowing light shone in Señora Conrad's eyes, and after a watchful pause she drew her young employee away from her post by the elbow.

"Come." The lady gestured to Henry. Then she led them to the rear of her establishment, opened the door to the storeroom, and pushed one and then the other inside.

The room was lined with crates, and the closed door protected Diana and Henry, if just barely, from the racket of an advancing evening. Both were bathed in the honeyed light of a single bulb muted with paper. Diana turned her chin up toward Henry, expecting a kiss, but for a while he could only manage a few disbelieving blinks. Relief, along with a kind of euphoria, had begun to seep into her chest, although Henry's presence had not yet begun to seem real. He stepped forward, and she parted her lips, but he did not put his mouth to hers. Instead his arms went around her torso, and he lifted her up above him, squeezing her tight. A deeply buried instinct told her to rest her face against his shoulder.

Sometime before the dawn they would begin talking and be unable to stop, and then their hands would roam all over each other. But for right then there was nothing she wanted but to hang like that, her feet suspended a foot from the ground, breathing in the smell that for her had ceased to be like anything but Henry. Not even her most fervent imaginings could have rendered him as good as this.

Seven

Those of us who thought that Elizabeth Holland—a girl most artfully groomed to be a bride—took a social step down in marrying her father's former business partner, Snowden Trapp Cairns, must now admit that she did not, in any event, grow poorer in the exchange, for she was spotted over the weekend directing new furniture to be carried into a very handsome Madison Avenue brownstone. . . .

—FROM THE SOCIETY PAGE OF THE *NEW-YORK NEWS OF THE WORLD GAZETTE*, SATURDAY, JULY 7, 1900

$\mathcal{B}$Y FOUR O'CLOCK ELIZABETH WAS FEELING RATHER fatigued, for she had risen at dawn to oversee the arrangement of antique sofas in her parlor, and the lighting of fires in her kitchen, so that something approximating an acceptable tea could be served to a few ladies who stopped by to wish her well at her new address. Among her guests were Agnes Jones, who turned over all the china to see if the stamps were authentic, and Penelope Schoonmaker, with whom she maintained a delicate façade of friendship in public, and who dropped by on her way to the department stores. It had been a lovely afternoon, but Elizabeth was glad when they were gone. The baby was restless inside of her, and there was still so much to do.

The house was arranged not unlike No. 17 Gramercy Park, where she had spent her first eighteen years. On one side of the main entrance was a large parlor with floor-to-ceiling windows that faced the street, and on the other a dining room of similar proportions. There was a more private drawing room in the back of the house, along with the kitchen and other quarters that only the servants used. The foyer was large enough to properly greet visitors, but it did not pretend to be the antechamber of a royal court, as in some of the ostentatious new constructions. A handsome flight of stairs was built against the north-facing wall, which turned onto a second-floor landing that offered a fine vantage of the bedrooms as well as the two social areas downstairs, when their pocket doors were drawn open. The house gave her tremendous satisfaction; just walking through its spaces made her feel that she was finally going to do right by her child and, by extension, her Will.

It was this sticky fact—that Will, the real father of her child, was never far from her mind—which made her resist lying down on one of the new chaises in her parlor, or in the frilly confines of her upstairs bedroom. For though Penelope had been perfectly gracious all through tea, Elizabeth could sense that she still remembered her old friend's queasiness when they had vacationed together in Florida over the winter, when it had only just been occurring to Elizabeth what she might bear within her. She suspected that the newest Mrs. Schoonmaker probably doubted the child's paternity, which was not a nice thing to be thought of any man, especially one who cared for his wife so well. And Snowden *did* care for Elizabeth well. The evidence was all around her, in the sturdy walls, the hammered black leather panels decorating them, and the polished birch wainscoting below.

That sensation of guilt, combined with her native orderliness, sent her rather heavily up the stairs and into the room that had been assigned as her husband's study. It was in the back of the house, where he would be less bothered by the noise of the servants or the noise of the street and, very soon now, the noise of a little child. She stepped into the masculine space somewhat timidly, for she had a strong sense that it should be his refuge. But Elizabeth, in her lacy, high-necked smock and black linen skirt, her blond hair rising like a hazy pillow over her fine forehead, was the product of a decade of assiduous grooming. The man whose proposal had saved her and her child deserved to benefit from her well-honed feminine abilities, too.

"Can I help you, Mrs. Cairns?"

The housekeeper, Mrs. Schmidt, a fastidious widow in middle age whose late husband had been for many years an employee of Snowden's, had come up behind her and was now lingering in the doorway. She appeared just slightly displeased that the lady of the house would be poking about.

"Mr. Cairns said I was to see that you don't overexert yourself, and to make sure that all of your needs are met while he is out on business. . . ."

Elizabeth rested her hand on her considerable belly and

tried to let a certain glowing kindness light up her heart-shaped face. Excepting the case of Lina Broud—who had been the final lady's maid of her life as a debutante, and with whom she had sparred mightily—she had always had a nice way around the help. With Mrs. Schmidt her gentleness seemed to hold no special power, however; the two women had yet to strike a natural ease in their relationship.

"No, I'm all right, but thank you." When the older woman did not budge, Elizabeth added, almost apologetically, "I wanted to put Mr. Cairns's study in order myself."

"Of course," Mrs. Schmidt replied, although still she hesitated until Elizabeth gave a firm gesture of dismissal with her pointed chin.

When she was gone, Elizabeth busied herself with the arranging of pens and paper on her husband's broad desk and the placement of several objets d'art. She turned over in her mind which of the taxidermied heads lining the walls she could persuade him to do away with, for though Snowden was an outdoorsman, and though she did not want him to abolish that aspect of his character, she felt that as his wife, she owed him the benefit of her rather excellent eye. The animal trophies did not, in her opinion, belong in such a genteel home. When the room was finally starting to appear tended to by a steady feminine hand, she turned to a box of papers that needed sorting.

The ordinary activity of putting a house together had calmed Elizabeth, but that steady, neutral feeling evaporated when, after carefully filing several bank statements and business documents in the drawers of the large walnut desk, she glimpsed her own name as it had been written during the first eighteen years of her life. And not just her name, but along with it the name that she chanted in her thoughts each night before going to bed—the name that she still thought of as hers, too. Her brown eyes grew large.

A letter to Stanley Brennan, who had once been her family's accountant, was clipped to the document, and the bit that caught Elizabeth's attention read: *Please have the deed for the California property transferred—immediately and jointly—into the names Elizabeth Adora Holland and William Keller.* The signer of the letter was her late father; it was dated a week before his death, and posted from the Yukon Territory. Her heart had begun to thud and her vision was growing blurry with tears. Still her eyes lingered there. Even the sight of Will's name brought to mind the picture of him in a new brown suit on the day they were married, the last time she remembered feeling anything like pure joy. It was another few moments before she was able to collect herself and read the rest, and thus to realize that the paper she held was in fact the deed to a bit of land she knew quite well.

She could not begin to understand why her father would

have put her and Will's name together on any document, much less one that connected them to the land that they had in fact lived on, quite happily, far, far away in a place called California. She had known that her father had told Will it might be a lucrative territory, but that he had owned it, much less deeded it to his oldest daughter and former valet, confounded her.

She rose to her feet with some difficulty, and then went as quickly as she could down the stairs, calling for Mrs. Schmidt.

"When did Mr. Cairns say he would be returning?" she demanded when the wide, flat face of the housekeeper emerged below her in the foyer. Elizabeth clutched the curved railing for balance. From below, her swollen figure must have appeared tremendous.

"I expect him home any moment now. . . ." The housekeeper was wiping her hands with a cloth. "What can I do to assist you in the meantime, Missus?"

"Please tell him that I am in the second-floor sitting room when he returns." She covered her mouth with her hand and tried not to feel woozy. "Tell him I must speak to him as soon as possible."

She did not know how long she waited. It might have been several hours or only a part of one that she reclined in the ivory wingback chair in the sitting room next to where she slept, and felt her heart rise and fall over recollections that she could not keep at bay. They were a deluge. By turns they washed her onto high, dry land and then back to rough waters. In moments she was there—making dinner for Will while he searched for the oil he believed would make them rich, her skin a little browned in the sun, her body warm—and in the next, she was on the platform at Grand Central Station with the sound of bullets ringing horrifically in her ears and the smell of blood turning her stomach.

"What is it, my dear?"

Snowden came rushing through the door, as though she really were his wife and it really was his child whose birth he was nervously anticipating. Elizabeth's pale lashes fluttered. But of course she was his wife, she reminded herself, as he knelt by her side. He grasped her hand, and she realized that he had scarcely touched her since kissing her in the carriage after he'd first shown her the new house.

"Please—can you explain this to me?" Her voice broke over the words as she thrust the peculiar document in his direction.

Snowden's small mouth twitched. Slowly it became a gentle smile. He wore a waistcoat of striped brown silk, which had not in the past been a fabric he favored. He took the paper, glancing over it before folding it away in his pocket.

"This is a deed," he began. "One of the ownership documents of a piece of land your father purchased, in California, near a little railroad town called San Pedro. . . ."

"Yes," Elizabeth whispered. She looked into her husband's eyes, imploring him to explain it all for her. "I know that land."

"Yes." Snowden's eyes darted across her body to the floor and back again. Then he went on in a rapid voice. "Your mother and I discussed it, of course, when you returned from California with—your first husband. He had mentioned there was oil on the land, and as a close family friend, your mother confided in me. I told her that of course oil speculation was a very complicated business, and awfully difficult to turn a profit on, but that Will seemed like a capable boy, and that if he didn't make it there he would make it some other way. . . ."

The sun was falling out of the sky, and shadows touched all the objects in the room. Snowden's face, a few feet away, was growing indistinct in the waning light. Breath had escaped her, and she had to remind herself to inhale. She nodded at him that he should go on.

"After . . . the tragedy, after Will's death, I began to piece together an explanation for an odd series of documents that I'd found amongst your father's papers, when I first came to help your family, early last winter. Of course I did not then know who William Keller was."

Elizabeth's eyes had become watery and her pale pink lips parted involuntarily. "He knew," she whispered.

"That there was oil? He must have believed so; why else would a man like Edward Holland have been interested in land like that?"

"No . . ." She bit her lip and swallowed hard as she took in her father's sanctioning of Will's love for her, so long after both men had died. "Father knew that Will loved me. That I loved him."

Snowden looked away.

In her more gathered moments, Elizabeth would have thought to apologize, but it did not occur to her now. "Why did you not tell me?" she pursued.

"My dear Mrs. Cairns, you were in no state to receive this kind of news. But you needn't have worried. I have been seeing to your interests. I've taken several trips to California to inspect the land, and it is in truth a rich oil field. Production has begun, and we've already seen returns on the property. How do you think I was able to secure funds for this house, my dear?" His hand swept through the air, and her eyes followed the arc it made, as though some detail in the molding would symbolize her father's prescience. "Of course, the natural treasure of the land will not be realized overnight, but very soon it will be paying us all—the Hollands, that is—quite handsomely."

"Oh!" Elizabeth took a breath; she had never breathed so deeply. Her long, fine fingers fluttered over her chest and she tried valiantly not to cry again. So it *was* Will who was caring for them after all.

The fatigue she had been dodging all afternoon was suddenly overwhelming. She fixed her gaze on the short, blunt stubble of Snowden's chin, which was a light color, and so caught the very last of the sun—and she tried to smile a little in gratitude.

"Thank you." She closed her eyes, and when she whispered it again, she was thinking of her father and the father of her unborn child, who were, perhaps, just at that moment, watching over her from heaven. "Thank you."

Eight

Now that Carolina Broad has shown all of society her splendid new abode, and all the wonderfully precious things she has managed to acquire for it, we suppose there will be no more doubting that she is at last one of us. Although the wardrobe that she ordered for her first summer season might have been taken as sufficient proof of this, or, for that matter, the fact that she retained her benefactor Carey Lewis Longhorn's famed box at the opera, and is regularly seen entertaining there.

—FROM *CITÉ CHATTER*, SATURDAY, JULY 7, 1900

ELITE NEW YORK WAS SITUATED IN A HIERARCHY of boxes, arranged around a grand horseshoe, high above a vibrant and melodramatic performance on a stage that few, if any, audience members were still paying attention to. The light of a giant chandelier played against their raised lorgnettes, which were adorned, like the hands that held them, with jewels of all varieties. There was plenty of drama to be witnessed, after all, by gazing through those ornamented lenses at the wearers of Doucet gowns, and at the gentlemen who had escorted them. Mrs. Henry Schoonmaker was out for the second night in a row, but nobody dared visit her box for fear of angering her father-in-law; Eleanor Wetmore, who was said to be desperate for a proposal since she had played maid of honor at her younger sister's June wedding, was twittering again beside that known roué Amos Vreewold. It was less than a year ago that Carolina had first come, wide-eyed, to this very box. But tonight she was no longer interested in what might be glimpsed or overheard around her, for she was sitting next to her first love, or her first real one, anyway. He was one of the favorite sons of the tribe that filled the parterre boxes at the opera, and so she knew that tonight, at his side, *she* was the girl to surreptitiously observe.

Earlier, they had dined in Leland's grand town house, a choice of venue that had initially disappointed her—for she was desperate to be seen out with her new beau—but which she had, in the end, found the beauty in. "It was so much more intimate that way," she could already imagine telling her lady's maid later, when her corset was being undone, and she would be telling the truth. For it had been much easier—sitting across from each other, the candlelight flickering in the darkened room, the prettily patterned white damask cloth between them—for Leland to stare appreciatively at her aubergine chiffon flounces and lichen-colored eyes. And he had felt comfortable enough to grow animated telling her about all the different places in Paris where he had thought her name to himself, and contemplated the qualities that set her apart from all the other girls he had ever known. His words received encores in her thoughts now, as she sat in Longhorn's traditional box, with glazed, rosy vision and a probably dopey smile. Any attempts to change that expression would have been useless. Occasionally Leland reached out, boldly, to squeeze her gloved hand under the cover of her shawl.

Now he bent in her direction, and spoke at such low

volume that she had to tip her head toward him. The rough-
ness of his skin came close enough that it tickled her neck,
which would have made the corners of her mouth flicker had
they not been already.

"You're far better in person," he said.

The tingling sensation that played along Carolina's
exposed arms and shoulders told her how strenuously she was
being watched from all angles, but Leland's vigor and apparent
obliviousness to the prying opera glasses all around them was
something she wanted to share in. She drew back and smiled
at him, straight on and adoringly. Moments had passed, or the
better part of an hour, she wasn't sure, when he spoke again.
The performers onstage were all different by then.

"How lucky that we live on the same block!" he went on,
disbelieving.

"Yes!" Carolina's head bobbed in ebullient agreement.
"What luck."

Stars bloomed in her eyes. Still Leland's presence there
beside her, and in her very own box, was something she could
only consume in small doses. There was his height, and
his solidity, and his overgrown, wheat-colored hair tucked
behind his ears, and his long legs in black dress trousers,
crossed and still almost too large for the small space, each of
which taken alone might have caused a touch of trembling in
her knees. She went on sneaking glances at him, but then he

would turn and gaze at her with wide-open eyes, almost as though he were feeling the same wonderful, scarcely credible thing. It was faint-making. Looking at Leland was almost too much for her—it threatened to overwhelm. Then she looked away.

Her glances fell across the capacious room: On her friend Penelope, whose blue eyes flashed in defiance; at Reginald Newbold and his new bride, Adelaide, who was wearing a diamond choker; at the Whitehall Vanderbilts, who rumor had it were not speaking to each other after their last trip to Monte Carlo, and whose postures in their box confirmed the tale. Then her gaze fixed itself on the face of Mrs. Portia Tilt and that lady's companion, who was a far younger, far thinner man than her husband. He had fine, architectural features and eyes of a hypnotic quality, although he held no allure for Carolina. No allure, except that she felt an immediate urgency not to give any clue that she knew him.

Tristan Wrigley was a Lord & Taylor salesman, but he was many other things besides: a hustler, the first man ever to kiss Carolina, and the person who had originally suggested to her that there might be a fortune in her friendship with Longhorn. Then he stood, and she realized she'd been caught staring. The possibility that he would enter her box, that she would be seen in front of all New York society talking to someone worse than a nobody, occurred to her with a crushing gravity. Slowly, delicately, she released Leland's palm and rose to her feet.

Luckily for Carolina, Amos Vreewold entered the private room behind her box just then. She saw, in a second, how easy it would be to absent herself, and avoid a visit from Portia Tilt's well-made companion.

"Why, Mr. Vreewold," she began, gathering herself. "You must excuse me, I was just on my way to the ladies' lounge for a freshening-up. Surely you will have much to discuss with our dear Mr. Bouchard."

"Vreewold . . . ," Leland said, turning, engaging the other man in conversation, "you haven't changed even a little!"

She put her fists into her skirt, to draw it back from her toes, and reminded herself that in this, her second social season, she already occupied the most coveted box at the opera. She had followed the lead of her friend Penelope Schoonmaker and chosen a signature color with imperial connotations; Penelope's was red, hers was purple. She was not to be trifled with. As soon as she stepped into the curving corridor, she came face-to-face with Tristan Wrigley.

"Can I help you?" Her voice was ever so low, ever so refined.

The man met her cool stare with a smile that spread slyly across his face and twinkled with charisma. He had a fine American jaw, and cheekbones that might easily convince an inexperienced girl that he came from good people. Like the real gentlemen in attendance, he wore shining black tails and a white bow tie, which fit him with certain flair. Though she would have known him anywhere, she maintained her indifferent, unresponsive gaze. Still, below her ribbons and her bows, underneath the bones of her corset, a layer of sweat began to collect on the skin of her ribs—for after all, it would have been impossible to completely forget how he entered her life, during that wild, impressionable period when she was just a lady's maid recently fired by the grand Holland family, making a fool of herself in all of Manhattan's best hotels.

His muddy golden eyes swept her figure, taking in the pearls at her décolletage and the tiers of chiffon that hung about her like delicate aubergine leaves. After an inappropriately long pause, he emitted a slow, appreciative whistle. "I would say so."

Carolina straightened. That angry, righteous feeling, which was such an inescapable piece of her personality, was seeping into her lungs. "Excuse me?"

He rested his shoulder jauntily against the curved wall of the corridor. The music of the orchestra sounded muffled and far away here. No one had yet passed them, but how long could that last? "I see my Carolina has done well for herself."

The phrase "my Carolina" came off his tongue purposefully, as though he wanted to remind her of the night he'd surprised her with a kiss on the mouth in an elevator, or of that brief period—after Mr. Longhorn had died, but before she knew the kindness he had bestowed upon her—when she had believed herself helpless, and had depended on Tristan for shelter and other things better now forgotten. That he would lord these events over her put a match to her rage, and heated the tender edges of her ears. But then she remembered herself, and glanced back toward the box. The curtains formed a sliver, through which she could make out, with relief, silhouettes of Leland and Amos bent in conversation.

"I am not *anybody's* Carolina," she returned.

Tristan shrugged and took a step toward her, leaning in close enough that she caught a faint whiff of onion on his breath. "I can't pretend I made you all on my own, but you know very well you couldn't have gotten here without me." The tone of his voice was lined with malice now. The smile became a grimace. "Longhorn was my idea, or had you forgotten? I believe you owe me some gratitude . . . Miss *Broud*."

Carolina's blood quickened, and she quivered a little at the sound of her true surname, and wanted very badly for it all to be over, for none of it to be true. She stepped away from him, as though that might make their past together, and all the other ways she used to be, disappear. Her movement was quickly mimicked, and he held her gaze as she backed away.

"Who is this?"

Carolina's heart thudded. Her eyes grew round. She turned, and saw Amos and Leland, stepping out from the box and into the corridor. Jovial expressions faded from their faces as they took in the sight of the handsome, flashily dressed fellow who was most certainly not one of their people. The boy she had been dreaming about for months was no less handsome when he wore an unhappy expression, Carolina saw. The suggestion of a territorial instinct lent an imposing quality to his features, which she discovered that she liked. In seconds, she knew that she would do anything to keep him from discovering what she really was—she would do anything just to keep him.

"I have no idea." The timbre of her voice was so light and sure, that she wondered for a moment if perhaps she was an actress at heart. When she turned back to Tristan, her face communicated nothing but a profound lack of recognition. "He thought he knew me, but he was wrong."

"Well, then, he should move on," Amos said.

Something murderous passed through Tristan's face, but she felt a little calm already. She could tell she'd silenced him. Perhaps, too, the image of two tall gentlemen from old families, looming in white tie and black tails, made him less intent on his mission than he had been in the previous minutes. In all their strange times together, Carolina had never seen Tristan intimidated. She was glad to see it now. He bowed curtly, and backed away.

When she turned again toward Leland, she saw that his broad, handsome features were still hung with a little possessive anger, and it gratified her. "Poor fellow," he said, trying to shake it off. "He read about Miss Broad in the papers and dreamed he'd have a chance of whispering pretty things in her ear."

"Maybe he thought he could get invited to her next grand fete," Amos added, laughing.

"Come, gentlemen, there is no need to mock a nobody." She tossed her head and gave an easy laugh. All of a sudden she wanted to be alone with Leland, to look at only him. "It was so kind of you to visit, Mr. Vreewold," she declared in gentle dismissal. "Good night."

Then she and Leland stepped back into the box, with moony faces and bright eyes that were only for each other. She beamed radiantly as if to say, unequivocally, that whatever had just occurred was nothing. Less than nothing. Meanwhile, she could see in his posture and his glances, she could feel in the way his hands brushed her skirt and arms, that a few little waves of jealousy had carried her even further into his affections. Several boxes to her right, she knew that Tristan must be retaking his seat, but she would not have deigned to look in that direction.

They remained in her prestigious box several more hours, being spied upon and whispered about all across the grand opera house. Carolina's face was lit with happiness, her movements were effortless, as though no threat had been posed. Only once, on the carriage ride back to Sixty-third Street, did her calm exterior falter, and for a moment she trembled at what a humiliating scene she had narrowly averted. Leland noticed it, and asked her what was wrong.

"Oh, it's only that occupying old Longhorn's box makes me miss him," she lied, pressing her eyelids together as if allowing a shudder of pain to travel across her body. "He was my father's good friend, you see, and had promised him that he would protect me, and now that *he* is gone I really am an orphan, and all alone in the world. . . ."

"My poor Miss Broad!" he exclaimed as he reached out for her. "But you see you have two strong arms around you now, and you must not feel alone!"

As the carriage rattled and shook in the direction of home, as she rested her head against Leland's shoulder, she felt something wonderfully opposite of loneliness. It had occurred to her that Tristan's interference had perhaps been fortuitous after all, for whatever little stories she had had to tell to make him go away had inspired Leland to draw her, protectively, possessively, closer to him. For the great majority of Carolina's life, she had felt a constant mute frustration that events would never go her way, but then, all of a sudden, her luck had changed, and now it seemed every charmed second was sure to unfold in her favor.

Nine

Meanwhile, I have begun to wonder whether Diana Holland is ever coming back from Paris to begin the craze amongst New York's well-dressed ladies for hair worn short.

—FROM THE "GAMESOME GALLANT" COLUMN IN THE *NEW YORK IMPERIAL*, SUNDAY, JULY 8, 1900

"HOW LUCKY I FOUND YOU JUST WHEN I DID, because I've been looking forward to seeing the poet's house, but I did not, in truth, want to go alone!" Diana Holland ceased her stubborn, boyish little march and turned to face Henry, wearing an expression of happy embarrassment for having babbled so long. He'd watched from behind as she walked away from him before, in anger, at times, or in sadness, but never had she moved the way the other girls of her set did, like Penelope or her sister—practiced, proud, as though their skeletons were made of platinum, and as though their heels never quite met the ground. Of course, at this particular moment, the place they were searching for was miles from rooms that demanded to be entered in such a formal manner. The scene was devoid of elaborate drapery, or dainty statues, or the kind of people who considered a lady's gait a worthy topic of conversation. Beyond Diana's figure, about which floated a dress of undyed fabric, there was only dense verdure and a steel-colored heavens. "I mean," she amended in a softer voice as she gripped the broad straw hat that covered her absent curls, "I am so glad I get to go with *you* particularly."

The poet was some old Spaniard, long fled or long dead. Henry couldn't quite grasp the name—it had a minimum of eight syllables, and in Di's fluid pronunciation it sounded like nothing more than lovely nonsense. Who the poet was did not matter to him particularly (Henry owned many books, but few with cut pages), for it was Diana's vitality he was pursuing, up the hill and away from the city; the literary shrine was, for him, incidental.

"I am glad, too," he replied simply. Then she took several steps back in his direction, gazed up at him with a face relaxed and glowing, and kissed him for perhaps the twentieth time that day. These were not the kisses of lawn parties, earned after hours of persuasion and the slow erosion of a debutante's sense of propriety. They were not stolen or hidden—they were easy, and full of joy. Diana had always possessed a kind of gorgeous, reckless innocence, which he would have liked to drink in; she was even more courageous to him now that he knew she'd traveled so far, and by herself. Earlier he had made an observation along these lines, and she'd gleefully responded: "I *am* seventeen now!" with such touching irreverence he could only laugh. It was as though his life had begun again late Friday evening, and every hour since then had been as wondrous and full as a day in the book of Genesis.

"There, I think I see it!" Diana withdrew her lips from his and pointed—pausing a kiss that seemed to go on endlessly from one hour to the next, with short breaks for speech or sustenance—up the hill, where Henry could just make out the jutting angles of a white walled villa. The city was below them, stretching out toward the sea, as well as the square where they had eaten croissants and drank *café con leche* that morning amongst languid gentlemen smoking cigars. The barracks lay between them and the crooked streets of the old town. Henry glanced back once, thinking fleetingly of his obligations there, and then hurried to catch up with Diana as she charged toward the house.

A few long strides and they had crested the hill. The ground dipped below them, and then rose again underneath the villa, a single-story structure that had once been white, ringed by an impressive terrace. Palms sheltered the area, which had fallen into disrepair, weeds colonizing the paths that connected the small buildings that dotted the property, and little turquoise birds darted in and out of the thick foliage. Henry followed Diana across the lawn and up the stairs of what must once have been the main house, where they encountered an impressive wooden door, carved and worn, and secured with a huge iron lock.

"We're shut out," Diana said, frowning, resting her fingers against the handle as though to confirm the fact.

"Perhaps we could break a window," Henry ventured, gesturing toward the glass panes to either side of the main entrance.

"No! No, no." Diana's eyes grew round at the suggestion. She took his hand and drew him along the terrace, which was covered with tiles that had, once upon a time, been painted with geometric blue and white patterns. "We can't touch a thing," she admonished sweetly. "I've heard from all kinds of people at Señora Conrad's that it's just as it was when he left it, all the books are in the same place, and God must be watching out for it because it is immune to thieves. They say," and now her voice sunk to a whisper, and she twisted her neck enough that Henry recognized a conspiratorial expression on her crescent face, "that he wrote his best verses here, that when he left it was over for him."

Around the house they walked, peering in at beaten leather armchairs and moldering book-crammed shelves. A peachy afternoon light broke through a sky that was otherwise a study in fearsome grays, illuminating the old candelabras and paintings and masks that adorned the walls that had once housed a sedentary life. It was the ruins of an existence very different from their own, and they moved around the grounds as though through the hushed halls of a museum. Diana became absorbed with the magic of the site, and he became absorbed in her, watching an aura of fascination suffuse her features. She glanced back at him, her shaded eyes wide open as though to say, *Can you believe we're here, in a place like this?*

Perhaps because she was so occupied in imagining the recitation of verses that had occurred there on long-ago evenings, while Henry remained distracted by the loveliness of her unselfconscious heart-shaped face—shadowed by palms, touched by breezes—neither at first noticed the drop in temperature or the moisture accumulating in the atmosphere. They had nearly traveled around to the front again, their hands still clasped as she led him from one window to the next, when raindrops as big as grapes began to hit the terrace.

"Oh!" she gasped in surprise, looking up at the sudden precipitation. Then they both broke into a run, hurrying across the wraparound terrace, which was quickly becoming slick, and down the stairs. But their instinct to run from the rain, Henry soon saw, had been a foolish one. By the time they had dashed across the field, the large drops were fast becoming an onslaught. Henry's shirt would have been soaked through, had they not so quickly reached the shelter of a garden shed with a thankfully broad metal awning. He tried the door, and found it secured from within, although by then all the fear and surprise had left Diana's face, and she was gazing out at the sheets of falling water, which were forming rivulets down the hill, in delight.

"We'll drown if we try to make it back to the city now. . . ." Henry dried his face with his hand. From where they stood, he could see all the way down to the bay, where children were no doubt running for the shelter of arcades and the sewers would soon flood.

"Yes," Diana agreed. "But how grand!"

"How grand," he repeated, realizing she was right. He had a sudden sense of the lushness around him, of the colors being unusually vivid, of each inhaled breath being impossibly full. Everything petty and extraneous in the world was about to be washed away. "And look—how lucky!"

A few feet to his left was a little round white iron table, and two chairs covered with the same chipped paint. Diana's pearl-like teeth emerged between her small, full lips as they stretched upward in pleasure. She undid her hat, and then they both moved to the chairs. Henry opened the covered wicker basket he had been carrying. Neither was hungry, so he pried open the two bottles of cola that Diana had packed for them that morning, when it had still been dry and sunny, and lit them each a cigarette.

"Isn't it amazing how the sun gets through, even in all this?"

Diana had settled into her chair. Her pink skin glistened with the moisture, and her hair clung, damp and dark, around her soft ears. Though he didn't want to take his eyes off her, he did, eventually, turn to catch the golden rays that were indeed visible despite heavy rainfall, despite the blacks and grays trying to outdo each other in the sky. The smell of earth rose up, mingling with drops fresh from heaven; water against the metal awning up above made for cacophonous music. He took a sip of the sweet soda, and a drag from his cigarette. His breath had slowed already, and after the long walk and the quick dash, his body was beginning to feel calm. Even though he was a volunteer soldier in the United States Army, he had perhaps never been so far from the comforts that had characterized every day of his twenty-one years. They were a good way from town, and yet he felt he had everything he needed. He turned his dark eyes on the girl whom he had dreamed of so often over the previous months. Beside him, at that very moment of existence, at the heart of a torrential downpour, she was exquisitely real, and she, too, seemed content to go on sitting there forever. She exhaled cigarette smoke into the humidity and reached out for his hand.

Consciousness came pleasantly over Henry. Faintly, beyond the door, he could hear boots, the distant voices of men, reveille. He was back in the barracks—it had been the nearest place for them to run to, the night before, when the rain let up. Though some part of him had longed, irrationally, to sit on that spot forever, drinking cola and smoking cigarettes and watching all the different ways that rain could sweep across a green acre, they had agreed they should try to get back to the city before darkness fell. But he liked being with Diana this way, too: sleepy and pliant, her face partially obscured by ill-behaved curls, the peachy arc of her shoulder just emerging from beneath a blanket. She murmured and stirred a little in her sleep, pushing against him in a way that brought to mind a newborn kitten.

When he'd first arrived in Havana, Henry had been at pains to prove that he was just like all the other troops stationed there, and he had risen early and run hard with the rest of them. But inevitably, as the colonel's leniency had grown more persistent, he had begun to slip. He kept trying to be up early, but it was never as easy after a night of rum drinking. Now that he had Diana again, he had given up the notion entirely; that morning, listening to his fellow soldiers exerting themselves out there in the wet morning, he felt not even a twinge of guilt.

"Schoonmaker!"

The gruff voice was followed by a shaft of stark morning light falling across the floor of his barracks room, and then the face of Colonel Copper, smiling idiotically as it jutted into the doorframe. At the sight of his mustache, Henry grabbed at the blanket and pulled it protectively over Diana, waking her in the process. He could feel her fingers seize up against his chest, and tried silently to communicate that he wanted her to stay very still, very silent.

No matter how little he had liked Colonel Copper up until that moment, it was nothing compared to the hatred he now felt as he watched the contortions of the man's face. His confusion over the second form under the blanket, and his subsequent surprise at finding Henry not alone, gave way— too slowly, and accompanied by a series of facial ticks—to lurid realization.

For the subsequent wink alone Henry could have killed him.

"Is something the matter?" he asked, after several moments in which the colonel stood mute, but apparently quite at ease, his eyes big as saucers.

"Ah—Schoonmaker!" The colonel boomed. The soft body beside him went tense at the sound. "I was worried because you've been absent since Friday, but now I see you were busy taking my advice!"

"Can I do something for you?" Henry prodded.

"You missed reveille," the colonel replied, mock-sternly.

"I thought—"

"Ha! Don't worry yourself, my boy. . . ." The colonel leaned against the doorframe. The daylight behind him illuminated Henry's twill jacket, which hung from a hook on the wall, as well as his second pair of trousers and shirt. Diana's clothes, muddy and wet after their hurried trek away from the poet's house, were in a heap on the wooden chair. "It has been lonely without you, though, with nobody but the uneducated classes to talk to. Of course, there will be no race this afternoon, owing to the storm, but I thought perhaps we could discuss . . ."

Henry watched him warily, and tried to make the face that would encourage the colonel to go away with maximum expediency. He seemed to have succeeded, for the colonel winked, muttered good-bye, and dragged his boot against the floor. If Henry had hoped that the man would disappear before really glimpsing Diana, however, he was soon disappointed, because she emerged slightly from his embrace then—showing, in the process, more of her naked back than he really felt comfortable with.

"*Hola*," said the colonel, his pronunciation stilted.

"Hello," went Diana's dry reply.

"You're . . . an American girl." The obnoxious cheer had disappeared suddenly, and whatever replaced it sent Henry spiraling to new depths of dislike.

"And if I were?" Diana ducked under the covers and pressed herself into Henry's chest again. Both of his arms covered her instinctively, but this gesture did nothing to head off Colonel Copper, whose brown leather boots—adorned with utterly superfluous silver spurs—were now striding noisily across the floor. He carried himself more sharply now, more like a military man than ever before, and when he reached the narrow, metal-frame bed in the far corner of the room, he stuck out his chest as though he had just taken part in a twenty-one-gun salute.

"And not just any American girl."

Henry watched immobilized as Diana slowly pushed back the covers and hazy layers of sleep, and turned to look at the colonel. If she appeared a little shocked it was no wonder, for no matter how many countless rules of decorum she had broken to be in that bed at that hour, so far from home, it was doubtful she had ever seen a man be so forward and boorish at her bedside. As far as Henry knew, he was the only man who had ever been in Diana's bedroom at all, and the widening milky whites of her eyes conveyed that the part of her that was raised by a mother always mindful of propriety was still alive inside.

"What does it matter?" she asked, trying to sound a little ribald.

"Oh, God—" The colonel took a step back. He met Henry's eyes. "I *know* her."

"No." Henry was relieved that the colonel had ceased his leering, but he distrusted whatever it was that had caused the change. "No, you don't."

"Yes. Yes, I remember her quite distinctly." The colonel was wagging his finger now. His voice had grown stuttering and obsessive, as though he were repeating information he had recorded in rote fashion in his daily journal. "She was at the party given for Admiral Dewey at the Waldorf-Astoria back in September. She was wearing lavender and she danced with Mr. Edward Cutting. I am sure, because I suppose I jotted it down. And I am doubly sure of it, because this morning when I was reading the social notes—it is the only way to know where in the world one's friends are—I saw a little section about how she was wearing her hair in a most peculiar short style, and you, miss, are the first girl I have ever seen with hair like that! The only trouble is," he went on, working his hands together, "you're said to be in Paris. . . ."

"You must have me confused," she returned with a brave giggle, but her heart wasn't in the lie, and Henry knew there was going to be trouble. The hours spent sitting a few feet from a torrent, smoking and waiting and telling each other stories of where they had been, were still with him, but he sensed there would be no more like them.

"Schoonmaker, what kind of an operation do you believe I'm running here? Do you find it farcical what I do? You can't bring a girl like her into a barracks, not a girl who is supposed to be attending balls in Paris or New York, a girl people are going to come *looking* for!"

Even now, Henry did not experience his superior pulling rank with him. Colonel Copper only paced the room, straightening his jacket nervously. He wasn't angry—he was afraid of losing some imaginary stature, and that boded worse.

"They'll come looking for her," he went on, more to himself now, "but it's my neck they'll want. They'll say I was running a high-class brothel down here and I'll be ruined. She'll ruin me. It won't stand, no, no, no, it won't stand."

Diana's expression had grown quizzical. She was asking Henry, silently, what he made of it. He wished he had reassurances for her, but all he could think to do was to reach for the blanket, pull it over her and hold her as tight as possible. It was plain to see that Colonel Copper's reaction was bad. What he'd seen frightened him, and he wasn't going to be able to sit still until he had done something about the debutante who'd snuck into the barracks like a camp follower. Her smile fell a little, and then they both turned their faces back in the direction of the colonel.

"No," he concluded, more decisively this time as he turned his gaze on the lovebirds. Morning light washed away the details of the simple room, as well as the older man's face, and there was almost a tinge of elegy in his words. "It will not stand."

THE WESTERN UNION TELEGRAPH COMPANY

TO: *William S. Schoonmaker*

ARRIVED AT: *The Schoonmaker House*
416 Fifth Avenue, New York
2:00 p.m., Monday, July 9, 1900

*Mr. Schoonmaker—Humbly to inform that
I am sending Henry back to New York
today on special mission. Please understand
this was necessary. I will explain more fully
in a long letter. Your friend—Col. Copper*

ONDAY AFTERNOON WAS THE TIME WHEN elegant people dropped by the Schoonmakers' Fifth Avenue mansion to utter polite nothings and view the expansive luxury amidst which its denizens lived. In the hour before the public was known to be welcome, the family gathered together, alone, so that their patriarch could be sure they all looked their parts. Penelope emerged from her quarters tentatively on the Monday following her reentry to society, and descended toward the main part of the house with a touch of caution. The mood behind her alabaster oval of a face was a mixture of defiance and trepidation. Henry had abandoned her to a crushing boredom, but some of the stuffier people had not taken her appearance in public very well. The papers were not commenting on the minor scandal yet, but if she continued to behave this way, they would. As everyone who knew her was well aware, Penelope was no fool, and she was acutely cognizant of how closely related were her social stature and her married name.

"Ah, Mrs. Henry," called the butler, as she approached the drawing room. "Mrs. Henry" was what the staff called her to distinguish her from the senior Mrs. Schoonmaker, and, Penelope couldn't help but feel, to subtly put her in her place. "These came for you," he informed, in a discreet tone, as he gestured to the marble tabletop. Her eyes darted. There, erupting from a huge gilt-inlaid vase, were hundreds of pillowy magenta peonies—so many stems, they seemed likely to overwhelm their container.

"Oh!" she exclaimed; the flowers constituted such a gorgeous still life that her façade instinctively relaxed.

"From the prince of Bavaria," the butler went on, averting his eyes, "who is currently a guest at the New Netherland Hotel. . . ."

"*Oh*," she repeated, though this time in a different tone, as she put her fingertips to the satiny petals clustered together. They were just like her: dramatic and rare and impossible to look away from, although frail, in their way, and she knew in an instant that the prince had recognized all these qualities in her person. The defensive foreboding she had so lately felt began to fade, and, as she experienced the sudden pleasure of being in the presence of beautiful things, her own high sense of self-regard came flooding back. She was still plenty alluring, those flowers reminded her, still capable of attracting a very fine species of man, no matter how poorly Henry treated her.

"Thank you, Conrad." She twisted the black agates set in white gold at her wrist. Like all the pretty things she had been given as a bride, it was from the elder Mr. Schoonmaker, whose money was old and greatly augmented by his youthful ventures in railroads and real estate and other areas that ladies like Penelope were raised not to be curious about. Her stepmother-in-law had once told her that a woman had the most fun after she was married, when no one cared very much about her purity anymore, and, staring at the breathtaking arrangement that her loveliness had garnered, she felt ready to finally accept this as the truth. Before—when she was cooped up in the house, or having to be constantly vigilant of her husband's questionable fidelity—she had been dubious. But now she saw that there were plenty of thrills to be had even with Henry away. Or—she amended her train of thought, thinking of the way the prince had admired her on Carolina Broad's dance floor—*especially* with Henry away. She gave herself a private, mischievous smile as she checked her simple, upswept bouffant in the walnut-framed hall mirror, and then turned in the direction of her in-laws.

"What a joy it will be to have all my family together again, under one roof . . . ," William Schoonmaker was saying as she entered the grand first-floor drawing room. He was not a small man, and all of his considerable size was richly garbed. Every detail of him commanded attention, but she was having difficulty feigning deference, or even paying much attention, at the current moment. Why should she, when she had so recently captured the attention of a prince? ". . . And just in time for the Family Progress Party's ball."

The only family whose progress old Schoonmaker was really interested in was arranged across a vast drawing room, reclining on the silk upholstered Louis Quatorze pieces, each at a safe distance from the colossal mahogany mantel where the patriarch stood surveying them. Isabelle, the second Mrs. William Sackhouse Schoonmaker, was closest, her elbow rested against the scroll end of the chaise longue she occupied. Her hair was girlish yellow and her cheeks a healthy pink, not unlike her dress, which ballooned in the sleeves but grew narrow in the wrists, and the chief feature of which was the giant satin bow across the bust. Facing Isabelle was Prudence, her stepdaughter, disappearing into her customary black silk dress with its priestlike white trim. Beneath them stretched the plum-and-ochre Hamadan carpet, upon which lounged Robber, Penelope's Boston Terrier, who everyone ignored. After crossing the threshold, Penelope chose a settee, walked to it, and quickly arranged herself so that the turquoise silk upholstery was obscured by waves of dress. She wore a voluminous skirt of salmon crepe de chine and a high-necked shirt of darkest gray with tiny iridescent lines across the chest; it puffed at the shoulders and grew narrow in the sleeves. A golden afternoon light fell across the Schoonmakers from the high windows that faced Fifth Avenue, lending a kind of splendor to all the marble statuary interspersed through the room, as well as the polished mahogany furniture, and the folds of the ladies' heaping skirts, which rose in gorgeous glittering crests and fell to shadowy canyons. Several servants wearing velvet livery emblazoned with the Schoonmaker crest were quietly posted in the margins of the room, where they could best be ignored, should anything be required.

Penelope let her made-up lids fall for a moment, and when she'd opened them again the bright blues of her eyes were refocused on her husband's father. "Which ball?" she asked blandly.

"Oh, Penny, you remember," said Mrs. William Schoonmaker, her voice a touch reprimanding. The chumminess between the senior and junior Mrs. Schoonmakers had slipped somewhat, ever since the junior had been less than helpful in facilitating the flirtation between her brother, Grayson, and Isabelle, who was in fact his same age. What she had failed to appreciate was how crucial Grayson had been to Penelope's scheme of ruining Diana Holland's reputation and stepping on her heart. Anyway, it was long ago, and none of it had gone as planned, and Grayson was back in London now, still irritatingly heartbroken over little Miss Holland and working for their family's firm there, and so the icy tone her stepmother-in-law employed was simply overkill. "The Family Progress Party ball, next Friday, when William's candidacy for mayor will be announced," she finally declared.

"And where the public will first get to see a reunited Mr. and Mrs. Henry Schoonmaker," the candidate concluded, with what Penelope supposed was an attempt at a friendly smile. If that farce of a kindly expression was intended to soothe, it sorely missed its mark; the long summer of entertainments she'd been imagining for herself had just been snatched away with a single sentence.

"*What?*" she snapped. Her face had fallen; she couldn't help it. She was again picturing Henry the last time she saw him, in his smart soldier's jacket and leather gaiters over polished black boots, completely indifferent to her suffering as he walked out.

"Show it to her," her father-in-law commanded, and then one of the servants came forward from the wall. Dutifully Penelope took the telegram and read what was written there on the yellow form, before placing it back on the silver tray. "You see?" Schoonmaker the elder went on. "Soon you will have your husband back."

Her eyes took in the telegram—already she could see just how it would happen. Old Schoonmaker would arrange for the less serious papers to write of Henry as though he really *had* behaved bravely in battle. The less serious papers were, of course, the ones her closest friends and most cherished rivals read, and they would all be congratulating her when they saw her next, for having such a very fine specimen for her mister, and for having him home in one handsome piece. But for Penelope, now quietly radiating hatred from her position on the settee, nothing could be more inopportune.

Penelope glanced up after a pause and offered her in-laws a supremely fake smile. She knew that if people were whispering about her, she should be grateful at the prospect of having the shelter of a husband's presence again. Yet she was unable to muster any sentiment of that kind. She liked to be always winning, and it seemed a long time since a game had gone her way.

"To the Schoonmakers!" William was saying now, lifting his afternoon bourbon so that the ice rattled and caught the light. "And to the Family Progress Party," he added. Penelope could not suppress an eye roll, although she was not alone in this, for Isabelle had recently stopped pretending to be interested in her husband's political ambitions—except when it allowed her to be snappish with her daughter-in-law. "And to the young couple who may now return to the important business of furthering our great line. . . ."

Bitter as it was for her, Penelope knew that this moment required a bereaved aspect, and so she did allow a little color into her cheeks and a light furrowing of her high, fine fore-

head. A tense silence filled up all the empty space in that opu-
lently cluttered room. Old Schoonmaker appeared to regret
the hurtful line he'd taken. Every one of the Schoonmakers
knew it had been a hostile gesture on Henry's part, to leave
when his wife was in a family way; to reference it now was
thoughtless at best. But in the bloodless way of their people,
the conversation would pause only long enough for the dis-
comfort to dissipate. Then the family would return to a safe
topic. Penelope blinked furiously, and then her eyes swept
toward the other members of the household, who stood still
and glistening in their bejeweled setting, like some very grand,
very dishonest portrait. The injuries the Schoonmakers had
brought on her were suddenly too much to bear.

"You must excuse me," she announced uncivilly.

Then she found herself a little shocked again, for as
she rose and strode toward the door, not one of them moved
to stop her. Not one asked if she were all right, if she were
feeling weak, or if her melancholy had returned to her. This
realization made her move faster, until her heels were making
a rapid click against the hardwood at the border of the drawing room. By the time she passed into the hall, her teeth were
set together, and the length of her spine had seized. Her eyes
had grown wild—it was almost difficult to focus—but then
she settled on the butler, coming toward her from the direction of the foyer.

"Mrs. Henry—" he began, but was cut off.

"Ah! Good." Penelope's voice was shrill, but that didn't bother her particularly. The important thing was that she was heard back in the plush quiet where the three remaining Schoonmakers doubtless persisted in uttering a deafening nothing. "My husband is coming back, as you know, but it will be necessary to set up a separate bedroom, as I am still much too weak to have my bed invaded. Make it far away from mine, perhaps on the east side of the house. Please have his luggage put there, and kindly inform the staff that I am not to be told of his doings. You can have the prince of Bavaria's gift put by my dressing table now."

Then she turned and walked with haughty fire back to her own quarters. Having been robbed of her first prospect of a good time in months smarted, and she was not about to make it easy for anyone even slightly complicit in the humiliating captivity her marriage had become.

Eleven

Sometimes ends are in fact beginnings; beginnings ends. Or that is how a few parties I have gone to fare, which is another reason I never travel without a varied wardrobe.

—MRS. L. A. M. BRECKINRIDGE, *THE LAWS OF BEING
IN WELL-MANNERED CIRCLES*

$\mathcal{D}$IANA WATCHED THE SKYLINE OF HAVANA DRAW away from her as though it were the coast of utopia, from which she had been banished forever. The baroque domes of the churches grew tiny and it began to settle in for her, rather darkly, that she would never again walk the arcades of the old town while the rain pelted the squares, or collect palm fronds in the hinterlands, or watch the sunrise over cobblestones after she had worked till dawn. Instead, it would be New York, a place she had left in the dead of night, where her lover's wife waited armed with all the secrets of all the bad things Diana had ever done. Still, for all that, she couldn't feel too sorry for herself. Henry was just behind her, his arms wrapped around so as to shield her from the wind up high on the hurricane deck.

Behind him stood two members of Colonel Copper's brigade, charged with escorting the society girl back to her mother. There had been much haranguing and pleading that morning, but in the end the colonel had not budged from his position that he would be failing his country if he did not insist on Miss Holland's leaving the foreign port of which he was, after all, among the most senior American military personnel. He had wanted Henry to remain in Cuba, but Henry had insisted that it would be improper for a girl not to have the protection of a family friend, who was after all a married man, on such a long sea voyage. And since the colonel's argument had been for propriety all along, he had been forced to acquiesce.

Henry wore his complete uniform that day, with all the buttons done up. Diana would remember him that way for a long time, she thought—his handsome face in a serious composition, his dark eyes alive with emotion, his shoulders broad under the blue jacket. Neither of the banished pair had spoken much since they'd been discovered in bed that morning. The enormity of what lay before them was almost too much to address. Anyway, they had first grown infatuated with each other when Henry was still engaged to Diana's older sister, though that seemed so long ago, and their love had never been the kind where communications were easily exchanged.

"I am sorry, my Diana," Henry whispered into her hair, which blew up around her face. They had passed out of the bay by then, and the ocean, which was growing choppy, yawned infinite beyond the ship's rail. "I ought to have been more careful."

She pushed her head back, so that his lips pressed faintly against the crown, and stroked his hand with her fingers. There were no accurate words for what she was feeling, and the rocking of the boat had put a sick twist in her stomach.

"I *always* ought to have been more careful," he went on, bending forward a little so that he could put the side of his face against the side of hers, and his lips against her cheek. "In Havana, in New York, after I was married, before. Especially before. If I had been more careful, I might not have been married at all."

Diana smiled a little at the memory of the morning after they first slept together. It was the only time he had slept in her bedroom. She'd given up her girlhood to him the night before, an act she'd never once regretted. But her maid, Claire, had come in through the door and seen them—she must have told her sister, Lina, and from there it had gotten to Penelope, who'd threatened to inform all the staid people who were the Hollands' supposed friends and relatives if Henry didn't marry her. Diana's ruination was the thing Penelope had traded to call herself Mrs. Schoonmaker; that was the bargain that had so effectively parted Di from the only man she'd ever loved.

"I was the one who was incautious," Diana replied after a minute, and laughed a little.

"But I was the older, the more experienced one," he persisted with a weary sigh. What he'd said was true, of course, but she couldn't help but think—without quite knowing how to express it—that she was older now, too, and that she had in fact traveled more than Henry at this point in their lifetimes. She could perhaps outdrink him now, too. The bones of her back rested against his chest, and so she felt how hard he swallowed before he spoke again. His tone, when he did, had the ring of destiny. "I'll never be so careless with you again."

She inhaled sharply. "It feels more true than ever now, doesn't it?"

"Yes." The sun would be gone from the sky soon, and for a while they watched the darkening sea smash up against the sides of the ship. They had rooms below—separate, of course—but neither wanted to go down under when the city where they had been so happily reconnected was even the slightest bit visible on the horizon. "It is truer. I can't imagine what my life was before. I can't imagine ever being without you for very long again."

The unsteadiness of being high up over rough waters became, in the next moment, confused with the particular dizziness that was for her so closely associated with Henry's attention when it was focused in her direction. She leaned against him for support and reminded herself to breathe. There was firm resolve in his voice, something new—there was power in it, and the beginning of a promise she had longed to hear for months.

"I can't stand the idea of going back to how things were, not after we've been together like this. Diana . . . it's you I always wanted. You I should call my wife."

The nausea faded at the sound of the word *wife*. The crisp sea air, which filled her nose and chilled the edges of her ears, was like cool clarity. Her insides felt dusted with sugar, and she opened her round little mouth to whisper sweetly back at him. "Once upon a time you gave me a piece of jewelry with the inscription 'For my true bride.' I took that seriously, you know."

"Yes, I know."

She turned away from the rail, twisting in his arms so that she could look up at the clean lines of his sun-touched face. The wind was harsh on his skin, and the outdoor light made slits of their eyes. "Anyway, it won't feel the same, not after we've been together like this. Not after I found you, one soldier of thousands, in a foreign city. How could it?"

Henry shook his head and exhaled gloomily through his nostrils. "But there are so many difficulties."

She half turned her face away from him, but held his dark gaze, and let her mouth curl up a little. She had never, even for an instant, seen Henry unsure of himself like that, unable to imagine how it would be for him, especially not over a girl, and one who'd known so little of love as she. It rather changed her world, for Henry was such a famous rake, and she was merely the second-best-loved of the Holland sisters.

"Henry . . . ," she whispered in her most caressing tone, as her hands reached for each other around his torso.

"Yes?"

"We neither of us can go back. Not to Havana, nor to the way things were before, not even if we wanted to." She was laying her words out carefully, each coming to her just before she said them. "We couldn't bend to all of New York's stringent ritual now if we tried. There are many difficulties, but how could any of their pieties or judgments keep us from seeing each other? We're in love, after all."

"Di . . ." He swallowed hard again—this time it was a sadness going down, and anguish was plainly visible in his face over all he had done. "I don't want you to be just my mistress."

The ship rose and fell with the water and, a little beyond them, across the blond boards of the deck, the two soldiers watched the scene of the huddling sweethearts as though, even now, they might take their chances overboard. But Diana had never felt steadier, surer. The sick feeling was completely gone now, and she knew she must be a great deal older for seeing, all of a sudden and so clearly, how men could be the weaker sex. Even a fellow like Henry was too sensitive in moments like these, and she understood that it was she who had to be brave and lay out how it would be.

Now Diana's smile was one of patience. She went on as

though she were telling him a story: "But it won't be forever, nothing ever is, and anyway I don't mind being a mistress so much if I'm *your* mistress." They leaned in to each other, so that their foreheads touched. Suddenly the prospect of sacrificing any amount of dignity for him, for the whole grand romance, seemed very heroic. "How could I mind being your mistress, when I love you so?"

He only nodded, their heads bobbing against each other to the rhythm of the ocean. A gull swooped, cawing, just behind her, and Diana found she was surprised that they were still close enough to land for all that. The sea was green-gray around them, and the place they were leaving was obscured by streaky clouds through which a few blades of fading sun shone for the last time that day. Or any day, as far as they were concerned. The place they were going, the stares they were in for—well, she couldn't imagine that yet. She clung to Henry in the in-between place, and found there was plenty of joy all over her little person right where she was.

Twelve

Elizabeth,

A most miraculous, most unforgivable event has occurred. Your sister has just been returned to my care, by two army men, arrived this day from Cuba. She will be punished, of course, and not allowed out of the house or my sight. I am relying on you to show her the error of her judgment. We are coming to your home for dinner this evening, and I want you to impress upon her how poorly your adventures outside of New York indeed proved.

Yours, Mother

*I*N THE CAIRNS BROWNSTONE, ON AN EMINENTLY respectable stretch of Madison, everything was in its place and an air of prosperous well-being floated throughout the rooms. The cook was preparing dinner, for all the Holland women would be dining there that evening. Elizabeth had had a busy week, but she'd finally managed some rest that afternoon, and now that order had been established, and the place was looking so much more like a home, a healthy aspect had returned to her cheeks. So Elizabeth thought, anyway, as she lingered a little while longer in front of the ormolu mirror with the embossed ribbon detail in her bedroom. Behind her in the frame were the white-canopied bed and garnet-colored wallpaper. Her complexion had always been pale, but as she studied her reflection, she thought she detected a hint of the pinkness that Will used to like, too. Ever since she had heard about the success of his oil field, she had been wearing black in a secret act of devotional widowhood, but it did not—she couldn't help but notice—make her look any smaller.

Soon Diana would be coming through the door—
Elizabeth could almost imagine how her soft little arms would
be thrown wide in the expectation of an embrace, as she cried
out: "But you're so gigantic!" Despite the tenor of their mother's
note, Elizabeth knew that the old lady was relieved, as she was,
to have Diana back. That was the main thing, and Elizabeth
felt extra lucky to have such a nice home to welcome her little
sister into. She had not paused the hectic business of making a
household all week, and she was glad that she hadn't, now that
she knew what a homecoming it would be.

Of course there was another, barely conscious reason for
her constant busyness, which was that whenever she paused
too long her thoughts turned to the document that linked her
and Will's names long before they were actually married. How
had her father realized, she would have liked to know. Had her
first love confided in him? But she would never have answers
to questions like that. The two men who could answer them
were gone from her. And then there was the issue that turned
her stomach a little sour, which was that her husband—the
one whose name she was called by in public now, the one currently pledged to protect her, the one who she'd most recently
promised to serve—had known of it for so long, and not told
her. There was a tiny voice in the back regions of her mind,
insisting that Snowden should get his hands off what had
been intended for her and Will to share.

Elizabeth gazed at her reflection a long time, like the vain girl she used to be, and not the mother she'd soon become. When the bell rang below, she tucked a few stray hairs back into the twist rising from the nape of her neck and tried to pinch some color into her cheeks. How had it grown so late?

But when she came—hurrying, and yet not particularly fast—out into the hall, which joined the second floor rooms and ended at the steep stairs into the foyer, she saw the sun streaming in through the stained glass fanlight and realized that it was far too early for her family to be arriving. She came onto the landing and looked down. The carpet, which she had chosen at the beginning of the week for its handsome oriental design of burnt sienna and teal woven threads, spread from below the landing to the front entryway. She couldn't help but pause, now, and feel a touch pleased with the choice. Presently Mrs. Schmidt walked across it and greeted the afternoon caller. Elizabeth stepped forward and rested a hand on the banister, but she couldn't see who was there; a hanging lamp obscured her view.

"I'm sorry, but he's not in," Mrs. Schmidt was saying.

Elizabeth stepped left gingerly so as to peek at the housekeeper's interlocutor. She felt an instinct, not yet fully comprehended, to be silent and secretive, even though it was her own house. As the man's face emerged beyond the intrusive porcelain shade, pockmarked and swollen, she was glad of that instinct. For she knew him—but how? He was large, and neither poorly nor richly dressed. He was not a man of her class, but he did not appear to be a servant, either. Snowden had a retinue of men who worked for him when he was leading explorations, but this fellow was none of these.

His face was not handsome, but it was not exactly ugly, either. There was something large and boyish about him that did not seem to warrant reproach. But for Elizabeth, that face and that man had a distinctly awful quality about them. It made her feel cold all over—and for weeks now she had been enduring the kind of heat that ceiling fans were useless against.

"I'll see he gets it," Mrs. Schmidt said, and then she placed a note on the pink marble-topped cabinet to the left of the entry. The door closed, and Mrs. Schmidt walked toward the back of the stairs without once looking up.

Above, on the landing, Elizabeth sucked in air. The man was gone, but his face hovered in her mind. She could not begin to understand what it was about him that made her want to cower and hide, or why she now felt so nauseated. The note he'd left remained idle on the table. It was just a little thing, folded and white, and yet she was drawn to the scrap of paper as though it had some gravitational power. She descended—slowly of course, one hand clinging to the banister, the other rested against her protruding belly. The sunlight in the foyer, when she stepped off the final stair, was momentarily blinding.

"Mrs. Cairns—are you all right?"

Embarrassment stuck in Elizabeth's throat as she turned, startled, to see Mrs. Schmidt standing in the shadows of the hall. Shame over her intention to read her husband's private correspondence, as well as any black notions she might have allowed herself to harbor, swept over her. The fatigue must have done it, she decided. She was so tired she was only half capable of logical thinking.

"Can I do something for you?" The older woman came out from the shadows. She wore an apron over the heavy black dress she donned, even now, during the extreme heat.

Elizabeth drew herself up with what dignity she could manage, and smiled softly. "I heard someone at the door—" she began in a feathery voice.

"It was a caller for Mr. Cairns. He left a note. Perhaps you—"

"Ah, good," Elizabeth replied with strained lightness. "Then I shall not have anything to worry about! I think I will go try to rest a little before my family comes."

Mrs. Schmidt turned away her face in subservient acknowledgment of her mistress's intention, and Elizabeth tried to maintain a superior mien as she moved heavily back up the stairs.

When she reached her room, she crossed to the bed, unable to meet her own eyes in the mirror again. She was, in truth, relieved that she had been interrupted before some nonsensical emotions led her to snoop in her husband's mail, for she had never wanted to be that kind of wife. Though she did lie down, she did not in the end manage to fall asleep.

Thirteen

If you're concerned about another

run-in like the one we had at the

opera, I would be more than

happy to make arrangements

face-to-face at the place and

time of your determination.

Affectionately,

T. W.

CAROLINA STEPPED INTO THE FIFTH AVENUE HOTEL in a cloud of expensive perfume, under a broad hat bedecked with cloth flowers, and felt the poetry of her selection of a meeting place. Her mission that afternoon gave her nerves, but she was wearing a fitted jacket of ivory-and-rose pin-striped linen and a matching skirt, both of which fit her exquisitely as only really expensive clothes do, and proved how far she'd come since the afternoon when she was run out of this very hotel by an unkind concierge. Now she knew better than to be intimidated by the Fifth Avenue, which faced Madison Square. It was not as modern or as fine as the New Netherland, where she had lived for a time, or the Waldorf-Astoria, which carried its royal associations in its name. In fact, she'd never returned because it had ceased to seem fancy to her long ago—and not because of any lingering fears about the concierge.

"Miss Carolina . . ."

She turned, surprised a little at herself for feeling so cool

despite the heat of the day and the identity of the speaker—
for there was no getting around the fact that he was a threat
to everything she had fought her way toward. But it was dark
and hush in the lobby of the hotel, and she had spent the
last week being courted by an incomparably eligible bachelor.
Her belief in her own powers of attraction, in her social grace,
had increased tenfold in those seven days. If someone on Wall
Street had put everything on her confidence the week before,
he could have retired like Carnegie today. Her bee-stung lips
gave up only half a smile as she confronted Tristan Wrigley's
golden gaze.

"Why, Mr. Wrigley." The flat delivery had become part
of her charm.

"Can I tempt you with a pot of tea, a pastry, perhaps a
late afternoon aperitif?"

His brown waistcoat and white shirt were similar to the
ones he'd worn the day they first met—she had been running
from the concierge, and he had been leaving his job at Lord
& Taylor, and they had collided on the sidewalk right there
in front of the hotel. She did not like to think of it anymore, but what followed had been rather dissolute. When,
on Wednesday, she had received the note from Tristan, it
had momentarily conjured all her old gauche selves, along
with several helpings of shame. But then she had noticed his
unschooled handwriting, his rather clumsy choice of words,

and told herself she should not be so worried about making him disappear.

She took a breath to steady herself. "No, Mr. Wrigley, I don't think you could."

Placing his hands behind his back, he bent his lean frame forward. It was a chivalrous gesture, but still a few seconds passed before it began to dawn on her that—though they were meeting because Tristan claimed he'd been cheated of a portion of her fortune—he was flirting with her.

"This is business, after all," she added coyly.

"As you wish." Smile lines emerged under his high cheekbones, and a twinkle passed in his hazel eyes. Then he swept his hand forward, like he was showing her around the glove department, and they moved together to the patterned velvet sofa best sheltered by potted palms.

She perched on the seat, her shoulders thrown back and her hands primly on her knee. Sweetly she began: "You feel you are owed something."

"We both know you would be back to working as a maid, or far worse, if I hadn't intervened," he answered in the same charming tone.

"Mr. Longhorn knew very well what I was, and still he thought I should be taken care of." She let her eyes drift to her skirt, and for a moment she stroked the fine fabric. When she spoke again, some of the sugar had gone from her voice. "But

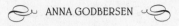

then, I know what *you* are, and I think you should be taken care of, too."

Now she turned in her seat to look at him straight on. He had been gazing at her, and she wondered briefly if the desire he'd felt for her the night he pressed her against the wall of that elevator had grown a little unbearable, now that she was such a polished version of herself. "I knew you would not forget me, Carolina."

"Perhaps you should tell me what kind of figure you had in mind."

He placed his elbow on the back of the sofa so that he almost might have draped it round her shoulders, and brought his mouth close to her ear. The lobby hummed with the low sounds of elegant hospitality, and bellboys pushed brass carts back and forth across the thick, wine-colored carpets. A few guests lingered by the front desk, but as she had suspected, there was no sign of anyone from her circle anywhere near what had only *once* been the best hotel in the city. He exhaled and then whispered a sum that, half a year ago, would have sounded so impossible as to be hilarious, but which now to her only represented a moderately decadent holiday. After all, she was a girl whose total earnings in a year as a lady's maid could not have bought her the suit she'd been buttoned into that morning.

She tipped her head so that her hat obscured the expression on her face, and then stood wordlessly. By the time her chin rose, exposing her features to Tristan, she had made them stony. His mouth opened, a dull, dark slot, and he watched as she extended a gloved hand.

"I will have a check made out to you for just that amount, and it shall be delivered to you at Lord and Taylor before the end of the day."

"Could you have it instead delivered to me at my apartment?" he asked, a little too quickly. Then she knew that he had debts and needed the money badly, and soon, and that he didn't want his employers or anybody else knowing about it. There was something hopeful and a little pathetic about him that she'd never noticed before.

"Of course."

In moments it would be over, and yet she found that she was in no hurry to leave. It was as though, now that she was winning, she didn't want the battle to be over already. She straightened her spine, and let her fist rest against her waist, proudly. This was a pose, and she had a sudden flash of how flattering the chandelier light was on her handsome figure.

"You look awfully pretty, Miss Broad," Tristan grinned. He was relieved, too, she guessed.

The compliment sent a girlish sensation washing through her, and she found herself wanting to say a sentence that had been brimming on her tongue for days, but for which she hadn't found the ideal listener.

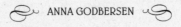

"What is it about you?" he pursued.

The smile that followed was involuntary, and she couldn't help the words that came out of her mouth next. "I'm in love," she very nearly whispered. "It gives a girl a certain something, isn't that what they say?"

Tristan's eyebrows levitated, and in the following seconds Carolina felt very tawdry for even having mentioned her blooming romance with Leland while in the same room as the salesman who had known her at her worst. "Are you now?" he replied in a manner more sly than chivalrous. The snakelike slenderness and the coiled way he carried himself were again obvious. "With that Bouchard fellow?"

She cleared her throat and stepped away from him, trying to summon her late hauteur. But her nerves had returned. "You can expect that check, Mr. Wrigley. I don't imagine we shall see one another again."

Quick as she could, Carolina twirled about and strode for the exit, suddenly wanting for that last bit to be true more than ever before.

Fourteen

Diana Holland—she of the newly shorn hair,
she of the storied starry eyes—will step off a
ship originating on the Continent and into
the waiting arms of her native New York today.
Welcome home, Lady Di.

—FROM THE "GAMESOME GALLANT" COLUMN IN THE
NEW YORK IMPERIAL, FRIDAY, JULY 13, 1900

"OH, NUMBER SEVENTEEN!" DIANA REQUIRED A DAINTY twirl to fully bring herself back into the room where so many of the important transactions of her life had taken place. All the details were the same—the embossed olive leather wall panels, the stained and carved wood ceiling, the Turkish corner heaped with pillows—but the overall effect seemed rather old to her after her travels, a mite dusty, and somewhat small. "I am seventeen now, too," she added with a giggle.

"I am your mother." Mrs. Holland, stationed by the tall, street-facing windows, employed a cold tone. "I am well aware how many years you've walked God's earth."

The house stood on the enclosed little park, all quiet leafiness, which secreted itself between Twentieth and Twenty-first Streets and Third and Park Avenues. That placid brown face with its large, watchful windows had provided shelter, as well as a certain understated cachet, to three generations of the Holland family. Diana's father, Edward, had been born there, and his younger sister, Edith—now occupying a sofa in the outer edges of the first floor parlor—remained a full-time occupant. The pocket doors still whined and stuck in their tracks, except perhaps somewhat less than before Diana had gone, for the brief poverty the Holland family had experienced last fall appeared to have passed, like a bad winter. It was difficult for the youngest member of the family to determine exactly how. In any event, the lady who was born Louisa Gansevoort, and then married Edward Holland at the rather ripe age of twenty-five, was looking petite, as usual, but had reclaimed some of the steeliness of posture which she had once been known for.

"Where's Claire?" Diana asked, noting an unfamiliar maid, who appeared almost too thin to lift a tea tray, cowering in the hall in a plain black dress.

"Who?"

"Claire Broud," Diana replied indignantly, for Claire, besides being a very genuine and soft-hearted person, had worked for the family for years, and was in fact the daughter of the Holland girls' childhood governess. The faux ignorance her mother had just indulged was nothing more than an exercise in status maintenance.

"She moved on," Mrs. Holland returned sharply.

"Oh." Diana's eyes darted to the place where her hands now came together, as regret stuck in her throat. She knew that Claire had felt guilty over telling Diana's secret, and the terrible consequences that had stemmed from its reaching Penelope. But

Claire could not have intended harm, she never intended *anyone* harm, and there was no way Diana could hold a grudge against her. Only—she now realized—she had never told her so.

"In any event," her mother went on coldly, "I do appreciate this trick you've managed, of setting up a false story in the papers in advance, to explain your absence and conceal your peregrinations—your sister never thought to do so much. . . ." Diana, close to the unlit fireplace, raised an eyebrow as her mother paused to examine her hands. For Elizabeth, when she had run away, *had* covered up her absence, and in a rather more extreme way: She'd made everyone believe she was dead. Their mother smoothed the rust-colored chiffon jacket, which she wore over a long black skirt; in the months since Diana had slipped out in the night, her mother must have ceased exclusively wearing widow's garb. The widow's cap, too, was gone, but this only exposed the fact that her dark hair, drawn up in a low bun, was streaked with gray. "I have talked to Mrs. Pennington Gore and old Granny Newbold and Odette, the manicurist, and nobody seems to be any the wiser to your ruse. That is *some* relief to me. But the worry you have caused"— emotion wavered, briefly, in her voice—"you have no idea."

Diana, in a dress of light blue chambray, which was fastened with a brown leather belt and ballooned airily around her arms and legs, moved forward through the old Bergère chairs arranged with affected carelessness across the faded Persian carpet. She had borrowed some of Henry's pomade, and her hair was now parted on the side and greased so that a dark section half covered her forehead and then ducked behind her ears, like a bullfighter's. The sensations within her were light and free. All her being wanted to run great distances, or drink vast quantities of wine, or speak too loudly, or dance for hours. She had successfully made herself far more interesting than any heroine in any novel—but she had not meant to cause her mother pain.

"I would have told you," she ventured sweetly, "but I didn't think you would have let me go."

Mrs. Holland turned sharply from the window, her onyx eyes shining. Aunt Edith, wearing white and cream seersucker, as well as features uncommonly like Diana's, smothered a giggle with the back of her hand. "You are correct on that score," the former snapped.

"And, you see," Diana went on, undaunted, "I knew it was absolutely necessary that I—"

"I will determine what is necessary for you!" Mrs. Holland was not a large person, but she was capable of tremendous vocal force. In a slightly quieter, but no less fearsome tone, she went on: "You are a child, you could not possibly know what is best for you. You are willful—but that is my fault. There was none of the usual tutoring, the finishing, a girl like you requires. If you have turned out a little wild—and clearly you have—then I must take the lion's share of blame."

The sweetness began to fade from Diana's face. She had expected this, of course, but she had traveled so far beyond her mother's petty concerns about propriety that she no longer knew how to respond.

"Mrs. Cairns has agreed to talk to you, tonight, at her new home—"

"Elizabeth!" Delight was resurgent within Diana. "Are we going there tonight?"

"Yes," her mother answered duskily, "because she is going to tell you how you must behave. Edith and I will accompany you. After that you will not leave this house until I deem it acceptable. And that will not be for a good long time." The stern tone was almost laughable to Diana, and she knew that amusement was visible in her coloring. She tried to turn her face away, toward Edith, with whom she'd always shared a girlish, unspoken understanding, but her mother sensed her rebellion. "And when that time comes, *I* will be your chaperone."

The afternoon light was slanting in through the windows on so much cherished, hoary bric-a-brac, showing it for what it was, just as the antiquated beliefs that Mrs. Holland clung to assumed a sheen of the absurd under Diana's bright, hard gaze. In a second or two she had seen that the old lady's methods of coercion were nothing more than postures of intimidation, and all her fixations with propriety were but nonsense spoken into a brisk wind.

"I've worked in saloons and slept in barracks!" Diana

threw her head back and put a defiant hand to her hip. "I can't even begin to imagine wasting my days fixating on embroidery, reading bible passages, day in, day out."

Mrs. Holland stepped away from the window on tense, fast moving legs, a long index finger cocked at eye level. "If you mean to suggest that—"

"I mean to suggest—I *am* suggesting—I am *saying*—that I am home for now, but don't expect me to wait for you to grant me permission before I do any little thing." Diana adjusted the collar of her dress, which formed a *V* over her chest, and inhaled to soften her voice. Then she offered a steady, almost wistful sounding justification: "I just couldn't live like that now."

Mrs. Holland's thin upper lip curled back over her top teeth. "You *will* go to your sister's with me tonight."

"Oh, yes."

"Yes?" The acid in Mrs. Holland's tone was trenchant enough to make Diana's stomach unquiet, and for a moment she wondered if she really was brave enough to act on all her big talk. But in the next instant she knew she'd called her mother's bluff, and that nothing would ever be the same.

"Yes, I'll go to Elizabeth's tonight. But first I am going to pick out some flowers for her. At the shop on Broadway. By myself."

Diana held her mother's gaze, lightning playing over

her chocolate-colored irises, and for a moment both women wavered there, amongst antiques that were the product of fifty years of the Hollands' collecting impulse. Her mother was stunned or furious or both, it was impossible to be certain, and Diana did not wait long enough to find out. She smiled wide and frank as she turned to leave the room.

Overhead, in a perfect blue sky, white clouds drifted, lazy and still in the heat. The façades of Broadway strained upward in their direction, with dollhouse-white columns and cornices, and row upon row of windows framing curious scenes. Signage blared from on high, and canes clicked against the sidewalk. The day was coming to a close, and the people in the street idled there as though they were too relieved just to be free of stuffy rooms to move with any kind of purpose. Diana charged through the crowds, full of joy to be out on the street, in her own city, by herself, and to no longer care who witnessed this indiscretion.

The chambray dress was old—it had been hanging in her closet at No. 17 since the Indian summer of 1899—but she wore it differently now. That shade of worker's blue set off her recently browned skin, and the looseness slavishly flattered the curves of her body. Everything was like that to her just then—familiar, but as though she were seeing it for the first time with all new eyes.

I am the mistress of a married man, she thought to herself as she made her way up Broadway. The phrase gave her insides a pleasant floating sensation. If a passing stranger had asked her to identify herself, she wondered if she could help that being the first response out of her mouth. *I am the mistress of a married man,* she thought again, and flexed her cheeks in private happiness as she entered the glass storefront of Landry the Florist's. Inside it was all tiny white hexagonal tile and mirrors etched with gold. She inhaled air redolent with petals and pollen, and searched out lilies, which were Liz's favorite.

A great cluster of pillowy magenta peonies, in an elaborate arrangement stationed next to the brass till, commanded her attention instead. She had never seen peonies that color.

"What are those?" she asked, approaching the girl behind the gray marble counter.

"Those?" The girl, who could not have been much older than Diana, looked innocently at the gaudy bouquet. Then her face underwent a series of transformations that had become familiar to Diana during her brief tenure as a gossip scribe: First her eyes grew wide with the secret knowledge she had just been reminded of, after which her brow grew together in guarded determination not to divulge, and, at last, her features relaxed with the happy, impulsive decision to go ahead and spill. The girl put her elbows on the counter, and leaned forward. "Those are for the younger Mrs. Schoonmaker, whose husband just came back from war—but can you guess who they are from?"

The name had caused Diana all kinds of anger and pain, but just now she found it overwhelmed her with curiosity. "No—who?"

"Not her husband at all, but the prince of Bavaria, who is a guest at the New Netherland! And it's not the first time, either. He has a standing order for a bouquet just like that to be sent to her every day!"

"No!" Diana feigned chummy shock. "Are Mrs. Schoonmaker and the prince particular friends?"

The girl drew her mouth down from her nose, and her brow rose high above her eye sockets; she opened her palms as if to say, *Who knows?* and then added, as though it explained everything, "They say they danced together at Carolina Broad's house opening."

Both girls exchanged satisfied smiles over this small transaction of information, and the pleasure of being mildly scandalized, and then Diana ordered two dozen deep yellow calla lilies. When she returned to the street, carrying a great bouquet wrapped in brown paper, it was with the distinct sense that someone on high was watching out for her. For she was a young lady who held both the means to plant a gossip item and an unsavory secret about her incomparably odious rival.

Fifteen

YOUR PRESENCE IS REQUIRED

AT THE WALDORF-ASTORIA

WHERE THE FAMILY PROGRESS PARTY

WILL BE CELEBRATING ITS

CANDIDATE FOR MAYOR

WILLIAM S. SCHOONMAKER

ON THE EVENING OF FRIDAY

THE THIRTEENTH OF JULY

NINE O'CLOCK

A HAZE OF CIGAR SMOKE HUNG OVER THE GILDED ballroom of the Waldorf-Astoria, where men in tails and ladies in brightly colored lawn crammed themselves against long banquet tables and danced under chandelier light. Pretty girls and drink were both aplenty, which would have pleased Henry at another point in his life, but he had just returned from a long journey that had left him forever changed. There was no pleasure for him in being on display at the raised table at the back of the room, and he had been bullied into continuing to wear his uniform, even though he wasn't even sure he was technically a soldier anymore. His father kept calling him a war hero; he felt like a clown.

The greasy remains and scattered crumbs of their feast lay across the satin banner of the Family Progress Party, which covered their table and hung down in front of it so that everybody in the room would be reminded who they were supposed to vote for come election time. The kind of families the party was supposed to make progress for were not on very great display that night—not even a token tenement dweller could be found. Henry's single moment of levity that evening was when he'd observed to himself that someone in that room had made a harsh and ironic political calculation, choosing a Schoonmaker to lead this particular party, and that it had proved a rather dark joke. To the right of him sat his father, voluble and imposing, and to his left was Penelope, who appeared dolled up and bored in equally extreme measure.

She was wearing peacock blue, the low square décolletage of her dress edged in gold, and her lips were a bloody shade of red. The bony points of her white elbows pinned down the tablecloth, and she wouldn't meet Henry's eyes. Or he wouldn't meet hers. It wasn't clear anymore. He did feel a little bad for Penelope—she was so proud, and the current circumstances had to sting. But then he remembered how ruthless she had been in mucking up the one pure and lovely thing in his life, and that thought made it impossible for him to even utter her name out loud. He was almost a touch jealous of Diana—for though it wasn't easy for either of them to be parted, she at least did not have to appear in public beside their victimizer.

"Henry Schoonmaker, how does it feel to be home in New York?"

Henry looked wearily up from the remains of his dinner at a slender man in an ill-fitting suit. He recognized him vaguely as a reporter from the *World* with whom the elder Schoonmaker was friendly, and guessed that he was at least partially responsible for the erroneous impression of the younger Schoonmaker's bravery, currently held in the public imagination.

"It must have been awfully fine, coming home to such a pretty Mrs. . . ."

The unruly noise from the dance floor quieted briefly, and it was possible to hear the ruffle of his wife's skirt as she fussed in her chair. She was listening, agitated, for his answer. Henry thought of Diana, and how unbearable it was not to know what she was doing after having spent so many continuous hours in her company. The Hollands should have been invited that evening, but he had looked in vain for her and concluded in the end that her mother would not have sanctioned her presence anywhere public. "How can I answer a question like that?" he replied impatiently.

"No, how could he possibly?" Penelope gasped. She had never been a girl with a surfeit of sweetness, but the sarcasm in her voice now could have severed limbs. "You see how tan he got from all the yachting he did out there, and wouldn't that be awful for any man to give up."

"The—yachting?" The reporter averted his gaze as though even he were embarrassed by the notion, and hoped no one else would be likewise discomfited. It was not the story he'd wanted to hear.

"Henry is just the slightest bit on edge after his months of service," the elder Schoonmaker interjected in a calm, commanding tone. "They both are."

The reporter nodded deferentially and scurried off.

The older man, leaning in to his son's ear, hissed: "Ask your wife to dance."

"But she just—" Henry protested.

"She's being sullen," William advised, sotto voce. "That's what women do. Now ask her to dance—she'll forget all about whatever it is you are squabbling over soon enough."

Henry closed his eyes and regretted ever having left Cuba. They could have run away, he now saw, they had still been free then. It had been an error, a colossal one, to let the colonel send them back. There had been so many missteps, great and small: He should have tried to like the colonel more, he might have been better at persuading him not to send the two lovers home. He shouldn't have let Diana out of his sight, he shouldn't have returned to the Schoonmaker mansion, like a cowardly dog, always returning to a stern master when he didn't know where else to go. Now here he was halfheartedly playing the role in which his father and Penelope had cast him.

"Go on," his father continued, in a tone not so much encouraging as insistent.

Henry tried to remind himself that making Penelope angry, tempting as it was, served no purpose, and that as long

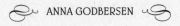

as he was by her side and not Diana's, he should do the thing that would protect his beloved, and make no waves.

"Penny—" he began, rising to offer her his hand, but she was quick and apparently operating with no small store of vindictiveness. Her foot jutted forward, tripping him, so that he lurched awkwardly. Had he not been able to get hold of the back of her chair, he surely would have fallen flat on his face. Henry grimaced in his father's direction, as though the old man might suddenly see the pathetic situation for what it was, but the expression his father returned indicated there would be no letting up now.

Henry drew his hand over his pomaded hair, smoothing his appearance, as though somehow this reference to his dashing exterior might make all the unpleasantness of the scene fade. He tried to recall how successful he had once been in making Penelope chase after him. "Mrs. Schoonmaker," he began again, though his teeth were gritted, and even he was a little surprised by the animosity remaining in his voice. "Won't you dance?"

She drew away from him, propping her chin against her palm, gazing out at the ballroom, pretending not to hear.

Henry leaned over her and said quietly, but—he hoped—forcefully: "I am your husband. I would like to dance with you."

She twisted hatefully in his direction. "You've never acted like it once," she spit.

"Well," he replied. The anger was scorching his throat and it was all he could do to keep his words from becoming ragged with it. "It was never a role I coveted."

Her eyes narrowed. "Perhaps not, but you promised just the same."

"You were in such a hurry corralling me to the altar that you barely noticed I didn't speak half the promises you assume I did."

Penelope slapped a hand against the table. "Why did you come back then? Just to humiliate me? Or do you think I am too dim-witted to notice that you returned to New York on the very same day as your little Di—"

"Stop," Henry interrupted just in time. Hearing Diana's name on such a vicious tongue aroused all of his protective instincts, which had become ragingly acute since their reunion in Cuba. The idea of what Penelope might have said infuriated him, and he fixed his teeth together so that she could see them. "Dance with me," he commanded.

Penelope lifted her face toward him. An arid smile lingered there. The sounds of the band, the low murmur of deal making amongst the political classes, the silent aggravation of his father, sucked up all the air in the room. A light passed across his wife's glacial pupils, and then she extended her gloved hand in his direction.

"Oh . . . *all right*." Her tone had grown girly, almost

flirtatious, but he knew her well enough to know that it was for the benefit of his father, who was after all the man who signed the bills for her new baubles, and that she was in fact speaking words of war. "But I won't like it."

Then she rose, and allowed him to escort her down past the other guests at the mayoral candidate's honored table, and onto the dance floor of the Waldorf-Astoria, where they had danced once or twice in simpler times, back when they still liked one another. Henry, in tails, bowed to his wife, and Penelope sank into a deep curtsy, after which they moved together. There were a few gasps from the crowd around them, and then the music swelled, and the crowd began to clap. For a brief moment, Mr. and Mrs. Henry Schoonmaker had created the illusion of a gorgeous young couple in love.

Sixteen

Tempting as it may be, you must never allow your daughters to chaperone or discipline one another. Such arrangements have always proved a recipe for mischief.

—MRS. HAMILTON W. BREEDFELT, *COLLECTED COLUMNS ON RAISING YOUNG LADIES OF CHARACTER,* 1899

DINNER HAD BEEN CLEARED AND PORT WAS being served in the front drawing room when the sisters Holland were finally able to separate from the rest of their family for a private moment. Like the well-trained hostess that she was, Elizabeth glanced back over her shoulder to be sure that there was contentment amongst her guests. They were lit by the low bluish glow from the gasolier—for it was not a new house, and though Snowden insisted they would soon update it for electricity, the time in which to do so had not yet presented itself. Inwardly, Elizabeth preferred the old way of illuminating a room, for it was subtle, almost ghostly, compared to what an incandescent bulb would provide. Dogwood erupted from tall bronze floor vases, and by the fireplace, Snowden spoke of serious things with Mrs. Holland, no doubt regarding the oil wealth of which his wife had until recently been ignorant. He had been extremely busy all day—dealing with Will's property was apparently a time-consuming endeavor, and he had only returned home just in time to greet their guests.

"You look like a pretty Spanish boy," Elizabeth whispered with affectionate disdain, as she drew her fingers across the dark hair that was almost long enough now to cover her sister's neck. It had been tamed and made to appear straight by some rather masculine hair product or other, and the new arrangement lent a special mystery to Diana's deep brown eyes.

"Well," the younger Holland sister returned with a devious little smile, "I do now know a lot about pretty Spanish boys."

"Oh, Di." Elizabeth tried to sound disapproving, but her relief at having her sister home was so overwhelming that she suspected her original intention was drowned out. The younger was wearing a pale yellow lace confection that made her skin appear all the browner; Elizabeth stood beside her in baby blue seersucker that enforced a rather severe silhouette despite her newly large bosom and belly.

"Oh, Liz, not really. I mean, I might have, except that Henry was all I could think about the whole time I was away, and when I found him he so fully eclipsed my life, I don't know if I would have noticed pretty Spanish boys if I were standing in a room full of nothing else."

Diana's voice was so loud, so rash—it tried her sister's

nerves. Elizabeth's blond head swiveled, fearful of being over-heard, but her mother and aunt and husband were engaged in conversation across the room, and the servants who waited upon them were too far away, even if they had wanted to listen in.

"You cannot speak like that," she whispered.

"But it's the truth!" Diana emitted a giddy laugh, and slid her arm around her sister's engorged middle.

"But he is a married man, Diana, and you are in a very vulnerable position. We have risked too much as a family already, and we are lucky to still have our good name. Mother wanted me to speak to you about—"

"Yes, she told me. She wants you to talk some sense into me, and hopes that perhaps a little decency will rub off, if only it's you doing the admonishing." Diana's sigh as she rested her head against her sister's shoulder was sweetly exhausted, amused. "But she's a fool for encouraging anything of the kind. Who are *you* to tell me not to risk everything for the man I love?"

The brown eyes of the elder Holland girl glazed, and she found herself silenced by this logic. She stared out the front windows. The air was still and damp, and the street lamps illuminated the hot darkness in yellow cones. Mrs. Holland had secured a new driver—that, too, was probably the product of Snowden's secret dealings—and the young man was lean-ing against the old coach wearily. He was not as broad as Will had been, and certainly not as alert in his waiting. But the very thought that this boy slept in the same old loft as Will, which she had crept down to on so many evenings, made her heart feel weak. Diana was right; she was in no position to admonish anybody.

"Do you really love him?" Elizabeth knew Diana loved him, of course—she had known since the brief, strange period when she herself had worn Henry Schoonmaker's engagement ring. What she meant was, did her sister love Henry as she had loved Will? Did she want the balance of her days to be about nothing but him? Once—just after Will's death—she had clung to the notion that Diana's feelings for Henry might be that profound, that such emotion was indeed still possible in this world, after all the horrors. She wanted to believe this now more than ever.

"Yes," Diana whispered, and for once her voice was serious. "Oh, yes, sometimes so much, it hurts."

"Ah," Elizabeth replied, her voice growing small with memory. "That's what it's like."

"I never knew I could love so much!" Diana went on, the giddiness creeping back. "And we *will* be together. He will find a way to leave Penelope. Only it may take a little while. But I have never in my whole life been so sure of something being so right, and I—"

"No." Elizabeth's eyes were still glazed, and her heart

had begun to thud. She spoke like a woman in the thrall of a vision. The well-appointed room behind her, with its blond wood accents and black trim, its polite occupants, its purposeful arrangement, ceased to matter. "You won't be with him that way, by letting time take care of it, by waiting and believing."

Diana turned up her rosy heart-shaped face at her sister. "But—"

"He loves you, doesn't he." It was not a question, and Elizabeth nodded in confirmation of her own statement. "Then you must leave."

"Leave—where?"

"New York." There was a swelling in Elizabeth's throat, which she tried not to give in to. All of her floundering had become raw for her again, and for a moment she would have given anything to be back in California, when she could still retract her foolish insistence that they return home. "The one thing I did wrong was come back here. All that fierce propriety—they would never allow a boy like him to love a girl like me, not in this gilded cage of a city." Elizabeth paused, and met her sister's eyes. "It won't be so different for you, Di."

A silence hung between the sisters. It was possible that Elizabeth had never spoken so forcefully in her whole life. She did not care who heard her, though it didn't matter particularly, as Mrs. Holland and Edith and Snowden had gone on talking all the while, anyway.

"Oh, Liz," Diana whispered after a moment.

Elizabeth shook her heard firmly, her fair brows taut, her small, round mouth cinched tight, and stared at the boy out there in the purple midnight. He looked ready to nod off against the worn black leather side of the carriage. "If you love him: leave. They'll never let you be together here."

The profound loneliness of the new house on Madison had not been evident to her until her remaining family members had filled it with their same old voices and poses and affectionate little sayings, and then returned home together to Gramercy Park. They had been gone for many hours, but Elizabeth had indulged emotions she had not intended to, and was having trouble sleeping. In the middle of the night, she found that her eyes were wide open, and that she was hungry, and that she desperately wanted to eat bread slathered in sweet butter. Apparently her attention was easily diverted, however, because by the time she climbed down the stairs, clinging to the banister to steady her unwieldy form, she had forgotten about food. By the time she finally stepped onto the first floor, all she could think of was the card perched on the pink marble-topped cabinet by the door. Snowden must have come in too hurriedly that evening to have even glanced at his mail.

Her moody fixation with that afternoon's visitor revived, and in her restless early-morning state she felt an extra, ticking urgency. She paused with her hand in the small of her back, and would have reached out to where the folded piece of paper still stood, like a tent on the marble, except that she noticed something else.

A blue box of very particular proportions and color sat beside the note, and she knew in an instant that it was a silver baby's rattle from Tiffany & Co. She knew because she had—in her previous life—ordered this particular gift for the children of several of her older, married cousins. The darkness within ebbed for a moment, and she let her fingers run along its edge, thinking how kind it was of Snowden to have known her well enough to guess how much she would appreciate this particular item. He was kind, of course he was, and she should stop slandering him in her mind. But then she set the box down and picked up the piece of paper anyway.

Mr. Cairns, Please stop avoiding me.
I know what you did in the Klondike,
and if you don't up my payments I will be
forced to make your actions public.
Sincerely, O.L.

Elizabeth placed the note back on the marble top, just exactly as it had been, so that nobody would know it had been read. The word *Klondike* had a terrible significance for her; it was where her father had died. He had enjoyed traveling to exotic locations and speculating far and wide, and he had never cared much if the world considered him a smart businessman or not. That was how he had met Snowden in the first place.

Snowden, her husband, who had known to purchase for her a silver Tiffany baby rattle. She stepped back from the note, ashamed of herself. The stairs and halls surrounding her were dark and empty, and she was relieved that nobody had witnessed her trespass. For the lesson was clear—one did not poke around at night, not unless one wanted to see ghosts.

Seventeen

Let's get out of here

THE NOTE SLID INTO CAROLINA'S FIELD OF VISION with such subtlety that at first she didn't comprehend its meaning, but once she had, her broad cheeks flushed pink. Her gloved hand darted the piece of paper, which had been ripped from the bottom of the menu, before Lucy Carr, the divorcée, could see it. Mrs. Carr had been one of her first friends as a society girl, and though the older woman had never been what you would call "nice people," Longhorn had always found her amusing. There had been several nights when Carolina and Lucy had screamed in laughter about something or other, while Longhorn nodded off over his cognac, and though Carolina had found little use for the twice-wed blonde now that she was truly rich, still she felt a little bad about dismissing her too quickly.

"Did I read that you are engaged again?" Carolina asked, hoping that her gauche blush was fading from her cheeks. Across the shiny parquet floor of the Waldorf-Astoria, skirts of organdy and satin twirled and men whose bellies filled out their paisley waistcoats congregated in colonies beside gleaming marble columns. She herself wore tiers of peach chiffon layered with tiny white lace appliqué and silver sequin edging, and her hair rose above her forehead and then lay in sausage curls, bound by ribbon, against her neck. Underneath the Grecian gathering of fabric at either shoulder, her freckled arms were bare.

"Oh, yes!" Mrs. Carr had once had very fine eyes, although they were ever blinking, and the blinking over years had created a network of lines like dry riverbeds that reached to her temples. "To Mr. Harrison Ulrich!" She giddily extended her left hand to show off the ring.

"*Very* fine." Once upon a time, Carolina would have meant it.

Mrs. Carr's lips pinched together in a poor attempt not to smile, and her eyebrows—which were painted on, and slightly too dark a shade—arched. Then her eyes rolled slowly toward Leland, whose note was still hidden under Carolina's hand, as though to ask, *And you?*

But Carolina simply responded with a bland and unaccommodating smile. In a few moments Mrs. Carr had moved on, which allowed her to crumple and drop the note under the table, where one hoped it would continue to go unnoticed.

"Come with me," Leland whispered into her ear with sweet, urgent emphasis.

Carolina put her hand over his and cast nervous glances across the room. She had been in the famous hotel several times in the months since she had become Longhorn's protégée and then heir, but it still held magical powers for her. The idea of absenting herself from its halls and ballrooms early caused her a slight shudder of scandal. Besides, she was there at Penelope Schoonmaker's invitation, and though the girls were not as close as they had once been, still Carolina owed no small part of her standing to their association. What would they all say if she left Penelope's husband's family's party so unexpectedly?

"But the evening is hardly over," she protested faintly. The Henry Schoonmakers had just taken the dance floor, which meant the night might yet produce glamorous and collectable anecdotes.

"*Come* with me," Leland persisted, and his tone was so firm and so sure that she found herself, despite the earliness of the evening, wanting to give in to him. To say yes to anything he suggested.

In moments they were hurrying out of the room where the Family Progress Party was honoring its next candidate for mayor, and down the bejeweled halls of the hotel. They passed the mirrored panels and amber marble coves, the gold crushed-velvet couches where common people sat and watched the parade of elegantly dressed ladies and gentlemen coming and going from one party to another. It was what the papers referred to as Peacock Alley—quite a show, in which a girl like Lina Broud should have been the observer, but was now, as Carolina Broad, the observed.

Carolina could now admit—privately, to her own self— what she had long denied: that if she'd had the courage, she would have come like the other girls with deadening worka-day jobs to watch the fine people strut past. Instead, she had acted too superior, and talked at length with Will Keller, the coachman, about the ridiculous vanity of all the drips of the leisure class. Those nights, and those sentiments, seemed a long time ago now, and it was partly because of this distance that she was able to glance over at the faces—rosy and imper-fectly arranged, with oversized mouths and chins that sloped to nothing—of the girls worshipfully observing the parade. She smiled faintly at them in passing, as though administer-ing a kind of benediction. But her smile fell when she saw a face she knew.

"Claire?" she exclaimed before she thought.

The girl gazed up at her, shocked and admiring from her place on a bench. She was squeezed between two other girls, clearly maids, wearing a black dress slightly more flattering than the one she wore while working for the Hollands. Her beautiful red hair was back in a simple bun.

"What are you doing here?" For a moment, Carolina was

so pleased with the idea that Claire could see her, so tall and grandly dressed and with the incandescence of a thrilling evening playing beneath her skin. Then she realized that Leland, a few strides ahead of her, had paused to look back, perplexed, and the smile vanished from her lips.

Claire's great big eyes shifted from the gentleman in tails back to her little sister. "Miss Broad," she answered hurriedly, her voice formal, respectful. "How kind of you to say hello. You look immaculate," she added, with a shy smile.

"Thank you." Carolina, suddenly mindful of Leland's presence, drew back her shoulders and did away with her familiar manner. "Are you well?"

"I am working for Mrs. Carr now." Claire glanced at Leland, and then back at Carolina. Her expression was almost pleading. *Enjoy yourself,* she was saying with those cowlike eyes. *Don't mind me.* "I was helping her, in the ladies' lounge, and she said she didn't mind if I waited here, to see the gowns, instead of being sent home as usual."

"How kind of Mrs. Carr." Carolina knew that if she lingered it would require an explanation—but oh, how she wanted her sister to appreciate her glory, how she wished she could just ask where she was living. "Then I trust I will see you soon?"

"Yes, I hope so, miss."

Carolina's heaping coiffure inclined forward, a little curtly, but by then her older sister's eyes were permanently averted, and Leland's expectant arm was already drawing her away, toward the exit.

"Who was she?"

"Oh—just a girl." Carolina's voice was off key; she listened to it echo woefully in her ears.

"It was highly unusual of you to stop and speak to her so familiarly." Carolina's face felt cold for a minute, but then Leland went on admiringly: "It was *very* kind. I've never seen a lady like you be so warm with a girl like that."

"Yes, well . . . I know a little of her troubles." Now her voice grew surer, having glimpsed the line she should take. "She was a waif Longhorn did a kindness to once. He saw her in the street and found her a job. He was always doing that sort of thing. And at the beginning, he asked me to see that she was all right, to go to her and look in on how she was faring, as only another girl can. It was not much."

They were nearing the wide busy entrance of the hotel, and it seemed to Carolina that they moved so lightly they were almost floating.

"How incredibly gracious of you."

The muscles of Carolina's back relaxed. He liked her more all the time, she realized. Then she blushed a touch for good measure. "Well," she whispered bashfully, "we all do what we can."

Their feet moved more quickly as they left the hotel

behind. Leland lifted her thin black cape over her, to shelter her from the public's eyes, as they hurried through the crowds and outside.

"Yes—you do, because you are lovely and good! But what bores! What bores the rest of them are!" Leland exclaimed, as he hopped up behind her into his waiting phaeton and signaled his coachman to drive. The flounces of her flesh-colored dress settled in against her long, strong thighs, and spilled down to the floor and over the legs of his trousers. She was a little taken aback that he would speak that way of the famous Schoonmakers and their associates, but in the next moment she realized it was true, that he was right, that all those people, despite their fancy names and elaborate clothing and heaps of jewels, had just spent an evening boring themselves to the point of absurdity in one of the very best rooms in the city.

"Oh, God, I'm sorry!" she laughed. The coach was pulling them up Fifth Avenue, and through the open windows they could see the orange light spilling onto the walks and all the very fine houses sitting quietly, somewhat spent with all the events of the long season. "How could I have insisted upon your attending such a tedious gathering?"

"I don't know," Leland chuckled. "I must have done something *very* bad, or perhaps you are still angry that I never wrote you from France. . . ."

"No! No, it was not meant vindictively at all. But, oh

dear, now that I've bored you to the brink of death, perhaps you'll cease to love me. . . ." The word *love* clanged and echoed in her ears, and the skin of her face and neck began to turn a shade of red she would not previously have thought possible. There it was, her tendency to blunder and misspeak, which she kept believing herself, erroneously, beyond. "I mean, perhaps you will cease to *like* me—"

"Love?" Leland's sincere blue eyes opened wide at her, and he straightened his broad torso against the carriage seat.

"Oh, I didn't—" Carolina stuttered.

"Do *you* love me?"

She found that she smiled at the very suggestion—it was an involuntary, awkward smile, which she hoped the dim light prevented her beau from examining too closely. They were arranged near each other on the seat, and though their faces were shadowed their breathing had grown quite noticeable. "Yes," she heard herself say, with courage from some inner source unknown to her.

"You know," Leland began, taking up her hand, "I have been saying that very phrase to myself, 'I love her,' 'I love her,' all day, but I didn't think it was possible you would love me in return."

"Not possible? How could you think . . ." But Carolina drowned out her own words with a disbelieving laugh.

"I'm not much for flirtation, and I have never paid ladies

as much attention as they long for. But neither have I ever met a girl like you. You are as lovely as any of them, but there is something so very unusual about you. You are more alive than any of them. More real. You are not so simpering or coddled. Oh—I don't know what it is." He shook his head, as though he were frustrated with his inability to express himself. He looked down at their hands, clasping each other on her lap. "Oh, Carolina—*how* I love you."

The movement of the carriage jostled both their bodies as it ferried them on, into the night. A lush, leafy darkness was tangible just outside the windows, but everything beyond the simple black confines of the carriage was uninteresting to either party at that moment. She pressed her lashes into her still-red cheeks, and let the sweetness of those words settle in around her tongue and into the back corners of her mouth. "Really?" she whispered.

"Do you not believe me?"

"It's only that it's beyond belief."

"I love you." Leland lifted her hands up, and began kissing each of her fingers. "But now I've said it three times, and you haven't really said it at all! Tell me."

"Yes." She kept her eyes closed, for the swelling of her heart was almost too much. It was a very lucky thing she was sitting right then, because the emotions within her were so wild that she knew her equilibrium had escaped her. "I love you."

Leland's head bent toward hers, and he moved one hand to cup the place where her dress made a rather narrow definition of her waist. His nose nestled into her hair, and his lips began to press gently against the skin of her neck. These soft touches sent such tremors all over her body that her eyeballs rolled back and her full lips parted and she felt she would have to be very still, lest she cry out.

"Oh, Carolina," he sighed, as he tipped her chin upward with a bent index finger and put his whole open mouth over hers.

They drove on like that for a long time, up Fifth and into the park, growing closer to each other and periodically pausing to repeat those wonderful words. Outside the windows of the carriage, the heat held quiet and thick, and up above, beyond the fragrant leaves, the sky was littered with stars. She hadn't known kisses could be like that, that they could last so long. In the matter of a carriage ride everything she knew about kissing had been quadrupled, and now she felt she truly understood why it was such a scandalous, whispered-of activity. She wouldn't have minded if they never stopped, although eventually they did, while Leland's coachman was still driving them over the little bridges and down the woodsy paths of Central Park.

The day had begun a long time ago, it seemed; she'd woken early to choose her dress and have it fitted and then prepare her person for the ball, as well as her coiffure, which now lay in beautiful ruins about her shoulders. There had been several dances at the Waldorf, and so many people she believed to be necessary social connections to talk to. There was the surprise of seeing Claire, and the stress of smoothing over the episode, and also a touch of sorrow to think that her sister had left the house where they had lived since they were children, and had had no family to tell of the change. All of a sudden, Carolina was tired—it was the kind of needy fatigue she had not experienced, or been allowed to experience anyway, since she was a child, and she did not waste another moment before putting her head against Leland. In seconds she was asleep, but in that hovering, half-awake place just before conscious thought slips away, she noticed that he pulled her lightweight linen shawl from the seat beside her, and drew it over her bare shoulders.

Eighteen

Mrs. Henry Schoonmaker, whose husband has so lately returned from serving our nation abroad, made a rather conspicuous reentry into the elite social whirl, and while her loyalists claimed she was merely breathing life into a dead season by dancing so scandalously with the prince of Bavaria, the prince's actions suggest otherwise. Word is he has a standing order for a daily delivery of rare blooms to be made at the former Miss Hayes's address, the Schoonmaker mansion on Fifth. Incidentally, there will be a dinner party given at that same address this evening, to honor young Henry's return. . . .

—FROM THE "GAMESOME GALLANT" COLUMN IN THE *NEW YORK IMPERIAL*, MONDAY, JULY 16, 1900

*P*ENELOPE ENTERED THE LARGE SECOND-FLOOR drawing room Monday afternoon, and labored to appear casual as she situated herself beside her stepmother-in-law. This was something of a struggle, as the *Imperial* was hanging from the brass periodical rack between the marble statues of Orpheus and Eurydice. Though nobody mentioned it, she guessed that several members of the Schoonmaker household now knew about her peonies. Penelope ordered tea with lemon for herself, and tried to glance over the columns that were unrelated to her as casually as possible. She was wearing a cerise shirtwaist whose decided architecture belied its summery weight, and a long slate gray skirt, which was adorned with three rows of ruffles near the ankle and then rose like a tower to her impossibly tiny waist. It was Isabelle's "day" again, and so she dressed in anticipation of seeing the visitors who would drop by throughout the afternoon, having already read the scandalous little item concerning her and the prince.

The magenta brushfire of blossoms had arrived as usual to replace yesterday's delivery in her bedroom, but Penelope could not help but feel somewhat less proud about them today than she had on the previous morning. She was a girl of exotic features and long, fine bones, and she was not shy of attracting attention to herself. But neither did she want—no matter how stupidly or caddishly Henry persisted in acting—to cease being the junior Mrs. Schoonmaker, a title that represented the pinnacle of her social standing and had, for a while anyway, silenced any accusations that she was the somewhat fast daughter of a nouveau riche. The Schoonmakers wanted a divorce in the family no more than the Hayeses did, of course—which was to say, not in the least—but she couldn't help but fear that if the "Gamesome Gallant" kept writing items about her and the prince of Bavaria, then the balance of sympathy toward Henry and his wife might soon shift, and not in her favor.

"Don't worry," Isabelle said indifferently, when nobody of consequence was within earshot. Her body emerged from the middle of a heaping grass green organdy skirt, and her blond curls were drawn back and then over her forehead in a kind of studied messiness. "Haven't I always told you that married women have all the fun? They'll forget soon enough; only, you could have been more cautious. Better not to let clues appear in the papers."

Penelope tried not to show on her face what she felt, which was irritation. For she had been a keeper of the elder Mrs. Schoonmaker's secrets regarding Grayson. And she knew perfectly well that, when the painter Lispenard Bradley (who presently entered the drawing room, knelt on one knee by the hostess, and began rhapsodizing about her beauty) lamented how long it had been since he had had an opportunity to sketch Isabelle, that he was speaking euphemistically.

Prudence, Henry's younger sister, sat glaring at Bradley and Isabelle from a neighboring chair, and Penelope might have wondered if some rather disgusting triangle had not been formed, if she wasn't so obsessed with her own troubles. Penelope had wasted weeks pining for Henry's return, knowing full well it would only mean that he would persist in being cold and indifferent to her. But the length of his absence had entrenched her bitterness toward him, and she now found it impossible to derive pleasure from his good looks, or to muster the will to try and convince him that she was the ideal wife, after all. He had been back a whole weekend, and he had not looked her in the eye more than half a dozen times. Meanwhile, everyone seemed ready to view *her* as the unfaithful party— the injustice of it caused her to set her teacup and saucer down on the mosaic-top table with a touch of violence.

A moment later, she saw that she had broken it. Brown tea ran over the table, and a wedge of lemon slid to the floor.

Penelope stood, shocked at herself for doing something so cloddish. She had always prided herself on her cool. "Oh!" she said, as a maid in black dress and a large white apron appeared from beyond her range of vision and began to clean it up.

Bradley stood as well, and Isabelle glanced at her with passing concern or disdain—Penelope couldn't be certain, and she depended so heavily on her ability to read a face.

"Penelope, are you all right?" Isabelle inquired.

"Yes, I—" She grimaced a little and tried not to feel vulnerable. "I think perhaps I'm just slightly faint and should—"

Penelope did not get a chance to announce her intention of absenting herself from the remaining social hours, because just then the butler arrived in the doorframe, paused for effect, and announced: "His Royal Highness, the Prince of Bavaria."

Isabelle stood, her cream-colored sleeves sweeping over her person as she smoothed her appearance. Prudence followed, somewhat more reluctantly, rising to her feet a few seconds later. Silent expectation swelled between the walls of the Schoonmaker drawing room. Then the prince entered, wearing an ivory suit and carrying his straw boater in his hand. He clicked the heels of his black dress shoes and made a bowing motion from his neck, before planting kisses on the hands of all the ladies, and whispering to each, *"Enchanté."*

He reached Penelope last, and lingered there, post-kiss, with the tips of her fingers resting against his palm. The maid who had cleaned up Penelope's spill was still hovering, her head bowed to show her frilly white cap. Penelope gestured toward her, and said, "Would you care for refreshment, your highness?"

"Champagne."

He released her hand but held her gaze. The maid, hearing his desire, took his hat from him and went to fetch the drink. The prince was taller than she remembered, and his eyes were bluer. They seemed not to blink, and they were fixed on her with such blazing intensity, for such an accumulation of seconds, that even she felt a little pleasantly shocked.

"Have you never been to our house?" she said quickly, when she realized they were being watched. "We have very good rooms here. My husband's family are quite avid collectors."

The prince's eyes roamed over the coffered ceilings and heavily decorated walls, finally breaking their gaze. "Yes, so I see," he replied eventually, in a blasé tone.

Penelope tilted her head, which was piled high with dark hair, and then he lifted his arm so they might take a turn about the room, casually examining the portraits and statuary. As they moved away from the others, Bradley took a seat beside the elder Mrs. Schoonmaker and Prudence returned, huffily, to her book.

"I cannot tell you how much I have enjoyed the flowers, Prince—"

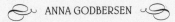

"You may call me Frederick."

"All right—Prince Frederick. I cannot tell you how much I have enjoyed the flowers, although I imagine you must feel a soupçon of embarrassment over the item that ran in the *Imperial* this morning, as I did, and I hope you do not think I would ever be so vulgar as to have made a public record of your thoughtfulness."

"It was not thoughtfulness." The prince smiled broadly, showing his large, healthy teeth, and Penelope found in the following moments that this was precisely the compliment she longed to hear. His nose was more robust than Henry's, which she supposed was owing to his royal blood. "You know my dear, on the Continent, when a man—a real man—sees something beautiful that he wants, he does not waste time feeling embarrassment over it. He shows it. That is all I have done."

Pleasurable buoyancy filled Penelope's chest, and she smiled, slowly but surely, for him alone. She had forgotten how wonderful it was to flirt with someone new. As they walked, they kept a safe distance between their bodies, except that her elbow did rest in the crook of his. That place where their arms touched began to hold a certain magic for her, as though it was a suggestion of how much more of him would like to be in contact with her.

"Is that what you are, a real man?" she asked in a faintly amused tone.

"I am sorry for you if your . . . acquaintance has rendered you so unable to recognize one," he returned in the same airy manner. "But I assure you, from this day forward, you will never again have trouble distinguishing between the real thing and the less solid variety."

They had come around another outcropping of antique divans and alabaster torchères, and turned back in the direction of the hall. The afternoon light played against her high cheekbones and the glossy hair of the dashing visitor. She smiled involuntarily, and when she looked in the direction from which they had come she realized Henry was lurking, just outside the drawing room. He had paused at the door, so that he appeared framed in the double height mahogany entryway, wearing a brown suit and boater not unlike the prince's.

"What a lucky thing to have a visitor who is not only charming but also so terribly instructive," she said, looking at Henry but speaking to the prince in a low, lush tone. "It is my sincere wish that your company will not prove an aberration."

The prince's blue eyes darted from Penelope to the figure in the hall, and he took in the scene without loosening his grip on her elbow, or otherwise trying to physically distance himself from her. For a married woman and a man who was known to be courting a French aristocrat, they were audaciously close.

"But why would I be so foolish as that?" The prince re-turned, just before Henry tipped his hat forward over his eyes and continued on his way.

Penelope turned her face toward her visitor and gave him a slow, purposeful wink. "I don't imagine you will be," she said, and then drew him toward a private corner, where they could talk without being heard, but where the light was strong enough that he would fully appreciate her beauty. As they settled in, and accepted refreshments from a liveried footman, she idly suggested, "You know, my father-in-law is throwing a party this evening, in honor of my husband, who has just returned from serving in the army. Perhaps you should come, and prove how very not foolish you are?"

Nineteen

Coney Island, that summer safety valve for the urban masses, that wild playground for grown-ups, where inhibitions are left behind and raw humanity always rises to the surface. . . .

—FROM THE *NEW YORK TIMES* EDITORIAL PAGE,
MONDAY, JULY 16, 1900

THE YOUNG COUPLE DESCENDED THE HIGH TRAIN platform and joined the droves moving down Surf Avenue and then toward the boardwalk, looking like any other couple, he in his soft brown suit and straw hat and she in white shirtwaist and a long navy skirt. The only detail that set them apart from the other shrieking, sun-touched pleasure seekers was her short hair, but one would hardly notice it, tucked under the matching boater she wore, which partially obscured her face. She kept a few steps behind him until they arrived on the boardwalk, and then he reached back and circled her waist in his arms.

"I've missed you," Diana whispered to Henry, biting her bottom lip because she meant it so much. Seeing him was sweeter now, she couldn't help but feel, after their unjust separation. "I can't stand being apart."

"It's unconscionable," he replied dryly. Then he laughed and gripped her under the shoulders, lifting and swinging her around him so that her feet flew in a circle above the ground.

His slender lips twisted up in a smile. "I think I'm losing my mind," he added, almost shouting now. "I miss you so much!" But no one on Coney Island cared enough to listen to another pair of sweethearts, driven to foolish excess by their love, and any self-incrimination was drowned out by the squealing and savage laughter, by the whir of the carousel and the crash of waves in the distance. The air was warm, despite the salty breeze, and it didn't take long for Henry to remove his coat and for the top buttons of his shirt to come undone. They were a long way from the parlors of Manhattan.

The afternoon was young, and for a while they were giddy. They rode the Steeplechase—Henry holding her securely in front of him as the mechanical horses lurched forward— and took in low entertainments. Diana had been all over the country by now, but still her stomach fluttered and her eyes popped at what she encountered there. They saw moving pictures and a bearded lady and a tattooed man and a dwarf and a giant, and afterward they rested under a striped awning and drank beer and ate fried clams. They looked at each other with happy, sun-washed eyes and soaked each other in over happy silences.

"I'd like to do this every day," Henry said after a while.

Women in flouncing bathing suits revealed naked calves as though it were all very regular, taking in the catcalls and lazy, appreciative smiles of gentlemen with handlebar mustaches, not a one of them appearing scandalized. Diana reached over and let her fingertips graze Henry's jaw, which had always been for her a favorite part of him. Since they were last together he'd shaved, and the skin was smooth as girl's now, which contradicted the taut pensiveness in his brow.

"But why shouldn't we?" she replied, affecting lightness.

"Because you have the strictest mother in all New York . . . ," Henry began, lifting his bottle of beer to clink it against Diana's.

". . . to whom I pay absolutely no attention . . . ," interjected his paramour, giggling as she brought her bottle up to touch his, before taking a long sip.

". . . and I am married to the most fearsomely controlling socialite this town has ever seen."

"Oh," Diana replied insouciantly. "Her."

"Yes, *her*. God, why didn't we elope when we had the chance?" Henry's voice was dark, although the blinding seaside light struck him with such loving force that his skin appeared all golden, and Diana could almost see through the thin weave of his white collared shirt. He was leaning back in his folding wooden chair, ankle rested against knee, and he would have appeared, to any casual observer, like a man in a perfect state of repose. But Diana had been at his side a great many hours by now, and she heard the worry in his tone. "We should never have let either of those harpies see us. We should never have come back to New York."

"That's just what Elizabeth says," she remarked, almost as an afterthought, as she gazed out to sea. "She says it's no place for us."

The wooden folding chair made a noise against the weather-beaten boards as Henry pushed it back. "You told Elizabeth about us?"

"Of course—she's my sister!" Diana laughed and put her hand, gently, on Henry's shoulder. "Anyway, don't make that face, she approves."

"She *does*?" Henry shook his head in bemusement. He paused, considering. "What do you suppose she meant, 'no place for us'?"

"New York, Manhattan, parlors and ballrooms, race-tracks, Long Island estates . . . ," Diana sighed, and shrugged happily, pausing to look out at all the merry passers-by. "She says we'll never be allowed to be together here," she added, and though she intended this explanation lightly, she heard her voice become low and portentous against her will. "That to be happy, we must leave."

Henry stared at her intently and brought his trousered ankle back to his opposite knee. He removed a cigarette from his shirt pocket and placed it between his lips, only looking away from her to strike a match. He shook it out and dropped it between the boards, and as he exhaled he met Diana's eyes again.

"Let's go," he said. The slow, summertime manner was gone, and she stared as his throat worked. Meanwhile the rest of him remained still and poised. Diana reached over and took a cigarette from his shirt pocket for herself. They held each other's gaze as he leaned across the small round table and lit it for her.

"Go where?" she replied in time.

His black eyes ranged to the waves, the activity on the sand, and back to her. "Where else do Americans go when they are sick of their own country? Paris."

"Paris?" Diana inhaled and exhaled quickly. Smoking reminded her of the silver streaking rain in Havana. Since running away she had become a more natural smoker, and she found she was glad of the habit now, for her heart was beating fast and the tobacco calmed her. She didn't know quite why his suggestion made her nervous; chasing after him all by herself had come to her so naturally. But she'd left, that time, with the hard knot in her belly of having committed a terrible act. She had been seeking something quite specific. What Henry suggested would mean giving up everything she had known for a place she had never seen, and a future she could not begin to picture. "But what would we live on?"

"I have a little money of my own, money my mother left

me. . . ." Henry exhaled a cloud of smoke that briefly blurred his fine, tanned features, and then flicked the rest of his cigarette away. "I can't stand pretending, I can't stand playing children's games with Penelope. I can't stand thinking about you all the time and not being able to have you. Please, let's go; the rest will fall into place."

Diana closed her eyes and let her assumptions about the rest of her life, and all the days that would fill it, slip away. She nodded to herself, as though to summon courage, and then she felt across the wooden table for Henry's hand.

"You want to go to Paris with me?"

Both his hands covered hers. "More than I've ever wanted anything. I'd go tonight, if you said yes."

"Then yes. Let's go tonight."

A slightly nervous practicality now entered Henry's voice: "The Cunard line transatlantic sails on Tuesdays. So we can't actually go until tomorrow."

When she opened her eyes, the rays of sunlight were too white, too extreme to see anything for several seconds, but she smiled through it, and soon enough Henry's face came into focus. For a long time neither said anything, while the blood pumped in and out of their chests at wild speeds. The afternoon had begun to fade by the time they left the little wooden table and walked back toward the train, moving more slowly than they had before but with greater purpose. This time they didn't bother finding seats on opposite ends of the car, and Henry extended his arm over her shoulder when they sat down beside each other. As the train lurched into motion, carrying them back toward their homes, where they would pack a few things and say good-bye to the people that mattered, Diana glanced out the window at the Ferris wheel rising like a full moon above the park. The rest of her life lay out below her, as though she were staring at it from an extreme height, from one of those trembling cages that the Ferris wheel brought up and around. The idea of everything that was yet to be made her feel dizzy, and alive, and terrified, and she was glad Henry was coming with her, wherever it was she was going.

THE WILLIAM S. SCHOONMAKER FAMILY

REQUESTS YOUR PRESENCE

AT A DINNER TO BE GIVEN IN HONOR

OF THE RETURNED HERO

PRIVATE FIRST CLASS HENRY SCHOONMAKER

MONDAY THE SIXTEENTH OF JULY

AT EIGHT O'CLOCK

AT THE SCHOONMAKER RESIDENCE

FOUR HUNDRED AND SIXTEEN FIFTH AVENUE

THE TWO MRS. SCHOONMAKERS STRODE ARM IN arm across the polished floor of the main hall of their family mansion. That afternoon, as they dressed for the dinner party, it had occurred to Penelope that her mother-in-law was in a particularly good mood, and they had over the course of a few hours grown sisterly again. The house was full of the smell of hyacinth and tuberose, and from the labyrinth of small galleries and parlors the sounds of polite social discourse could be heard. They were robed like goddesses, the elder woman in a column of pale purple crepe de chine, with a deep oval neckline, her fluffy blond hair descending diagonally on either side of her doll-like face; the younger, in an empire waist dress of gauzy white with a black velvet bodice and beadwork of shimmering gold. The sleeves billowed, but her phosphorescent shoulders were entirely bare, and her dark hair rose up from her unblemished forehead and was gathered in an elaborate bun festooned with ostrich plumes. Pink gold and diamond earrings twinkled against her jaw.

"I like your prince," the elder Mrs. Schoonmaker whispered as they approached the first floor parlor, where already their guests were sipping aperitifs and waiting to be greeted.

"Oh, he's hardly *mine*," Penelope protested, but faintly. She was feeling terribly regal after the attention he had paid her during his afternoon visit. Each of her gestures since then had been theatrically self-confident. "Anyway, the papers say he is soon to be engaged to the Comte de Langlois's daughter."

"All the better, my dear." Isabelle giggled, and then continued in a self-indulgent rush: "I myself am quite sick of Bradley. I have been for a year now, but I always go back to him when I have nothing better to do. I thought artists would be more interesting than gentlemen, but they make love with the same words other men do, and when it comes to giving tokens of affection, they have less money at their disposal. You are very clever to be flirting with Europeans, and noble ones at that."

Then they entered the oak-paneled room, where men in black jackets and women in tulle and ribbons and jeweled chokers burbled admiringly at the vision of their hostesses. String music played in the next room, and bushes of cherry blossoms emerged from gilt inlaid vases, erupting above the heads of the guests.

Penelope cast her bold blue gaze across the room, meeting the eyes of the newlywed Reginald Newbolds and of Isabelle's handsome brother, James de Ford, along with a few others, although she did not bestow the compliment of a wink on any of them. Her father-in-law was several drinks in already, she guessed from his ruddy aspect, although it would be a while before dinner was served—the cooks were working on rather short notice, she believed. He exited by the adjoining gallery along with a small fleet of similarly dark-clad gentleman, who looked as though their waistcoats had been puffed out with wind. They were off to do what men did alone, she supposed—smoke cigars and talk of entertainments they didn't let ladies in on.

"And where is your handsome husband?" Penelope turned disdainfully to Agnes Jones, who was a good deal shorter than she. Penelope would not have thought the guest list would be so inclusive.

"It is something of a battle to make him presentable, now that he is a soldier," Penelope answered curtly, before striding forward into the room.

She and her mother-in-law moved in opposite directions, working their way slowly through the assembled guests standing on the camel hair carpet. There were about thirty people in the room—all of the men with distinguished names, and all of the ladies with heirloom necklaces. The younger Mrs. Schoonmaker managed a semicircle, cooing in delight at the faces of old friends, delicately extending her bracelet-clad wrist so that gentleman guests could place kisses there, offering carefully phrased compliments to gowns that fit less well than her own. She still had half a room to cover when she saw Mr. Schoonmaker—the younger one, who was supposed to be her husband—entering from the main hall. Her mouth dropped open at the sight of him, for he wasn't wearing a jacket, and not even one of the buttons of his vest was done. From across the room, Isabelle flashed her a look of alarm.

Everyone else noticed too, it seemed, as the din subtly descended a notch or two. Henry, impervious, refusing to meet her eyes or anybody else's, crossed toward the gallery on the east side of the room. It was the direction his father had gone, toward the smoking room. Penelope smiled demurely, or as demurely as she could manage, at Nicholas Livingston, with whom she had been discussing an upcoming weekend party to Long Island, and hurried through the burgundy club chairs and clustered bodies in pursuit of her wayward spouse.

"You smell like beer," she observed in a quietly heated tone when she caught up with him, just on the threshold of the adjoining gallery. The brownness that he had achieved while abroad had begun to fade to a respectable tawny shade, but she could see now that his nose had been turned red by the sun over the course of the afternoon. "And you are late."

Henry stopped, hesitated, staring at the shining parquet before him, and it was only after several seconds that his eyes rolled back in Penelope's direction. "I'm afraid I cannot play the part of Henry Schoonmaker, war hero, this evening," he said eventually, and though the sarcasm was somewhat buried, it did not escape Penelope.

"Your father won't like that." She took a step toward him, so that they would appear more like a loving couple to the curious spectators who were, no doubt, stealing glances. The words, however, were spoken as sharp warning. She could hear them behind her, chatting at normal levels about the latest boat races, whispering in more subdued tones about how peculiar their hosts were acting.

"No," Henry returned. "But there's no need for you to concern yourself about that, as I'm on my way to tell him myself now."

For a moment it was as though she'd breathed in ice crystals. When Henry took a few steps deeper into the gallery, she matched them exactly.

"On your way to tell him what?" she demanded. Henry's shirt was unbuttoned to midsternum, and she could see the dark marks of sweat around his armpits. Wherever he had just been was still all over him. He was awfully handsome, she couldn't help but think, and then hated both of them equally for allowing this line of thinking to begin again in her mind.

Henry sighed and his head swayed back and forth. The impatience he'd expressed in the previous moments evaporated, and when he spoke again it was in a flat, almost broken tone. "That I'm leaving you."

"No. No you're not."

"Yes . . ." Henry nodded. His gaze, when he met hers, was unflinching. "I am."

Penelope's mouth constricted and she tried to force back hot, angry tears. But the fearful rage this information at first elicited simmered down quickly, until, in a matter of seconds, she found it a more manageable sort of challenge. "Henry," she whispered through a tight smile, "all *those* people think you're a war hero, but I know the truth. I doubt very much you have the courage."

"That's all right, Penny," Henry said wearily. "You'll see in a minute or two, anyway. I don't love you, and you know that, so it's rather ridiculous to go back and forth like this. I love Diana, and I'm going to be with her—really this time. I'm not even sure why you care, as I doubt very much that you're still in love with me. I saw you, today, with that prince, you know. . . ."

If Penelope hadn't been so bent on her task of persuasion, she might have wondered if there wasn't a faint quality in Henry's tone suggesting that she might have inspired some territorial instinct in him. Her words were rapid-fire now, however, and she went on with a dismissive wave of her gloved hand. "Oh, *Henry*, that was nothing. Of course I love you, and anyway we made those promises in front of too many well-regarded people. This is what marriage is Henry, for people rich and good-looking as you and I. So you imagined yourself in love with little Diana Holland, so I accept pretty tokens from Prince Frederick . . . they're all just diversions, Mr. Schoonmaker." Her elegant nostrils exhaled authoritatively. "This is what we *do*."

Henry's expression was a mystery. He was staring into her eyes, and might have been confused, although that didn't seem quite right. "That is what you do," he said eventually, and turned on his heel. "Not me."

Penelope's first thought, in the next moment, was to rush after him and throw one of her scenes, anything to get him back before he stormed into his father's presence and started talking stupidly. But some impulse made her turn around just then, and she saw, in the warm light of the drawing room, through the visual clutter of ornate coiffures and erupting cherry blossoms, the figure of the prince. His chestnut hair was polished and thick over his regal brow, his blue eyes glittered with amusement, and his mouth was just slightly crooked on one side, suggesting a smile that only a girl like Penelope would notice. The prince was wearing a smart navy blue jacket with gold tasseled epaulets and a red sash across the chest, for as he had told Penelope that afternoon he was a commissioned officer of the Prussian Army. Henry's footsteps were fading across the hardwood floor, but she was no longer worried. Either his resolve would fail, or the old man would put him in his place—it didn't matter particularly to her.

The younger Mrs. Schoonmaker felt entirely confident that the threats her husband had just made were exactly like all the rest of his threats—hollow, and with no greater objective than to cause her pain. He could stalk about the house and make noise all he wanted; she was no longer going to allow his moods to interfere with her fun. Across the room, the prince's eyes found hers, and she lengthened her fine white neck, lifting her chin up slightly to the left. Then she let the heavily blackened lashes of her right eye lower in a slow and smoldering wink.

Twenty One

Carolina—

My apologies, I won't be able
to meet you before dinner and drive
you—I'll meet you at my family's
house, at No. 16 Washington
Square North, at eight o'clock.

—L.B.

*B*UT WHY HAD HE NOT COME TO MEET HER?

Carolina's eyes grew watery and darted about as she rode downtown in her own coach, cheek rested against fist, watching buildings roll by and chasing this question around in her thoughts. She wore a little fitted jacket of ash-black silk, with ruffles at the sleeve and just below the ruching at the fitted small of the back, over a dress of white faille layered with grapefruit-colored lace that bunched up near the hips and fell rather epically down around her feet. Her intention had been for a subdued appearance, but now, as she traveled by herself toward the Bouchard family residence, she wondered if it wasn't obviously the kind of dress that the sort of girl who rides around in carriages with boys at night chooses, in an attempt at merely *looking* subdued. Then there were all her other blunders, and surely the worst of them she was still ignorant of, and weren't people always saying how ephemeral love was? Maybe having said the word aloud had made all of Leland's affections disappear for good.

The Bouchards were old banking money, and Leland's mother was the product of a union between a Lusk and a Cortland, making her prestige and wealth older still. The Everett Bouchards lived in two conjoined townhouses on the north side of Washington Square Park, along with four of Leland's six younger siblings. The family had lived there for several generations, and so worshipped tradition that they would not dream of moving to a more fashionable part of town. That was why they had colonized a neighboring property, when the original house proved too small for such a large clan. Carolina had known all this for years, even when she was a maid, from the gossip columns Claire used to read aloud to her. She knew also that Charlie, who was two years younger than Leland, was away in the navy, and that Katherine, Charlie's twin, had recently been married to Peter Harwood Gore, though she, according to Leland, would be at the family dinner that night.

All day Carolina had felt overjoyed that her beau was going to introduce her to his family—it was a step that could only bode well. That was what she told herself as she prepared for her evening with her lady's maid, roping herself into her corset, curling and pinning up her hair, darkening her lashes, and lightening the freckles on her cheeks with powder. But then his note came, some hours before he himself should have arrived to escort her, and her mood had become increasingly dark and paranoid in the intervening period.

She had hoped against hope that he would appear and tell her it had been a mistake, that he *would* accompany her, but this fantasy never became manifest. By the time her driver helped her up to the seat of her carriage she had become completely convinced that she would die of nerves before she'd be capable of entering a room populated by such grand people. Because, after all, she had rode around in Leland's phaeton being kissed in a way she was pretty sure virginal debutantes were not supposed to be kissed, and wouldn't they all know, the high and mighty Bouchards—who, unlike her, were *real* society people—with a single glance?

At her destination she paused and hovered behind the door of her coach, and was only persuaded to come down when her driver asked if maybe she didn't look a little pale and want to be taken home, at which point she became annoyed at him for saying so, as well as at herself for giving him any cause. Through the lush trees of the park she could see the marble arch that the society architect Stanford White had built, cast a little orange by the dying light of the day. That was where Fifth Avenue began, she thought to herself with a shiver, before turning to climb the white stone steps of the redbrick structure with the Greek columns on either side of the entryway.

The door opened before she had a chance to ring the bell, and she was greeted by the shell-pink face of a blond child, whose merry smile revealed two missing front teeth. The child wore a simple blue pinafore over a dress of white eyelet, and for a moment Carolina wondered if she wasn't one of the servants' children. But then the girl addressed her.

"You're Carolina!" The girl beamed for a moment, but then an unexpected wave of shyness overcame her, and she hid her face. "I'm Olivia," she explained from halfway behind the door. "Leland's my brother."

Carolina tried to muster a smile, but her jitters had grown so bad that it took all her concentration just to stand still and upright. A woman with graying blond hair in a simple arrangement, dressed in a high-necked dress of pewter-colored fabric, appeared behind the girl. "Olivia," she said, "who have you found?"

"Carolina!" Olivia answered, her shyness abating somewhat.

"Welcome, Miss Broad. I'm Mrs. Bouchard," the older woman said in a low, smooth voice, drawing her guest indoors and kissing her warmly on either cheek. "Leland has told me so very much about you."

Carolina, who had been expecting a butler or housekeeper or some other uniformed middleman, found that she couldn't remember a single phrase, or even a word, appropriate to the situation. She did manage to part her lips just slightly, but if this succeeded in looking like a smile, then she was a lucky girl indeed. The foyer was paneled with wood and dark, and the ceilings were somewhat low, as they often are in old houses. As her eyes adjusted, she saw through a wide doorframe into the front parlor, where the last light of day illuminated a room as cluttered with old paintings and bric-a-brac as the Hollands', but populated with many more people besides.

A maid—wearing not livery or a black-and-white uniform, but a plain black dress of the variety Carolina had once donned every day—moved away from the mantel, where she had just set a large brass candelabra ablaze, and came into the foyer.

"I'm sorry, Mrs. Bouchard," the girl said hastily. She was about the same age as Carolina, and yet she seemed infinitely less beset by anxiety.

"That's quite all right, Hilda," the mistress replied.

Hilda gestured toward the Bouchard's guest, and a moment later Carolina realized she was supposed to give up her jacket. Once it had come off she saw that the curves and flounces, the lace and detail of her dress, were almost blinding with ornament. She was painfully overdressed.

Leland's mother approached and hooked her arm through Carolina's in an elegant, easy manner. With her other arm, she drew Olivia along by the shoulder. "Where is Leland?" she asked her guest.

"I—don't know," Carolina answered stupidly.

"What a cad, to send you here alone."

Perhaps the older woman was joking, but there was a sharpness in her tone—Carolina thought so, anyway—and it suddenly occurred to her that she was a young woman out, sans supervision, amongst an old and very traditional sort of family. "My chaperone . . . ," she stuttered.

"Yes?" Mrs. Bouchard looked at her, the light from the adjoining room dancing in her blue eyes.

"I don't have one," was what came out of Carolina's lips.

"Oh, nonsense!" Mrs. Bouchard laughed. "*I* will be your chaperone, if you are worried, and if the police stop by to see that everything is in order here, I am sure they will approve of the job I am doing. Now come."

They stepped across the threshold and into the low, wide room, which was filled with wingback chairs upholstered with patterns of pineapples and palms, and paintings that depicted the stern faces of a previous century. Black cloisonné vases filled with pale pink chrysanthemums were stationed around the room, and beautiful textiles hung from the back of every sofa. The Bouchards were indeed a clan, Carolina saw, and they were so many that they nearly blotted out the Persian carpets. The gentleman who must have been Leland's father sat by the fireplace, a friendly giant of a dog with a brindle coat prone at his feet. The Bouchard patriarch was oversized and gangly, the way Leland was, and though his hair had gone completely white, he had the younger man's well-defined nose. He did not rise at the sight of the guest, as everybody else did, and she guessed from the sight of him that he was ten years older than his wife, and not in prime health.

"Come here, Miss Broad!" Mr. Bouchard called, extending a long arm toward her. His voice was booming, his smile grand.

There was a moment of graceless hesitation, after which Carolina did as he said, stepping timidly away from Mrs. Bouchard and between the stuffed ottomans and colonial side tables to reach him. He clasped her hand and stared up at her for a long minute with such fierce attentiveness that her heart began to thud again at the prospect of being found out.

"Th-thank you for inviting me to dinner," she said awkwardly.

"She's too pretty for that ugly son of mine," Everett Bouchard declared, ignoring her timidity, and laughing with uproarious joy. "But she's made of very good stuff and I'd like to keep her around, so you will all have to do your part to charm her!"

Then the rest of the Bouchards laughed with him, and for the first time since receiving Leland's note at four, a natural smile broke across Carolina's face. A woman with honey brown hair, dressed in an ivory shirtwaist and a topaz-colored skirt of exquisite material and very fine, simple tailoring, stepped away from the other side of the fireplace and came to Carolina's side.

"I'm Katy, Leland's sister," she said as she embraced the guest. She could not have been much older than Carolina, a year or two. "And that's my husband, Peter," she said, gesturing to the smartly dressed fellow on the other side of the fireplace. "That's Beatrice . . . ," she continued, presenting a tall, skinny girl in white, sitting shyly on a settee, not quite old enough to have come out yet, "John . . ."—the boy sitting next to her, with the height of a man but a face that indicated he could not be much more than twelve—"Harold . . ."—still a child, sitting on the floor with a toy train—"and of course Olivia, the youngest, you met at the door. We are seven, you know."

Carolina beamed, and they all beamed back. "Yes," she said. "Leland told me, and how jealous I was! I'm an only child," she lied. How much easier it would be, she thought in passing, if she *were* an only child, and then felt a pang of guilt, and hoped Claire's bed at Mrs. Carr's was more comfortable than the one they'd shared in the Hollands' attic.

"How unfortunate! But you must sit, my dear," Mrs. Bouchard commanded from her position at the edge of the room. "And since you are a very special guest, we shall break our habit of drinking only at table, and have a little champagne before dinner. . . ."

But before she could sit, or Hilda could be sent for the

champagne, the door opened again, and the tall handsome figure belonging to Leland Bouchard strode into the entry-way. For a moment his gaze held Carolina's, and she saw that his failure to escort her was not out of any deficit of love. Then the youngest children ran to Leland and threw their arms around him, as though they hadn't seen him in months, and he bent to kiss each of their heads.

"You look very well, Leland," Mrs. Bouchard said, in a tone of perfect equanimity, as she kissed his cheek.

"So do you, Mother," he replied.

An older male servant appeared in the hall, and Leland quickly moved to take off his blue coat with the wide lapels. As he handed it off, he leaned in and whispered something in the old man's ear that made the whites of his eyes grow large. The servant patted the eldest Bouchard boy on the back and disappeared with his coat, as Leland entered the room and walked from one of his siblings to another, greeting them with a kiss for the ladies and a handshake for the gentlemen. When he reached his father, he lowered his whole body down for a bear hug.

"Is she all right, Dad?" he said.

"You may proceed," answered Mr. Bouchard.

Watching his path across the room, Carolina's pulse had grown fast and her knees had become a little weak. It was the very picture of everything Carolina herself had never had, and

she felt her love for him growing sweet and heady in the handful of minutes it had taken for him to reach her, just beyond
his father's throne.

But whatever this vision of him amongst his family
had done to her internal registers of emotion, it was nothing
compared to his next act. For he turned to her, caught her
gaze, and then sank to one knee. The room went silent, and
for the first time since he had entered the house he fumbled.
He was trying to get something out of his waistcoat pocket.
He glanced away, and when his eyes met hers again his lips
were parted and he was holding a small box aloft. Until the
lid flipped back and he spoke, her stubborn brain refused to
believe that this scene could be what it seemed. But there were
three diamonds set in yellow gold staring up at her, and the
words, "Carolina Broad, will you do me the honor of being my
wife?" hanging in the air.

The entire Bouchard clan stared at her with shiny eyes
and bated breath.

For Carolina, it was a struggle not to cry. The moment
could only have been made more perfect if her own mother,
with her hands worn and chafed from a lifetime of doing
other people's laundry, were there to witness this triumph. But
perhaps she was, from on high.

"Yes," she said with simple, beatific clarity. The light
outside had gone completely from the sky, but perhaps some

of it had been transferred to Carolina's face, for she was now glowing like a country sunrise. Hilda and the old man and a few other servants had come in from the hall to see what was happening, and the rest of the Bouchards began to smile and clap. Leland slipped the ring onto her left finger and then he stood, cupped her face between his hands, and kissed her— somehow it appeared chaste, but was experienced otherwise— on the lips.

"You will make a very lovely Bouchard, my dear," she heard Leland's father say as he rested his hand against her arm and smiled in congratulations. She nodded in stunned thanks. Nothing about her dress or bearing seemed remotely off anymore; already she felt like one of them.

Twenty Two

Our era has produced many great men— robber barons, masters of innovation, beasts of business—whose staggering wealth, incomparable ruthlessness, and personal legends would seem to prove they are the dominant of the species; but then one has a look at their sons, and doubts the theory of evolution entirely.

—DR. BERTRAND LEGMAN COPPER, *PROBLEMS OF SCIENCE AND SOCIETY, POSITED BY ONE WHO HAS KNOWN BOTH*, 1900

ENRY STARED INTO THE ALABASTER OVAL OF A face that belonged to the girl who one way or another had become his wife. There was a warm hue at the edges of her sharp cheekbones and on her wide, plump lips, but everything else was glacial. He was momentarily stunned into silence by the outrageously callous thing she had just said, and it occurred to him, for the first time, that it did unflattering things to a person when affection was taken away from them. For there had been a time when she had seemed gorgeous, and fun, and all of her naughtiness had had for him a kind of irresistible pull. It was only after he decided he didn't want her anymore that she became such a shrew, and obliterated his memory of the girl she used to be with her despicable behavior.

"That is what you do," he returned firmly, when he had recovered himself. He turned from her, not wanting to see any more hatred on her features, and as he walked away he added, almost to reassure himself of the greater capacity of his own heart: "Not me."

He half expected her to come tearing after him and was relieved when he realized that he was being followed only by the echo of his own footsteps. The route he took was not entirely familiar to him, for though he had lived in the house all his life it was a large and complicated one, and anyway his years as a young man-about-town had rarely brought him to his father's chambers of business. They were sacrosanct rooms to the old man, so Henry hadn't been interested. In any event, there had always been easier ways to get money when he needed it. But he was seeing to something serious now, and his instincts didn't fail him. He came upon the smoking room soon enough, with its ornate carved ceiling—Italian craftsmen had been transported from their homeland for this single, specific purpose—and cognac-colored club chairs.

"Yes, every widower thinks he wants a young wife to replace the one he has lost," the elder Schoonmaker was bellowing. "But that is before she starts giving away all his money to her dressmaker, and stops caring about managing a household, if indeed she ever did!"

Henry stepped across the threshold and into a space filled by men in dark jackets who chomped cigars and appeared haloed by their own moody smoke. They were mostly older than him, associates of his father or more recent cronies acquired along with his political ambitions, and you could see their corruption in their bloated middles and ruddy faces. His father, whose nose was in full bloom, was no exception.

"Henry . . ."

His father had noticed him before he had a chance to speak, and the elder Schoonmaker's tone indicated that he was unsure whether to act jovial at the sight of the guest of honor, or to instead be furious that the young soldier had not taken the time to dress properly or comb his hair before the beginning of the evening.

"A cigar?"

"No, Dad, I have something to say to you, and then I'll be on my way. But I don't think I'll be able to attend your party."

The men turned their heads, eyes wide with interest. They plugged up the holes of their mouths with cigars, and waited for the inimitable William Sackhouse Schoonmaker to reply. The big man flexed back his shoulders and watched his son. After a minute, a grin broke across his face. "What . . . is there a battle you have to get to tonight?"

The others erupted in guffaws. Henry looked at the floor and placed a hand in his trouser pocket. He let the laughter die down before meeting his father's eye. "I'm not much of a soldier, am I?"

"Come, Henry, I only meant—"

But Henry was not searching for reassurances, and he cut

his father off before he could apologize. "I can't stay because I'll be leaving New York tomorrow. There's a ship that sails for Paris at noon. I'll be on it, and Diana Holland will be with me. I'm in love with her, you see, not Penelope. I married Penelope because I thought it would allow us all to go on living quietly, under some false façade of respectability, but I can't stand it anymore."

The elder Schoonmaker's face had gone white—with rage, one assumed—and his big bear's hand, and the cigar in it, moved slowly below his waist.

"I can't stand lying about my marriage or about my tour of duty. I don't want to pretend I was a hero in the Pacific, when in fact you all know I was just another soldier who went to Cuba after the Spanish had been defeated, and never fired his gun. Penelope can divorce me if she likes, or she can go on with the sham of calling herself Mrs. Henry Schoonmaker." Henry waved his hand dismissively, and realized he was glad that so many of the old man's associates were there to witness him becoming his own man. His voice had risen continually as he laid out his intentions; it was glorious thumbing his nose at his father, telling him to do his worst, that all his bullying and threatening to withhold Henry's inheritance held no power anymore. It was the freest Henry had ever felt, except maybe in Diana's arms. In a small act of showmanship, which he would come to regret for the rest of his life, he reached forward, plucked the half-smoked cigar from his father's lowered hand, and placed it between his teeth. "I don't care," he concluded, "and I won't be here to see it, either way."

The room had gone silent. The wall of men in black dress jackets loomed steady and still behind the elder Schoonmaker. William's broad face hung open. At one time it had been notable for the same clean, aristocratic features that had always made his son so irresistible to debutantes, but it had since been ruined by a life of anger, competition, rich food, and stiff drink. The expression that face now wore was unreadable; whatever mysteries it contained, however, did not undercut its severity. He took a lumbering step forward, and for a moment his son thought he was about to be wrestled for the remainder of the cigar.

Then Henry felt a tremendous weight against his shoulder, and in the next instant he realized that his father could no longer stand on his own. He tried to hold him up, and for a moment they really were wrestling, William's massive body pushing for the ground, and Henry's young, slim one fighting against gravity to keep it upright. The old man wheezed and gasped for air. Seconds passed, and Henry couldn't support him anymore; the father fell heavily to the ground, and the son sank down beside him.

"Help!" Henry yelled at all the elegantly dressed men standing around, their pocket watches gleaming in the low, pretty light. "One of you go and call the doctor!"

There were murmurs, shuffling, and then somebody did finally do as he said. The elder Schoonmaker's artificially blackened hair was all out of place now, and his face was pinched by his inability to breathe. There was fear and rage in his eyes, but that faded into a steady something else as he stared up at his son. Henry blinked at him like a little boy, and put his hand against the old man's heart, as though somehow that might help. One of the men separated from the others and came to stand over the fallen patriarch.

Henry glanced up and saw the long tall figure of Jeremiah Lawrence, his father's lawyer. "He's gone," Lawrence announced, and by the time Henry had turned back to his father, he knew that it was true.

Twenty Three

To match a European title with American dollars is so tried and true a matrimonial route, it is hardly worth commenting on, although it ought to be remembered that they do things differently there, and a mother should be wary during the courting process, lest the young lady catch a little Continental moral lassitude.

—MRS. HAMILTON W. BREEDFELT, *COLLECTED COLUMNS ON RAISING YOUNG LADIES OF CHARACTER*, 1899

"So which one of these fellows is my rival?" the prince asked, bending in Penelope's direction with an air of conspiracy, allowing his eyes to linger on the soft white skin of her décolletage before glancing at the other guests. The gauzy white part of her dress floated down around her feet, and the chandelier light played at the rings and bracelets that adorned her hands.

"Mr. Schoonmaker is acting strange this evening," she answered, liking the word *rival* more than ever. It made her feel all doused in gold. "So I don't expect you will meet him."

"Ah." There was glitter in the prince's eyes when he met hers again, and though Penelope could not be sure, she thought she felt his hand brush against the back of her upper thigh. His appearance, in the blue military jacket, was especially crisp and robust. "All the more for me, then?" he went on in a quieter, more carnivorous tone.

The Schoonmakers' guests were accepting second glasses of champagne now, and the ambience had grown festive. It was the height of summer, and they all wanted to see and be seen before they went off for Riviera cruises or to their cottages at Newport for August. Isabelle was whispering something to Bradley behind her fan, and Penelope realized as she watched that none of her confidences were safe with her mother-in-law when that lady had taken a paramour. Even now she was probably repeating verbatim things Penelope had said about the prince of Bavaria, and to a man with no reputation to keep.

"Everyone is looking at us, you know," Penelope said after a pause, enunciating each word to let him know she believed they were, indeed, in the midst of something quite worth looking at.

"But all of their eyes are averted," he countered.

"Yes, that's how we do it in this country."

"I am not unfamiliar with the technique." The prince surveyed the people before him, lifting his champagne as a kind of punctuation, so that the light shot through the pale liquid. "But what could we possibly have done to inspire such interest?"

The large blue disks of Penelope's eyes floated toward her upper lashes as she averted her gaze in a false display of modesty and confusion. "Do you suggest, my prince, that we have not done enough?"

She briefly wondered if she had again gone too far, but

then a smile flickered at the corner of his mouth. "My darling, one can *always* do more."

He kept his eyes on her as he swallowed the rest of his drink, and then he took her arm and placed his lips near her ear and instructed, in a voice growing pleasantly gruff: "Show me the grounds, why don't you?"

Penelope glanced back at the guests she was leaving behind—slyly, from the corners of her eyes—as she and the gentleman in epaulets strode out into the main hallway. She made no attempt not to be seen. Earlier in the evening, when she still had yet to encounter the prince, she had held a suspicion that she looked especially well put together, and an inclination not to waste such a pretty showing. But her sense of her own beauty had reached another level entirely, and as she walked arm in arm with her first royal admirer, she felt as though she were traveling a foot above the ground.

"As you can see, we have very fine tapestries in this house . . . ," she said as they moved down the hall. She had returned to a rather distanced manner of speaking, as though she were any young matron showing off the family treasures. "But then I suppose you are a little sick of tapestries."

"Yes," he answered in a banal tone that belied the movement of his hand from her elbow to her waist, "we have far too many tapestries in my own country. I did not, my incomparable Mrs. Schoonmaker, come all this way to search out more."

They had walked through a series of corridors, and the chatter and the music of the party had become far away and indistinct. Around the corner and down a short flight of stairs was the entrance to the greenhouse, which had been a favorite assignation spot for Henry, back when he still wanted her. "What would you be interested in seeing? We have plenty of statuary, and all manner of hothouse flowers—"

The prince dropped his arm and drifted away from her for a moment, as though he really were considering what part of this fine home he was most curious about. He batted down a smile and lifted a well-manicured finger, placing it against Penelope's exposed clavicle. Then he drew it down, across the smooth skin of her chest, to the elaborate gold embroidery at the edge of her black velvet bodice, and then slowly along the embroidery until he reached her right arm, at which point he began tracing a line upward to her opposite clavicle. He had taken his time, and when the gesture was over her chest was rising and falling rather more quickly, and his mouth stood open.

The noises from the rest of the house had grown clamorous, and she realized the mood of the party was ascendant. She was the hostess, and she would soon be missed. The fragrance of flowers and loamy earth emanated from the greenhouse, which for her had always meant one thing. She was inclined to show the prince the rest of her, but knew there wasn't time.

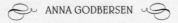

She extended her neck and waited for his kiss. When it came, it was with such force that she felt the wall against her back and the medals on his jacket sinking just slightly into her skin. That, she thought to herself, just before she heard the servants shouting from down the hall that both Mrs. Schoonmakers were needed, was how kings must kiss. Footsteps were growing closer, and she knew that she was at a very great risk of being found out, but she remained in place, staring into the prince's eyes, feeling him press in against her, for as long she possibly could.

Then Jesus said unto his disciples, Verily I say unto you, That a rich man shall hardly enter the kingdom of heaven. And again I say unto you, It is easier for a camel to go through the eye of a needle than for a rich man to enter the kingdom of God.

—*MATTHEW 19:23–24*

*T*HE GHOSTLY GASOLIER LIGHT FELL ON MR. AND Mrs. Cairns, as the gentleman of the house gazed silently onto the street and his lady read from an open Bible propped against her full belly. Neither had spoken much since dinner, which had itself been a rather wordless affair. She had never stopped to think very much about what occupied Snowden's thoughts; the realization made her feel even more of a churl. He had done so much for her—the perfectly chosen silver rattle was only the most recent example—and she had never so much as stopped to consider what preoccupations might plague him.

And then of course there was the word *Klondike,* written in that childlike scrawl, which kept returning to her thoughts. She tried to put it away, and then laid down the small Bible and crossed the floor. The avenue framed in the tall windows was darkly purple, except where the street lamps illuminated it, and was populated by subdued carriage traffic. It was a Monday, but she knew from the servants' gossiping that the Schoonmakers and several others were holding parties that night. The season would be over soon, and Elizabeth knew very well from years past, when she had been at the center of things, the kind of reckless energy that must be overtaking all social functions just then.

"Is everything all right, Mr. Cairns?" Elizabeth asked, hovering just slightly behind her husband, and watching their two reflections in the glass.

He nodded.

"I have a confession to make," she went on, in a small voice that twinkled just slightly. This was the way she said things when she was playing the hostess, the little lady of the house, the lovely and demure girl who set about defining perfection for her peers.

In the reflection she could see his brow lift, and then his head rotated in her direction, although not far enough that their eyes met. "Oh?"

"Yes." Her words fell sweetly into the air, although she was speaking too quickly now. "I saw the rattle—I mean, I didn't peek, but I have given the same gift, so I knew what it was. I am sorry, but I have been feeling such gratitude all day, it is such a *lovely* thing for you to have purchased for me, and I wanted to thank you."

"Oh. I am glad you like it," he said in a tone she had never before known him to employ—like relief, except not exactly that. "Or that you will, rather," he corrected.

He had not turned to look at her, and so she rested a reassuring hand on his arm and allowed the touch to lengthen, compassionately, into the quiet. He did not offer a word or a glance, but still she thought that she was being admirably wifelike, and when she felt that her hand upon his arm had served its purpose, she left the room to search for something soothing to serve him. Tea perhaps, or better yet, brandy, which the staff had not yet found time to decant into the crystal bottles that she'd intended for the regency huntboard in the front parlor.

Every day now she seemed to be growing larger and slower, the child within requiring more of her energy. It took her a long time to find a tray, the brandy, and a snifter. The kitchen was quiet at that hour—for Mrs. Schmidt was fastidious and saw that everything was cleaned and put away almost as soon as dinner was cleared—and Elizabeth was distracted from her task by the look of the hanging copper pots and the brick-sized white tiles of the walls. Her new home had been built in the same era as the house she'd grown up in, and the coal range with its iron hood, the porcelain sink, the hot water tank, all of it was reminiscent of the room in No. 17 Gramercy that she had known so well. Not because she had ever spent much time in the Holland kitchen, but because she had had to go through it when she was sneaking to see Will at night. What anticipation it had always held for her—the faint smell of cooking grease, covered over with soap, which she would experience just before stepping down and into the carriage house that had been Will's domain.

These pleasant associations had largely eclipsed the guilt and anxiety she had felt toward Snowden by the time she returned to the hall, and she caught herself almost smiling in the oval mirror that hung across from the staircase. That was when she heard the voice of a man that was quite plainly not that of her husband, followed shortly by the more familiar timbre.

"It's late," Snowden said dismissively.

"It's late, it's late—*I* know that." The accent, Elizabeth realized, was not what one usually found in drawing rooms like hers. "That's how I was sure you'd be here."

Elizabeth, in the shadow of the stairs, knew she should announce herself. She glanced down at the glass on the tray, its contents sloshing silently back and forth, and didn't budge.

"Make it quick, then—what do you want? Though one would think I've given you enough already, seeing how you've bled me all these months."

"Ah, but that was for services rendered, and now there is something new, a little story I've discovered about you that I think you'd rather not have told. In fact I think we'd *both* sleep better having experienced that reassuring feeling of money changing hands."

"Hurry up then. This is my family's home," Snowden said.

The other man made a noise like a laugh, but it was the most horrible, sneering thing Elizabeth had ever heard. "Family," the man repeated, and then she realized that the noise had been in reference to her, her child, their arrangement here. She felt nauseous.

"It's about what you did in the Klondike—"

So this late-night visitor was the man who'd written the note. A shudder traveled hard across Elizabeth's body, from left to right, and though the summer heat was as stifling as ever she felt for a moment as though she'd been standing out in a winter gale for several hours. But the feeling was not just within her; her hands shook, and in another moment her tray, and the full glass upon it, capsized. She grasped for them helplessly, but this only caused their trajectory to be more violent, and when they hit the floor the glass shattered loudly and the sickeningly sweet smell of the brandy filled her nostrils.

She looked down at the mess, her mouth forming a small, tremulous circle. In the next moment, her husband appeared on the other side of the pocket door. Behind him was the man with that large, boyish face that had been so marred by pockmarks. When he met Elizabeth's eyes, he appeared as surprised to be confronted by her as she by him, and after that she was sure they'd encountered one another before. He should be wearing a uniform, she thought to herself, as she began apologizing for the noise and bent to pick up the large shards of glass at her feet.

"Come visit me tomorrow, when you will not be such a disturbance to my wife, and we will agree on an arrangement then," she heard Snowden say, followed shortly by the sound of men's shoes moving toward the door, and then the click of the lock being turned.

The man was gone quickly, but the sight of him had caused her such a fright that she could not get her fingers to stop shaking. She tried to pick up the shards with both hands, but it didn't help the shaking, and in the next moment she realized that she had cut herself and drops of blood were falling from her palm onto her white cotton dressing gown.

"Are you all right?" Snowden was looming over her now.

"No . . ." She was not in the least all right. The phrases "services rendered" and "what you did in the Klondike" and "money changing hands" were all ringing in her ears. "I—I know that man."

"That isn't possible," he replied curtly.

"Yes, no, of course . . . I don't mean that I'm acquainted with him. But I've seen him before. He's a policeman, and he was one of the men who—" The nausea was wracking her body now, and she slumped against the wall. "One of the policemen who killed my husband."

"I am your husband."

"Will." She was having trouble getting the words out. The horror and fear were as fresh for her as though she were still standing on the platform in Grand Central, under the great glass train shed, the sound of bullets ringing in her ears and the smell of fresh blood spilling from her husband's body. When the smoke had cleared, the policemen came forward and swept her up—that man, with his pockmarked face, he had been among them. "He was one of the men who killed Will."

Snowden reached down and pulled her up to her feet. All of her was limp, and once upright, she had to be supported. "You are overtired, my dear; you are under too much stress—"

"No! I *know* that face. I have seen that face in nightmares. I have relived those moments so many countless times." Her voice was growing shrill, and she had to hang onto Snowden's shoulder for support. "But what was he doing here? What does he want with you? Oh . . . *God.*" Her voice fell to a tragic growl as she realized just what kind of service the man had done for Snowden. "Oh, God, oh,God, oh, God."

"You hallucinate, my love."

Now she pulled away from Snowden instinctively, as though from something vile. "He killed Will, because you told him to," she whispered. She had to put her hand out for the wall again, as she backed away from her husband. "That's why you were paying him. You paid him to kill Will so that you could marry me. So that you would own the land in California, so that you would own all that oil we're living on now."

There was an unnerving calm in Snowden's still, watchful pose. He was listening to her, but he was no longer trying to convince her of anything. His light hair was like a beacon in the dark hallway, and she could not make out his eyes.

"But what about the Klondike? Why did he want to see you about the Klondike? What could possibly have happened in the Klondike?" The bile was rising in her throat, and she had to reach up and cover her mouth with her hands. For only one thing had ever happened in that part of the world that Elizabeth cared about, and that was that her father had died. She knew, without quite understanding how, that Snowden was responsible for that, too. She kept stepping backward, one hand against the wall for support, piecing it together out loud as she moved. "That money you gave my mother last fall, you had stolen it, hadn't you? You weren't going to give us father's share. You killed him for it, and would have kept it all, if you hadn't realized there was more money to be made by keeping up relations with his widow and daughters. By marrying into the family." She brought her hands up to cover her eyes as she let out a moan. "Oh, *God*."

In the next moment Snowden had moved in close to her and ripped her hands away from her face. The light from the moon, shining through the window over the fanlight, now illuminated his eyes, and she saw in them the plain, forceful avariciousness which had led him to prey on her and those she loved best.

"You are overtired, my dear," he repeated, all persuasion gone from his voice. Now he was telling her how it would be. "Your condition is not good, you are unwell, and it can be so dangerous, carrying a child. How many young women die trying to bring their precious babies into the world? I think we had better put you to bed and keep you there, as long as possible."

Elizabeth tried to move away from him, but he was holding tight to her hands. What the man she had been living with for so many months was capable of was finally beginning to dawn on her, and the sick feeling faded as the panic set in. Those unremarkable, blocklike features had, in a matter of minutes, come to hold impossible menace for her, and though she told herself that she should cry out, the fear spreading through her was so great, it seized her throat. The last thing she knew, before the faintness overcame her and she lost first vision and then consciousness, was that he had roughly scooped her into his arms and was carrying her up the stairs.

Twenty
Five

The Cunard Line steamship *Campania* sailing New York Southampton Le Havre departs
at noon from Pier 54, with many notable
passengers on board, including Grace Vander-
bilt en route to Monte Carlo, and the Duke
and Duchess of Marlborough returning to
their ancestral home.

——FROM THE SOCIETY PAGE OF THE *NEW-YORK NEWS OF
THE WORLD GAZETTE*, TUESDAY, JULY 17, 1900

ON TUESDAY THE HEAT BROKE, AND FOR DIANA ALL OF New York had that dazzling quality of any place one has decided to give up and has already begun to appear softened by nostalgia. The leaves blanketing the little park were as thick and green as they had ever been.

"The Schoonmakers have always been lovers," Edith said in a quiet voice. They were sitting side by side on the threadbare jacquard-upholstered chaise longue nearest the window in the front parlor, finishing their coffee, Diana in the blue chambray, her aunt in simple white. The morning light was almost blinding where it struck the porcelain cups and the elder lady's delicate fingers. *Everything is beginning to disappear,* Diana thought, rather melodramatically. Breakfast was over, it was just past eight, and in an hour, perhaps two, she would make her way west, to the piers, where Henry would be waiting. They had agreed that he would book passage for them at the last minute so as to avoid any report in the papers, and that they would spot each other and then board together just as the last call was being made.

"Not old William Sackhouse, he couldn't possibly have been," Diana replied distractedly. She could not keep her thoughts away from the small case, currently hiding under her bed, which held a few favorite books and other necessaries, and how she was going to get it from there out the front door.

Mrs. Holland eyed her daughter and cast arch glances at all the whispering that was being done on the chaise. Diana had always had much in common with her Aunt Edith, and in a strange way she felt that the older lady would understand what she was going to do that day. Yet she hadn't told Edith about her and Henry's plan. Some deep and abiding super-stition kept her mum on this topic, and so she only fed her aunt little snippets of what she'd seen while she was abroad, and hinted, in a very general way, of all that would be between her and Henry.

". . . Ah, but when he was young," her aunt was saying, to the window as much as to anybody else. "Henry is the spitting image of him. . . ."

Diana had become distracted by her mother's approach from the back of the room, where she had laid down the morning papers. She wore a burgundy shirtwaist with mini-mal ruffles, and an exacting black stare.

"What are you two talking of?"

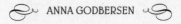

Edith looked up at her sister-in-law as though at an acquaintance that she had, until just that moment, forgotten, and her high cheekbones rose as she put on a faraway smile. "Oh . . . ancient history," she replied.

"Diana," Mrs. Holland continued, ignoring Edith's comment and moving to separate the two romantics in her midst. "We have entirely too many pastries left over from breakfast. Will you bring them over to your sister's, please?"

In Diana's view, Mrs. Holland was framed by the clutter of generations: the portrait of her late husband above the mantel, the many worn Bergère chairs, the leather paneling and little decorative tables, the Turkish corner on her left. With that one simple command, Diana saw how she was going to remove her suitcase, and herself, from her childhood home. Only she would be leaving sooner than she'd imagined, her remaining minutes in the house harshly abbreviated. It was a shock, and her sauciness failed her momentarily. She stood lingering, glancing from her mother to her aunt as she adjusted the wide belt at her girlish waist.

"Well, go on, then," Mrs. Holland commanded. "You may have the coach."

Diana averted her eyes before leaving the room—the only way to leave forever is to do so as quickly as possible.

When Diana reached Elizabeth's house, she told Donald, the new driver, that she would really rather walk home, seeing as the day was so clear and temperate, and then she took the large paper bag of baked goods and her small case, which was concealed under a long coat—not that Donald was paying attention—and ascended to the front door. Although she knew her sister was not in love with Snowden, Elizabeth did seem very happy with her new life, and anyway Diana was relieved it was the older and not the younger of the Misses Holland who had traded her maiden name for the title Mrs. Cairns. For there had been a time, last winter, before Liz returned, when Mrs. Holland had bade Di to be a little good to her father's former business associate, since he had done so much for them. So it was with tender relief—for all the things he had saved her sister from, and all those he had *not* deprived Diana of—that she greeted her brother-in-law.

"You look a little tired," she said sweetly, noting the bruised color around his eyes and taking it for proof that he was as worried about the arrival of Elizabeth's child as though it were his own. They stood facing each other quietly for another moment, in that entryway that looked, to Diana's eyes, too empty and a little harsh—the hammered black leather panels and polished birch wainscoting in sharp contrast to each other.

"Yes . . . ," he began. "Your sister hasn't been well. The

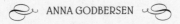

doctor was here last night. He ordered her on bed rest until the baby comes, and gave her something so that she could sleep more easily."

Diana couldn't help a brief flare of irritation as she realized that her sister's health might imperil her escape plan. But when she asked, "Is Elizabeth going to be all right?" she was met with an immediate and confident nod, and her fear of being stalled faded almost instantly.

"Of course, so long as we follow doctor's orders and keep her lying down."

"Well, then I will give you these," Diana went on blithely, feeling entirely reassured. She passed him the bag of morning buns and breads that was her excuse for visiting her sister one last time. "And give my sister just a quick kiss—"

"I don't know that—"

"Mr. Cairns," Diana interrupted, undoing the ribbon at her throat that secured her hat, "you are married to a Holland girl, so I expect you know I am not going to take no for an answer." Snowden looked as though he might persist in preventing Diana from disturbing Elizabeth, who after all carried so much on her shoulders, and now in her belly. But Diana was leaving in a few hours, for a long time and without any plan to return, and there was no nervous young father-to-be who could possibly have stopped her. She pushed past him and up the stairs.

"Miss Diana," he called, on her heels, "I must insist. . . ."

From the doorway into her sister's room, Diana turned and smiled graciously at Snowden, in that confident glowing way Liz used to have with suitors. "A little time with me won't harm her. I'll just sit a minute, and be on my way."

Then she stepped in and pulled the door behind her.

Elizabeth laid in the white-canopied bed, which was heaped with fabric, her protruding belly only somewhat visible amongst all the coverlets. Her head was sunk back in the pillows and her ash blond hair streamed out around her head, and she breathed—a little noisily for Elizabeth, who Diana had always believed followed rules of decorum even in her sleep. There was something pungent, almost sickeningly sweet, in the air, which she couldn't quite place, until she remembered that the doctor had been there. That was precisely the smell: as though the doctor had been there.

As Diana approached and perched on the corner of the bed, she saw that the garnet-colored wallpaper reflected on her lovely, sleeping sister, and lent a little color to her pale cheeks.

"Oh, Liz," Diana said as she picked up her sister's hand. It was limp to the touch, but then Elizabeth had never had a particularly firm grip. Her sister's mouth opened and closed and she exhaled, and Diana took that as encouragement enough to go on. "I have taken your advice, I'm leaving—*we're*

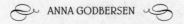

leaving," she went on in the loudest voice she could manage, which was not much more than a whisper. It was so incredible to her, what she was about to do, and even with her considerable powers of imagination she found she could not conjure what her life would look like in even a month's time. "I am so sorry I won't be here to greet your baby. But we will write often . . . and, as you said, it's the only way Henry and I can be together."

For a time she prattled on—quietly, for she supposed it was really better not to wake Elizabeth if her health was indeed very poor. Her words almost slurred together, so heady a mixture of emotion was she feeling: anticipation, nerves, and now a touch of guilt for leaving her very pregnant sister behind. She might have gone on longer, even though the day was advancing and she had an appointment to keep, when her sister's fingers strengthened against her palm.

"Liz?" she whispered.

"I'm not feeling well," Elizabeth said dreamily, without opening her eyes.

"I know," Diana answered sympathetically. "But you'll feel better soon. Can I get you anything?"

"Teddy."

"What?"

Then, in the same soft voice: "Could you get me Teddy Cutting, please?"

Diana's mouth fell open. This was very odd. She might have dwelled longer on it, or on memories of her sister and Teddy walking arm in arm several months ago when they were all in Florida, but the door opened just then. Diana swung her head around to see the full figure of the housekeeper.

"Hello, Mrs. Schmidt," Diana said. "Liz *really* isn't feeling well. She's talking nonsense."

"Yes." The broad-faced woman stepped into the room. "I think you had better let her have her rest, miss."

Diana sighed and glanced a final time at her sister, who pushed one side of her face and then the other into the heaping pillows. "Don't forget, Di," she whispered into the down.

"Good-bye, Liz." Diana bent forward to kiss her sister's forehead, as though suddenly she were the older and more mature of the two.

"It's time to go," the hovering Mrs. Schmidt said, and Diana knew that she was right. It was time to leave it all. Diana put her hands down on her thighs in a small gesture of readiness, and then she allowed herself to be escorted out of the room and down the stairs.

"Is my brother-in-law still in?" she asked at the front door.

"He has gone out," Mrs. Schmidt replied.

"Well, please tell him good-bye for me," she said. Then, in a less convincing voice, "Please tell him I look forward to seeing him soon."

"Very well."

Once Diana had fixed her wide straw hat back on her head, she picked up the case, still hidden under her long gray coat, and went out into the day. Young girls who worked in grand houses were passing on the walk, and carriages and streetcars hurtled down the street in competition. She took a deep breath for courage, but before she could descend the stairs she had not been vigilant enough, that her plan had required greater caution. Standing near the curb, wearing a fitted brown jacket over her white dress and a plain cloth hat, was Edith.

For a moment, Diana convinced herself that the distance was sufficient, that she would be able to escape unnoticed. But then her aunt gestured to her, and there was nothing to do but attempt a smile and step in her direction. Once the two women were close enough, Edith put an arm around her niece's shoulders, and drew her away from the Cairnses'.

"Have you heard the news?" the older lady said. Despite the blue sky above, there was grimness in her tone.

"No . . ." The possibility that her mother had known, all along, what she was up to began to dawn on Diana, and she was ashamed when she realized that she was still afraid of Mrs. Holland's wrath.

"Last night. William Schoonmaker . . . he passed."

"What?" Diana's eyes became wild. Her aunt's face had

gone pale in the search for words, and her gloved hand flew to cover her mouth.

"This came for you. I managed to get it before Mrs. Holland, and thought you would want to see it before you . . . before you did anything else."

She handed over a small scrap of paper, which Diana unfolded without hesitation. All of her nervous trembling had left her; a kind of silence began to settle within.

Dear Di —

A tragedy has occurred which I am sure you will read about in the papers, if not today, tomorrow at the latest. This series of events prevents me from meeting you this afternoon. I will come to you soon, and we can do as planned next Tuesday.

—H.S.

So it would not be today. She looked up at the buildings around her, familiar in their square arrangements, standing shoulder to shoulder along the avenue, as they did on all the avenues, which ran straight up and down the island.

They were not going to disappear before sundown after all. Then she crumpled the note in her hand. There was almost an absence of feeling within her—moments ago there had been such surging anticipation, and she could not yet tell if it was relief or disappointment or something else that had taken its place. A terrible event had occurred in the life of her lover, and for many hours now she'd had no idea. The light was no longer nostalgic—it seemed almost strange.

"In my day, we used to swallow notes like that," Edith said.

The sense of disorientation began to ease for Diana, and she heard herself laugh. "Do you really think that's necessary? I thought I'd just leave it in the gutter."

Edith smiled now, too. "It would be a little overdramatic, wouldn't it? Come, you've had a surprise. I promise not to ask you any questions, but I do insist we go have a long lunch somewhere where they serve champagne all day. . . ."

Diana let her shoulders rise and fall in agreement, and the two ladies held tight to each other as they made their way downtown. After all, when would she again have a free afternoon with her aunt? She would be leaving next Tuesday, and there are never as many hours as one hopes for in a week, as they always go by too quickly, and one never knows how one could possibly have spent the time.

Congratulations are due to Mr. Leland Bouchard and Miss Carolina Broad, whose engagement is being announced far and wide this morning. Invitations will, by all reports, go out today for a Sunday wedding at the Grace Church. While we long to be believers in love at first sight, the skeptic in us wonders if this mad dash to the altar is owing to motor car enthusiast Mr. Bouchard's need for speed, or if it has more to do with the rather vast social difference between a girl whose connections do not go back even a year, and an august family who might, given enough time for reflection, come to think better of the match?

—FROM *CITÉ CHATTER*, WEDNESDAY, JULY 18, 1900

"IT SIMPLY WON'T DO," CAROLINA SAID, STARING INTO a reflection that she had come, in a few days, to like more than she would ever have imagined. Was it possible she had grown taller in only a week's time? Of course she was standing on the dressmaker's box, and the six-foot triptych mirror now elongated her figure three times over. But surely her eyes were a purer shade of green. Her dark hair was pinned above her head, so that Madame Bristede—the dressmaker Longhorn had chosen for her during their short friendship— could better see to the elaborate lace- and buttonwork of the high neck, which Carolina knew to be very flattering even as she disparaged it. She and Leland had agreed, in the rush of their engagement, that they didn't care what anybody thought, and that they had wasted too many years apart already. In less than a week they would be married.

"I am doing all I can, Miss Broad," said Madame Bristede from her position by the pearl-encrusted hem. The elaborate dress had already been under construction for Carolina, but it had not been intended as a wedding dress, and so in the last twenty-four hours black netting had been painstakingly removed form the full, flouncing skirt and replaced with ecru *point de gaze*. Two young ladies in the corner with fatigued but agile hands were busy constructing a train embellished with ostrich feathers and opal beads. Near them sat a red-haired maid, who Carolina had insisted upon borrowing from Mrs. Carr for the week, watching the proceedings in quiet amazement and holding her temporary mistress's street clothes folded in her lap. Ever since glimpsing her at the hotel, Carolina had been obsessed with finding a way to have her sister closer to her, and after the proposal, to see that Claire witnessed the wedding. Now she had. "But I have less than a week to finish, and so I am very sorry to say that it will have to do."

Then the dressmaker looked up at Carolina, as though she had just remembered that she was no longer talking to a lucky nobody, but the future Mrs. Leland Bouchard. Part of Carolina wanted to rail about the monumental importance of this gown, this wedding, and, indeed, of herself; but the majority was too full of bliss at the impossible direction of her life to sustain anger. The memory of Leland's quite public proposal rushed back for her—as it did several times an hour—causing her lungs to swell and her eyes to grow pleasantly moist, and then she found it impossible to persist in being difficult with

Madame Bristede. She smiled. Madame Bristede smiled, and then returned to her task. No, she would save her exacting impulse for the florist and for Isaac Phillips Buck, who she had hired to oversee everything about her last-minute wedding, and who was now looming by the wall. It was very lucky that Penelope had not needed him for anything that week, she had commented earlier, to which he had responded with a politic silence that she simply had no time to interpret.

"Delivery for Miss Broad," said the dressmaker's assistant, poking her head around the door. It was true that Carolina had come to possess everything a girl might want, but her ears tingled pleasantly at these words anyway. "From Mr. Bouchard. The Lord and Taylor salesman is here to deliver it."

"We are quite busy." Madame Bristede did not glance up from her work. "Just have him leave whatever it is."

"He says that he has a particular message, and that it is for Miss Broad's ears only."

The dressmaker looked up at her demanding client with weary, questioning eyes.

"It will only take a minute," Carolina told her. She still felt nice about the idea that something was being given to her, although the phrase "Lord and Taylor" had not been a welcome one.

Sighing heavily, the dressmaker stood and motioned to the girls in the corner. Claire followed them, to her sister's chagrin—but of course, both girls were extremely cautious of not appearing to have a special relationship. "Be very careful," Madame Bristede said to Carolina, gesturing at the detailed skirt, after which they all left the room.

The bride-to-be stepped gingerly down from the box and walked to the worn blue velvet sofa in the corner.

"My dear Miss Broad, how enchanting you look."

She twisted her neck to see, over her shoulder, Tristan's familiar figure as he swaggered into the room. The sight of him did not do kind things to her mood.

"Mr. Wrigley, I hope you are delivering something very nice, as I have already paid you quite handsomely so that I might be spared your presence."

"You did, it's true, and promptly." Tristan's smile did not waver, and his gaze burned on. "But I'm afraid the bit about the package was a ruse."

"Then I think you'd better leave," she replied coldly.

"Ah, but we have business."

"I think not. We *had* business, but that transaction has been completed."

"Yes. That transaction has been." Tristan moved forward with that same easy and attentive manner that made him so successful with silly women shoppers at the department store. "But that was before you became engaged to Leland Bouchard, which I should say makes you richer by at least half,

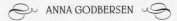

not to mention brings you into one of those families who do still care about things like breeding, and would probably be less enthusiastic about their son's choice of bride if they knew what she really was."

Carolina's stung lower lip fell, and a fresh dose of outrage began to course through her. "That's robbery," she replied indignantly.

Tristan shrugged. "Call it what you like. It doesn't mean you don't want me quiet and happy."

He had ambled quite close to her. Now he leaned forward, bringing his face near enough to hers that if he spit a little when he spoke, she would feel the wetness.

"You revolt me," she hissed, pulling away.

"I find that hard to believe."

She reached for the small purse, which she had idly placed in the corner of the sofa upon her arrival, and removed a twenty-dollar bill, which she kept there in case of emergencies. "Here," she said, without meeting Tristan's eyes. "It's all I have. I charge everything these days, you know, so I'm afraid you'll just have to consider yourself lucky."

"Ah, but Miss Broad, don't you think—"

"Buck!" Carolina yelled shrilly. Tristan instantly drew back. Buck, meanwhile, came hurrying through the door, as fast as he could manage, considering his rather large person.

"Yes, mademoiselle?"

"This man is harassing me. Please see that he is not allowed near me again."

She kept her eyes averted as Buck hustled Tristan from the room. His feet shuffled against the floor, but he went without a fight. Then she took a breath, and waited for the unpleasantness of the phrase "what she really was" to fade.

Carolina remembered how, as a child going to sleep, her mother would whisper she had been made for better things, and that if only her father had lived longer, he would have seen to it that she had a different kind of life. Mrs. Broud had been a beauty, and so Carolina had harbored the belief that she herself might someday be admired for her looks, and considered rather grand. But it was no longer merely a belief. She was a Bouchard, so it was a fact everybody would have to plainly acknowledge. Or anyway, she would be in a few days, she thought as she came up to her full height and stepped onto the dress box, dividing her reflection into three perfect pictures of a bride. After that there would be no questioning what she really was.

Today William Sackhouse Schoonmaker, one of the great men of his generation, will be laid to rest in the Trinity Church Cemetery in upper Manhattan. He would seem to have been at the height of his powers, and rumors have circulated about what his son might have said to him, just before the fatal episode, that could have given such a shock.

—FROM THE SOCIETY PAGE OF THE *NEW-YORK NEWS OF THE WORLD GAZETTE*, WEDNESDAY, JULY 18, 1900

"WHAT DOES SHE THINK SHE'S DOING HERE?"

There was no wind, and the sky above the cemetery at 155th Street and Riverside was truest blue. The large green leaves on the trees were motionless, like the white headstones that stood in their eternal rows, up and down the hill, from Broadway on toward the Hudson, which was visible over the black hats of the fine ladies who surrounded Diana Holland as she quietly observed the solemn occasion. She was too far from the reverend to hear what he was saying; of course the burial of a man like William Schoonmaker would be a crowded one. Motes of pollen hung in the air like gold dust. They were telling, Diana thought, and if she were writing about the funeral in a literary way, instead of from the perspective of a society gossip, she would have described them just as they were.

"They say she and Henry Schoonmaker were in India together, and that she cut her hair in a Hindu ritual. . . ."

Diana turned her face sharply, so that her eyes met with

Mrs. Olin Vreewold's. She had been talking to Jenny Livingston, the old maid, and though the look Diana gave was enough to silence them, both ladies persisted in assuming sour expressions under their black brims. The story of what Henry had said to his father was being passed around, although happily the papers were shy of printing so untoward a story during the week of the old man's funeral. Diana couldn't be sure if they would feel the same way next week, but by then she and Henry would be gone. In the meantime, she wanted to make as much money as possible. Her old friend Davis Barnard, who wrote the "The Gamesome Gallant" column, had long ago told her that death has a way of flushing scandal out, or else burying it forever.

"Perhaps he *wanted* her here," Jenny whispered when Diana's gaze was again averted.

Before she could decide on another way to respond, the plaintive drone of bagpipes picked up and the crowd began to disperse. As the elegant, black-clad mourners turned and walked away from the fresh grave, she saw others like Mrs. Vreewold and Jenny Livingston, who stared at her with piercing scorn. The onset of a blush was heating Diana's cheeks, and she lifted her chin defiantly at the silent scolds. She had always been unconventional in her way, but she had never received stares like these.

Then Henry came, wearing his black frock coat, which

must have been unbearable in the heat, and a black crepe mourning band on his left arm. His handsome face was exhausted and sad, and he met Diana's eyes for longer than he probably should have, considering the scene. It took only a moment for him to communicate to her that he would have cleared a small village to be alone with her right then, and she tried to return the sentiment with a tiny, darting smile. Penelope hovered there beside him like a loving wife, just as she had all afternoon, but her face was covered with a black veil, and so it was impossible to see if she was sincerely aggrieved or merely clinging to her position as Mrs. Henry Schoonmaker. On his other arm hung his stepmother, Isabelle, who—one could see, even through her veil—had the face of a woman struck by lightning. By then Henry was gone, moving up the hill, to where the family coach waited.

For a moment Diana stood watching the Schoonmakers' backs stupidly, but then she reminded herself that she must not be obvious, and also that she too had lost a father, and that she ought to be patient with Henry. He was doing the best he could, and probably experiencing awful things. Anyway, she would have him to herself soon enough.

"Miss Holland?"

Diana swiveled. She hadn't realized how alone and vulnerable she had felt in the crowd until she saw the proffered arm of Teddy Cutting, just slightly down hill from her. He was wearing his officer's uniform, and the aristocratic forehead under his fair, slicked hair was riven with entirely new lines. If it were possible, there was even more sincerity in his gray eyes than when she'd seen him last, at the Royal Poinciana in Palm Beach, Florida. She was vaguely aware that he was in the army, but she had been away, too, and it seemed somehow fitting to her that they would both be standing there now.

"Mr. Cutting, what a happy sight you are," she said, gratefully accepting his arm.

"And you, Miss Holland." They began to walk up the hill, along with the others. "I've only been gone for five months, but it seems the whole world, or New York anyway, has been turned on its head. I can't believe Mr. Schoonmaker expired so quickly. And your sister . . . is soon to be a mother?"

Diana glanced at Teddy pityingly—for he had always been sentimental when it came to Liz—and tried to change the subject. "Yes, it must all seem very parochial to you now that you have been to the Philippines and seen the world and had great adventures?"

"Adventures . . ." Teddy emitted a strained, tired laugh. His eyes darted over the greenery, the averted faces, the hill sloping down toward the water, as though he felt guilty standing there now, in one piece, amongst so much quiet tranquility. He went on presently, in a voice deepened by his seriousness, "There is no such thing as a splendid little war. I saw things in the Pacific. . . ." He paused, shook off a memory. "But you are a lady, and should not think of it. Suffice it to say, I will not be going back. But tell me of yourself, and your family. Is everyone well?"

"Mother is her old self, taking tea with only the most important people and forming backroom alliances," Diana began, attempting lightness. "I saw Elizabeth yesterday morning—she had seemed well until then, but the doctor said she should be on bed rest until . . . until the baby comes . . . and she was so exhausted, she could barely speak."

Teddy seemed pained by this news. "I wish I could see her."

"Oh, but you should." They were moving away from the grave, gravel and dirt scattering underfoot, and Diana was regaining some of her exuberance, despite the sad day. "It was curious—she didn't say a word to me the whole time I sat with her, but then when I was getting ready to leave she said your name. I thought I had misheard, but then she instructed me, as clear as day, to get her Teddy Cutting."

"But I couldn't, it would be so improper to visit her in her condition, and—"

"Teddy," she interrupted. They were coming up a flight of stone steps that were rather worse for wear, and he supported Diana as she stepped ahead. All around them women were whispering about her, saying that she would be ruined by what she had done, hoping that it would come true so that they could have a little entertainment to twitter over in their identical drawing rooms, which were all decorated in the same self-important colors and littered with the same useless objects, made twice as useless for having been gilded on every surface. "Don't be ridiculous. You are her friend, and if you are her good friend, you will visit her when she is ill, no matter what anybody thinks."

They had come onto the street, where the carriages waited, and for a moment he fixed those sad gray eyes on Diana and considered what she had said. "Thank you for that," he said after a while. There was something chastised and yet hopeful in his face now. "You are right, of course. Can I offer you a ride home?"

Up ahead, the Schoonmakers had already pulled away. The bagpipes wailed on by the newly placed headstone, and further off, boats made their way down the Hudson. Nobody else was going to drive her, she realized, and anyway there was solace in the polite company of Henry's best friend, who at various points had played witting and unwitting supporting roles in their romance. In any event, he was already guiding her to his coach, much to the disdain of the hateful hens presently deriving disgust and fascination from what they imagined had occurred between Diana Holland and Henry Schoonmaker.

Twenty Eight

The living are made of nothing but flaws. The dead, with each passing day in the afterlife, become more and more impeccable to those who remain earthbound.

—MAEVE DE JONG, *LOVE AND OTHER FOLLIES OF THE GREAT FAMILIES OF OLD NEW YORK*

*T*HE REVEREND'S DRONING HAD CEASED AND THE bagpipes had picked up. Henry's eyes went skyward. The air was full of life, but he felt washed out inside and unsure what emotion belonged there. The crystalline blue above and delicate green of the leaves looked all wrong to him, as did the rich earth he'd just helped to shovel over the body of his father. The old man had always seemed so frightfully imposing to Henry—from the time he was a motherless boy hiding behind his governesses' skirts until the day Schoonmaker the elder had insisted his son marry Elizabeth Holland or be disinherited. Now the father was powerless; he would soon be dust. They had never been close, and Henry knew that if anything he should feel as though an oppressive winter garment had suddenly been removed from his shoulders. But as he stood there, blinking at all those sympathetic faces, he began to feel that the summer sunlight was, bizarrely, rather cold.

A few days before, he had longed for Paris. Today he

would have given anything to be there already, sleeping in Diana's arms in some garret room where no one would think to search for him.

When he saw her, it required everything he had not to halt the Schoonmaker family's ascent and go bury his face against her breast. She was standing there, petite and beautiful, her face even more rosy and gorgeous than usual against the black crepe dress she wore. A black ribbon, which held her hat in place, made a dramatic line under her small, pointed chin. Those soft brown eyes, protected by thickets of lashes, stared into his until he almost couldn't bear it.

"It's time to go," said Penelope, at his side. She wore a fitted black dress and a hat of gleaming feathers, and yet she had been surprisingly subdued and dutiful all day. Henry glanced over at his best friend, Teddy Cutting, who was standing with the other pallbearers a little way off. This was one fact that Henry felt unalloyed gratitude for—that good old Teddy should have returned to New York just then. Later they would have a drink and set things right. Now, with a nod, he communicated to his friend that his mistress needed company, and then he took his stepmother's arm, and began to move up the hill with the others. In a few moments he was accepting a final round of condolences from various business associates of his father, loitering by the family coach, who he, in truth, had difficulty distinguishing from one another.

"Henry," Isabelle wailed, once they were situated in the coach. She blew her nose loudly into a black handkerchief. "Whatever will we do now?"

The horses were urged into motion; soon they would be making the long trip downtown via Broadway. He glanced behind him over his shoulder, through the small window in the back, at the hordes paying their last respects, and at the river, which glittered reflecting the afternoon sun. He had no idea what she should do now, and yet a strange voice—unfamiliar to him, and yet decidedly emanating from his own throat—said, "We are Schoonmakers. We will carry on."

To his left, from Penelope's general direction, came a barely audible snort. His sister, Prudence, sitting across, gave him an aggrieved and skeptical look.

"He was a man," Isabelle went on, in the broken, awed voice of eulogy. "A great man. He was *too* good."

Henry's dark eyes glanced to his right, where his stepmother sat amidst an abundance of black crepe, her complexion gone pale as never before, her girlish yellow curls invisible under her hat and veil. Nobody had ever called his father too good, even without the heavy emphasis on the intensifier, not even when he was a child. He was surprised by the thought that perhaps Isabelle, who was after all a second wife of only a few years, who had not borne her husband any children, felt that her position in the family was vulnerable. There was something profoundly stricken in her aspect, and he decided after a moment's reflection that it was more likely that she felt guilt for her romantic antics in the months before she became a widow.

Then her hat came off, and he realized for the first time how bizarre the heart is. For he could see, in her red eyes and ghostly pallor, that amongst whatever other emotions, she had, once upon a time, loved him, and that the memory of that lost affection would haunt her forever. "Oh, Henry, you *must* carry on. He had so many hopes for you. He talked of how his Henry was a Harvard man and how he would take over the family business and what a charmer he was"—here, Penelope snorted again, although the older Mrs. Schoonmaker paid her no mind—"and what a good representative of the family he would be, once he grew out of his wild stage."

The carriage hit a bump in the road, and all four were jostled. Isabelle was thrown forward and then back against Henry, who could not have felt more shock if the carriage itself had sprouted wings and taken flight. He couldn't remember a time when he was not painfully aware of his father's dim view of his louche lifestyle, nor could he recall the old man offering him a single encouraging word. His stepmother, meanwhile, had rested her head against the breast of his black coat. "You will see," she went on, her tears beginning to soak through to his shirt. "He was hard on you so that you could be great too, and you will learn in time that he was always right."

Henry placed a hand on her tremulous shoulder, and tried to sit up, straight and powerful, as though he were trying on the part of the son his father had always wanted.

Twenty
Nine

Is it true that one of those sons of top-drawer Manhattan, who went very publicly to enlist, was not in the Philippines at all, as had been reported? If so, what was he doing, and is his wife now wondering what kind of man she really married?

—FROM *CITÉ CHATTER*, WEDNESDAY, JULY 18, 1900

*T*HE RIDE BACK TO THE SCHOONMAKER MANSION on Fifth was interminable, and nobody spoke except Isabelle, whose words were almost indecipherable through her sobbing. It was a rather maudlin and over the top display, in her stepdaughter-in-law's opinion, and had entirely to do with the fact that the young widow had spent the afternoon of her husband's demise flirting with that letch of a painter Lispenard Bradley. But she had nothing to worry about—for dead husbands could not, after all, seek divorces. Henry could, as Penelope was painfully aware, and he no longer had the rather forceful disapproval of his father to dissuade him from such a scandalous course. William Schoonmaker would have kept Henry in line, but now Henry was the head of the household, and could be as improper as he liked. Already his intention of leaving his wife, which he had apparently stated quite plainly just before the old man croaked, had become a story and made the rounds. If Penelope had known her father-in-law was in such poor health, she certainly would have thought twice about lingering in the hall so long with the prince of Bavaria pushing amorously against her.

As there was no longer any way of correcting that, she had tried today to play the good wife. This was not a coveted role for her. Even when she had been in love with Henry, the idea of seeing that his suits were pressed and that the maids were bringing him fresh coffee and that someone was seeing to his correspondence bored her. It was a little insulting now, and made her feel menial, second rate, which she absolutely was not. But what would she be if she was stripped of the title Mrs. Henry Schoonmaker, when she had not even been married a year, when there were no children to tie her to the family? Her dearly won position in the social firmament would evaporate as surely as William Schoonmaker's last breath.

All of genteel New York had seen her that afternoon, patiently and humbly keeping to her grieving husband's side. She did have that. They would remember, later, if Henry persisted in making his affair with the Holland girl public. But if Penelope was to seal a sympathetic impression of herself in their minds, she was going to have to keep up the act. How difficult this might prove to be did not fully occur to her until they had stepped down from the coach, and she heard her name being called out.

"Yes," she turned. The day was fading, and it was difficult to determine who had spoken.

"Mrs. Schoonmaker, over here." By then she recognized the voice, and in the following moment she saw Prince Frederick, waiting inside a fashionable black phaeton with the cover raised up. There was no driver, and he held the reins idly in his large, gloved hand as though he might, at any second, take off. She glanced behind her, hoping nobody had yet noticed the visitor, but Henry had already traveled some distance up the steep limestone steps of his grand family home, with his stepmother leaning heavily against him.

She kept her eyes on the ground as she approached. "You should not have come today," she said, and then flicked back her lashes suddenly, so that despite her shy posture, her blue eyes would be revealed with sudden drama.

"No . . ." He was smiling at her, again, in that impossibly subtle, urbane manner he had. "But I couldn't help myself. Anyway, you are *the* Mrs. Schoonmaker now, and I expect you need a drink."

"I do," she replied, letting him see what an effort it was for her not to return his smile. "How very clever."

"Why don't I escort you to dinner then? Take it from me, your husband will be busy with paperwork this evening, and I think he would appreciate my showing you a good time."

Penelope raised an eyebrow and pretended to mull his offer. The tangerine light of an advanced day was especially lovely on the defined jaw of her royal friend. His eyes darted up toward the Schoonmaker house, where the windows had been draped in black, and then back at her. The tactical matron in her knew she should stay inside and tally condolence letters, but then Henry had not said two words to her over the entire day, and the part of her that was an angry, snubbed girl of eighteen overwhelmed the rest.

"All right—if you insist. But know it is against my better judgment, and only because you are here in our country for such a devastatingly short time. Only, wait a little, will you? I hate these black clothes."

The prince rested his elbow on the polished side of the coach and leaned forward to reply, in a serious voice she had never previously known him to employ, "I would wait for you forever."

She winked and turned to follow her husband. She was already inside by the time she realized how completely this last comment had lifted her mood.

In the late afternoon, Penelope had hoped Henry wouldn't notice as she slipped out of the house dressed in elaborately draped carnelian organdy and a pearl-encrusted aigrette. By the time she was being swept across the dance floor of Sherry's by a certain strapping royal, however, this was no longer among her concerns. Because, as her companion had pointed out a few times already, only a fool would ignore so incandescent a wife, and she wouldn't at all have minded if Henry had had to watch, for a few moments anyway, the appreciative glances Frederick kept bestowing on her bare shoulders and lean form.

Indeed, everyone was staring at her, and as Frederick rested his hand on the small of her back, she felt the thrill of a low murmur circling the room and the sensation of being talked of once again. He was wearing black tails and his hair was slicked—he looked like Henry, like any very handsome gentleman of the upper class, except that there seemed to be more of him than her husband, and he was focused on her with such delightful intensity. She knew they made a very pretty picture. Long before she had played the ingénue in order to marry into one of the oldest and best families in New York, she had created minor stirs like this one for sport. It felt good to do it again, good to be moved about on the floor by such a nicely put-together gentleman. But then, when the music stopped, she saw that even the divorcée Lucy Carr did not bother to hide her disgust.

"I have been very bad," she said, not as defiantly as she had intended, as he escorted her back to their table, where nearly eight courses had passed with the young Mrs. Schoonmaker taking nearly as many bites.

"I hope your countrymen will not judge you too harshly." The prince pushed her chair in as she sat, before taking the cushioned seat beside her. He drew the bottle of champagne from the silver ice bucket, which was sweating at the center of the table, and refilled their glasses. He cast his blue eyes across the vast room, which was filled with round tables and the busy skirts that overflowed from underneath them, the chandelier light falling in flattering gold speckles across the merry diners. Prince Frederick very nearly glittered.

"Of course they will." Penelope adjusted the white gloves that reached several inches beyond her elbows, and then rested her chin on her fist. She had had more champagne than usual, and it was causing her to wallow, which was terrible for her complexion, and not otherwise an activity she liked to be noted for. Still she spun her glass about, melancholically, before sipping.

"My poor Mrs. Schoonmaker," the prince lamented. "She is so impossibly sad."

"I am not sad," she returned. "Only a little tired. It has been a very long day."

This was true. It had been sad and lonely, and had required a great deal of poise. Meanwhile, she had stood for much too long, and she had been wearing her new black shoes, leather with grosgrain trim, and they had pinched her toes. Though the fatigue did not bother her half as much as the idea that the prince might pity her; she was not a girl to be pitied.

But in the next moment she stopped caring about that, for he placed the back of his hand on her shoulder and drew it down her arm, his nails gliding along her skin, and then the silk glove, so that little tremors spread over the rest of her frame. She hadn't been touched like that in a long time. Her eyes closed, almost involuntarily, and she found that she wanted to be kissed by him again very badly. This desire, she realized with a slight chill, had not a thing to do with making any husband jealous, or causing any diverting scandal.

Then she felt his warm breath by the dark strands of hair, which were brushed over her ear. "You would not look so sad if you were a princess," he said.

There was no collection of words that could possibly have been more delicious. Though spoken with purpose, they created a giddy, girlish sensation, of a variety that Penelope had not experienced in a year or more. It was wonderful, and she kept her eyes closed for another few moments, as the room began to spin with an emotion not entirely unlike love. For the first time in some years, she wondered if the title Mrs. Henry Schoonmaker wasn't the highest she might attain.

Thirty

Sergeant Teddy Cutting has returned from the Pacific, which was cause for Gemma Newbold, who people used to say was old Mrs. Cutting's first choice to become her only son's wife, to wear a smile yesterday, along with a very fashionable bonnet, even though the occasion upon which he reentered society was the solemn burial of Mr. William Schoonmaker....

—FROM THE "GAMESOME GALLANT" COLUMN IN THE *NEW YORK IMPERIAL*, THURSDAY, JULY 19, 1900

"THE PUBLIC DOES LIKE THIS SORT OF THING," Davis Barnard said from the sideboard where he was pouring whiskey into coffee cups. The newspaperman was referring to the funeral tidbits Diana had fed him the day before. He had a dark, dramatic brow, a rather pinched nose, and he filled out his waistcoat in a way that, from his own, oft-expressed point of view, symbolized good living. "But it is my personal belief that at this point they would be far more interested in the personal diary of Diana Holland, *avec* illustrations. You, my dear, could sell papers."

Diana smiled distantly from the daybed by the window, where she lounged in a long navy skirt and a shell-pink blouse that fluttered around her small, curved frame. She had come to know Mr. Barnard's narrow quarters, on the third floor of an apartment building on East Sixteenth Street, quite well: the cracks in the twilight blue paint; the rows of framed prints covering the fissures as best they could; the large cut-glass punch bowl on the cabinet; the boxing gloves strung up over the fireplace, which, in the summer, was used as a storage place for books. There were several books in that pile that she had a mind to rescue before her departure on Tuesday. "Ah, but that is all talk," she replied, and turned toward the window, where great puffs of white clouds were wandering across a devastatingly clear sky.

Davis gave her a look and then brought her and his friend—George Grass, the writer, sitting on the cane-backed chair on the other side of the window from Diana's daybed—their coffee. "I don't believe a word of it, do you, Grass?"

Grass put his long, horselike face close to his mug and drank. All of him was long and horselike, and his far-reaching legs were crossed in the manner of a seasoned flaneur. Upon his arrival half an hour ago, Diana had determined he was ugly, but interesting.

"I have no idea what you two are talking of." He extended his porcelain cup, in a congenial gesture, so that it made a clinking noise against Diana's. "Gossip is just a tool to distract people who have nothing better to do from feeling jealous of those few of us still remaining with noble hearts."

Diana tossed her head of abbreviated curls and laughed; Davis made a sour face. "It is the tool that bought the whiskey you are enjoying," he retorted, but Diana could see that he didn't really mind. That he was a hack was one of Davis's favorite jokes.

"Don't think I am not grateful." Grass smiled, revealing his brown teeth. "Art never paid for anything."

"Come, though, Miss Holland," Davis went on, ignoring the sad turn of his friend's comments. "The next time you run half way around the globe, I don't want to find out via a telegram asking for money, and demanding that I print your official alibi in the papers."

In days she would be gone again. She could hardly wait. To her, it felt like years since she had been alone with Henry; it was a special kind of agony, being so long removed from their secret society of two. At night, she fell asleep imagining just what kind of kiss would join them together again. Plus, disapproving eyes and vitriolic murmurs followed her everywhere these days, and her mother charged around the house in silent fury, waiting for the story to officially break and for her family to be ruined once and for all. It was not a situation in which she longed to linger.

"I can see the joke, Miss Holland, playing just under the surface." Grass's piercing gaze was on her, not unkindly. Diana tried to put on an enigmatical expression, but a glowing quality gave her away. "You're up to something!"

"Don't be angry, Mr. Barnard." Her eyes darted to her old friend, standing just beyond the cane-backed chair. She sank her teeth into her plump lower lip at the thought of what she was confessing. "But I *do* have an escape plan."

"Where are you going?" Davis asked sadly. She had long suspected that his affection for her was too large to be based solely on her ability to collect stories about the doings of the well-heeled classes, and tried her best to be not *quite* so lovely.

"To Paris, this time for real."

"Alone?"

She blushed.

"Don't ask her that," Grass put in. "We will know soon enough," he added philosophically.

"Will you still send me telegrams, when you are eating snails and trading romantic secrets with the viscomtesse de blah-bitty-blah?"

"No, she will not." Grass's voice had grown excited with the picture he was conjuring. "She will be busy writing novels. As soon as she has gotten far enough away from this frighteningly puritanical country, her mind will be set free, and she will be able to turn all of her observations into richly drawn characters and intricately themed stories."

"But what will she eat, dear Grass?" Barnard leaned against the wall, his arms crossing his chest skeptically.

"Baguette and red wine, pure art, filthy air. Look at her, she is made of rose petals, the world will take good care of her. And if it does not, we will have our hearts moved by such an exquisitely gorgeous tragedy." He put down his cup and leaned toward the young lady in question. On his breath, there was the hint of a tooth going rotten. She was surprised by the urgency with which he addressed her case, although she knew she should be flattered, and after all, it was a very lively life. "My dear, you have made a good decision. Here you would be a pretty wife who everyone would forget in time. There—there you will become some ultimate version of yourself. Take it from me, no American can really see himself, or understand his country, when he is here, in the middle of all the brutal hubbub and hectic commerce. It effaces everything. You will see when you go. France is a very different country—each and every cobblestone there has played its part in history. Your eyes will be wide open."

When he had finished, his mouth remained open a few seconds, and his eyes were shining with the intensity of his words. She tried to appear worthy of such an impassioned speech. She wished Henry were there, to hear about their future home, to grow excited about the cobblestones and baguette and red wine. Then her head filled up with Henry, and she began to wonder if he was too miserable, if Penelope was being really horrible, and how many times that day he had paused to imagine Diana disrobed. "To wide-open eyes, then," she said, raising her coffee cup.

They all toasted again. "To wide-open eyes," Grass and Barnard repeated in tandem.

"But you must promise you will miss me, Mr. Barnard, or I shall cry myself to sleep all across the Atlantic Ocean and doubt my choice," she went on gaily.

"Ah, Miss Di, we will all of us miss you more than words can convey." As Barnard and Grass turned to other topics, she found that her imagination kept drifting to a small window, above a twisting little street, which she pushed open in the early morning, when her body, like Henry's beside her, was still soft with slumber.

Thirty One

When a lady is in a family way, she keeps her name out of the papers and her person out of sight. In recent years, some women have welcomed visitors when they were quite visibly with child, but it is not a practice I look very kindly upon.

—MRS. L. A. M. BRECKINRIDGE, *THE LAWS OF BEING IN WELL-MANNERED CIRCLES*

HE WALLS WERE DEEP RED. A LACY WHITE CANOPY obscured the ceiling above her. There was the framed mirror with the decorative bow, the chest of drawers with a high shine. She felt with her hands: Her belly was still swollen under the dressing gown she wore. It was summer. It was hot. A light sheen of sweat clung to her forehead and underneath her lower lip. Elizabeth opened her mouth, and tried to make a sound with her dry throat. She was exhausted; she had been in bed for days. Then the rest of it came flooding back.

In her dreams, Snowden preyed on her family. He snatched coins from their pockets and made off with her child in the night. But when she came to and saw the real him, he never had that air of lecherous, crouching evil. His humble features assumed a calm expression, and then he would douse a white hankie with a clear liquid, and put it over her mouth and nose, and in a few moments everything would go black. Occasionally he would leave her conscious long enough for

Mrs. Schmidt to bathe and feed her. Then it was back to sleep, where Will would sweep from heaven, as strong as ever and now winged, and scoop her up and take her to see her father, who was sitting on a cloud, watching over them, smoking a pipe and reciting long-forgotten poems. Sometimes the Will role was played by Teddy, the concerned eyes gray instead of pale blue, but it was always with the same tenderness that the male angel lifted her out of the white coverlets and carried her away.

Perhaps it was for this reason that she was unsurprised by the sound of a familiar voice in the hall quietly insisting upon seeing her.

"But, Mr. Cutting, as I said, it is highly irregular for a gentleman to visit a woman in her condition, especially when she is not well enough to receive in her parlor. If Elizabeth were awake, I am sure she would be mortified by the idea of you seeing her in her bedroom. . . ."

"Mr. Cairns, I am sensible to your concerns, and believe me I have no interest in offending you or your wife. But Elizabeth is one of my oldest friends, we have known each other since we were children, and I am only here in the city for a short time. I am familiar with her tremendous sense of virtue, but I know she would make an exception this time. And with her own husband as chaperone, I think even Mrs. Hamilton Breedfelt would approve."

Elizabeth's eyes were huge. Her breath was short. She waited, listening for more. When she heard nothing she tried to scream, but her unused vocal cords failed her. Then the door opened, and into the deceptively sunny room walked Snowden, followed shortly by Teddy. The simple sight of him at that moment was the kindest thing she could have hoped for herself. She gazed at the slender but pronounced facial features, which were the hallmark of his class, the sad gray eyes, his blond hair greased as usual but trimmed shorter than before, his cheeks soft, recently shaved. There was that patient, almost polite quality in his pose, and she saw—even from across the room where, for propriety's sake, he lingered—that he was wounded by the sight of her sick bed, or maybe by the idea of her now being married to someone else. It made her want to cry, seeing him like that—even though she knew she should be begging him to help her—and she felt her throat constrict.

"Hello, Lizzie," he said quietly. He was wearing his uniform, and he looked so solid and capable in it that her body relaxed a little. He'd come for her. He had made it through the door. Her state of duress would be easy for him to read; he was going to save her.

Now Elizabeth began to move her lips, but still she failed to make sound. *Help,* she was trying to say, but it was inaudible, and Teddy was all the way across the room. Finally she managed to produce a weak croak, but it didn't sound like any kind of language known to this world.

"You see?" Snowden said. He had noticed what she was attempting, and he crossed the room quickly to her side, blocking Teddy's view of her, and hers of him. "She is truly not well, and can hardly speak. As you say, you know her very well, and so I am sure you are aware how delicate a lady she is. Please. I fear you will cause her a great shock."

Then he bent forward, pretending to put his face close to her mouth as though he were listening, but in fact covering her lips. Panic seized Elizabeth, as it occurred to her that Snowden might somehow or other manage to keep her quiet until Teddy was gone. Her heart raced. She managed to say something like help, but it was drowned out in the heel of Snowden's palm, which was pressing down against her sluggish mouth.

"Yes," Teddy said then. There was something stunned and low in his voice, as though it had been too much for him to see the girl he had on more than one occasion asked to be his wife. "Yes, I have been most improper. I am sorry. I will show myself out."

"No," Elizabeth tried to cry out, but the plea was smothered by her husband's grip. Already Teddy's footfalls were moving away. She blinked, and Snowden looked down at her with a most patient fury. He waited another few moments, and she brought air into her nose sharply, trying to maintain her breath. She could hear Teddy on the stairs. Snowden lifted his hand off her mouth, and she parted her lips to call out. But her husband was too quick, his other hand was ready with the soaked cloth.

The picture of Teddy standing there like her savior was still fresh in her mind. Yet in reality he was on his way to the door, and anyway her eyes were drifting closed, and everything was growing fuzzy and dark.

Thirty Two

With the passing of William S. Schoonmaker, the city has lost one of its most esteemed merchant princes. Barely more than half a century in age, Mr. Schoonmaker made prodigious gifts to many of New York's finest institutions, and was a fixture on its social scene. He is said to have left his second wife, née Isabelle de Ford, with whom he had no children, and his daughter, Prudence, each an amount of $100,000, which, while certainly a handsome inheritance, is nothing compared to the rest of the estate, which will go in its entirety to his only son, Henry.

—FROM THE FRONT PAGE OF THE *NEW YORK TIMES*,
FRIDAY, JULY 20, 1900

"THANK YOU, GENTLEMEN."

Henry stood on the threshold of the Schoonmaker mansion, his hands thrust in the pockets of his black trousers, and his face drained of color by the events of the week. His father had left holdings far vaster and more complex than he could possibly have imagined, and he had spent many days trying to come to understand them. It seemed to him that his father owned a not insubstantial slice of everything in the city, and maybe in the nation. They were all his now, as was the house with the theatrical limestone steps stretching down below him. It was twilight, and the carriages of many of his father's associates waited by the curb in a deceptive quietude. These men had come to see what it would mean, for them and their interests, this calamitous, startling event.

"Thank you, Mr. Schoonmaker," each replied, one after the other. They gave him sympathetic pats on the back and handshakes as they moved, in a stream of dark bowlers and jackets, through the entryway and down to their waiting drivers. He was beginning to be able to match their faces to their names.

"You have put their minds at rest," Jeremiah Lawrence offered, from Henry's side, once the others were out of earshot. The lawyer's sleeves were rolled to his elbows, as though they had been shucking corn all this time.

"They think I am too young." Henry sighed. He, too, had done away with his jacket, and now wore only his black waistcoat over an ivory dress shirt with an undone collar. The night was muggy, lavender, and he could hear the cooing of an especially loud pigeon, fluffing his feathers and rubbing his wings together somewhere overhead.

"Yes, they thought you were a puppy when they arrived. You surprised them, I think. Your seriousness, your attention to the details of the estate—they were impressed."

"I surprised them by being there at all," Henry remarked dryly.

Lawrence laughed, and rested a hand against Henry's black jacket. "Well, they know you didn't have to be. You could have absented yourself from these proceedings, and you would still be a very rich man tonight."

"That thought had occurred to me," Henry confessed, "but I suppose we all have to grow up sometime, don't we?"

"No." It was Lawrence's turn to be wry. "Not *all* of us do."

For the first time that day, a kind of smile came to Henry's face.

"Your father always thought you would have a good head for business, though," Lawrence went on, growing serious again, and assessing Henry as though he were not a man of twenty-one. "I think he would be pleased with how you are conducting yourself."

This notion was no less shocking to Henry today than it had been yesterday, on the tongue of his stepmother. Since then he had replayed countless arguments with his father, searching for hidden clues, and though he could detect a kind of harsh affection in some of his memories, it still baffled him. But the week following a man's death did not seem like the time to question his secret trust or magnanimity, and Henry had told himself that he might as well see if Schoonmaker the elder had been right to believe in him. "So it was not some oversight that I was the chief beneficiary of his will? He was always threatening to cut me out, I half thought he already had somewhere along the way."

"Your father did not make oversights like that. He did not make oversights at all." Lawrence chuckled. "Nor will you; I will make sure of that, though I expect in time you will be after me about my failures of attention. But these have been long, hard days for you. The old man's legacy has been well taken care of. We should give it a rest and pour ourselves a drink."

Perhaps the emotions of an entire staggering week showed in Henry's finely chiseled features then, for Lawrence quickly changed his expression.

"I mean, of course, *you* should have a drink, young man. With your friends, or your Mrs. . . ."

Henry's eyes drifted as Diana entered his thoughts. They had exchanged a flurry of notes but had not seen one another since gazing from a distance after his father's burial. Frequently he found himself picturing those shining eyes and that twisted little smile, and yet he felt a kind of quiet orderliness settling within him and all around. To his surprise, these days of responsibility, the answering to people and finding that they listened to him, had a rigid rightness to them. He didn't want to disturb this feeling, which was a new one for him; he did not, just then, relish any thrills.

"You would be as good a companion as any," Henry returned, after a pause. They had begun to walk slowly across the marble floor of the main hallway, which was washed with golden light from the chandeliers hanging above. Behind them, a footman sealed the door. "It's only that I don't feel much like celebrating."

"No, sir. Of course. I'll just put things away in the office so that we can pick up again tomorrow."

"Thank you, Lawrence." Henry bowed his head appreciatively, and took the lawyer's hand, shook it firmly. When

the older man had disappeared, he began to slowly walk the
halls and stairwells of the house, not knowing quite what he
should do. He could be anywhere, he knew, and yet these were
his walls, his roof. As he ambled past the grand parlor, where
Mrs. William Schoonmaker had long been known to welcome her visitors on Mondays, he heard the quiet sobbing of
his father's young widow.

"Isabelle . . . ," he said, crossing to the settee where she
curled, under layers of black crepe, her face hidden in cushions.
He knelt by her side and rested a hand against her shoulder
and thought, not for the first time that week, how she seemed
to have grown smaller over a very short period.

"Oh, Henry." He could only see half her face, for she
covered her mouth as she turned frightened eyes upon him.
Her gloves were stained dark by her tears and running nose,
and her eyes were swollen and red with sorrow and self-pity.
"What will become of me?"

The blond hair that she always kept so elaborately
curled was pulled back severely under a black widow's cap.
He realized, seeing her in mourning garb in the place where
she had collected clever people and amusing anecdotes, that
she had been diminished, perhaps forever; that she feared a
permanent loss of status. Remembering how repeatedly he
had pushed his father, how continually he had infuriated him
until the end, he felt a pang of guilt. He had never coveted

responsibility of the Schoonmaker fortune, but, for better or worse, he had it now.

"It is an awful period," he began slowly. Reassuring was not his most natural mode, but he felt that he must say something. "But you will see, in time, you'll hold your Mondays again, you will wear fine dresses in colors other than black. You are Mrs. William Schoonmaker, and you must carry on, just as I must."

Her pupils moved rapidly back and forth. She sniffled, and tried to dry her cheek with the back of her hand. "I can stay here?"

"Of course."

"You will maintain the house?"

"I think father would have wanted that." She nodded emphatically. "I certainly do," he added softly.

Her face crumpled, and she pulled her gloves off, yanking each finger with a touch of aggression, and cast them aside. Then she rested her little palm against Henry's cheek.

"He was right about you, you know, Henry," she said when the risk of a fresh cry had passed. "Now, will you be a darling and help me to bed?"

Once Henry had seen his stepmother to her suite, and called for her maid to undress her, he went to the room that used to be his study, where his own monogrammed stationery was kept. It was next to the room that he used to sleep in, but which now belonged to Penelope, and so was naturally done up in white and gold as though Marie Antoinette had outfitted it for her children. There was no light from under her door, as there had not been for some days. The servants told him, in their most circumspect tones, that since Tuesday his wife had been coming in late, sleeping through the morning, dressing and then going out again. They made concerned and loyal faces at him, but for Henry this was only another sign that his life was adhering to some perfect, as yet invisible design. He turned on a lamp and searched out a monogrammed piece of card stock. Then he wrote a quick note—*My Diana, when can we meet?*—and went to find someone to deliver it.

Thirty

Three

THE EVERETT BOUCHARD FAMILY

REQUESTS THE PLEASURE OF YOUR COMPANY

AT THE WEDDING OF

MISS CAROLINA BROAD

TO THEIR SON

MR. LELAND BOUCHARD

AT THE GRACE CHURCH

THE TWENTY-SECOND OF JULY,

NINETEEN HUNDRED

ONE O'CLOCK

*T*HE BELLS HAD RUNG ONE O'CLOCK, BUT ALL OF the notable, elegant, very rich people occupying the pews of Grace Church sat quietly waiting, in their heavily ornamented hats, for the union of one of their own and a rather new heiress. In the small room on the side of the church, which Isaac Phillips Buck had arranged like the dressing room of a visiting princess with soft chairs and flowers everywhere, the flutters had arrived. It was as though Carolina's physical body might disintegrate at any moment and go floating away on the wind. This feeling was in no way trepidation about marrying Leland—that part could not come soon enough, especially after the separation of a few days, which his old-fashioned family had insisted upon, and which had been unbearable for both bride and groom. The fear was entirely to do with her having possibly misstepped in some way, now, when she was about to take her grandest stage yet, and when it was too late to fix anything.

"Miss Broad, are you ready?"

Over her shoulder, in the gold framed mirror's reflection—it was full length and had been so heavy that it required three men to carry it in and position it—hovered Buck. Her eyes, paler green than usual, flashed in his direction, and then back toward herself. The antique lace fit tightly around her torso, to her chin and down to her wrists. A belt of white satin embroidered with pearls marked her waist; below that swept a vast and complex skirt with a train worthy of a coronation. Because of that train and that skirt, she had not sat down for some hours, and her legs felt just a little weak. Her dark hair was parted at the center and swept down over her ears and into a low bun. Sprays of white flowers and tiny diamonds decorated the headband that secured a gauzy veil in place.

"Your groom," he went on gently, "is waiting."

"But do I look all right?"

She knew she did. It seemed to her that in the last few days some final rough edges had been scrubbed from her features, so that what was truly lovely and original about them was now allowed to shine. The dark freckles that lay across an otherwise pale complexion no longer seemed a liability, but rather like a seal of authenticity. Buck, who surely knew a thing or two about status anxiety, came forward to her side and rested a hand upon his shoulder.

"You are the loveliest bride I have ever seen," he said.

"And you know I have assisted not a few in the hours before they walked the aisle."

For the first time that day, she managed a smile at the thought that Buck was comparing her favorably to Penelope Schoonmaker. But she owed much to that other lady, who was no doubt waiting among her and Leland's guests, and she knew it would be indecorous to press further, to try and extract more pleasure from the compliment. Especially not on a day as important as this one. She tucked her lower lip under her top teeth and declared in a voice barely above a whisper, "I think I am ready."

Everything had come together, she reminded herself. Madame Bristede had completed her dress and the bridesmaids' peach-colored confections—for Katy and Beatrice and Eleanor Wetmore and Georgina Vreewold—in just the right amount of time. The papers had all reported extensively on the bright and shining couple. Even God seemed to have done his part, granting her one of those perfectly temperate summer days when the sun is a golden disk against a backdrop of eternal blue. She had succeeded in having her sister there, even though it had meant inviting Mrs. Carr; Claire had assisted her regular lady's maid in dressing her, and stood in the shadows now, watching these final moments before the ceremony with quiet reverence. Soon the pomp and circumstance would be over, and Carolina would officially be Mrs.

Leland Bouchard. She and her husband would walk down the church steps, smiling at their own, gorgeous weather. All of those fancy New Yorkers she so wanted to impress would judge her or not judge her—it wouldn't matter much anymore, she suddenly realized, because in days she would be on a steamship, sailing for Europe and her honeymoon.

Buck turned his smooth, larded face at an angle. "Shall I get Mr. Bouchard?"

As soon as she nodded, Buck summoned the two lady's maids with a flick of his hand. Claire did not meet the bride's eyes on her way out the narrow, arched doorframe. The sisters had barely been able to speak, as there were always so many attendants about that week, but Carolina could see in her older sister's glances that she was happy for this fairy-tale ending, even if she herself was still wearing a dress of plain black. She had done her red hair up in a braided and more ornate arrangement than usual; that was something. What was important, the younger sister told herself, was that Claire was on the premises, that she would be present in a secret way, when her last remaining family member was married.

Since there was no father figure in Carolina's life, her fiancé's father had kindly offered to play that part in the ceremony. She thought, sadly, of Mr. Longhorn, and how he would have enjoyed doing her that service, and of her own father, who she could scarcely remember, and who surely would have been shocked by the news that his younger daughter would ever be wed on such a grand scale. All of a sudden she found she was in a hurry to begin the processional, and she felt that every moment separating her from that first kiss with her husband would be a kind of torture. The little smile she had given Buck now suffused her entire face.

"My, Miss Broad, you *do* make a lovely bride."

Carolina's smile fell when she realized it was not her future father-in-law who had appeared in the far corner of the reflection, but rather the unfortunately familiar figure of Tristan Wrigley. He was dressed in black tails and slacks, a gray waistcoat, and a dress shirt with an arrow collar, just like a guest at a very fine wedding. He wore the costume well, and with the handsome modeling of his face he probably did look to the ushers standing sentry on the church steps like the product of an august lineage and extensive breeding.

"How did you get here?" she whispered.

"Oh, Miss Broad," he replied in the same cozy tone. "Everybody in New York knows that you and Leland Bouchard are getting married at the Grace Church today. I just walked in, along with the rest of your fancy friends. Or did you think you were really going to get rid of me with a twenty-dollar handout, as though I had just been some fellow you let hold your wrap one evening long ago?"

His knowing, congratulatory smile did not fade once

during this speech, but Carolina could hear the threat in his words. "You're going to have to leave now," she began a little shakily. "My father-in-law will be coming. It would be most improper if you were here when he arrived."

"Indeed it would be. Although—he is not your father-in-law *yet*."

"He will be shortly," she snapped back, hoping he hadn't noticed the unsteadiness in her voice.

"Well, all right. But I thought you deserved fair warning that I was here, and that *if* the reverend should ask whether or not any of the assembled knew any reason why the man and woman in question should not be wed, that I *may* feel compelled to speak. . . ."

"No." Carolina's gaze broke with the reflection in the mirror now, and she turned to stare at Tristan. "You can't. Don't."

"Don't?" Tristan's fair eyebrows rose delicately. "But why would I do you the favor of not telling what, you must acknowledge, are the facts of the situation—that you are a former maid and an impostor and that your current wealth was derived from a most improper relationship—when you have been so very cold to me?"

"It was *not* improper," she returned, heat rising to the skin of her cheeks. For there was one fact of her personal history that made her an ideal bride and also happened to be true, and that was that she would come to the altar a virgin. Some angry instinct reared at the thought that Tristan might somehow rob her of this.

"That is not for me to judge," her tormentor replied with an easy shrug.

"What do you want?" All of her was ticking, and she tried to remind herself of the self-possession and resolve she had acquired along with those other jewels and paintings and stocks and bonds. He may have been hustling longer, but he was stupider than she was, and she knew that if she kept her head she could handle him.

"I am not greedy," Tristan answered evenly. "I just want to be compensated for my part in making you a very rich lady."

Carolina took a sharp breath in through her nostrils, and willed the color in her cheeks to fade. She spoke slowly and seriously, looking into those glittering eyes. "I swear, I will make it worth your while. Only, leave now, please—"

In the moment before the door to Carolina's dressing room burst open again, she saw in his face that she had persuaded him. That he was ready to go peaceably and let her have her wedding. But before they could shake hands, loud voices closed in on them from the antechamber. Both froze in anticipation.

"He is probably nobody, Leland, I will take care of it." Her heart dropped when she recognized the older Bouchard's voice. "Only, you must not see your bride!"

"Father, all due respect, she is *my* bride, and if I suspect she is being chased by some old beau . . ."

Carolina's lips parted. Perhaps, if she thought quickly, she could conjure a convincing story. But before anything came, Leland had charged into the room and grabbed Tristan by both lapels, pushing him backward, beyond her, against the huge mirror. It shuddered with the impact, throwing beams of light across the stone walls. Leland's father and Buck hovered, silent and concerned, just outside the room.

"You bastard!" Leland shouted. His broad face had turned a shade of red not unlike his fiancée's a few moments before. Carolina realized he had harbored a jealousy toward the handsome man at the opera all this time, that the idea of his girl belonging to another angered him. The drama in the capillaries of his face made his eyes appear especially blue. His dress and hair were more smoothed than usual, and she couldn't stop herself from thinking, in the middle of it all, that he looked awfully handsome in his groom's finery. "How dare you come here today—on our wedding day! How dare you harass my fiancée at all, much less in God's house!"

Tristan's face fell, unpleasantly, into confusion and fear. He glanced toward Carolina. Leland loomed over him— he was by far the larger of the two. She was distracted for a moment by the idea that the first man she'd ever kissed and the man she was about to marry were on the verge of coming to blows, and couldn't help but feel a little exhilarated by the chest beating. *Not bad for a girl who a year ago nobody paid any attention to*, she couldn't help but think.

"What are you looking at?" Leland was yelling at the Lord & Taylor salesman. Carolina glanced at Buck and old Bouchard, hoping they would intervene, but neither would meet her eye. Meanwhile, Leland struck Tristan across the face with the back of his hand, using enough force to split his lip. "Tell me why you're here!"

"Miss Broad?" Tristan said, helplessly.

But she was distracted by the blood that had been knocked from Tristan's lip and onto the perfect white front of her skirt.

"Don't speak to her!"

Tristan had begun to struggle now, but Leland was too strong for him. They pushed back and forth against one another, but had soon toppled over, falling to the ground at Carolina's feet. She watched, with horror, as more blood was smeared against white silk, and feathers and pearls began to come dislodged from the fabric.

"Please, Lina . . . ," Tristan said again. He had been fully overpowered, and his adversary was holding his head down against the stone floor; there was a truly helpless quality in his voice now, and something familiar, something that suggested how well they had known each other. Leland was shaking him, banging his head against the hard gray surface of the floor. If he kept it up, she realized, Tristan would soon be knocked out cold.

"Stop!" She wailed, her hands rising to her cheeks.

Very slowly, Leland turned his blue eyes on his bride. All three parties were panting a little. It was not only her gown, but Leland's white dress shirt that was now rumpled and bloody. They were no longer going to be married that afternoon, not with their wedding finery undone like this. For several seconds, he stared at her before quietly saying: "Why, my love?" When his question was met with silence, the softness left him, and he asked in the voice of dawning realization: "What is he to you?"

Her hands crept over her eyes, but that did nothing to prevent the reality of what was going to happen, what had already happened, from settling into her consciousness like a winter chill. She asked her tears to hold awhile, and found that they obeyed.

"Mr. Bouchard, Mr. Buck, will you leave us?" she said, bringing her hands from her face to her corseted waist. Now, with the truth brimming in her throat, a strange calm overcame her. "Tristan, go—you have done your worst."

Leland stumbled, slowly, to his feet. The man he had struggled so roughly with crawled in the direction of the door, and then pushed himself up and began to run. Leland's father and Buck nodded to each other, and absented themselves from the room. All this time, Leland had maintained an intense and wary gaze in Carolina's direction. She could not bear to go on meeting it.

His face was full of questions, but all he said was, "Tristan . . . ? When we saw him at the opera, you told me he was nobody."

"Darling," she began, casting her eyes down on the ruined dress and clasping her hands nervously together. The term of endearment echoed false in her ears; it was not the sort of word a girl like her used. When she spoke again, it was in her own voice, and to tell the whole, messy truth. "There are a few things about me that I really ought to have told you sooner."

Thirty Four

Perhaps the heat has gotten to the city's most well-heeled citizens, for it has been a month of rushed weddings, bizarre coiffures, and unforgivable behavior. In the final case I am speaking of Mrs. Henry Schoonmaker, of course, who has been seen all around town with the visiting prince of Bavaria, without the slightest attempt to feign even a modicum of subtlety about it. What peculiar cocktails has the demimonde been drinking?

—FROM *CITÉ CHATTER*, SUNDAY, JULY 22, 1900

$\mathcal{M}$RS. HENRY SCHOONMAKER WAS PERFECTLY content to step outside the gothic church on lower Broadway and into a brilliant afternoon. She wore a pert little smile, despite the whispering and hissing that followed her everywhere, and a hat that was as broad as her shoulders and festooned with cloth roses and other delights. The wedding of Carolina Broad had been called off most abruptly and unusually, but it was just as well, for the outfit she wore—a fitted ivory bolero with gold stitching, and a dress of pomegranate-colored crepe de chine, cut to best display her naturally tiny waist—was too flattering to waste on God. Although there was something faintly disappointing about having a girl whose reputation she had allowed to be associated with her own make such an embarrassment of herself, she wasn't particularly bothered. Nor was she ruffled by the unkind stares of women who, a week ago, had considered her the wronged party in the Schoonmaker scandal. Soon she wouldn't need any of their friendship, or even that hard-won surname, which had in the last few days begun to chafe.

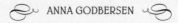

They had been intoxicating days. She and the prince had dined together every night, and stayed up long past supper dancing wherever the champagne was cold and expensive. How many aspects of herself had she recognized in this strong, sparkling nobleman! For he was tall, like her, dark-haired and blue-eyed, and he knew with great certainty that his life should be about having the best of everything. She had dreamt of meeting her match in looks, in taste, in wealth—she'd thought Henry had been that match, but Henry didn't have her vision, and anyway it didn't matter anymore because even if he got it, at this late date, he still couldn't make her a princess. Not a real one.

"Now that old Schoonmaker is dead, the whole household has gone to pieces . . . ," said Gemma Newbold, exiting the church behind Penelope on the arm of her older brother, Reginald, and using a speaking voice that, despite its decorous quiet, was not meant to go unheard.

Penelope exhaled noisily, and shrugged in a way that ensured that Miss Newbold, who had not yet received any marriage proposals, despite her supposed beauty, would not miss it. Europeans, she had discovered in a few days' time, were flashier in the way they cut their rivals, and did not fall all over themselves when a married woman had a little fun on the side. Let them talk, the prince had said to her whenever she put on a little modesty, and by Sunday she was beginning to think as he did. That was how she was going to live from now on.

Without turning back, she descended the Grace Church steps and let her driver help her into her polished phaeton. Then she told him to take her to the New Netherland.

Late last night, Frederick had been telling her about his family's winter castle in the Alps, where he planned to spend that Christmas, skiing and exchanging rare gifts with his many cousins, and he suggested that it would be far more enjoyable if she were there at his side. December was soon, she'd thought, as the idea of how much bigger and fancier her life was going to be started to settle in; but then, she had never been a girl who was shy of working fast. On the ride to the hotel, she composed a note to Henry.

"Peter," she said, once her driver had helped her down to the street, "please deliver this to Mr. Schoonmaker."

"Yes, ma'am," the boy said. They all referred to him as a boy, even though he was practically her father's age. "When would you like me to come back for you?"

"Oh—that won't be necessary."

There was only one piece of her seduction left. Her dramatic red lips pressed up into a smile, as she passed Peter a fifty-cent piece. She was telling him good-bye.

The prince's suite overlooked the park, and was decorated with exquisite antique furniture that, taken together, suggested a British hunting lodge of a hundred years ago. It was a room that Penelope had come to know well over the last week, but she had never been there so early in the day. The heavy drapes were mostly drawn, and a diffuse light did only a little to illuminate all the sturdy mahogany furniture and brass fixtures. She paused, feeling the slow tick of a mild irritation as she realized that the setting was not the ideal one to display herself—her skin would seem too phosphorescent, her dress would appear not nearly red enough.

"The prince is still in bed," said his valet. He was British, his age impossible to determine, and his manners were impeccably unfriendly. "Shall I wake him?"

Penelope descended the four steps into the sitting area, on her way to the window. "By all means," she said, as she disengaged her hat and tossed it onto an armchair upholstered in green and gold jacquard. She made her way through end tables and carved ashtrays as though these sundry pieces belonged to her already, and pushed aside the drapes.

"This is more like it," she heard the prince say from behind her, as the light of midafternoon flooded the room. "I'd like to wake up to you more often, Mrs. Schoonmaker."

She turned and parted her lips suggestively. Frederick was wearing a silky wine-colored robe, tied at the waist, and his hair had not been combed into place. It rose above his forehead in a robust, chestnut brush. The robe had been tied indifferently, and this afforded her a greater view of his chest than she had ever had before. As she stood, staring at him, feeling her heartbeats increase despite her specific intentions to the contrary, he put on the cockeyed grin that she had begun to think of as just for her.

"Does it please you?" she replied slowly and purposefully.

"Very much so."

The valet reappeared, and without letting his eyes stray to either the prince or his visitor, he placed a tray with croissants, coffee, orange juice, and a bottle of champagne on the low, carved table in the middle of the room. Frederick thanked the valet and instructed him which clothes would be needed for his and Mrs. Schoonmaker's evening revelry. The valet bowed and absented himself, and then Frederick walked to the center of the room and took up the bottle of champagne. The corked air was still wafting over the mouth of it, as though just opened. He poured himself a glass, sat down on the sofa by the table and reclined.

"To things that please me," Frederick said, raising his flute and taking a sip.

Penelope's fingers moved to the delicate buttons of her little jacket. One at a time she undid them, and then dropped the garment on the floor. Frederick's eyes were fixed on her now. She strolled across the floor and paused, standing over him, holding his gaze. She reached for his glass and drank until it was empty. Then she sank down to her knees in front of him, throwing her arms forward around his waist. The blue lakes of her eyes, she knew, were at their most persuasive when viewed from above.

Before she became Mrs. Schoonmaker, she'd only been kissed by three boys, and Henry was the only one of those who she had allowed to do anything more. But already she felt a kinship with Frederick, like she too was one of those debauched Europeans who took lovers as they pleased, and she wanted him to understand how completely they were two of a kind.

She blinked at him innocently. Then she pressed up, between his legs, putting her face close to his and inviting his kiss. There followed an exquisite moment of hesitation. He reached forward, as though he might cup her face with his hand, but instead pulled the pins one by one from her hair so that it fell, in a glossy, dark ribbon, and burst upon her shoulder. Only then did he put his mouth against hers. There was such size and warmth to him, and she felt a surge of desire to burrow in against that. His firm fingertips moved from her hair way down her back, and then he gripped her, pulling her up.

"There," he said, when she was situated on top of him and his hands were deep in her ruffled underskirts. "I don't think I will be needing those clothes tonight after all, do you, princess?"

Thirty Five

H—

It's been an awful week, and I find
myself, at the end of it, tired
of chasing you. If you want a
divorce, you shall have it, and I
won't even be difficult.

—P

ENRY HAD WAITED ON THE STOOP OF NO. 17 Gramercy Park in all kinds of weather, but none so fine as this. He was still wearing the mourning band for his father, and he had dressed, in a dark jacket and bowler, thinking more of serious topics than of the sunshine. Diana had told him, through notes written in her lovely scrawl, that he was welcome to come by her home anytime, and to hell with what everybody thought, but he had had so many things to see to that it wasn't until Sunday that he found the time. It did not occur to him, until he was standing at the door with his finger on the bell, that it had been almost a year since he had lingered on the same spot, waiting to reluctantly propose to the older sister of the girl he would come to love. His father had insisted upon it, and told him that Sunday was the Hollands' day for receiving social visits—if he had not obeyed, who could guess what might have been.

A slight girl with big teeth appeared on the other side of the glass. In the moment before she accepted his hat, he mistook her for the maid who had intruded on him and Diana the first night they lay together. He wondered what that girl had traded for her secret, and where she was now, and if she would have been shocked to hear that Penelope Hayes, who had once paid a no doubt dear price for the information, had now become indifferent to her marriage. Or so said the note, folded up in his pocket, which he'd now read countless times.

"Is Miss Diana in?" he asked.

"Yes," she replied hesitantly. "And Mrs. Holland and Miss Edith Holland, as well," she added, as though in warning.

"Could you please tell them that Mr. Henry Schoo—"

"I know who you are, Mr. Schoonmaker." She bowed her head awkwardly, as though she regretted the confession, and then walked to the pocket door, which groaned as she pulled it back. He waited to hear her announce him, and then stepped into the small, old-fashioned parlor where the Holland women received.

"Why, Henry," said Mrs. Holland, rising from her place by the window.

Edith, positioned closer to the dusty mantle, stood also, and Diana, who was tucked into the pillows of the Turkish corner, pushed herself up on her elbows, appearing a little breathless and rosy as always. The mistress of the house had not spoken in a particularly warm tone. Henry knew from the way she hesitated—she kept the full length of a Persian carpet, from which years of traffic had mostly worn away the pattern, between them—that she had heard the unpleasant stories about his affair with Diana. Of course she didn't convey this in any overt manner.

"I am so sorry for your loss," she went on coldly.

"We all are," said Diana's aunt, in a voice that sounded meek in contrast to that of her late brother's wife.

"And I am very sorry I wasn't able to attend the funeral," Mrs. Holland continued, ignoring the other lady. "But I thought Diana would make a suitable emissary for our family." She sniffed, and then he realized that she hadn't known Diana would attend, and that if she had had her way none of the Hollands would have come anywhere near the Schoonmakers while rumors about them were in circulation.

Diana was watching with dewy, dark eyes, which darted between Henry and her mother. So she had gone without her mother's permission to see his father put in the ground. To his surprise, he found that it was possible for him to love her even more, when he thought of the courage and carelessness that had been required for her to stand there, still and sincere, in the background, but close enough for him to sense her presence.

"I understand, of course, these are not difficult times for me alone," he replied. "We have all lost. Although I hear that things are better in the life of Elizabeth—while our engagement did not end as planned, I hope you know I am very happy for her."

"Thank you."

"It was a great comfort to me that the Hollands were represented at my father's funeral—I know he would have liked it—and Miss Diana, in particular, was a sight for sore eyes after my many months at war, and after this very sudden tragedy."

Mrs. Holland briefly closed her black eyes, acknowledging this lie, and then refocused them on her guest with even greater fierceness. Henry, however, did not flinch. He had struck his own tone, and he found that he was able to stand before this imposing little doyenne with the full confidence of any very capable man of his class.

"I wonder if you might let her walk about the park with me? She always says the most comforting things, and I do not have many comforts these days."

Diana had already come to her feet. Pale pink seersucker covered her still faintly brown chest and arms—it was almost a surprise to see her in a proper dress like that, after their time away, as well as to notice that her rich brown hair had grown long enough to curl under her ears. She never could be hemmed in by her clothes, and the vivacity and girlishness that he had always adored in her was evident in the way the fabric conformed to her movements.

"I do not control my daughter." Mrs. Holland's words were dry with just a hint of ire.

"I will have her back to you soon," he replied. Then he gave a slight bob of the head good-bye.

Diana moved through the clutter of the Holland parlor with great poise, although he knew her well enough by now to see what a struggle it was for her not to rush straight to him. For his part, it took all of his concentration not to smile at the absurd good luck of having had such a beautiful girl fall in love with him. She was prettier every time they met again. He followed her out through the pocket door, and watched as she fastened her flopping straw hat to her head.

Then they began to amble around the park, her arm resting lightly against his. It was just the walk he had done with Elizabeth, the day he had proposed to her, when he still had no idea how delightful her younger sister would prove to be. He had been so awkward then, and he felt so natural now. Of course he was careful not to seem too familiar, since her mother was surely watching from the windows. He wouldn't have minded if they didn't say anything, he discovered presently, so long as they could keep moving together through the warm summer air.

As they rounded the northwest corner of the park, she said, in a very proper tone, "What a shame we haven't seen you much lately, Mr. Schoonmaker," as though she were amused by the idea of pretending, for the sake of any spies or gossips, that they hardly knew one another. He wanted to share in the game, but he found that it made him a little sad. There wasn't anything funny to him about their separation. It suddenly seemed to him such a waste of time, to speak this way, all style and subterfuge. "But then I know you must have a lot of business to attend to after this strange turn of events."

He glanced at her face, mostly covered by the shadow of her hat, and wished that he could show her some real affection. "I miss you," he replied quietly.

"And I you," she answered in the same affected tone as before. Then, in a whisper: "You have no idea how."

"I might agree with you . . . ," Henry said as they strolled through the open gates and into the verdant park. Gravel scattered under their feet as they passed benches and flowerbeds. ". . . except that I feel the lack of you so intensely myself."

Beneath the straw brim, he saw her mouth twist into a smile. This did please him, although the larger part of him needed to look her straight in the face. "Well, very soon, Mr. Schoonmaker, you and I shall be on a ship bound for a country where neither of us will know anyone, and so you shall have me to yourself quite completely."

Henry's eyes closed involuntarily. "About that . . . ," he began.

"Oh, Henry." Diana stopped and turned, so that she was

finally looking straight up and directly at him. "Don't put it off another week. I couldn't stand it."

"But everything is different now!" He had not planned a speech, and now wished he had. Somehow he had believed that Diana would have already come to realize, on her own, what luck had befallen them. His excitement over the neat design of it all was profound, yet he felt uncharacteristically tongue-tied now that he had to make her see. "My father dying so early was tragic, but if one good thing comes of it, let it be that you and I can finally be together. Really together. His political ambitions, his influence—none of it matters anymore. With him gone, with my inheritance secure, there is no reason for me not to divorce Penelope, aside from a few old-fashioned naysayers, who will at any rate be thoroughly demented long before our children take their first steps." Henry smiled at the thought. "Not even Penelope will stand in our way anymore."

He reached into his pocket and withdrew the crumpled note, which he had fidgeted with on the drive to the Hollands'. She read it, and though it could not have taken her long, still she would not show him her eyes.

"Diana, it's wonderful, isn't it? You see—a week ago it was all so complicated. But not today." He reached for her little hands; he was practically singing this news. "I have my own money now, and my own house. Everyone will do as I say.

And they will call you Mrs. Henry Schoonmaker, and you will be the lady of that house."

Finally she brought her chin up and met his gaze. He was relieved to see her face but was confused by the blankness he found there. The future he was describing was so clear, so brilliant, in his own mind, and yet it had only produced confusion in her features. She seemed to be laboring to understand. The sun was high in the sky, and it strained her eyes.

"That is what you wanted, isn't it?" he asked after a moment.

"Henry, I'm sorry but . . ." She had let go of his hands. "No. That's not what I want. What I want . . . what I want . . ."

There was a storm brewing in her brow, and he realized in the next moment that she couldn't complete her sentence because she was on the verge of tears. The word _no_ stunned him, clanging in his ears. It was as though great cymbals had clashed beside his head.

"But . . . ," he began. He didn't finish. Already she had run from the park, leaving him alone and stunned in the incongruous sunshine.

Thirty Six

A year ago there were murmurs that Miss Penelope Hayes and Miss Elizabeth Holland were not so much best friends as rivals for the attention of Elizabeth's fiancé, Henry Schoonmaker. Now the latter is Mrs. Snowden Cairns, and it seems that Penelope Schoonmaker's rival may have been the younger Miss Holland all along.

—FROM THE SOCIETY PAGE OF THE *NEW-YORK NEWS OF THE WORLD GAZETTE*, SUNDAY, JULY 22, 1900

$\mathcal{D}$IANA UNDID HER HAT AND DROPPED IT ON THE piece of furniture by the front door, where a silver tray collected the cards of visitors and invitations to teas and musicales. There had been less traffic there since the death of old Schoonmaker, probably because of the rumors that had stemmed from Henry's final words to the old man.

Diana did not look back through the glass to see if he had followed her. Perhaps he was still in the park, in that same posture, appearing vastly older and all of a sudden like the kind of specimen one could call a gentleman with a straight face. The skin of her face tingled with the impulse to hurry back outside, to see if she could catch him and tell him that she was his, forever, on any conditions. Instead she stood there, her brows tense. She glanced down at the dress she wore, a pink frock that she had picked thoughtlessly from the wardrobe in her room that morning, and which now seemed completely ill suited to the rest of her, like the costume of a little girl on a woman who commands a staff of twenty. Then she went upstairs.

What he had proposed was everything she had been dreaming of: to show Penelope and the world that Diana had been Henry's true love all along, and then to go on proving it forever. And yet her heart had shrunk, and her spirit burrowed somewhere shadowy within her. The idea of proving Penelope wrong seemed lackluster to her now. She paused in the upstairs hall in front of the high, north-facing window, and glimpsed Henry striding to his coach on long, lean, dark-trousered legs. He hopped inside as though he had somewhere else very pressing to be.

"Mrs. Henry Schoonmaker." She pronounced the phrase out loud and frowned. Neither the floorboards, nor any one else, moved at the sound of it. Then she returned to her little bedroom, which had been the sight of so many wild imaginings of all the places she would go, and all the people she would meet, and what the whole incredible arc of her life would look like once her biographer finally sat down to try and do it justice. Perhaps they would start here, in this place. There was the faded salmon-colored wallpaper, the narrow mahogany bed, the bearskin rug where she had made of her whole self a present for Henry, giving him everything. Important events had transpired between these four walls—but they were nothing compared to the stories she had told herself lying beneath that rather low ceiling.

She wished Claire still worked there—she would call for her, and the redheaded maid would help her undress, and they would discuss love and destiny and other topics they secretly suspected they knew nothing about. She did consider calling Gretchen, the new maid, because the buttons that ran from her tailbone to her neck were complicated and hard to reach. But everything was irrevocably altered now—she was more alone than ever—and in the end she undid the buttons herself and laid the garment across the chair by the carved vanity, where angels and lilies emerged from stained wood around an oval mirror. There was a silver case secreted amongst the perfumes and powders on the table, and she took a small cigarette from it now and lit it with a match. She lay down on the floor in her white cotton bloomers and bodice, which were decorated with pale blue ribbon, placing beside her the glass ashtray which she had taken as a souvenir from Señora Conrad's. She rested her head against one palm, and inhaled and exhaled lazy, contemplative puffs in the direction of the plaster filigree on the ceiling.

Just to find Henry—to know him just a little better, to make herself his beloved—she had traveled a great distance. Now, with a few lucky strokes, he was all hers, and not just in some secret, insupportable way. He wanted to marry her. So why did her throat grow tight at the thought? She wondered if it wasn't some malign element in her personality that sought out what was difficult and couldn't help but take umbrage with anything that came easily. Maybe her dramatic streak was leading her to trouble, and making her suspicious of a great bounty.

She smoked another cigarette and then another until her mouth was dry and her chest hurt. When a small pile of burned tobacco and ash had collected in the glass tray, she stood up and went to the bed. She pulled out the case that was still ready for departure, and in which she kept a few items of clothing and a very magical bowler, and removed her journal. Sighing loudly, she flopped down on the white matelassé bedspread. For a moment she felt very juvenile, and a little silly, for spending her afternoon like this, when somewhere out in the city her wealthy lover was making monumental decisions that would later on affect the doings of hundreds, maybe thousands, of men. But once she began scribbling words she didn't stop until she had filled pages. She began:

What kind of Mrs. Schoonmaker would she be? Vicious, frivolous, or too soon in the grave? Would she be vain, or happy, or quickly forgotten? Not by the gossips or the quick to judge, of course, for they have the longest memories, and they are the record keepers of our kind.

The person who advised that it is always best to tell the truth undoubtedly led a very sound life, although it is difficult to imagine that he would have lasted very long in a society like ours, where appearances are so savagely maintained.

—MAEVE DE JONG, *LOVE AND OTHER FOLLIES OF THE GREAT FAMILIES OF OLD NEW YORK*

BY THREE O'CLOCK CAROLINA HAD REMOVED THE veil, although she still wore the white dress that had been the pricey product of a week's frenzied labor. She had stopped worrying about rumpling the back, and had sat down in the comfortable stuffed chair that Buck had placed in her dressing room that morning. There was a polished silver tray with sandwiches and tea, but she had not touched them. She could not think about consuming anything. She had often heard of delicate ladies suffering from complete lack of appetite, but she had never before this experienced anything of the kind. All her uneasy thoughts gravitated toward Leland, wherever he was. When they were alone, she had begun to explain who Tristan was, with the half-formed notion that she could serve him just a sliver of the truth and smile contritely and hope for his forgiveness. But before she could help it she had told him everything, down to her real name, her place of birth, her real family, her former position as a lady's maid, her meeting with Longhorn. He had listened carefully and taken everything in, and then he'd told her, in a calm voice, that what he wanted was to be alone and walk. But he would come back. He had promised to come back.

A few hours ago she had feared some small embarrassment of wardrobe or wording. She could not have anticipated anything as mortifying as what had come to pass, and yet, in the event, she found that she thought only a little about the contempt of her well-heeled guests, or of the scandalized reports that would no doubt run in the papers the following day. If she could, she would have traded the whole of Longhorn's estate for the assurance that Leland still loved her. She would have given away her house just to know what block he was on at that very moment.

The loneliness of waiting was more profound than any she had ever known. It occurred to her that maybe her sister was close by, that perhaps Claire, with her reserve stores of reassuring goodness, would make soothing company until her groom's return. But along with the cool cleanness of confession had come the realization that asking one's natural-born sister to play a silent maid on one's wedding day was a very callous thing to do, and that she deserved none of Claire's comforts anymore.

There was no urge to cry. As desperately as she wanted some piece of Leland, there was another part of her that had become quiet and settled during her hours of waiting. Since she had become Carolina Broad, her every minute had contained a lurking paranoia that she might somehow betray her past and her secret, cloddish, low-born self. But now she had revealed those things to the only person whose opinion really mattered to her anymore, and that fact—while horrid—made her feel that she might, at last, be able to put her feet up.

The room was small and quiet, but the ceiling soared, and there was something cathedral-like and hushed about the space. She ought to pray, but she didn't know how. Yet, even with no prostrations on her part, Leland kept his promise. He walked back into her dressing room presently—far less animated this time, and with an ashen complexion. She gazed at the deep black jacket he wore and the fine weave of his dress shirt, which, even wrinkled and smeared with blood, hung handsomely on his large frame.

For a while neither spoke. She stood, all of the fabric and lapidary detail rustling as she brought herself upright. The noises her finery made seemed especially loud in the monkish silence of that room, between those two souls. The man who should already have been declared her husband looked at her with pale blue eyes, but perhaps it was painful for him to do so, for he quickly averted them.

"Carolina—" he began, just as she blurted:

"I am so sorry—"

"Don't be."

"What?" Her heart, and all the other delicate tissue within her, swelled upward, as if with a summer breeze.

"I understand," he went on, sounding quiet and defeated and keeping his eyes on the floor. "I understand why you lied about who you were. Who you are. In a way I think it was quite audacious of you, really, to put those ninnies on and make them think you were just as grand as any of them."

"You do?" she whispered, stepping forward, listening to the stiff petticoat brush against the stone. The shadows on his face were driving her mad, for she wanted nothing so much as a clear vision of him and the chance to show him her full, true self.

"Yes. But of course none of those people ever really impressed me particularly, and I never cared for their parties and clothes and conversation all that much. I guess I always knew you were different from them, and that's what made me want to have you. I've been walking for hours asking myself, if you had told me from the beginning that you were a maid, and not an heiress, would I have fallen in love with you in the same way?" Now he did finally bring his face up, so that the natural light of the high window could fully illuminate his features, so that his eyes were cast directly at her. "I think I would have, Carolina. I think I would have loved you anywhere."

Her lips parted and a noise unlike any she had ever

heard—something between a gurgle and a wail—came up from her throat. She wanted to be able to say something back to him just as beautiful as what he'd said, but there were now tears brimming on her lower lids, and even if there hadn't been, there was no possible way words could have approximated the magnitude of her feelings at that moment. Already she was picturing a very small ceremony, perhaps onboard a ship, as she and her husband sailed away from the city and its vitriol. She stepped forward and reached for his hands.

"I wish you had told me from the beginning. Or once we had gotten to know each other a little." His hands gripped hers, and squeezed. Then he let them go. "But that you called yourself an only child, when you have a sister. That you pursued Longhorn's friendship for financial gain—even if only in a small way. That you grew up right here, so close to me, and thought you could conceal the fact over a whole lifetime together. You lied to me for too long, and I don't believe I'll ever be able to forgive you that."

"No . . . please!" she gasped. In seconds it had all gone to pitch inside. She threw herself forward, reaching for him, and he took her up and let her rest her face against his chest. The tears were a flood now and the sobs rocked her whole body. She was soaking his shirt, but she couldn't care about that anymore, and he didn't seem to mind. When her emotions were somewhat less violent, but no more bearable, he began to rock her. "But I love you," she wailed in that stupid, futile way of hers.

"I loved you, too," he said, and then for a long time they stood there, silent, as they were.

She was glad of his arms around her, but she sensed that already the quality was different. As long as he let her, she went on pressing her face into his chest and tried to store up whatever comfort she could, for she knew the devastation, within and around her, was only just beginning.

Thirty Eight

Hysteria is a condition very common in women of the upper classes; the symptoms include nervousness, an inclination to fainting, shortness of breath, insomnia, irascibility, and a tendency to cause trouble. Quacks will prescribe sensory deprivation and all manner of doodads. The best cure, in fact, is heavy consumption of rich foods and several hundred hours in bed, after which the delicate flowers of teatime will come back in as vigorous a state of health as ever.

—*WOMEN'S SUPERIOR HOME HEALTH MANUAL*,
1897 EDITION

$\mathcal{T}$HERE WERE NO MORE ANGELS FOR ELIZABETH, not even in the cloudy waters of deepest sleep. In her few conscious moments, she whimpered and prayed and begged. She had tried to pretend to herself that it was all a delusion, and believe that Snowden really only did care that she got her rest. But then she saw the cruel calm with which he put her down again and again, and she remembered that he had killed with awful calculation before. This fact she knew with some frightened, primal certainty. Perhaps her father had given a fight, and she knew that Will had faced his death with the same dogged bravery as he had everything else in his short life. She would be easy for Snowden—he would make it seem that she had died giving birth, and then the heir to everything the Hollands had would be his to control. For why would anyone doubt that it was not his child, once she was turning slowly to dust below the ground and could no longer speak?

It was well past midnight when her eyes flew wide open,

and she found consciousness upon her like a frost. There was no way for her to know what day it was. Her heart, which had suffered such abuse already, was now churning like some heroic machine. The memory of a few very hard facts came first, and then sensation followed, all the way to her fingertips and toes. She was thirsty and hungry and would not have minded an encouraging smile from just about anyone, but she needed nothing so badly as she needed to be out of that bed and out of that house.

Everything was blurry, indistinct, bruised. She blinked hard, trying to make out the contours of the room, trying to think what was best for her to do. But she knew she wouldn't get many chances like this one, that it must have been some oversight that she was allowed to wake now, and that her husband was not given to many of those. In her dreams, Teddy had come to save her, but in real life he had made it to the door and his profound sense of decorum had blinded him to her situation. All she could think was: *the stairs, the door, the street.* Then she brushed aside the heaping covers and stumbled forward on trembling feet.

She had always stepped lightly. It was one of the pretty things that used to be written about her in the society pages. She moved with such grace on the dance floor, one wouldn't even know she was there, except that of course one could never take their eyes off her. That was how Elizabeth Holland had been, and she found those qualities served her well now as she moved like a ghost into the hall.

There was a touch of moonlight coming through the fanlight above the front entry. Everything else was a spreading darkness. Perhaps, she thought as she came onto the second-floor landing, her training to become a very marriageable debutante would one day make her a great cat burglar, too. But this was a whimsical direction, and her situation was very grave, and she wondered what that clear, cloying stuff that Snowden soaked his handkerchief in before smothering her mouth and nostrils was, and whether it didn't make her a little daffy besides causing her to fall asleep.

This distracting notion allowed her pulse to slow just slightly as she came, almost, to the top of the stairs. Then she heard the creak of a board not far below her, and all of her instincts lurched. She knew it was Snowden, though she could hardly see anything. A trace of moonlight caught in the bottle of clear liquid he was carrying. So it was only his being a little late in coming to put her down again that had allowed her this opportunity. The vileness of his intention swept over her. The man whose home she'd promised to make for the rest of her life, before God and everybody, was engaged in nothing less than the extermination of her family. She had never experienced rage of the kind she felt now. It coursed through her like electricity.

In her mind's eye she saw Will just before he was gone, his face so full of fear and confusion, his whole body trauma- tized with pain. As Snowden was nearing the top of the steps, his movements slowed, perhaps because he had only recently woken up. She could make him out now, his eyes cast down but his purpose plain in his limbs. He hadn't noticed her—but then she hadn't so much as dared inhale since hearing him on the stair. His breath was full and even, like that of a man who slept soundly in a soft bed. He still had not seen her as she took hold of the banister. That she was there, upright and watchful, didn't fully occur to him—his eyes growing pop- eyed at the sight—until after she put her arms forward and pushed hard against his chest.

There could never be a contest of strength between these two. He was solid, and she was practically a wraith, unbal- anced by her immense belly. Was it her rage that gave her such force, or some mother-wolf instinct, or had God's hand worked through her in that moment of peril? Later, when her body was no longer so storm-tossed by terror and emotion, she would come to see that it was Will who had been there, in her, like the winged angel she'd dreamed about, protecting her one final time.

The impact of that push was sudden and great. Snowden's slippers skidded against the step, and then his arms wheeled. The whites of his eyes grew huge, and he looked at the small, blond thing he had so easily kept subdued for many days now. But it was too late for him; the earth pulled him down hard, and not in any kind way. He hit the bottom of the stairs with a thud and a bone-snapping crack. After that Elizabeth took several quite audible breaths and still felt no kind of calm. She placed her hand on her belly, to try and stop the trembling there. The rest of her was a lost cause.

Then she tiptoed forward, to see what she had done.

Thirty Nine

. . . and can't you just imagine those women glaring at us for sport, calling me the second wife and criticizing my hostessing style? It's not a game I have any interest in playing, or a place I have a taste for anymore. I can't be without you, but I can't stay here. Come to Paris with me. I will wait for you on the pier for the noon ship tomorrow.

With all the adoration my beating heart is capable of,

—D.H.

ENRY HAD STAYED UP ALL MONDAY NIGHT GOING over documents having to do with his father's railroad interests, but by the time the first peachy hint of dawn was spreading from the corners of the sky, he and Mr. Lawrence had cleared the matter up satisfactorily and he was ready to address some paperwork of real importance. He was anxious about Diana—it was now more than a day since she'd run away from him, and he was eager to show her that everything was over with Penelope officially, legally, and in every other way. The staff had reported that Mrs. Schoonmaker had not come home the night before, or shown herself today, and his lawyer was ready to draw up divorce papers on the grounds of adultery. It could be kept out of the columns, Lawrence assured him, especially if it was done hastily and while the ghost of William Sackhouse Schoonmaker still held some sway over the city's newspapermen.

A footman brought him the letter just as he and Lawrence were getting into the particulars. He glanced down at it, and knew immediately from the lovely looping scrawl who had written these pages.

"When did this come?" he demanded.

"Yesterday, Mr. Schoonmaker."

"Why was it not brought to my attention sooner?" He had not realized with what force he was speaking until he saw the trepidation in the young, thin face.

"We thought you were busy. . . . We—"

"Never mind," he said. "It's done now. Don't worry," he added, trying to sound a little kind. He was overtired, and the staff couldn't help but be somewhat confused and intimidated by him now. His features had hardened with fatigue, and his lean frame was down to a white collared shirt tucked into dark slacks; his jacket and waistcoat were somewhere, but he had, in the last few days, stopped thinking so much about his clothes. He was carrying himself differently; he knew he walked through the many halls of that house with a proprietary attention that he had not formerly possessed. "Don't think any more of it. You may go."

When the footman was gone, he stood and spread the pages out against the massive dark-stained wood desk with the simple bucolic imagery carved on its hefty sides. His father had bought it at the auction of the contents of some English lord's country seat; in its previous life, it was the great bulwark peasants had had to face when they came to pay their tithes.

His father always liked to keep in mind the piece's history, and to see to it that when associates and underlings and rivals came to visit his offices, they felt a little peasantlike, too. In the last few days, Henry had come to really know this section of the house for the first time and had discovered to his surprise that he felt at ease there.

My love, how do I begin? read the first line of her letter, after which tumbled unwieldy paragraphs of yearning and fervent feeling. Despite the desperate situation she was laying out in words, he found himself smiling. She was such a vivid, passionate little thing. There was so much emotion in every remote part of her, in each drop of her blood. She loved him—so said all of the sentences of her letter, even if they purported to be an ultimatum. There had been so many moments, over the course of the previous year, when he had fumbled hopelessly in the case of Diana. But there had been a shift inside him, and he was able to read her arguments and pleas without his confidence flagging even slightly. This he could make right.

When he finished reading, he folded the pages of her letter and put them away in the top drawer of the desk. He hated himself for being unsure, for not acting sooner. Now he understood why she had run from him in the park—it was because he had been beastly. He had presumed that he had Di's affections, rather than asking, humbly if she would be his wife. How he wished he had shown her, clearly, what a transformation he had undergone. In this sad, hectic week he had glimpsed the man he would become—a man she would be proud to call her husband. Lawrence—sitting in one of the black leather and wood chairs, which his father had acquired at the same auction, down near the corner of the mighty desk—glanced up. His eyes were watery and wrinkled, and he was waiting in a pose of expectation, as though acutely sensitive to some coming order.

Henry strode across the room to the large, square windows that looked down from on high at the most famous avenue in the city. There was nothing doing at that hour, except in the sky, which was growing brighter with every passing moment. He stood pensively, his feet spread apart, and watched the day beginning. Presently he placed a cigarette between his slender, patrician lips, hesitating some moments before striking a match. Afterward, smoke curled up in his line of vision, blending with the smoke from all the fires that were being lit in that hour in all the best kitchens of New York.

"Mr. Lawrence," he said after several moments of quiet reflection. "How soon can the divorce papers be ready? Could we perhaps serve Mrs. Schoonmaker this afternoon?"

"I see no reason why not," the lawyer replied.

"Excellent." Henry dropped his cigarette on the floor and stubbed it out with his toe. "In that case will you send someone to call Tiffany? They're going to have to open early for me today. . . ."

Forty

Mrs. Snowden Cairns has been known for
a weak constitution since the days when she
still went by the name Elizabeth Holland. Of
course she has not been seen out since it was
reported that she was in a family way—but even
her best friends, like Miss Agnes Jones, have
not glimpsed her, and one wonders if her frail
life can survive any more disruption. . . .

—FROM THE SOCIETY PAGE OF THE *NEW-YORK NEWS OF
THE WORLD GAZETTE*, TUESDAY, JULY 24, 1900

$\mathcal{D}$AYLIGHT HAD BECOME SHIMMERINGLY VISIBLE IN the fanlight over the front entryway of the Cairns house. Soon the morning deliveries would begin to arrive, and outside, there was a summer day in the making. Halfway up the steep staircase that ran along the north-facing wall, Elizabeth Holland sat, frozen and shivering despite the heat, and incapable of going up or down. At the bottom of the stairs lay the lifeless body of her second husband, his head bent away from his body at a horrific angle. Ash blond hair fell from her bowed head and all around her shoulders. Both her hands were placed over her protruding belly, as though to shield her unborn baby from seeing, for the first time, what ghastliness the world was capable of.

For a girl who was raised for the exclusive purpose of appearing lovely and exercising correct behavior, she'd done some bad things in her life. But nothing had shut her down like this. Her hands, her will, had snuffed out a human life. She knew that soon one of Snowden's men, or his housekeeper, or another person who might pose a threat to her, would come along. But to run from that place, to do anything, was to acknowledge her unspeakable act. And so she sat, rocking, and the hours passed.

She was so distraught, so curled in on herself, that she barely noticed the sound of the door opening. Once she had, she realized that the unidentifiable noise she had been only dimly aware of for the preceding minutes must have been the doorknocker, and someone taking it in his hand.

"Why—Elizabeth . . ."

The gentleness with which her name was pronounced was so like a much-needed caress, that by the time she had lifted her head and met the eyes of Teddy Cutting, her own were filled with tears. He was wearing a fitted navy blue jacket with brass buttons up the front and black trousers; his soft face was torn open with a mournful kind of yearning. There was a pistol at his hip, in a leather holster—it was so odd, seeing something like that, on her decorous, fair-haired friend.

"Oh, God," he said, glancing at the broken body lying between the bottom step and the ornately patterned carpet. "I'm too late."

"No," she whispered. He was just on time, she wanted to tell him, but the words wouldn't come. He hurried toward her, stepping over Snowden and taking the stairs two at once. She tried to stand up, so as to better greet him, but her legs were faulty, and in another moment she had collapsed into his waiting arms. She allowed all of her weight to fall against him and found that he supported her completely. "You knew," she whispered eventually.

"The other day, when I came to visit. I saw that you were asking for help," he began, almost apologetically. He rested a palm on the back of her head and secured her around the waist with the other arm. So drained was Elizabeth, she believed she could have fallen asleep, just like that. "I could smell the ether in that room, which I felt sure you didn't need or want. But your hus"—his voice broke over the word—"husband was so vigilant at your bedside, and I feared that if I went to your mother she would not believe me. After all he was your hus—your husband, and why should I know any better?"

He shook his head, lines deepening on his brow. Elizabeth knew she should say something, but speech was impossible for her, and in a moment he continued.

"But days had passed. I couldn't sleep I was so worried. This morning, I still didn't know what to do, but I knew I couldn't go another day without coming for you. So I decided I would talk to your husband myself and try to take you away without causing a scandal. But I called the police and told them to come in a little while, in case . . . I wasn't successful."

Teddy adjusted his stance on the stairs, leaning back against the wall so that he could better hold Elizabeth. She wanted never to move from her resting place against his chest. She sighed, and pressed closer. It was strange, she recalled, and awfully irregular, to stand there letting some gentleman acquaintance hold one up. But she couldn't care about a thing like that at a moment like this, when everything was grotesquely on its head, and anyway, manners had already been the cause of far too much pain and misunderstanding between her and Teddy.

"But I should have been here sooner. Before this . . . before . . . what *did* happen?"

Elizabeth's brown eyes widened as she tried to think how she might possibly explain. She looked up at Teddy, whose face was as smooth as always, and you might have almost thought he was still a boy of sixteen, if it weren't for those creases above his brow, and his height, and the gun at his hip. "It seems impossible, but—" she began.

"You don't have to," he interrupted, gently, when she hesitated.

But she wanted to, and might have gone on to explain, had not the knocker sounded against the door again. They were both paralyzed by the noise.

Presently the squat figure of Mrs. Schmidt, still in her dressing gown and moving on sleepy feet, emerged from the rear of the house and swung back the door. Two men in police uniform were visible just outside, their brass badges gleaming on their chests. Mrs. Schmidt stood away, and the officers removed their hats and stepped across the threshold. Then the faces that express welcome and grateful greeting fell, as they took in the strange tableau of the lady of the house nearly hanging from the arms of Teddy Cutting, at the middle of a flight of stairs—her hair a wreck, her body swollen with child—and her husband's body smashed at its foot.

"Oh!" Mrs. Schmidt exclaimed, her hands flying over her mouth. "Mr. Cairns!"

"What's this?" said the first policeman. "Someone's done a murder."

Elizabeth shuddered, not so much because the officer was searching for a culprit, although that thought did occur to her, but because his face was the face she had seen just before she was forced to bed. It was that boyish face, cratered by some childhood illness, which had, in a matter of seconds, unraveled all the horrors that had befallen her over the last year. The face was even more abhorrent to her now, and she held on to Teddy. His grip on her grew firm. Then he began slowly moving them down the stairs, supporting her all the way.

"Mrs. Cairns has had quite a shock," Teddy said once they had stepped gingerly over Snowden. The dead man's chest was against the floor, but his head was still turned up, his face frozen in that final moment of shock. "I'm afraid I am to blame. I came to visit the lady this morning, and Mr. Cairns refused to let me see her, and she is such an old friend of mine you see, and there was a bit of an argument I'm afraid, I really don't know how it happened, and then the old boy just lost his footing and—"

The officers and Mrs. Schmidt stared at Teddy, confused and disbelieving. He had never been much of a liar, Elizabeth reflected. The policeman she recognized from the day Will died glanced from the dead body, to the fibbing gentleman with the fine way of talking, anger taking hold of his expression. But of course he was angry—he had been trying to extort money from a man who was no longer capable of writing checks.

"Did you try to embrace his Mrs. *before* or *after* you shoved him down the stairs?" the policeman snarled. He took a step in Teddy's direction, reaching as he did for the handcuffs at his belt. "I'm going to have to take you in, sir."

"You'll do no such thing." Elizabeth could not stand on her own, but her voice had all of a sudden become strong and clear and fine. "You won't come one step closer to him."

The policeman's brow soared, and he addressed her contemptuously: "He's a murderer, Mrs. Cairns. You may not think that people like you can be arrested, but I assure you, that is not the case."

"My husband fell accidentally," she went on, keeping her words even and calm no matter how her heart raced. "This is not a matter the police need concern themselves with. It is a sad fact, nothing more. You will speak no further of what you have seen here. I am sure you won't, because otherwise I will be forced to contact your superiors and tell them how you were blackmailing my husband. I will see to it that your career is ruined. And I won't stop there. Because you perpetrated a far greater crime, which I was also unlucky enough to be witness to." Here her voice grew low, and she found it necessary to let her eyelids droop. "Remember that boy you gunned down in Grand Central? For your own *profit*? If you ever bother me or Mr. Cutting or any of our family again, I will see that you are tried for the murder of William Keller."

There was such a wild beating in her chest now, she felt sure everyone could hear it for five blocks. Her features, like those qualities of her personality that refined people used to always praise, were diminutive. But in that moment, she knew that all the ferocity and agony that had been trapped within her since the dream-shattering violence of New Year's Day was bold on her face. "I loved that boy you killed, and if you think that I am too proper to say so on the witness stand, to tell everyone what he was to me, and what you did to him, you will find that you are dead wrong."

There was not a shard of regret or remorse in that horrible face. The policeman stared at her for another moment, and though she could see he didn't like what she'd said, he eventually gestured with his chin to the other officer, and then they backed out of the room in defiant silence. She knew she had only a little of this resolve, this fighting stance, left, and so—still hanging from Teddy—she turned to Mrs. Schmidt. "I am going to go home now. When I come back, or when I send somebody in my place, you will be gone. Is that clear?"

Mrs. Schmidt had the kind of solid face that has been so marred by hard things that it no longer betrayed fear or intimidation. But she nodded, and Elizabeth knew that she understood what she was accused of, and that she would cause no more trouble. Then Elizabeth turned her chin up toward Teddy, expectantly, as though he were her husband instead of the man who lay a few feet from them. "Will you take me home?" she said.

The fine, architectural planes of his face crumpled a little at the simple intimacy of her statement. His eyes were tender with concern. "Yes, Lizzie, I'll take you home," he answered.

She went forward, her body propped against his, but found that she had spent all her strength. Her legs trembled and she sagged against him.

"Don't," Teddy almost whispered. Then he bent and scooped her up, carrying her in his arms away from the sordid scene and into a bright new morning.

Forty One

When the *Lucida* sails for Europe today, it will have amongst her saloon passengers Mr. and Mrs. Reginald Newbold, their guest Jenny Livingston, the prince of Bavaria and his retinue, the painter Lispenard Bradley, traveling in a party with the Abelard Gores, and the countess de Perignon and her daughter, who are said not to have enjoyed our shores as much as they had hoped. . . .

—FROM THE SOCIETY PAGE OF THE *NEW-YORK NEWS OF THE WORLD GAZETTE*, TUESDAY, JULY 24, 1900

"*I* DO HOPE IT WON'T BE A BOTHER," MRS. HENRY Schoonmaker said with uncharacteristic contrition. She let her eyes dart about the high entryway of the Schoonmaker mansion for perhaps the final time, her red mouth crookedly smirking on one side. The bother she was referring to were the eight or nine trunks packed with her best clothing and jewels currently blocking the way to the main hall. It was only early that morning that she had finally left the prince of Bavaria's bed, and she had taken the opportunity to make herself lovely for him again. She had bathed and changed with the assistance of her maid, and now stood, fresh and clean and tall in a fitted ivory jacket and matching skirt, her long neck encased in baby blue lace, her dark hair done up and mostly covered by a broad straw hat, prettily festooned with fake sparrows. "I have arranged for Mr. Rathmill, who is my family's butler, to have them picked up shortly."

The Schoonmakers' butler nodded coldly.

"Good-bye, then," Penelope concluded as she pulled on

her gloves. She had been trying not to be difficult, for even though she and Henry desired the swift annulment of their marriage, one never knew how families would behave in a situation like this one, and there were several hundred items that she would really rather have at the Hayes house if any trouble began. But the day was advancing and her goodwill had run out. She walked through the front door and descended the limestone steps without looking back.

Girls like her were not supposed to ride in hansom cabs, but this was an awkward period when she could no longer use her husband's stable and did not yet have the use of her lover's coach. Anyway, she was not a debutante, but a married woman who had seduced a prince. And surely *he* would be her husband in time for Christmas in the Alps. Right there on Fifth, in front of passing carriages full of spying eyes and wagging tongues, she flagged one down. Then she asked to be taken to the New Netherland.

As she entered the lobby of the hotel, with its gleaming mosaic floor, its aroma of flowers and tea, the bellboys in Royal blue uniform darting from one end to the other, she couldn't help but think how she might one day return to stay there— she would be a little older then, vastly more soignée, and in possession of a new title or two—and experience a flood of memories of her first love affair of any real importance. Because it was clear to her now, from her elevated position, that Henry had only been a kind of practice for her.

"Madame, may I help you?"

Mr. Cullen, the slight concierge, was gazing up at her. He gripped his hands behind his back, and it struck her as peculiar that he had approached her, in the midst of the hushed busyness of that lobby, when he surely knew that she had stayed there the previous two nights, if only so that he could be discreet about it.

The oddness evaporated into her smile, however, as she pronounced the words, "I am here to visit the prince of Bavaria."

For a moment there was no reply, and so she decided to specify. "Frederick."

Mr. Cullen took in a breath. "The prince is no longer a guest at the hotel, Madame."

"You must be mistaken," Penelope replied, confidence and irritation mingling in her tone.

"Quite sure, Madame, but his valet is over there. . . ."

Penelope's neck twisted sharply around and she saw, on the far end of the lobby, by a grove of potted palms, the prince's man guarding a mountain of luggage. Without glancing back at the concierge, she strode across the floor.

"Where is Frederick?" she demanded, once she had arrived beside the great piles of leather cases and packed crates.

"Ah . . . Mrs. Schoonmaker." The valet looked up from a

folded broadsheet. In his polished British pronunciation, she could hear all the backward American associations her married name held for him. "He has departed already, I'm afraid."

"What do you mean, departed?" Her shoulders had become frozen, tight and high under her little jacket. "Departed where? To another hotel? Was something amiss with the service here? Because my family often throws parties at the Netherland, and if you need my father to speak with the management—"

"He sails for Europe today."

"Did he leave instructions for me?" Her desperation to have this vexing news explained was not subtle in her voice, and she hated herself for it, even while she was helpless to fix the unpleasant sound. "Shall I meet him on the dock or—"

"The prince is sailing today," the valet went on, placing each word carefully after the last. "He has become engaged to Therese, the future countess de Perignon, and he wants to travel to see his family as quickly as possible. He hopes to tell them before the engagement becomes too generally known."

"But—" Penelope's eyelids fell shut as a sensation of utter abasement swept over her. "I thought—" she began, and managed to silence herself before saying, *I thought he was in love with me.*

Surely the valet noticed the shock and humiliation draining what color there was from her oval face. And perhaps he even pitied her a little, for he continued in a whisper: "You ought to consider it a compliment, for the prince is known in his own country for the artfulness of his seductions, and ladies who have laid down their honor for him are known to brag of it for years to come."

"Oh, God, what a *fool*," she spit. She had to put her hand on her famously narrow waist to steady herself. It would be a useless waist to her from now on, for she was not even twenty and already damaged goods. A ruined girl. She was not going to be a princess after all; that future would never be. She'd have to stay in New York, where everybody was already whispering viciously about her bad behavior, and where her husband was poised to trade her in for his preferred vintage.

"You might yet catch him, I suppose." The valet gave her a doubtful look. "The ship sails at noon, but he wanted to hurry ahead to be sure that his fiancée and her mother were comfortable."

But Penelope had no desire to go to the docks. The humiliation was already too heady for the girl the prince had used up and promptly discarded. She had spent so much time with him that week, and every second since the afternoon of Carolina Broad's canceled nuptials—it seemed impossible to her that he could have found an hour to propose to the little French woman, but then she realized that he had perhaps already been engaged when she arrived on Sunday. In a matter of minutes, her slender body had been thoroughly depleted by a very crushing shame. It was too much for her; her great blue eyes disappeared under thick lashes. The tall white column of her wavered, then crumbled, as though into pieces on the ground. As her head slumped to her shoulder, and her sense of her surroundings began to fade, she heard feet rush in her direction. Someone called out for a doctor. The last thing she heard was the arch voice of a lady saying, "My word . . . if it isn't the fallen Mrs. Schoonmaker."

I have followed with great interest the story of Carolina Broad, the Western heiress whose name was first introduced to the demimonde in this very column. The rise of her social star was proved indeed too good to be true on Sunday, when her wedding to one of the most sought-after bachelors in the city was called off in spectacular fashion. Apparently she was, all along, nothing more than a lady's maid from New York who wanted to dress up as her mistress did. Though she has lost her chance to marry into one of our most esteemed families, she is still rich—Mr. Carey Lewis Longhorn left her plenty of very real money—and we cannot but acknowledge that we have glimpsed in it the future of high society: wealth without class.

—FROM THE "GAMESOME GALLANT" COLUMN IN THE
NEW YORK IMPERIAL, TUESDAY, JULY 24, 1900

"MISS BROAD, IS THERE ANYTHING I COULD GET for you, perhaps tea or—"

"No." Carolina—posed limply on a pink upholstered silk settee, below the window in the second-story drawing room of her town house—did not so much as blink an eye as she rejected her maid's offer. She wore a dressing gown of coral-colored lace that piled up around her torso and rose and fell in listless folds. It was too late in the day, she was dimly aware, not to have put on real clothes, but she could not bring herself to care. She had grown weary staring out the window at Leland's house, but there had been nothing doing. One of the girls who worked in her kitchen told her that she had heard from one of Bouchard's parlor maids that the master had already left town, for a long stay at his family's country home on Long Island. "Nothing."

Ever since her return from church on Sunday, she had found it difficult to put more than one word into a sentence, or to want very much of anything. "Nothing," was what she heard herself saying over and over. Food, tea, drink, flowers, gowns, jewelry, sunshine, stars—all seemed like so many varieties of pointlessness to her. The only thing she wanted in the whole wide universe was Leland, and he was the least possible for her to attain. Her eyes were sore from crying. It was as though her whole body had gone dry, after such a vast expenditure of tears.

It no longer seemed possible to her that she could be one of the richest girls she knew. And yet she was. There was nothing Tristan could do to her anymore, and perhaps sensing this, he had not again tried to claim some compensation for his knowledge of her past. The modest town house near the park was still hers to live in, except that it seemed entirely too big for her, now, when she was so unbearably alone; just as her wealth seemed a kind of perversion, when it could not purchase her lone desire.

"But would you perhaps like a book, some cake, the papers—?"

"No papers." Carolina drew her prominent, round shoulder—white flecked brown by the sun—to her cheek, and closed her eyes. "Please just go."

The maid shuffled away, leaving Carolina to attempt sleep. She tried, but could not transcend that sad room, that impossibly fraught street, into dreams. The sourness in her stomach was too great; the regret seized her brain every time she thought it might be possible to doze. Time passed, she had no idea how much, and then she heard the stairs from the first floor groan as someone came up from below.

"Miss Broad, I'm sorry to disturb—" the maid began.

"I said go," Carolina muttered without opening her eyes.

"But Lina," said a third voice, "you can't just lie there being useless all day."

Carolina's lids fluttered back. The sunlight fell like a path of gold across the long parquet floor, leading to the spot where Claire had put down a small black leather case, beaten almost gray by the years.

"Oh, my dear," the older girl sighed. Her red hair was pinned under a simple hat, and she wore the black boatneck dress that had been both Broud sisters' uniform for years. "Oh, what has become of you?"

For a moment, the mistress of 15 East Sixty-third was angry that her sister had been allowed to witness her in defeat. But then the need for human warmth overwhelmed. One and then the other of Carolina's enfeebled arms reached out. The older girl arrived at her baby sister's side and pulled her in close for an embrace, just as she always had when they were children, in the days after their mother was gone, when Lina had had a nightmare.

"I was a lie," Carolina whimpered.

She was being kissed, on the forehead, at the hairline.

Feeling was coming back to her, but this only made fresh for her all that she had lost, and she began to cry again.

"They took it all away from me," she wailed, as her sister tried to blot the salty droplets staining her cheeks. The tears were no longer the main thing, however; her whole body was being wracked with sobs. "They took him away from me."

"Oh, my little Lina, my little Lina," Claire whispered, as she rocked her younger sister. "You really loved him, didn't you?"

"Yes."

"But at least you have experienced such things," Claire reasoned, kindly. "At least you are not like me, who has never even *been* in love. . . ."

The intention was kind, and yet there was nothing to say after a thing like that. For Carolina it colored the situation even bleaker. She wailed again, and burrowed against her sister.

"Listen," Claire went on, once the sobbing had quieted. "I have brought something to cheer you up." She paused to draw a piece of newspaper from her pocket. "It's ridiculous, isn't it, a girl following her sister's every move in the papers? You must think I'm an awfully silly, simple sort of person."

Perhaps a few days ago Carolina would have responded to this confession with a mixture of imperiousness and embarrassment. But her whole life had been turned upside-down, all its contents spilling out and a scattering across the floor, and the notion that someone might want to read about her, much less be considered simple or silly for doing so, seemed the height of absurdity. She almost wanted to laugh—and then, through her misery, she did manage something like a guffaw. "I am silly, or the world is. *You* are not."

A slight glow of relief came into Claire's fair, round face when she saw her sister laugh. "*Listen,*" she insisted. "It's from Mr. Gallant's column: 'We cannot help but acknowledge that we have glimpsed in it the future of high society: wealth without class. And while I am sure many will bemoan the death of an era, I for one think that the inbred old families of this city have reigned long enough, and that if new blood comes from a girl who, no matter her other qualifications, so charmed a connoisseur like Longhorn that he left her everything, I am inclined to say that is not altogether a bad sign.'"

Carolina watched her sister's cheeks swell up in smile, and the daylight reflect in her cheerful eyes. Behind her, the room was full of the ghosts of parties and little evenings she'd had, or planned to have. She remembered sitting in just this spot on nights when Leland appeared, on the landing, with his excitement at seeing her clear in his face. For a moment she feared this house would always make her sad. But then the beautiful rosewood paneling, the dangling crystal chandelier, the fine parquet all twinkled at her, and she saw that it was just as fine a home as it had been the week before.

"Don't look dour, love. It's not so bad really, don't you see? Imagine, my Carolina in the 'Gamesome Gallant' column. He thinks that no matter what is being said about you right now, you have your independence, and you represent the direction the fancy world is headed in. Carolina Broad is the future, he said. That's you!"

"No." Carolina took her sister's hand, and forced her bee-stung lips into a kind of smile. Her dark hair, which not so long ago had been arranged in curls, fell across her shoulders and chest. Once her face had assumed a happier expression, she realized that it was not so far from her feelings after all, and that perhaps her circumstances did, in the end, warrant some joy to chase the melancholy. The dressing gown was pleasant against her skin, and the air around was fragrant and warm, and the person at her side loved her no matter what she had done. "That's *us*. I hope you brought everything you want from Mrs. Carr in that old case, and told her good-bye, because you live here now, with me, and—you and I? We're going to have an absolute ball."

Forty Three

The return of Teddy Cutting is quite a boon to mothers with debutantes to marry, for he has long been one of their most prized quarry.

—FROM *CITÉ CHATTER*, TUESDAY, JULY 24, 1900

"*I* DON'T KNOW THAT I AM READY TO GO IN THERE," Elizabeth said, gazing up at the simple brownstone façade of No. 17 through the window of Teddy's carriage. She had brushed her hair with her fingers and braided it in the back so that she would be slightly more presentable. But she looked a fright, she knew, and didn't want to worry her mother. In the small dark enclosure of the Cutting coach, on its soft, worn blue velvet seat, her heartbeat had returned to something like its normal rate.

"You don't have to," Teddy said. "You can stay here as long as you like."

"Thank you." The air was sweet with the life of deep summer. It wafted into the carriage along with so many slow moving motes. The indirect light, filtered through clumping green leaves, did little to illuminate her delicate shoulders, still clad only in a white cotton dressing gown, and the small round fruit of her mouth. "But of course you have done so much for me today, and listened so generously, and I am sure you have so many other places to be."

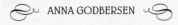

Teddy, beside her on the bench, replied with a kind of stunned expression. "Where could I possibly have to be?" he said after a minute.

"Oh, I don't know," she went on, in a voice that probably would have been better suited to a year ago, if perchance they had met in her family's parlor. "You are a soldier now, so perhaps you have soldierly things to do? And anyway, I am sure there are many *un*married girls in this city, who deserve your company far more than I do," she went on lightly. She did not feel remotely light about it, but she knew that the steady comfort of his presence could only last so long, and that even if he did, somehow, in his way, love her still, that there was the large belly, in which another man's child grew, between them. She had already taken up too much of his time explaining what Snowden had done to her, and to her father. "You must not worry too much about me, I am stronger than I look."

Teddy's mouth opened, a narrow glinting prism, but the importance of what he was trying to say seemed to overwhelm him.

"I know how much strength you have," he began eventually with a wistful shake of the head. "I've always known how much stronger you are than I, and only sought to be worthy of it. I went to war thinking I might prove myself, that I might come back deserving you . . . but I saw and did awful things there, and I know I am no soldier. I only wore this today"—he gestured to the blue coat with the brass buttons, smiling wanly—"because I thought it might intimidate Mr. Cairns."

This confession made him seem to her, for a moment, like the bashful young man who used to visit her for tea on Sundays. She replied sweetly: "I am sure it would have."

"It doesn't matter, anymore, Lizzie. He's gone, and thank God. I don't know if I will ever forgive myself for waiting so long to come rescue you. . . ." He nodded firmly to himself, as though dismissing a futile line of thought. "But what matters is that you, and your child, are all right."

Outside there was the chirping of birds, a horse's hooves against the pavement on the other side of the park, a low rumble of traffic from the avenues.

"When I came back, and heard you were married . . . that, too, was something I thought I'd never forgive myself for. I realized how foolish it was to think I could make myself into the man you wanted by going all the way around the world. I belong here, anyway, and I think, in my way, I can lead a noble life in the place I was born. I will, no matter—" Teddy broke off, clearing his throat. His face had grown slack and pale, and Elizabeth realized he was nervous. Meanwhile, the blood just below her skin had begun to hum. "But the surest way I know my life will be noble is if you would agree to be my wife, and to be with me for all the rest of my days."

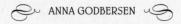

The dainty manner of speaking that Elizabeth had recently assumed abandoned her now, and her mouth quivered in a little circle. "You don't want *me*," she whispered. She had meant to say something more articulate and persuasive, but the threat of tears was too great.

Teddy's reply was rushed, nervous: "We are neither of us new, Elizabeth. I assure you that I am not as perfect a gentleman as some would have me, either." He squeezed his eyes shut, as though he was allowing some excruciating pain to pass. When he opened them again, his voice was steadier and he met her gaze. "But I have never for a moment wavered in my belief that we would make each other very happy, and I swear to you, with my whole being, and no matter the circumstances, I do absolutely *want you*."

Now it was Elizabeth who had to look away. The sight of Teddy's earnest eyes, the sincerity with which all of him addressed her now, was too much. It caused a tide of emotion within her; it created almost too much feeling. She wanted to tell him nothing but yes, but her sense of propriety, never flagging, reminded her there were a few more things he deserved to be told. "You know Cairns wasn't my child's father. I was never . . . with him that way."

"I know. I knew you wouldn't have married, like that, so suddenly, to someone merely convenient, if it hadn't been a desperate situation. And I realized, a long while ago, that there must have been more to your kidnapping than was reported in the papers."

Elizabeth bent her head. She didn't want to tell Teddy the whole story, but somehow she sensed that he was her friend, too, that he would understand. "His name was Will Keller; he was my father's valet and coachman. I fell in love with him when I was a young girl and I had to be with him. It was impossible here, of course, so we went to California." It was strange, after so much secrecy, to say these facts out loud. This was her history now, she realized; soon it would be in the past. "My father knew all along, I discovered, and he had tried to arrange something for us to live on. If my family hadn't pulled me back . . . ," she trailed off as Teddy brought her hands firmly into his grasp.

"Lizzie, I have loved you a long time." The intensity of his gaze told her no more information was necessary. "I will always love you."

In the time it took him to speak these words, her whole face had become wet with tears. Her nose glistened with moisture, and she would have wiped it, but she didn't want to let go of Teddy's hands even for a second. "I was thinking, if the baby is a boy, that I'd like to call him Keller. Could we do that?"

Finally a smile broke Teddy's serious aspect. "Keller Cutting? I think it would be a very handsome name for a boy— or a girl. You know, when I picked out the rattle for you, I couldn't help this feeling, that no matter who your husband was, or how sorry I felt for myself that I couldn't have you, that it was a fine thing to see you become a mother, and that I was going to enjoy sending gifts to your child for many years."

"The rattle from Tiffany? *You* sent that?"

He nodded. She opened her mouth to tell him what she had previously believed, but the joy in this realization—that it was Teddy who knew her so well—was too natural to require explanation.

"When we were in Florida," she went on, crying and laughing at once, "I wanted to kiss you so badly. It was only that there were so many complications, I felt so guilty over everything, and my life seemed so . . ." There were a hundred things she wanted to tell to him, but all of a sudden, in her rush of words, she realized that there was only one that mattered. "I love you," she whispered.

"You have no idea how long I've waited to hear you say that."

He pulled a monogrammed handkerchief from his coat pocket and tried to wipe away some of Elizabeth's tears. Then he took her face in his hands, and brought it close to his. She gazed at him, seeing in this fractional moment of pause all the years when he had longed to do exactly this. She felt weak with the sweet expectation of a first kiss, and after that a whole life together. Their breath mingled, in the summertime hush, and then he turned his chin and touched his lips to hers.

A girl who has lost her reputation will, eventually, be let back into the fold of society's little gatherings and grand showy parties, but she will never be allowed to forget her transgression, lest younger ladies fail to understand her cautionary tale and be tempted to repeat her mistakes.

—MRS. HAMILTON W. BREEDFELT, *COLLECTED COLUMNS ON RAISING YOUNG LADIES OF CHARACTER*, 1899

*T*HERE HAD BEEN DAYS, AND MAYBE EVEN WHOLE years, when it had not occurred to Diana that she lived on an island. The pier that jutted off Eighteenth Street and into the Hudson was not so far from the house she was born in, and yet the breeze, the salt air, the shouting, the heavy traffic of luggage and crates, the hundreds of passengers moving up the swaying planks, seemed another world entirely. No wonder, she thought, as she looked out on the Hudson—so populated with barges and tugboats and skiffs on a cloudless July day—she had felt trapped there; old New York was hemmed in by water on all sides, and it was only when a girl ventured to its borders that she saw how vast was the landscape over the high walls.

A thin, khaki coat, belted at the waist, protected her from the wind and half covered her long, dark skirt. She wore a black bowler of magical significance, and she carried her little case in one hand and the booklet with her second-class cabin ticket and brochure and passenger list in the other. She had booked passage with her own money, which she had earned while traveling, and from selling news to Davis Barnard. Grass, her writer friend, had given her the names of friends to call upon in Paris, and of several hotels where she could live cheaply upon her arrival. Barnard had encouraged her to send him items, and promised that once she had established connections in her new city, she could write a weekly "Letter from Paris." She was glad of the coolness rising from the water, for it numbed her a little; if not for that, she might have begun to really feel the fear and anticipation of leaving so much behind.

She had put letters in the mail to her mother and aunt and sister; they would receive them tomorrow, or the following day, and hopefully they would understand what she had to do. Henry, she knew, had already received his letter, for she had delivered it yesterday in person, climbing the imposing stone steps of his monolith of a house, a kind of final act of improper behavior in her short career as a marriageable girl of old New York. It stung that he had not come for her sooner, but she had the gift of imagination, and some remote part of her knew that any second he would appear, each strand of his dark hair in place, walking at a fast, urbane gait, whispering an apology to her about all the loose ends he'd had to tie up before he could leave his old life behind, and then drawing her under his wing and up the plank.

All the while, the great iron hulk rose many stories above

her like some monster of the deep, its impenetrable black walls, the white paint above, all the portals and ropes and smokestacks up higher. Pretty soon they would be shouting for any lagging passengers, and then she really would be leaving for good. It took her breath away, the impossibility of this leap, and yet she couldn't believe it. She wouldn't really believe it until she was on deck, and the water between her and land was too much to swim.

She turned on the weather-beaten pier and let her eyes drift across the great collection of people who had arrived with all the trappings of travel, and all those who had come to bid them bon voyage. There was so much excitement and trepidation and sorrow in those faces—round, long, fat, youthful, or worn. There was such a concentration of waiting and expectation. She saw a man, striding through the crowd, his black jacket unbuttoned so the waistcoat was visible beneath it, his hair brilliantined to a fine sheen.

Her lips parted and then a smile broke, as their eyes met. The fixated quality of Henry's gaze indicated he had seen her a long time before she did him, and in a moment all her fear was gone and she knew she'd been right. Of course he had come. They were going to Paris together, and she need not worry or fret. Above them, benevolent clouds moved swiftly and silently over a concentrated blue. The shouting and movement continued all around, as though there was nothing remarkable about these two people, meeting this way, in front of a steamer bound for Europe. By the time Henry reached Diana, she was beaming. He took the ticket from her and put it in his jacket pocket. Then, wordlessly, he reached for her gloved hand and sank down on one knee.

"I have not behaved as I should have—not this week, not ever. But neither have I ever met a girl I loved so much as you, and if you would agree to be my wife, I promise that I will spend the rest of my days correcting those original failures." He looked up at her, his dark eyes—which were sometimes so hard to read—full of sincerity. There was no smile on his face. It was all a very serious variety of desire. In a few moments he presented a small box. "Diana, will you marry me? Stay here with me and be my wife? I promise, there shall be a proper engagement, and a great church wedding, and they can say whatever they want, damn them, but I will stand by you. Never again will I take your affections for granted."

Then he drew back the lid of the box, and Diana saw the ring he had picked. It was not like the one he had given her sister, or the one that Penelope wore in some sad pretense of a romantic engagement. It was shaped like a flowerhead with a giant sapphire at the center of a ring of diamonds set on a delicate yellow gold band. There was a femininity to it, but it was also bold and defiant, just like her. She knew that Henry had thought about her carefully as he made his choice, and this softened the tightness in her shoulders. Her lungs billowed with sea air. But in the next moment she heard the commentary that would soon begin, from women who called themselves her mother's friends, or from Penelope loyalists, or from any number of people with too much time on their hands. "Who does she think she is wearing a ring like that?" they would say, for as long as she wore it, which would be forever if she and Henry wed.

Forever, Diana thought, as though learning the word for the first time. Without waiting for a reply Henry removed her glove, stuffed it into the pocket with her ticket, and slipped the ring onto her finger. He stood and placed his hands on her neck so that his fingers thrust into her curls. She closed her eyes, and felt all of her swoon a little with the idea of Henry coming for her this way, persuading her to be his. His lips met hers in another few seconds, and the old magnetism between them came back in a rush, and she felt herself begin to give in.

They might have gone on like that, kissing on the pier, despite the height of the sun and the number of people about, had not the wind picked up. But it did, knocking the hat off her head, rearranging her rich brown hair, and carrying the bowler sailing. She gasped unhappily. It was Henry's hat, and he had given it to her when they had only just begun to play little games with each other, before they had come to truly love each other. The loss of that talisman was momentarily excruciating.

"My hat!" she said, her brows drawing together disappointedly.

"Don't worry, I'll get it back for you." She gazed up at Henry's face in profile, at his long jaw and defined cheekbones, as he gave the crowd and the docks a serious look to determine what had become of the wayward item. The way he stood, his appearance—so like a man that all of New York envied and desired—made her heart beat several times too fast. The anxiety of losing the hat faded; she was shocked by how quickly. A sheen came over her brown eyes, as though she might cry, and yet she was not remotely at risk of shedding tears.

"No," she said, grabbing his hands and holding them.

He gazed down at her and for the first time a smile began to spread, as though she had just said something secret and a little bit naughty to him. "I should let it go?" he asked.

"Yes." She smiled back at him, feeling the warmth of a small and private moment. "Yes, let it go. But no—no I can't marry you. Not here, in New York, like this."

"What?" the happy expression fell, immediately, from his face.

"Oh, Henry." The traces of a smile were still visible on her lips, but she could no longer look him in the eye. The certainty of what she had to do had come quickly, before words capable of explaining. "I wasn't threatening to leave because you hadn't made a romantic proposal. What courtship could

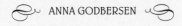

ever be more romantic than ours? It's that if I married you I would always be the compromise second wife, the one ladies warned their daughters not to become."

"What do they matter?" Henry's voice was quick with urgency. "What can their thoughts possibly matter when I love you so well and need you by my side? My life is different now—I have responsibilities in this world that I must meet— and yet I don't know how I'll meet them if you are not behind me, my wife. I don't care what they say or do."

She nodded and pretended to consider. If there were onlookers, neither she nor Henry would ever have known. "It's not that I care what they say, and I know you do not. But I don't want to live in a place where all I can hear is the whispering about what a little tramp I am. They don't matter so much, except that they are New York, the people we would have to dine with over and over again, and their way of thinking is so impoverished, and being among them makes me sad. I want to hear other noises, other voices, I want to look down vistas that . . . ," she trailed off, for the crooked streets of ancient cities overwhelmed her thoughts, and she knew that the man before her could not see them. She bit her bottom lip and batted back her lashes and met Henry's eyes. "I *want* to go to Paris."

"Then I shall go with you," he replied, but she could see this was just what he felt he ought to say.

"No, Henry. You belong here." She removed the ring from her finger and placed it in his palm. Then she took the ticket and glove from his pocket. That golden quality, which had always marked him as rakish and lucky, abandoned him now, and she realized she'd struck him dumb. This was just as well, for she craved no more inducements. There was only a long solitary path up the ramp, and then the sensation of a whole building coming unmoored beneath one's feet. "Don't worry," she went on. She gave a little laugh that was made husky with sadness and wisdom. "You will fall in love again. Only know that wherever I am, I will always have the marks of you on me. You were my first love."

"But—"

Her arms clasped each other around his neck, silencing him, and the kisses came in sudden, intense bursts. They were soft and moist and repetitious, as though both were trying to drink something in for the final time, and might have gone on indefinitely had not the crew started shouting for any last passengers. Then all around them loved ones erupted in shouts and cheers to their husbands and children and friends high up on the saloon deck, and Henry and Diana were engulfed in confusion and movement. There was nothing more to say, so she clutched his hand and whispered, "Good-bye." Then she picked up her suitcase and ran for the plank before they took it down.

Forty Five

I have seen it often: For many couples, all the golden splendor of a marriage occurs after the love has been lost.

——MAEVE DE JONG, *LOVE AND OTHER FOLLIES OF THE GREAT FAMILIES OF OLD NEW YORK*

TO HER HORROR, PENELOPE WOKE TO THE VIEW of her own white-and-gold bedroom. She was at home, or whatever the Schoonmaker mansion was to her now. She wasn't sure how she had come to be here, and the mental task of retracing her steps contained no small amount of dread for her. Someone had taken her hair down and her corset off, she discovered, as her hands moved over her person. There was a small egg-shaped bump on the side of her head, under her undone dark locks, which was tender to her fingertips, and when she rolled over to better see her environs she noticed the ivory skirt she had been wearing earlier cast across a chair. That was the skirt she'd selected to meet the prince of Bavaria, when she had still believed he would make her a princess. *Oh, God*, she thought, *the prince of Bavaria*. Then a wave of revulsion came over her as she remembered how publicly pathetic she had been. On the side of her bed Robber, her Boston Terrier, sat panting, his beady black eyes cast up at her as though in accusation.

"Shut up," she said, throwing back the blankets and wheeling her legs overhead and then bringing them down hard on the floor. The animal, frightened, went skittering forward across the carpet. She was dressed in a thin white silk chemise and her wedding rings. Her dark hair, without restraints of any kind, fell almost to her waist. She was thirsty, and for once in her life, felt more fear than hate. "What's to become of us?" she asked Robber self-pityingly. But he was now half-obscured behind a hassock; at least he too seemed scared, although not as much as their desperate situation warranted. Penelope walked forward through the room— really it would be more accurate to say she stumbled, for she felt a little dizzy after her fall in the hotel, and her legs were bandy—searching for something to quench her thirst.

They had left her nothing. No pitcher of cold water infused with apple slices, no tall glass of lemonade. She knew perfectly well, with a staff as competent as the Schoonmakers', that it would not be misinterpretation to call this a hostile gesture. Nor was it unexpected, really. She had always been a foreigner in this house, and she had flouted the servants and tried their goodwill. If she ever had the good luck to be married again, Penelope swore to herself, she would be sensible enough to play the diplomat. She turned to Robber and bent toward him with the half-formed hope that he might provide a little warmth to her open arms. But he saw her coming and dashed away.

At the beginning of that day, Penelope had believed herself nearly in possession of a prince, but by late afternoon, she was so thoroughly demoralized that she saw no reason not to chase after a dog. Robber went running up the little flight of stairs to the adjacent room, which had once been Henry's bedroom, and later a kind of study for him. There he had slept, most nights, before he went off to war. She hurried after Robber, barefoot, and into that shadier room, where no lamps had been lit, and the glow of summer dusk shone in through the west-facing window. Her disobedient pet went in that direction, disappearing beneath one of a pair of large black leather-and-mahogany chairs, where to her surprise, she saw a figure frozen in rumination.

"Oh . . . Penny. It's you." Henry, sitting in one of the chairs, turned away from her and went back to gazing out the window. It had been a long time since her husband had seen her in anything but full dress, and for a moment Penelope felt embarrassed that her skinny legs were visible below her ruffled undergarments. His legs were crossed and his elbow was placed against the polished wood armrest; she was surprised, and yet there was something natural about his presence.

"What are you doing here?" she began. "I would have thought you would be off with your little lover, Diana," she added, more cruelly.

"No," Henry said. He let out a sigh of uncharacteristic melancholy and defeat. "That's all over."

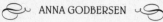

"All over?"

"Yes. She went to Paris this afternoon. In the end, being the wife of Henry Schoonmaker didn't sound so grand to her." The pink-and-orange sky lent a special warmth and shadow to Henry's face, as though to spite the sad workings of his mouth and brows. She hovered behind him, unsure what exactly there was to say. She supposed it boded well for her, however—if he was heartbroken, he would have less energy to throw her out on the street immediately, and perhaps her total degradation could be stalled until she came up with another plan. "I suppose you are surprised to be here? The servants told me you had your best things sent to your parents' house."

"Yes . . . ," she acknowledged cautiously.

"Are you feeling all right? Apparently staff from the New Netherland brought you here. They said you fainted, but that was all they would say."

"Oh . . . yes. I don't know; I can't remember." An ache shot through her head, the way an earthquake sends fissures through the earth. She did not want to be made to think of the incident. "I mean, I remember the New Netherland of course, but why I was there, and the being brought back here, escape me now."

Henry did not reply. Perhaps he simply did not care enough about her shameful activities to bring attention to them. There was a kind of dispirited honesty about him, and she supposed that after all the havoc they'd wrought, neither had very much left over for anger or deceit. Her eyes darted to his black jacket, in a heap on the floor, and beside it a small suede jewelry box.

"May I look?" she asked, tiptoeing forward and picking up the box.

"Why not?" Henry replied flatly. He reached into his breast pocket and removed a cigarette. The sweet smell of tobacco smoke filled her nose as she drew back the lid and saw the huge sapphire set in a corona of diamonds.

"Oh!" she gasped.

"It was for Diana."

Penelope's dark eyebrows sailed into a perfectly alabaster forehead. "Even after this, she wouldn't stay?"

"No." Henry exhaled, as though to cut off a path of conversation. "Where is your prince?"

A thousand lies played on Penelope's tongue, but none of them seemed likely to restore her dignity. "He departed for Europe this afternoon," she began matter-of-factly. She winced, remembering how thoroughly she had been used, how foolishly she had believed him to be in love, and all the other fantasies of a very far-flung life she'd allowed herself to cultivate. But there was no getting around facts that would soon be printed in the columns. "He went back to tell his family that he's engaged to the daughter of the count de Perignon."

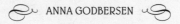

"Oh." Still Henry did not look away from the view of the skyline, which cut geometric shapes out of that array of dying color. "I'm sorry you lost him," he added, and she thought he was, perhaps, sincere.

"Yes, well, men are ever fools," Penelope returned, some snappish pride returning to her tone at last. "Give me one of those."

Henry twisted his neck and assessed her. Then he offered a cigarette from a slim gold case, and lit it for her with a match.

"What a wreck we've made of everything," Penelope said as she exhaled into the growing darkness. There was still a throb in her head, but she found that it calmed her to stand like this, taking smoke into her lungs, speaking in tones of exhaustion and regret with the boy whose attainment she had once upon a time believed would fix everything.

"Yes," Henry replied, although he didn't sound particularly remorseful. He sounded broken, and tired, and indifferent. They didn't speak again until their cigarettes had burned down, and then he lit another two and handed one to Penelope. She took it, and was grateful. "Whoever would have imagined," he went on eventually, with a rueful laugh, "a year ago this time—it was hot like now, remember? And you and your family were living on Fifth Avenue, and we met in hotel rooms all over the city and neither of us took anything very seriously. And now we are married, and miserable, and everything is in tatters."

"At least you wear misery well, Mr. Schoonmaker," she replied dryly.

He responded with the same sad laugh. "What does any of it matter?"

"You mean, what does it matter if we wear our misery and humiliation hideously or gorgeously? It doesn't, I suppose. But as long as we're both miserable and handsome and here, we might as well have a drink." For a moment she feared she had been too friendly, and that he would finally tell her to leave. "I could use one," she added hastily.

"Yes." Still Henry wouldn't meet her eyes. "I think that's the right idea."

She placed her cigarette between her lips and walked over to the collection of cut glass bottles on the sideboard. She poured them each a glass of Scotch, and then returned to the window, handing Henry a glass and then lowering herself into the chair beside his. She did not care anymore that she looked a little worse for wear—her hair simple, parted in the middle, undone. Her defenseless slip. Without all the padding of a gown, she knew, she sometimes appeared too thin, but what did it matter now? Henry had taken his cuff links off, and he wore the well-tailored white shirt unbuttoned at the collar.

"Cheers." She raised her glass, and attempted a wicked smile. Their drinks made a clinking sound. "To broken hearts."

"To broken hearts." His black eyes darted to her for a moment, and then he took a sip. "Perhaps we deserve each other," he added, shifting his weight and letting it relax deeper into the cushions of his chair. He appraised her and then sighed, as though he were waiting out some pain, like a stubbed toe, that seems monstrous for a moment but is forgotten soon thereafter.

Penelope lifted her long legs, crossing her delicate ankles and resting them on Henry's thigh. There was no response from him, but neither did he brush her away. She bent her neck and looked down on Fifth Avenue. The sun faded from the sky and the light around them grew purple and soft, and she began to feel that they might go on, just as they were, for a very long time.

"*I* AM ALWAYS RELIEVED TO SEE IT SHRINK."

Diana Holland turned her hatless head of abbreviated curls, which had become completely wild in the wind high above the *Lucida,* to see a girl of about her own age, well dressed, utterly unpretty but nonetheless possessed of some quality that wanted to be looked upon. "When what shrinks?" Diana asked.

"New York," the girl replied, not unkindly but as though it were obvious, and then went back to watching the figures, their handkerchiefs aloft, growing blurry, indistinct, minuscule as the ship pulled out into the river. In another moment Diana found that amongst a multitude of emotions, she too was experiencing a kind of relief. Of course there was a humming exhilaration as well, and a bruised longing for Henry, and for the other things she had loved well and given up. She had watched him for a while, standing on the dock in his slim-fitting black clothes, gazing up at the ship as though it might somehow explain to him what he had lost. She believed he was still there now, but it was impossible to be sure, once he had become so small and the churning white wake behind the ship had grown so big. For some time she told herself it all would have been bearable if she had still had his hat, but then she realized that from a literary perspective it was far better that she had lost it then, on the docks, and not later on in the years to come, when she would be moving from one garret to another and always misplacing things of sentimental value.

They would be restless years packed with mistakes and ardor. She would mend her broken heart, only to find it broke easily again. Different men loved differently, she would discover, and every one would leave her a little older, a little wiser, and with more feeling to translate into the pages of her notebooks. She would receive letters from Henry over the years, and though the strength with which he urged her to return would wane over time, he would never lose that tone of regretful desire. She had not lied on the pier—he would always be her first love.

Diana lingered on the saloon deck and examined the passenger list, for among them would be notable people who might invite her to parties in her new city, or provide little stories to telegram Davis Barnard about. There were several names she knew, and others that she recognized—all occupying finer cabins than she. Among them were Governor Roosevelt's niece, Eleanor, who was born the same year as Diana and was on her way to finishing school in England. There was also the prince of Bavaria, traveling with the countess de Perignon and her daughter, who was said to be about Diana's age, and not remotely the same flavor as Penelope. And though Diana felt no joy at this denouement, she couldn't help but smile wanly. For no matter how worldly the former Penelope Hayes believed herself to be, she still had a particularly American naïveté, and it was a good joke that she had been so blinded by her desire to bed a royal that she had allowed herself to be completely taken advantage of. It was fitting, really, like the ending of a good story. That girl's fate was to go on, married to the handsome husband she had wanted so badly at eighteen. They would never be completely faithful again, or understand each other for any very extended period of time. They would appear together at parties and occasionally share a laugh, and they would betray each other again and again, in that curious mating ritual of their kind.

Perhaps it was the weather up high on the open ocean, or maybe the little tremors over what she had done, but Diana was experiencing a heightened sensitivity to everything at just that moment. She believed it to be born of a profound relief that this kind of marriage was not her own fate, in the way that colors appear especially bright to a person who has just cheated death. Of course, Elizabeth's marriage would not be like that, for she had finally found herself with someone so entirely devoted to her that his eye would never wander and his tongue would never be capable of cruelty. They would have a child, Keller Cutting, and then several more. They would use the Holland oil windfall to decorate beautiful homes in New York and Newport. There would be grand parties, to rival Mrs. Schoonmaker's, with whom Mrs. Cutting would maintain a wary, knowing camaraderie. The columns would always refer to them as rival hostesses, although in truth Mrs. Cutting never took the socialite part of her life so seriously again.

That world was over, anyway. The most talked-of parties of the coming years would be those thrown by the Broad sisters, Claire and Carolina, whose humble origins everyone was happy to forget under a great swell of champagne and exotic party favors and the sort of antics that become calcified into legend almost as they occur. Names like Holland and Schoonmaker and Hayes would soon sound old-fashioned amongst that new, fast set.

But those stories are in the future. The city of Diana's birth grew miniature in the distance, like a diorama for schoolchildren. It was manageable that way; she could explain everything she had seen and done there. In time, she would: There would be intricate novels of drawing room betrayals and love that couldn't be. Her brain was beating with them. From far away, on a clear day, she saw how all those mighty mansions were only temporary delusions, and how fashion would march on, and the chateaus and palazzos of American merchants would fall to the wrecking ball so that department stores might rise above.

Slowly the sky turned from the color of cornflower to that of hyacinth, and the Ferris wheel at Coney Island appeared like a ring of diamonds against the twilight. New York—that city made of canyons between tall buildings, and ornate houses filled with glittering things that might trap a girl forever—was nothing more than a few dots on an infinite landscape. The atmosphere was crystalline and afforded her a perfect view. Only from this place was she able to see how limited the city was, after everything, and how wide open the world could all of a sudden become.

Acknowledgments

I am incredibly grateful to everyone who has worked so hard to turn The Luxe series into real live books. Thank you, thank you, Sara Shandler, Farrin Jacobs, Josh Bank, Les Morgenstein, Andrea C. Uva, Nora Pelizzari, Lanie Davis, Joelle Hobeika, Allison Heiny, Kristin Marang, Cristina Gilbert, Melissa Bruno, Kari Sutherland, Barb Fitzsimmons, Alison Donalty, Ray Shappell, Elise Howard, Susan Katz, and Kate Jackson. And thanks also to James McLeod, for always asking what Hem would do.

TURN THE PAGE FOR A SNEAK PEEK AT
ANNA GODBERSEN'S ALL-NEW SERIES

SET IN THE ANYTHING-GOES ERA
OF THE ROARING TWENTIES. . . .

PROLOGUE

IT IS EASY TO FORGET, NOW, HOW EFFERVESCENT AND free we all felt that summer. Everything fades: the shimmer of gold on White Cove; the almost-above-the-knee dresses the girls wore on the decks of yachts; the lavender early morning light on the faces of skyscrapers, which had become so heroically tall. And so I will try to tell you, while I still remember, how it was, before everything changed, that final, hot season of an era that roared. . . .

By the summer of 1929, prohibition had been in effect for so long it ceased to bother anyone very much. We did whatever we liked and dressed in whatever we thought smart and broke rules for the sport of it—diving into public fountains, carrying flasks in our garters, mixing social classes as insouciantly as we mixed cocktails. There were no longer exclusive balls given for a few people with old money and good names, and even if there were, no one would have cared to go. Nice girls wore the kind of makeup that thirty years before would only have been seen on actresses, and actresses were escorted publicly by the scions of shipping fortunes. Women took to dressing like boys, and though we'd obtained the vote, we had swiftly moved on to pursuing the flashier freedoms— necking in cars and smoking cigarettes and walking down city streets in flesh-colored stockings.

New York was the capital of commerce and joy, and young people sought us from every direction. They came in droves, to join the kind of party only a great metropolis can host. They came from wealthy families and farming families from the North and South and West. They came to avoid kitchens and marriages, to a place where they could reasonably claim to be twenty-one forever. Or for the foreseeable future anyway, which seemed to us the same thing. They came, mostly, for the fun—especially the young things, especially the girls.

I can't remember very many now—although there are three, from that last incandescent summer—who I resist forgetting. They were all marching toward their own secret fates, and long before the next decade rolled around, they would each escape in their own way—one would be famous, one would be married, and one would be dead.

That is what I want to tell you about: the girls with their short skirts and bright eyes and big city dreams.

The girls of 1929.

1

THE MARSH ESTATE WAS DECEPTIVELY NAMED, FOR THE
grounds were expertly manicured by a team of ten gardeners
so that its appearance had none of the wildness the name might
otherwise conjure. The place was called Marsh only because
the man who had built it had been called Marsh. It sat on the
lovely finger of land that marked the eastern border of White
Cove, on the north shore of Long Island, a short drive to Wall
Street and all the money that was made there, but a long way
from the city's more sordid quarters.

The impossibly green lawns were populated as far as the
eye could see by a hundred varieties of tree imported from the
English countryside, and beneath the arbor of their branches
walked a girl wearing loose-fitting, pale peach, silk pajamas, an
old tennis visor, and a mink jacket that was short enough to
reveal the fast cadence of her slim hips. Visitors uninitiated in
the ways of New York might have found themselves confused
by the sight of her—for it was both late enough in the day that

somewhere people were already dressing for dinner, and a season when fur is hardly necessary.

Her name was Astrid Donal. She had a full head of egg-yolk yellow hair, cut so that its tips curled against her jaw, and the soft, heart-shaped face of a girl young enough to still have a taste for sweets, but old enough to have been quite frequently kissed. If she had been asked the time, she might have guessed from recent experience that it was no longer morning, but it would have been impossible for her to name the exact hour. As for the coat, it was merely an aberration of Astrid's temperament that she often felt cold when no one else did. But now, as she wandered across the lawns, she began to feel truly warm, and let the mink slip from her shoulders and fall onto the ground.

"Miss Donal!"

Astrid squinted in the bright sunlight to make out her maid on the stone veranda of the home belonging to her mother's third husband, Harrison Marsh II.

"Telephone for you!"

Astrid's feet carried her up a gentle slope, ending her meander sooner than she'd really intended. "I lost my jacket somewhere somehow," she announced a little breathlessly, when she reached the maid's side. "Do send someone out to find it, dear?"

"Yes, Miss. Telephone for you."

4

"I heard you," Astrid replied hurriedly but not unkindly as she went into the dimly lit first floor and tried to make her eyes adjust. Her bones had that delightful weightless quality of having not been awake very long, and she smiled a little to think that she could simply skip over the hours when one wore daytime clothes. Was it only one week ago she had returned from her all-girls' boarding school in Connecticut, arriving by a private ferry that carried her and her fourteen pieces of luggage across the sound? She had another year left at Farmington, but somewhere over the course of the last seven days she had acquired the fatalistic notion that she would not be returning there. She wasn't exactly sure why, for she could be a very good student when she bothered to concentrate. Perhaps it was that her life here seemed to swallow her so completely, and then everything outside it began to seem vague and unimportant.

Crossing through the library with its leaded glass windows on either side, she arrived in the main hall at the front of the house. No lamps had been turned on yet, and there was only the bluish natural light coming in from the great windows that flanked the door. The receiver of the cream-colored telephone lay on its side atop a little polished rosewood table. She paused a moment before picking it up, and noticed that her pajama pants, which were too long for her, had become slightly muddied at the hems.

"Hello?" she finally said, resting the receiver next to her face.

"Hello, baby."

Astrid's eyelids sank closed, and a small crescent emerged at the left corner of her lips. The sound of his voice always made her feel like a tiny, precious doll. His voice was like him, big and impressive, and it immediately brought to mind all the places they had been and all the things they had done last night. "Morning, Charlie. Are you just waking up?"

"No, baby, I can't lounge around like you all day." On the other end of the line were the voices of men speaking in three-word sentences.

"No . . . you've been up for hours, I suppose, seeing to very important things," she teased. Her eyes were still closed, and she swayed dreamily in the cool quiet of Marsh Hall's foyer. It must be more than a year now that she'd been calling Charlie her boy-friend, since the beginning of the previous summer. "Not me. Me, I have been exquisitely lazy, until I got very ambitious and went to see what the grass felt like between my toes."

"Good. You're getting some beauty sleep. I want my girl to be the best-looking girlie at the party tomorrow."

"What party?"

"The party my father is throwing. It's his birthday." Every-one in White Cove knew that Charlie's father was one of the big-gest dealers of illegal liquor in New York, and he used his nearby estate as a kind of advertisement for the lifestyle his wares made possible. "I told you last night, don't you remember?"

"Did you? I guess I forgot," she lied, because she hated ever doing anything according to a plan.

"Wear the silver dress I sent you when you were at school. I'll have a car come 'round to pick you up."

Astrid tilted her head dreamily to the side. The silver dress he was referring to didn't fit her, of course. Charlie always bought things two sizes too large, as though he couldn't quite comprehend how much smaller than he she was. But she could have it taken in by tomorrow, she supposed—one of the maids could do the work that night.

Astrid opened her eyes then, and realized that she was not alone in the room. "Are you lost?" she said to a young man wearing a worn denim shirt tucked into worker's pants. He was long and ropy and his skin was brown from the sun, and he had pretty, sad eyes.

"Who's there?" said Charlie, suddenly at greater attention.

"No one. Never mind. Send a car 'round tomorrow, cocktail time. Good-bye." Then she put the receiver back in its ornate cradle. "Don't I know you?" she purred, though this seemed unlikely.

To her surprise he nodded. His dark hair was falling in his eyes, and he pushed it back a little shyly before answering. "Yes, ma'am. My name's Luke. We rode together a few times when we were young. My pa ran the stables at Count de Gruyter's place over in Great Neck."

"Aha, knew it!" she lied. "We must have been about eight," she said, because her mother had only been married to the count—her second husband—for a year and a few months, around 1920. "Anyway, what brings you here, Luke? You couldn't possibly be working for us again."

"No . . ." He paused awkwardly and looked at his feet. "I work over at the White Cove Country Club now."

For some reason this made her smile, and when he saw it he smiled, too. Then she decided she didn't want to know anything about the series of events that preceded him being in her foyer on that particular afternoon—it was one of her virtues that she was often content to know little—and shrugged happily. "I'm suddenly so hungry, aren't you?"

"Actually, yes."

She moved breezily to his side and took him by the hand, and they hurried together through the quiet rooms of the house to the kitchen, where the cook and her assistant were busy making bread. The cook glanced up—she had a kind, fat face, just as all cooks should—and there was only a brief moment where a little scandal lingered in her eyes to see the young miss wearing pajamas in the late afternoon and holding the hand of a strange man in work clothes. She had been employed by old, rich families a long time, and could remember the days when a girl's reputation was ruined over much less. But all the rules had changed in the last decade, and in Marsh Hall, as on many of the surrounding estates, people with fine names were always having meals at unusual hours with people who were not at all like them.

"Martha, we're hungry," said Astrid, showing her lips in their full poutiness. "Won't you make us some eggs?"

"'Course, dearie," Cook answered as Astrid draped her arms around the older woman's neck, happily receiving a kiss at the hairline. "Only, sit down and don't be in my way. There's coffee on the stove."

Astrid winked at her new friend and poured them each a cup of coffee in delicate china cups. He took a tentative sip, and glanced at her as though he was unsure whether or not it was his place to speak.

"I remember you now," Astrid mused, forgetting that a moment ago she had pretended to know him for sure. There *was* something familiar about him; she saw it now, a quiet boy in a plaid flannel jacket who used to lead her pony for her. "There were three of you, weren't there?"

"My older brothers, John and Peter." His eyes were shining, and she realized that it pleased him to be remembered.

"And you used to walk my pony Arabella around the corral for me. You and I were the same height then. . . ." A mischievous smile crept onto her lips. "You used to look back at me sometimes," she whispered sweetly.

His own smile fell at this, and his face colored. Then she knew that his childhood self had had a crush on her childhood self. She was perfectly aware that the cook was giving her a disapproving look for being such a flirt, but she didn't care. It was Astrid's way—she loved Charlie, of course, but she was an incorrigible flirt. It was glorious, making a man blush like that.

"Oh *there* you are."

The cook's eyes darted up first, and then Astrid and Luke glanced over. There, framed in the hall doorway, was her mother, Virginia Donal de Gruyter Marsh, whose strong features conveyed any displeasure that her tone might have left in doubt. Her physical presence was composed of brittle parts, but the overall effect was one of fierceness. It was very generally known that the lady of the house enjoyed a party as much and maybe more than her daughter did, a fact that always made the latter wince.

Indeed, Astrid's mother was in full evening dress now, but it was apparent, especially in the natural light streaming through the large windows, that she was still wearing what she had gone out in the night before. The quality of her pale skin was dull, and her sleeveless black dress, with the black sash tight at her narrow waist, hung off her in limp, wrinkled tiers. Her hair had surely been done up for whatever fete she had abandoned her husband for last night, but now it sat around her shoulders like weeds. The buckles of her high-heeled shoes, which involved diamonds and emeralds, were the only part of her that shone. It was only after several seconds that Astrid realized it was not she, but *Luke*, her mother had misplaced.

"I have been looking everywhere," she added unnecessarily.

The exact circumstances under which Luke had met her mother and been invited into Marsh Hall would never be fully explained to Astrid, but a vague outline of what must have happened had now taken form in her mind—after all, her mother was very frequently at the White Cove Country Club, and people on their third marriages are rarely sentimental about fidelity—and the idea inspired a wave of nausea through her. Although Astrid had inherited her mother's flirtatiousness, she was not nearly so cavalier. She gave Cook as true a smile as possible before standing up.

"Thank you, Martha, but it's just occurred to me how late it is, and I must have my dress fitted, for the party tomorrow night at Charlie Grey's," she announced. Without meeting the eyes of anyone in the room, she advanced toward the hall; on the threshold, her mother grasped her wrist.

For a moment Astrid imagined she was about to be admonished for having slept so late, for so clearly planning to skip dinner in the formal Marsh dining room, for ruining a very expensive pair of pajamas, or for announcing so casually that she was going to socialize at a house that belonged to a known bootlegger.

But instead her mother parted her thin lips, caught her daughter's gaze, and asked, "What time is the party?"

Chris Mottalini

ANNA GODBERSEN

was born in Berkeley, California, and
educated at Barnard College. She
currently lives in Brooklyn, New York,
where she is at work on her new series,
Bright Young Things.

For LUXE secrets and gossip, go
to www.harperteen.com/luxebooks
and to visit Anna online go to
www.theluxebooks.com.

For exclusive information
on your favorite authors and artists,
visit www.authortracker.com.

LAST SUMMER
A SUMMER BOYS NOVEL

Also by Hailey Abbott

SUMMER BOYS

NEXT SUMMER

AFTER SUMMER

LAST SUMMER
A SUMMER BOYS NOVEL

HAILEY ABBOTT

SCHOLASTIC INC.

New York   Toronto   London   Auckland   Sydney
Mexico City   New Delhi   Hong Kong   Buenos Aires

No part of this publication may be reproduced, stored in a retrieval system, or
transmitted in any form or by any means, electronic, mechanical, photocopying,
recording, or otherwise, without written permission of the publisher.
For information regarding permission, write to Scholastic Inc., Attention:
Permissions Department, 557 Broadway, New York, NY 10012.

ISBN 13: 978-0-439-86725-2
ISBN 10: 0-439-86725-8

ALLOYENTERTAINMENT

Produced by Alloy Entertainment
151 West 26th Street
New York, NY 10001

SCHOLASTIC and associated logos are trademarks and/or registered
trademarks of Scholastic Inc.

Text design by Steve Scott
The text type was set in Bulmer.

12 11 10 9 8 7 6 5 4 3 2 1   7 8 9 10 11 12/ 0

Printed in the U.S.A.
First printing, May 2007

"Congratulations, graduates!" cried the principal of Martin High, directly into the microphone. The sound reverberated out from the small stage and echoed across the June morning, over the heads of the seniors sitting in rows across the football field, and back up over the stands where the parents sat, applauding wildly.

On cue, the entire graduating class let out a long cheer. They weren't allowed to toss their caps in the air, or they'd have to pay a penalty fee, but one brave — or crazy? — soul did just that.

Beth Tuttle knew it had to be her ex-boyfriend, George.

But, whatever. Beth tilted back her head and let loose a banshee howl of her own. Then she reached over and hugged the kid nearest her: Michael Tutweiler, to whom she had previously spoken exactly once in their entire twelve years of Martin, Massachusetts, public schooling. It had been at graduation rehearsal one week ago, and had consisted of exactly four words: *Is this my seat?*

But Beth didn't care. And neither did Michael. The moment was bigger than either of them. She and Michael cheered wildly and pounded each other on the back.

"We did it!" Beth cried.

"We rock!" Michael replied at the same volume.

Then they let go of each other, and Beth grinned as Michael was swallowed up in the black-gowned crowd of seniors all around them.

Never to be seen again, she thought, *except maybe ten years down the road at a class reunion.* Somehow, though, she was okay with that. Michael Tutweiler would be her private graduation-day memory.

Beth pulled the black mortarboard hat from her head, shook her shoulder-length blonde hair free, and sighed.

High school was over.

After a moment, she turned to follow the chaotic surge of her classmates back across the football field and toward the brick school building, where their families waited on the wide school lawn.

"Tuttle!" One of Beth's younger swimming teammates

launched herself at Beth. "What are we going to *do* without you next year?"

"Kick some ass," Beth replied with a smile. "Life'll go on, I guess."

The other girl looked like she couldn't imagine that, but Beth was already moving on, picking her way through the crowd of celebrating new graduates, looking for her parents.

Life *would* go on, Beth mused. She would meet new people; maybe become a new person herself — as if the eighteen years that had created the person she was right now were just a *base* for everything that would come after.

Beth was leaving for college in August. She knew that going to college meant changing her whole world. She'd watched her cousin Kelsi change in a major way this past year at Smith College. Beth watched the CW Network. She knew that high school was where people dreamed about things, and college was where people actually *did* them.

She almost wished she could go straight to college, without having the summer to wait and wonder about it. She wanted her future to begin *now*.

"Bethy!" cried her mother, and then Beth was swept up into her arms. Her mother couldn't stop hugging and congratulating her. Her father stood to the side and snapped picture after picture: Beth with her mother, Beth with her diploma, Beth grinning and holding on to her braided gold tassel. Beth knew it was only a matter of time before these pictures were in frames all over their house.

"Okay," Beth said when her eyes were dizzy from the flash, and her jaw was beginning to ache. "I have to return my cap and gown or they'll charge me."

"We're so proud of you, sweetheart," her mother said with a big smile, and then kissed Beth on the cheek. Beth hugged her mom back, hard.

"Take as much time as you need," her father told her in a gruff voice.

Beth felt a surge of emotion as she looked at her parents, and tried to imagine *not* living with them anymore. She was an only child, and she had a relationship with her parents that was kind of different from the ones she knew her friends had with theirs. She knew it was dorky, but she *liked* hanging out with them sometimes. So thinking about going off to college and leaving them felt a little bittersweet.

"I'll see you guys in a bit," Beth murmured, feeling like she should say more, but not knowing how. The way her parents smiled at her, she thought maybe they understood.

She turned then, and headed away from them.

The past several months had been like this, Beth thought, making her way through the crowd once more. Different. Strange. Surreal. If she thought back to this time last year, it was like thinking about an alternate reality. She'd been Beth Tuttle, but a completely different version of herself.

A year ago, she'd still been with George. He'd been more than a typical boyfriend — he'd been Beth's best friend. They'd inhabited a little world that was all about the two of them. Their own games, secret nicknames, a whole private language of jokes, dreams, and silliness. As Beth walked down the hallway of her school, she shook her head. She'd had no idea that last summer would tear them apart — that Beth would do the tearing herself — or that they'd break up for good at Thanksgiving.

Beth would have assumed, a year ago, that losing George would kill her. It nearly had, last summer. Then the autumn had arrived and they'd grown so far apart, and she felt like she needed to lose George completely in order to really live.

It still hadn't been easy. It was like she had transferred to a new school these last few months — that's how different things felt without George. But she'd concentrated on her college applications. She'd spent Christmas visiting her cousins, Ella, Kelsi, and Jamie, who were like sisters to Beth. Instead of treating the prom like a big romantic thing, Beth had gone with a big bunch of single girls — and they'd had a blast. She'd kept on swimming. She'd run track. She'd gotten into college.

"I did it," Beth said out loud then, attracting the notice of one of the parents near her. She smiled when the man looked at her, mostly because she saw that he was the father of Steve Wilson, captain of the soccer team, and one of Beth's old friends.

"Congratulations," Steve's father said to her politely, which made Beth want to giggle.

"Thank you," Beth said very formally. She had to bite back a laugh at the look on Steve's face, as his mother took what had to be the zillionth photo of him in his cap and gown.

"*Mom*," Steve complained, "I have to find my friends."

When she heard that, Beth admitted to herself that it felt the tiniest bit weird to finally be at graduation day without George. Well, not *without* him. She'd heard his name called during the ceremony, and it had surprised her how much she wanted to cheer and scream for him. Since she hadn't really wanted to *see* him in the past six months, it was a change.

Beth shrugged it off, then ran down the flight of stairs that led to the auditorium. Inside, the chaos was extreme. Kids were lining up to return their graduation outfits, but were using their last moments as classmates to branch off into groups, sign yearbooks, and make promises about staying close.

"Beth Tuttle! Come over here and sign my yearbook!" called a guy who Beth knew from track. His name was Paul, and he had the distinction of being both the tallest and fastest kid in their class.

"I have to return these," Beth called back, indicating her cap and gown with one hand.

"Don't think you can get out of it," Paul warned,

pretending to brandish his yearbook at her. "Remember, I *will* catch you!"

Beth was laughing as she turned back toward the line, and she definitely wasn't paying attention.

So that was how she bumped into George.

Literally bumped into him. Like, with her entire upper body.

They both shot their hands out to steady themselves, and then dropped their hands abruptly when they saw who they'd collided with. It looked practically choreographed.

"Hi," Beth said, diving right into the awkwardness. "Sorry. And, uh, congratulations."

"You, too," George said immediately, and more politely than she remembered him ever being. He ran a hand through his wild dark curls.

"Guess you made it after all," Beth said, trying to smile, though it felt a little forced. Because they'd joked a long time ago that the numerous Enemies of George might bar him from participating in the graduation ceremony, simply out of spite.

Beth had a weird thought. Maybe *she* was one of the Enemies of George now. How depressing was that? She felt anxiety pool in her stomach. This was *exactly* why she'd been avoiding him for months.

George gave her a half smile. "Yeah. What a relief."

"Uh-huh. So, what are your plans?" Beth asked quickly,

aware that her face felt a little heated. She was embarrassed to be asking *George* such stiff questions, like they were strangers.

But maybe that's what they were now. Strangers. It occurred to Beth that George probably didn't know what her actual life plans were either. Because why should he?

"Oh, you know," George said airily. "World domination, battling evil, an occasional dragon slaying, the usual. You?"

"Nothing quite as exciting as your Xbox," Beth said, feeling a spark of her old wit as she raised her brows at him. "I'm going to Georgetown in the fall."

George looked at her for a moment, and then his eyes warmed with that wicked humor she hadn't seen in a long, long time.

"That just proves my theory, you know," he told her.

"I'm afraid to ask what you mean by that," Beth said, rolling her eyes in the way that only George could make her roll them.

"You shouldn't be afraid, Beth. After all, you can't help it. It's only natural."

"Help *what*?" she demanded.

"Once you go George, you never go back," George said happily. "I'm going to enjoy thinking of you wearing Me Town sweatshirts for the rest of your life."

Beth shook her head at him, but she couldn't contain her grin. "How about you?" she asked. The *George*town irony had nagged at her ever since she'd gotten her acceptance letter.

"After much consideration," he replied solemnly, "I decided that Pittsburgh, Pennsylvania, will be the lucky recipient of all that is George come fall. I'm going to Pitt."

"Cool." Beth nodded. She'd guessed that George might go there, since his older brother had as well. "What are you doing this summer?" she asked then, pleased that their conversation felt more normal now.

"It's funny you should ask." George pulled his graduation gown off, and folded it messily in his arms. Beth did the same, and they stepped into the returns line together. "My friend Dean —" He paused. "You don't know him — we painted houses together last summer. He invited me up to his grandparents' place, for a summer of total relaxation. It's a cool little town in Maine. You might have heard of it. Pebble Beach?"

Is this really my life?

"It sounds familiar, yes," Beth said drily.

George looked at her, then away. When he spoke again, his voice was lower.

"I didn't want to just, like, appear in Maine. That's your place. I wanted to respect that." He shrugged. "I kept wanting to talk to you about it, but it never seemed like the right time."

"Things have been weird," Beth acknowledged.

"This is pretty much the first conversation we've had

since . . ." George shrugged again. It was like he didn't want to admit that it had been cold outside with snow on the ground the last time they'd spoken. Neither did Beth. "In a long time."

"Things have been *really* weird," Beth clarified.

"Yeah, they have."

They stood next to each other in the slow-moving line, quiet for a moment.

Beth thought about how tense and strange it had all been — the months of not talking to him, not sharing everything with him. Not sharing *anything*. She'd pretended not to see him in the halls. Ignored him in their classes. Acted as if they'd never had a history.

Which seemed kind of silly, now that it was all over. Now that high school was over, and everyone had to move on to something new, what did the past matter?

"I think you should go," Beth said, tossing her hair back. "Pebble Beach wouldn't be Pebble Beach without you."

She almost said, *Look what happened last summer*, but thought better of it just in time. Why would she want to remind George that she'd fooled around with that lifeguard?

"Are you serious?" George asked, his dark eyes searching her face.

"Of course I'm serious," Beth said, not sure if she meant it entirely, but wanting to come off as the bigger person. "I don't think you should avoid the nicest place on the Maine coast just because I'll be there. Pebble Beach isn't *that* small. We might not even see each other."

"Like you could stay away from Ahoy Bar and Grill," George said, shaking his head at her. "I was having this recurring dream where you stumbled over me sitting at one of the booths." He shuddered. "Not pretty."

"Ahoy by definition is not pretty," Beth replied. "Try crowded and crazy."

"You love it there," George teased her.

"Can't deny it," Beth agreed.

They got to the head of the line, and had to split to their separate ends of the alphabet to return their armloads of graduation attire.

"Guess I'll see you in Maine," George called out, lifting a hand.

"See you," Beth called back, still dazed by the direction her summer had taken.

So much for normal.

Kelsi peeked out the window for the eighty-seventh time in three minutes, but the driveway in front of her mother's Colonial-style house remained empty. The suburban Connecticut street at dusk looked exactly the same as it had always looked throughout the entire course of her childhood: the lawns well-manicured, the houses serene, the yards festooned with oak and linden trees.

And no sight of her boyfriend's car.

She propped herself up on her knees and turned around so she could see herself in the mirror across the room. She assured herself that she still looked as cute as she had when she'd gotten ready, hours ago. Her short hair was glossy and nut-brown, and she'd outdone herself with lip gloss, thanks to a panic attack and a trip to Sephora earlier in the day.

Kelsi was not normally the lip gloss type, but she thought a reunion with her boyfriend deserved something a little more special than her usual Burt's Bees lip balm. Paired with her new favorite flowy halter top from Anthropologie and the Chip & Pepper jeans her fashionista sister, Ella, had given her for her birthday, Kelsi thought she looked exactly like the Bohemian princess she aspired to be.

If only Bennett would hurry up and arrive, so he could fully appreciate it.

Kelsi flopped back against the cushions on the couch and let out a rueful sigh. She was *almost* embarrassed for herself. She was glad her mother was away for the weekend, and that her sister had gone to her boyfriend's place in Philadelphia, so there was absolutely no one around to watch Kelsi run to the window over and over again. She'd completely lost her cool — and all because of a boy.

Nothing about Bennett had been what she'd expected. That was one of the reasons Kelsi had fallen in love with him in the first place. She certainly hadn't expected it to be so hard, not being with him for the eternity between the end of finals and the middle of June, when the Tuttles headed up to Maine and summer officially began.

But now the wait was over.

Kelsi took a few deep, calming breaths, and thought back to where everything with her and Bennett had started.

She'd had the most amazing first year at Smith College.

A year ago, she'd felt so lost and worried about her future. Now that she knew how it all turned out, she couldn't believe she'd been so stressed out. Hindsight was definitely 20/20.

For example, Kelsi couldn't have known that instead of finding herself awash in homesickness and fear like many of her classmates at Smith, she would, by pure coincidence or the grace of the housing gods, find herself living with Taryn Gilmour.

The thought of her irrepressible, pixie-like, irreverent best friend made Kelsi smile as she shifted into a more comfortable position against the soft cushions.

Taryn and Kelsi had fallen into a friendship quickly, but unlike many other friendships they'd watched crash and burn throughout the year, they had only gotten tighter. So tight that Taryn had been thrilled when Kelsi started dating her brother, Bennett, who went to school at nearby Amherst College.

Though not as thrilled as Kelsi had been, of course.

Kelsi couldn't have predicted that what had seemed like such a great relationship with hot, snarky Tim from Pebble Beach would turn out to be just a summer thing. Back in Maine, Tim had seemed to transcend his frat-boy roots. At school, though, it turned out that Tim really *did* enjoy all those keg stands and drunken toga parties. It wasn't that he had turned into a different person, necessarily. It just seemed that he and Kelsi had both emphasized other parts of their personalities when they'd met each other. Maybe Maine had brought out the best in them, Kelsi thought charitably. But dating while Kelsi was at Smith and Tim was at UMass had made their essential differences entirely too clear.

Kelsi had broken up with Tim just before Thanksgiving, in the middle of midterms. When she'd returned to school, it seemed like Taryn was on a mission to help Kelsi discover what she'd been missing while she'd been occupied with Tim.

"There's a whole world of men out there," she'd told Kelsi in her knowing drawl. "Not all of them think the pinnacle of life is a packed keg party with half-naked girls. Some of them like art. Books. Music, even."

Taryn felt that her artistic brother was the perfect person to usher Kelsi through this new, collegiate world of Men Who Liked Other Things. The three of them went to a Pedro the Lion show over at Amherst one weekend. Then the next weekend, they road-tripped around the area to check out local galleries for a paper that Bennett was writing in his art history class. One afternoon, just Kelsi and Bennett had driven into Boston to watch the entire Krzysztof Kiesowski's *Three Colors* trilogy. As they headed back home, Kelsi's head was filled with French cinema and Bennett's delightful raspy voice, as they talked about films and ideas the whole way.

It was probably right then that she'd fallen in love with him, with winter racing by outside the windows and all that warmth and sexy intellect inside the car.

But it wasn't until a few weeks later that things really happened between them. Kelsi had found out that the Smith Studio Art department was having a Make Your Own Art night. She'd invited both Taryn and Bennett, but only Bennett was free. They'd laughed and laughed as they'd collaborated on their first sculpture: a metal and wood rendition of Taryn — all edges and motion. Later, they'd walked across the Smith campus in the dark, crunching their way over the frozen ground with their breath coming out in puffs. Kelsi couldn't remember what they'd talked about that night. She just remembered the big moon overhead, and how soft and perfect Bennett's lips were when he finally leaned close and kissed her.

Taryn had loved the fact they'd gotten together only slightly more than she'd loved the sculpture, which she'd placed in the center of Kelsi's and her room for the remainder of the school year. The three of them were like their own little family unit these days.

The best part was that Taryn had agreed to spend the summer in Pebble Beach with Kelsi and the assorted Tuttles. It would be like having another cousin to hang around in Maine with, and Kelsi couldn't wait. She imagined the two of them sprawled out on the beach, gleaming in the Maine sunshine, and she just knew that the rest of her family would love Taryn the way that she did.

Kelsi thought that Ella, particularly, would adore Taryn. Especially since Kelsi's sister would get to spend the summer on the old sunporch that doubled as a guest room. Whenever the sisters shared the bedroom — which was every past summer — they spent half their time fighting. Thanks to Taryn, Ella would finally get what she wanted: her own space. The thought of the inevitable Taryn-Ella bond, and the havoc they would wreak, should have scared Kelsi, but instead it made her laugh.

"Anybody home?"

At the sound of that familiar, beloved voice, Kelsi jackknifed into a sitting position and let the rush of joy sweep through her body. It was always this way. Every time she opened her eyes and saw Bennett, she felt like she glowed.

"Did I leave the front door unlocked?" she asked, drinking in the sight of him from her spot on the sofa.

"You did," he said, "and I walked right in. This is not the safety-conscious girlfriend I thought I knew, Kelsi. I'm disappointed."

He was nothing of the kind, as the mischievous glint in his eyes attested.

"You took a very long time to get here," she chastised him, still not moving, still wanting to soak in the anticipation of his nearness. She wanted to prolong the separation, so it would be that much sweeter when she reached out and touched him.

Kelsi studied Bennett as he stood there in the entryway to the family room, looking slightly disheveled from the road. She hadn't known it was possible to love every single cell of someone else's body. She loved Bennett's slightly messy, slightly longish coppery-red hair, and the emo-kid cut he wore it in. She could sink into his warm, intelligent dark eyes behind those adorable Buddy Holly glasses. She loved the stretch of his arms and the way his butt looked in his hipster jeans. She loved the way his smile seemed to light up his whole body, and the way he cocked his head slightly to the left when he aimed that smile at her.

"I had to make a few stops," Bennett said, and then Kelsi couldn't take it any longer.

She bounded to her feet and threw herself across the room, connecting with his body in a big bear hug that swept him back a few feet and brought her up on her toes. Finally close to him, Kelsi could smell the warm scent of his skin. She closed her eyes and just inhaled him. He smelled like sun and heat and Bennett. Like love.

"I missed you," she murmured, her eyes still closed.

"These were some tough weeks," Bennett agreed. Kelsi opened her eyes as he pulled back slightly and grinned down at her. Then he lowered his head and kissed her, his lips hot and soft and familiar. The kiss grew in intensity, and they were both a little breathless and giddy when Bennett pulled away again. "But I have a surprise for you."

"Who needs a surprise?" Kelsi protested when he pulled even farther away, breaking all contact except for his warm hand around hers. "You're here!"

"You'll love it," he assured her, and tugged her along behind him into the hall, where Kelsi saw he'd stashed a picnic basket. "Everyone's away this weekend, right?" he asked in a low voice. Kelsi nodded. "Excellent," he said.

Bennett led Kelsi down the hallway, out the back door, and into the warm Connecticut night. In the center of the backyard, he let go of her hand, and set about creating a ridiculously romantic nighttime picnic right there in the grass near her mother's rhododendrons.

Kelsi could only stare and then laugh in amazement as he shook out a blanket, and set out tea candles in adorable little lanterns all around it, bathing the blanket in a soft, romantic light. When he was finished, Bennett held his hands out to Kelsi, and pulled her inside the ring of light he'd created.

"First, dinner," he said as they sat down together on the soft blanket. "Then I want to talk to you about something."

The picnic hamper was filled with all of Kelsi's favorites — roasted eggplant sandwiches and vegan potato salad, olives and cherry tomatoes, with brownies for dessert. Kelsi was sure it was the best meal she'd ever eaten. As they ate, Bennett told her stories about his recent art projects and his father's well-meaning, if bumbling, attempts to understand things, such as finding his only son half naked in the basement at two A.M., covered in purple paint.

"I think he'd have been a lot happier if I'd been covered in beer," Bennett told her, laughing. "You know, *beer* he could comprehend. He was the president of his fraternity back in the day. Me — all wild-eyed and clutching my paintbrush? Not so much."

"What did he do?" Kelsi asked. She put the remains of her brownie aside (dairy- and gluten-free, because Bennett was good at details, she thought happily), and stretched out on her back, her feet across Bennett's lap so she could see the stars. It was only the stars above and this little ring of light, with the two of them in the center. And Bennett's sweet, deep voice, which she felt she could listen to forever.

"He hemmed and hawed and left me to it," Bennett said. "Which is the most you could ask for, I think. Right?"

"Definitely," Kelsi agreed. She'd met Bennett and Taryn's parents several times, and was always struck by how normal they seemed in comparison to their madcap children. How the four of them handled one another so well was one of life's great mysteries.

"So that's kind of what I wanted to talk to you about,"

Bennett said gently, moving her feet aside and stretching out next to her.

"Purple paint at two A.M.?" Kelsi laughed at him. "I don't think I need any further details to enjoy *that* visual!"

"Very funny." Bennett propped his head up with one hand, and Kelsi stopped laughing as his gaze went serious behind his glasses. "Do you remember me talking about Carlos Delgado?"

"Carlos Delgado," Kelsi echoed, as if she had to think about it. She wrinkled her nose. "I think I might have heard you mention him five or six thousand times. Since he's only your favorite contemporary artist in the entire world . . ."

"So, you remember," Bennett said drily.

"I'm still not sure," Kelsi teased him. "I remember going to Manhattan for the weekend and visiting his gallery show no less than seven times. But besides that, I don't think I remember."

"So there was this internship," Bennett said quickly. Kelsi got the sense that his excitement was too unwieldy for him to even respond to her teasing. "And one of the seven times we went to the gallery, I picked up the application, and don't be mad, Kels, but I decided to apply." He let out a breath.

"Why would I be mad?" she asked, shaking her head at him.

"Because I hid it from you." Bennett reached over and traced a pattern slowly along her arm, up her neck and to her cheek, as if she were his canvas and his finger were a paintbrush. "I thought that if I pretended it wasn't real, it would hurt less when I got rejected. Is that crazy?"

"It makes perfect sense," Kelsi told him, turning her head to kiss his palm.

"But the most amazing thing happened," he whispered. "And now I'm afraid that it isn't real, but I'm going to tell you, anyway."

"You got it." She knew from the sparkling wonder in his dark eyes, and the joy in his voice.

"I got it." Bennett stared at her, shaking his head. "I'm going to be Carlos Delgado's personal assistant for the whole summer."

Kelsi let out a little whoop of joy, and grabbed him into a hug.

"This is terrific!" she cried. "I'm so proud of you!"

"I'll visit you every weekend, or maybe you'll come down," Bennett added hurriedly, hugging her back. "I don't want you to feel like I'm blowing off our summer together —"

"We'll work it out," Kelsi assured him, cutting him off with kisses. "This is going to be the best summer ever. You're going to learn so much!"

"I can't believe it," Bennett confessed. "I mean, that's

actually true, I'm not just saying that. I'm *incapable of comprehending* that I'm going to be spending day after day with my idol. I can't get my head around it!"

"You're an amazing artist yourself," Kelsi said staunchly. Not only because she loved Bennett, but also because it was true. "Someday someone's going to say the same thing about you."

"I think maybe you're biased," Bennett said with a laugh, and they kissed out there under a canopy of summer stars.

They kissed and kissed, rolling back and forth on the soft blanket, and once again Kelsi thought about how special and safe Bennett always made her feel. She knew that she wanted to stay with him forever. She knew it deep down in the pit of her stomach. She knew it in her fingers and her toes. She knew it with every breath she took and every blink of her eyes.

Which was why she decided, as she felt love course through her in waves, that she wanted to *really* be with him. The way they never had been, in all the time they'd been together.

"Hey," she whispered, smiling up at him in between kisses. "I want it to be tonight."

"You want what to be tonight?" he asked, gazing down at Kelsi with tenderness.

That was just one more reason to love him, Kelsi thought, her smile widening.

Unlike every other guy she'd ever dated, sex wasn't the first, last, and only thing on Bennett's mind.

"If you want to," she went on, feeling suddenly a little bit shy, "I'd really like to . . ." It was ridiculous that she was going to be a sophomore in college and didn't know what to call it. "Sex" seemed so scientific. "Making love" was just a weird thing to say and she couldn't speak it without cracking up. In her head it was just . . . *It*.

The *It* that she hadn't done, despite being pressured by every guy before this one.

The *It* that she'd thought about so much and worried about so much, and now it just seemed like the obvious thing to do. The right thing, even.

"Oh," Bennett said in a hushed voice, getting what she meant. They looked at each other.

"What do you think?" she asked. Because it wasn't just her choice. It would be the first time for both of them, if it happened.

Kelsi suddenly wanted it to happen, so much so that she thought she might be shaking.

"I think," Bennett said slowly, carefully, "that it would be perfect."

They both laughed again — nervous and excited and hopeful laughter. Kelsi helped him blow out all the candles and then they climbed to their feet and she led him inside, up the stairs to her old bedroom. Once inside, they kissed again, long and sweet. Again and again, as if they were relearning how to kiss each other. Their bodies pressed together tight. As they kissed, they pulled off each other's clothes and then they were naked, and then they were in the shelter of Kelsi's bed.

"Do you want to change your mind?" Kelsi whispered, when it seemed like Bennett was hesitating.

"No, no," he whispered, holding himself above her. His smile was slow and wonderful. "I just want to make sure I remember every second. Every breath."

Their warm skin together felt so soft and so natural. Kelsi arched her back and twined her arms around Bennett.

It was funny how Kelsi had always wondered why something in her didn't want to take this step. She'd thought something was wrong with her. Maybe she was frigid, or dysfunctional.

Now she knew better.

Now she knew that she'd been waiting her whole life for this moment, this boy, this night.

"I love you, Kelsi Tuttle," Bennett whispered.

"I love you, too," she whispered back.

They smiled at each other, and then, just like that, they were no longer virgins.

Her first night in Maine, Ella Tuttle tied the ribbons on her platform espadrilles and inhaled the familiar smells of the cottage all around her. It smelled like the beginning of every summer as far back as she could remember: wooden and salty, old and comforting.

What did not smell familiar was the sunporch, where Ella was being forced to sleep this summer. Ella looked around the strange space that she'd never spent too much time in as she got to her feet. This was the guest area in her father's cottage, and aside from making out with Stevie Lewis on the couch once when she was thirteen, Ella had never really paid it much attention. But Kelsi had brought a friend with her this year — Taryn — which meant Ella got to pretend to be okay with being banished from *her* summer bedroom.

Ella might have *appeared* cool with the situation, but the truth was, she missed Kelsi. Kelsi was so wrapped up in her new college life during the year that she'd bailed on family functions and hardly had time to call or e-mail her little sister anymore. Ella had been looking forward to the summer as a chance for her and Kelsi to play catch-up.

At least, the whole extended Tuttle family was in Maine, too, so Ella knew she could turn to Beth or Jamie when Kelsi was off entertaining her friend.

Ella ran through the cottage, waved a good-bye at her dad as he sat with his mystery novel in the armchair by the fireplace, and then burst out through the screen door and into the Maine evening.

"Take it easy!" her dad called, but she ignored him.

She couldn't take it easy — she was too filled up with love.

She loved the pine needles that crunched beneath her totally inappropriate yet undeniably kick-ass wedge heels. She loved the pine trees themselves. She loved the sweet, salt smell of the coming dusk and the not-so-far-off sound of the waves in the bay hitting the sand of the beach. Her family had rented cottages in this small clearing for as long as she could remember. Ella felt as if she'd finally come home, after the long year with all its Catholic school restrictions and annoyances, strict nuns, and dreary detentions. She'd always loved Pebble Beach, but tonight it seemed as if that love had tripled in intensity.

She loved *everything* about Maine, she decided, but especially the fact that her long-distance boyfriend, Jeremy, was now just a few minutes' walk away. Not a couple of hours away in Philadelphia. Not a phone call here or there. Not a text message or a weekend. Just down the road and up the hill. *A few minutes.*

A few minutes that should, Ella felt, begin immediately. She felt that restlessness inside that she'd always thought was just uniquely *her*, but now she knew could be focused.

In this case, on to Jeremy.

She hadn't seen Jeremy since he'd dropped her off at her dad's cottage earlier that afternoon. That was a whole handful of hours they'd been apart, and it was too long. They'd already spoken on the phone twice. Ella loved the little buzz it gave her to know that he was every bit as excited as she was to have the whole summer to enjoy each other — a whole summer without the ticking clock that had been the focus on all those weekends during the school year. It was like the summer was a long, hot bath of Jeremy-time, and Ella couldn't wait to start soaking.

All she had to do was motivate her little posse.

Ella headed toward the picnic tables out on the lawn that served as the central area of the Tuttle family's collection of cottages. Kelsi sat on one of the tables, surrounded by their cousins and the college friend she had brought with her for the summer. Ella enjoyed looking at her family, all together

28

the way they were supposed to be, laughing at some story Kelsi was telling, looking like they all belonged in an Abercrombie ad, only with slightly less bare skin. No one was off at any summer programs this year, Ella noted approvingly. She preferred all the Tuttles present and accounted for, as they were tonight. That was the whole point of Pebble Beach.

Ella took in a lungful of sweet Maine air. How lucky was she that her cousins were her best friends as well as her family?

Ella and tall, toned Beth were the blonde Tuttle cousins, though they looked like two entirely different versions of the "blonde girl" stereotype. They both had long hair, though Ella's was more golden than Beth's and Ella wore hers down around her face in loose curls, while Beth preferred her sporty ponytail. And, apparently, Beth preferred outfits to match that sporty ponytail, despite years of Ella's attempts to trendy her up a little bit. Which, Ella admitted reluctantly, suited Beth's athletic figure best.

What suited Ella was the tight little tank top and short-shorts she was wearing, which she knew accentuated all her curves. It was fun to be a blonde, curvy stereotype, Ella felt, and she had always been about having fun whenever and wherever possible.

Ella's sister, Kelsi, had also been a blonde once upon a time, but had decided to dye her hair a rich, dark brown before going off to college last summer. Now she and her friend Taryn looked sort of alike — both with short, dark hair and intelligent eyes. The similarities didn't stop there. Both Kelsi and Taryn were wearing different versions of the same ratty jeans, flip-flops, and floaty tank tops. Kelsi's was floral with spaghetti straps. Taryn's was a halter top in Kelly green. Ella wasn't sure how much she liked the fact that Taryn and Kelsi looked like peas in their college pod.

Last, but not least, was Jamie, Ella's gypsy cousin, with her dark curly hair, smattering of freckles, and bright green eyes. She was rocking her trademark thrift-store look, with her usual long, belted tunic and a raggedy skirt that show-cased her slim legs. Not to mention the roughly seven hundred necklaces hanging around her neck and spilling down her front. Ella suspected Jamie had found the entire outfit for less than five dollars at some garage sale, which she supposed made it even more amazing that Jamie actually looked cute in her secondhand rags.

Ella liked the fact that everyone looked so good, actually. She wasn't one of those girls who liked to hang out with less attractive girls in an attempt to make herself look good. In fact, she thought she got a lot more attention when everyone was equally hot.

"Let's go, ladies!" she commanded, walking up to the little circle and inserting herself into the middle of it. She clapped her hands together like a coach.

"'Let's go'?" echoed Beth. "Are you kidding?" Beth, her smooth athlete's arms bare in the summer evening, laughed up at Ella from her seat on the wooden picnic bench. "You went inside to change all of twelve seconds ago. Literally."

"This is the new, improved Ella," Kelsi told Beth, as if Ella wasn't standing right there. "The one who can get ready for the annual party on the pier in five seconds flat — because she wants to see her boyfriend."

"Cute Jeremy, right?" Beth confirmed. "He was so nice at Thanksgiving. Didn't he bring a casserole?"

"He has *many* talents," Ella bragged with a saucy wink.

"Ella with a long-term boyfriend," Jamie said with a smile, her green eyes dancing. "The mind boggles."

"Boyfriends are overrated," piped in Taryn.

Ella cocked her head to one side.

Taryn smiled at Ella. "Unless he's the right one, of course," she added, possibly remembering that Kelsi also had a boyfriend. Who happened to be Taryn's brother.

Ella chose to interpret that as appeasement on Taryn's part, and therefore decided to be gracious. She smiled back.

"But I still can't believe she got ready that fast, even for Jeremy," Beth continued, shaking her head. "*I* don't even get ready that fast anymore. Did Ella and I switch places? How scary is *that*?"

"We have *not* switched places," Ella told Beth loftily,

and then let out a little sigh, as if she were annoyed. "You are wearing what looks like a Nike running shirt and Gap jeans from, like, six years ago."

"They're not that old!" Beth protested, although Ella noticed she frowned down at her jeans, obviously not sure. "And this is *not* a Nike running shirt!" She paused, considering. "Though I have gone running in it once or twice, now that you mention it."

"Meanwhile," Ella continued, pleased with herself. "I am wearing retro Zara." She indicated her outfit with a little flourish of her hand.

"Can Zara *be* retro? By definition?" Taryn asked Kelsi, who laughed a bit harder than Ella thought was strictly necessary.

"You both look adorable," Jamie said, standing up from the table to link her elbow with Ella's, tugging Beth to her feet with her other hand. "You look exactly like yourselves."

"Thank you," Ella said, because that was exactly what a free spirit like Jamie would say. "Now I would like to hit the pier before it sinks into the bay. If everyone's finished talking about how fast I can change my clothes?"

"Oh, please," Beth teased her. "You love the attention."

"I know," Ella whispered, as everyone got up and started moving in the direction of the dirt road toward town. She gave her cousin a little wink. "But it's fun to pretend."

All the cousins — and Taryn — walked together down the uneven dirt road, through the woods, and then spread out a little bit when they hit pavement on the other side. Ella found herself walking in companionable silence with Jamie, down along the road that ran into town.

They looked at each other and smiled knowingly. Then they both took deep, dizzying breaths the way they had when they were little girls, to suck the summer straight into them. They broke into giggles.

"Are you psyched about Amherst?" Ella asked when she could catch her breath again.

"Yeah, it's been my dream college," Jamie replied, but there was a strange note in her voice. She looked out toward the boats bobbing gently on their moorings in the dark water.

"I remember how much you loved it last summer," Ella mused. "I, personally, find it difficult to imagine that *I* could ever love a *school*, but whatever. You and Kelsi are going to have so much fun, hanging out up there in Northampton."

"It's a terrific place," Jamie agreed, running her hand over the top of a well-pruned bush outside a clapboard cottage.

This time, Ella *knew* Jamie's tone was off. Amherst was all Jamie had talked about since doing that writing program there last summer. Shouldn't she be a little bit more excited? Kelsi had been beside herself when she'd gotten into Smith, and she had never been crazy about that school the way Jamie had always been about Amherst.

Weird, Ella thought.

And then she forgot about Jamie, because they were finally nearing the pier. The entire town of Pebble Beach seemed to be there, reveling in the first big summer party. Ella found herself smiling at nothing in particular, as she breathed in the atmosphere.

Ella could clearly remember other summers. Summers when she'd found the big inaugural party on the pier or the bonfire down on the beach boring. Summers where she'd felt restless and almost needy, like she wanted something thrilling to conjure itself out of seaweed and sand to sweep her away. But this summer she just wanted to embrace all of it. The packs of summer boys with their gleaming eyes and sun-kissed skin. She just liked looking at them. The urge to touch didn't seem to be there at all. They were like pretty scenery.

"I'll meet you down by the bonfire," Ella told her cousins.

"*Please* go find Jeremy," Kelsi said, rolling her eyes. "You're practically jumping up and down."

"Like this?" Ella asked her, jumping up from her toes a few times, mostly so Kelsi — whom Ella totally loved, but who had this whole prudish side to her — could look horrified at the possibility that one of Ella's breasts might fall free of her skimpy tank.

A very high possibility, but then, *Ella* was not a prude. And, clearly, neither was Taryn.

"La Perla, right?" Taryn asked casually, motioning to Ella's pink bra strap under her tank. "Best lingerie in the world."

"Uh, yeah," Ella said, taken aback by the input.

Grinning, Kelsi shook her head. "I knew the two of you were soul mates," she said teasingly to Taryn.

"I should go," Ella said, blowing kisses to her sister, Beth, and Jamie. Then she turned and headed for the spot where she'd arranged to meet Jeremy, trying to brush off the suspicion that Taryn kind of annoyed her.

"Sorry, boys," she singsonged at a deliciously disheveled surfer dude and his completely Chad Michael Murray friend, both of whom grinned at Ella as she passed. "I have a date."

"I could be your date," Chad said with a twinkle in his eye.

"I have a *hot* date," Ella clarified, but with a little smile to take the sting out of it.

Then she forgot the cute surfer boys entirely, bobbing and weaving her way through the crowd. She headed toward the stage where the band was playing something very Death Cab-meets-Sufjan Stevens, but didn't give the band members a second glance — she wouldn't make *that* mistake again. Farther out on the pier, couples huddled together against the wooden railing and groups sat around fishing lines, apart from the madness of the party. Ella made her way to the farthest corner, her pace — and her pulse — quickening as she saw Jeremy standing there, waiting.

When he saw her, a smile flashed across his face and he started toward her, slowly.

He looked so good, Ella couldn't believe it. She felt as if she hadn't seen him in days instead of just hours. He was so deliciously Seth Cohen-ish. That dark hair and sexy, lopsided grin. His amazing lifeguarding body that he concealed perfectly in baggy jeans and long-sleeved T-shirts. She wanted to eat him up.

They finally reached each other.

"Hey," Jeremy said, and pulled her into his arms.

"Hey to you, too," Ella said back, which made them both laugh a little bit. Ella was usually so forward with guys and the last couple of summers were perfect examples. She had pursued Peter and Ryan with all the confidence in the world. But she couldn't figure out what it was about Jeremy that made her nervous and yet so excited all at once.

"You look so beautiful," Jeremy said, looking down at her. "I mean, you always do, but even more so here."

Ella smirked, ready to snap back with a flirtatious, sarcastic comment.

Until she looked up at Jeremy. He gazed back at her

with his deep brown eyes as if he could never stop looking at her. Ella felt her breath catch in her throat.

Every other guy Ella had been with had obsessed over her looks. Ella had loved it, but part of her had always wondered if that was the only reason they were so interested in the first place. But with Jeremy, she actually *believed* that she was beautiful. And she knew that it was all the more special because he actually cared about her.

Slowly and softly, Jeremy tipped up her chin and leaned in to kiss her. She relaxed for what felt like the first time in days. Jeremy smiled at her softly as he pulled her closer and kissed her again and again, sending a zing of electricity through her body. She slid her arms up around Jeremy's neck, letting her hands run through his messy dark hair, and gave in to the freedom of summer.

No clock, no school, just the two of them and a million stars overhead.

Finally, Ella thought.

Pebble Beach and Jeremy.

She was home.

4

Beth looped her hair back into a ponytail, and stretched in the lazy morning sunshine that lit up her room in her family's cottage. She took in a few deep breaths — filling herself with the scent of cedar from the chest at the end of the bed. The patchwork quilt on her bed was ragged and perfectly familiar, and Chauncey the cork figurine held his customary position on the shelf above her light switch. Outside, wind chimes made soft murmurs in the breeze, and Beth could smell the fresh kick of the sea wrapped in the scents of woods and earth.

She had been in Maine for two weeks so far. She was happy here. She loved it here.

But something was missing.

Beth headed out into the bright June morning, waving

at her younger cousins, who raced around the grassy central area of the Tuttle compound, playing Capture the Flag. They waved back, but then turned their attention back to their game.

"You have to surrender!" Jessi commanded her brothers, making Beth smile at her bossy tone.

Beth had been something of a loner so far this summer. Kelsi and her college friend were inseparable — constantly making little outings to various places in Pebble Beach, or driving to the outlets in Freeport. They'd invited Beth along, but the few times she'd taken them up on it, she'd felt like a third wheel. The two of them had lived together for a whole year in college, and now spoke in a sort of abbreviated code about their common experiences and friends. Which was mostly funny, but sometimes kind of overwhelming, too. Beth didn't like having to ask for explanations every two minutes.

Jamie, who Beth had imagined would be as interested in finding things to do as Beth was, was instead proving to be hard to pin down this summer. She disappeared for hours at a time, or was always reading. She marked up big books with her pen and copied huge passages in her journal. Beth couldn't tell if she was up to something, or was just relaxing in anticipation of her freshman year at Amherst. She also didn't think Jamie's version of reading looked relaxing — it looked a lot like homework to Beth.

Meanwhile, Ella, who was usually the life of any given party, was completely wrapped up in her lifeguard boyfriend. As far as Beth could tell, Ella spent all day, every day, lounging around the beach, waiting for Jeremy to have time off.

Okay, Beth thought then, heading down the dirt road away from the cottages, that wasn't entirely fair. Ella had spent entire other summers doing exactly the same thing, just *without* the lifeguard boyfriend. Ella simply liked to lie around on the beach, doing as little as possible.

Beth couldn't imagine living that way. It was just one of the reasons she and her cousin were so different. Today, for example, Beth decided to walk over to the local high school so she could work on her times on the track there. She usually just ran in the woods and on the walking trails all around town, but she wanted a change of pace.

It took her about twenty minutes to walk inland across town to the high school. Only the summer people built houses so close to the water, Beth knew. Locals had a much healthier respect for the winter sea, and kept their homes and other important buildings at a distance from the water.

Beth made her way through the bleachers to the track, passing what looked like a summer camp set up on the nearby baseball diamond. Kids were performing calisthenics to the barked commands of a very convincing-sounding drill sergeant. But it was obvious by the way the kids were laughing and having a ball that they loved the guy. Beth had a flashback to some of her favorite times as a kid — at soccer camp with her hard-ass, completely cool, college-age counselors, who were Beth's idols. She could immediately see how much the drill-sergeant guy fit that same image.

Beth grinned to herself, and then scrolled through her iPod playlists to her collection of Training songs, which were differentiated from her Running songs, which were in turn different from her Weight Room songs. She took a couple of breaths as Franz Ferdinand's "The Fallen" began, and then set off running as the drums kicked in.

She was nearing the end of her ninety-minute mix when a baseball bounced onto the track in front of her, then rolled. Beth slowed her run, and pulled her earbuds out of her ears. Any closer and it might have hit her.

She bent over to pick up the baseball, and had a sudden, perfect memory of the years she'd spent playing Little League way back when, in Martin. She wound up, and then threw the ball as far as she could, back in the direction of the baseball diamond —

And directly over the drill sergeant's head.

Not that he was really a drill sergeant. As he walked closer, Beth could see that he was actually a cute auburn-haired guy maybe a year or so older than she was, who happened to be wearing the same uniform as all those kids.

Beth couldn't help but notice his tight T-shirt that emphasized the long, captivating muscles of his torso, and shorts that rode low on his narrow hips. He was grinning at her.

And to her surprise, Beth found herself grinning back.

"You have a great arm," he said, still smiling. "If I'd known that, I wouldn't have walked all the way over here."

"Thanks," Beth said. Then the strangest thing happened. It was like the spirit of Ella rose within her, and Beth found herself saying almost the same thing her cousin had two weeks ago: "I have *many* talents."

What? Had she really just said that? To this total stranger who might think she was flirting? *Was* she flirting?

"I bet you do," the guy said with another smile. "Unfortunately, I have campers." He looked back over his shoulder, where at least fifteen ten-year-old boys stood at the edge of the baseball diamond, singsonging high-pitched teasing rhymes. He turned back to Beth. "But maybe I'll see you around."

"You never know," Beth said, again as if she were someone else — someone who flirted, someone who enjoyed being flirted with — and he laughed at that, and then jogged back toward his campers.

Beth stuck her earbuds back in her ears and started to run, but she couldn't pretend that her mind was really in it any longer. She couldn't remember the last time she'd even *noticed* a cute guy. It was as if she'd put that part of her life in storage after she and George had broken up last fall. She'd been a boy-free zone for a long time now.

And she'd kind of thought that might be a permanent condition.

But look at her now! Beth felt a little bit giddy, and also impressed with her own boldness. She hadn't had any idea what was going to come out of her mouth.

And the truth was, it felt great.

Because if she was honest with herself, Beth realized as she rounded the track once more, she'd spent a long time getting over George. She didn't regret breaking up with him. But breaking up with him wasn't the same thing as being over him.

Maybe today signaled a new phase in her life, when she'd least expected it.

Maybe she was finally moving on.

Naturally, Beth ran into George exactly four days later.

It was a gorgeous Maine afternoon, with not a cloud in the deep blue sky, and Jamie had actually put her books aside for a change. She and Beth had walked into town together and had lunch down on the beach. They'd gotten hot dogs and waffle fries from their favorite greasy snack vendor, taken their flip-flops off, and walked down to put their toes in the wet sand near the water's edge.

"Wow," Jamie said, swallowing reverently. "I can feel the grease, like, *congealing* inside my body."

"And it's delicious," Beth replied around a mouthful of crispy fries.

"A*mazing*," Jamie agreed happily.

When they were finished stuffing themselves, they washed their hands off in the bay, and then decided to wander around town.

They darted in and out of the cute little shops that dotted the main street of Pebble Beach. Jamie became entranced by some crystals in the New Age store, which, Beth knew from experience, could keep her occupied for hours.

Beth looked out the back door of the shop, to one of the many courtyards that made the town so cute. You could access them from small gates along the main road or from the back doors of the shops, and it was like a whole other layer of Pebble Beach goodness. Across this particular courtyard was one of the village's ice-cream stores, and there was a big commotion outside at the plastic tables.

Intrigued, Beth walked over, and eased her way into the middle of the crowd so she could see what was happening.

Two guys sat at the table, bent over two huge platters of ice cream. Beth knew exactly what they were doing. Every summer, Benny's Ice Cream offered a deal: If you could sit down and eat the entire platter of ice cream — which was like Emack & Bolio's Mack Attack and featured a scoop of every single flavor of ice cream in stock — it was free. But if you didn't finish, you had to pay for the whole thing.

Beth knew all about the contest because George had attempted — and failed — to get his free thirty-seven scoops of ice cream on several occasions.

So really, she shouldn't have been at all surprised when one of the guys lifted his head and she saw that it was her ex-boyfriend-ex-best-friend-ex-everything. She would have recognized George earlier if he hadn't been wearing an out-of-character baseball cap that covered his unmistakably wild hair.

"I am the man!" George shouted to the crowd all around, but mostly to the other guy, who Beth assumed was his friend Dean.

"Ohhh," Dean moaned. "I think I might hurl."

George had done it. He had actually cleared his plate. He had smears of chocolate and strawberry all over his shirt, but his platter was clean. Dean hadn't fared nearly so well: At least ten scoops of ice cream remained, melting sullenly on the platter in front of him.

"I told you not to eat that waffle for breakfast," George told his friend. He whooped. "It's all about pacing."

Beth felt a rush of conflicting emotions. On the one hand, she knew better than anyone how excited George probably was, because he'd been trying to achieve this goal for years. On the other hand, she sort of felt like she was spying on his life. A life she wasn't a part of anymore.

Beth tried to blend back into the little ring of observers, then started for the New Age shop's back door — until she heard her name.

She couldn't exactly make a break for it without looking like an idiot, so she turned around instead.

"Hey!" George looked thrilled. "Did you see what I did? I ate an entire Benny's Big One! Finally!"

"I know," Beth said quietly. "Congratulations." She felt like they were at graduation again.

George rocked back on his heels, and tipped the brim of his cap up, so he could look Beth in the eye.

"You weren't running away in my moment of ice-cream glory, were you?" he asked. "Without even saying hello?" His tone was light, but Beth knew him too well. She could hear the hurt beneath.

"I didn't want to bother you," she said, shrugging.

George shook his head, but his eyes had that glint in them. "Come on," he said. "You alone understand the torturous history of George and Benny's Big One."

"That's true," Beth conceded, and found herself smiling a little bit. "I was there the first time you made the attempt, and bailed after a mere seven scoops."

"I was just a boy, Beth," George said wistfully. "Just a

boy who today became a man." He nodded wisely, and rubbed a hand down along his belly, which had to be killing him. Beth couldn't help laughing.

"Manhood is thirty-seven scoops?" she asked. "Because *I* would have called that insanity."

"Manhood is knowing that thirty-seven scoops are insanity, and figuring out the best strategy for consuming them, anyway," George told her, his eyes dancing with merriment.

"My mistake," Beth said with a sigh, which made him laugh.

"Hey," he said, suddenly serious. "We should hang out some time."

Beth felt her smile slip.

"George . . ."

"In a totally platonic way!" he shook his head at her. His eyes were clear and warm, but nothing more. "Not everybody is as much fun as you, that's all. I drove by the mini golf place the other day, and remembered our hard-core tournaments."

"I haven't played mini golf in a long time," Beth mused, mulling it over. Of course, she should tell George no. There was no point dredging up all that old stuff again. Hadn't she *just started* to feel like she could move on?

But then again, she told herself as George launched into an impassioned description of how he was, in fact, the Tiger

Woods of mini golf, it was *just* mini golf. And maybe the fact that she was starting to move on was why it would be okay to hang out with George. After all, he was still the funniest guy she knew. The funniest *person*, in fact. She missed laughing the way they'd always laughed together.

"Please stop talking," she said, interrupting George's treatise on how his swinging style had developed over the years.

George paused, and bit his lip. "Sorry."

"I think mini golf might be fun," she said, eyeing him with one part hope and another part apprehension. His expression looked the way she imagined hers must: wary, but kind of pleased, too. Because if it wasn't awful, it really would be fun to hang out with George again.

"Yeah?" He nodded. "Um, okay. Cool."

"I guess you should call me," Beth said, feeling awkward. And then she realized that she didn't want to sound like she thought it was a date or anything. "Or I can call you, whatever."

"Sure," George said quickly. He looked at her and smiled that fully George smile. "But we'll definitely do it. It'll be fun."

"Fun," Beth echoed. "I'm looking forward to it."

They smiled at each other, and it was nice, but kind of tentative, too.

"Okay, well, I should go find Jamie," Beth said, beginning to feel awkward.

"Yeah," George agreed. "I think Dean might be in an ice-cream coma."

"See you later." Beth knew she sounded stilted and strange, but didn't know how to change that.

It had never really occurred to her that trying to be friends would be so hard.

Kelsi pushed her way off the subway train, and let the crowd carry her along, up the stairs and out into the sweaty, humid June evening.

Once free of the foot traffic, she backed up to the nearest building, looked all around her, and let the thrill of it all snake through her: She was in New York City!

The plan had been for Bennett to drive up and spend the last two weekends in Pebble Beach. The first weekend he'd cancelled, because his new job at the gallery involved a ton of overtime hours, which he hadn't expected. Then this weekend he'd been supposed to come up again, and when he'd called late last night, Kelsi had steeled herself for yet another cancellation.

"I have to cover all these galleries for Carlos," Bennett had told her. "So I can't come up this weekend."

"It's okay." Kelsi had tried to sound supportive, even though she was crushed. She didn't even know what "covering galleries" meant, or why it was so much more important than his coming up to see her, but she didn't think she should ask that question. She suspected it would sound needy, and she really wanted to sound completely behind him — one hundred percent.

"It's not okay," Bennett replied immediately. "But you should come down. There's no reason why you can't come with me while I do the coverage and, anyway — I want to see you."

And so here she was.

Here being the actual island of Manhattan, which Kelsi could hardly believe she was standing on. She'd been to New York before on various field trips to the Metropolitan Museum or a Broadway show — and even once on an ill-advised night out with Ella — but it had never been like this. She'd never been completely on her own, planning to stay in her boyfriend's *apartment* and cover *art galleries*. Bennett was living in such an amazing world this summer, and now she got to be a part of it, too.

Kelsi pushed away from the wall and started down the street, admiring the sweep of skyscrapers above, and the jam-packed streets spread out in front of her as she headed south. New York was so dramatic, from the eclectic citizens who marched with such purpose, to the bright yellow cabs that zoomed toward certain disaster at top speed only to stop *just* in the nick of time. The sour summer perfume of garbage and hot asphalt rose up from the pavement beneath Kelsi's feet.

Truth be told, Kelsi wasn't sure why anyone would *want* to spend the summer in a place as relentlessly hot and gritty as New York City. She'd foolishly worn flip-flops tonight and could practically feel her feet collecting all the grime and dirt from the hot street. But maybe that was the price for all the restless, exciting energy of the place.

In Maine, the sunset brought lower temperatures. The nights were cool, even cold, and the air was clear. If there *were* stars up above Manhattan, Kelsi couldn't see them past all the bright lights. It was as if Manhattan made its own light, and didn't even need stars. Kelsi laughed a little and turned down the side street that led to Carlos Delgado's gallery.

And Bennett.

At the thought of her boyfriend, Kelsi felt the usual excitement and delight roll through her body. It competed with the clatter and rumble of the city around her, and won, until she was smiling ear to ear.

She didn't really mind that Bennett's job had turned out

to be so much more demanding than he'd anticipated, Kelsi told herself, because he was gaining so much experience and it was going to be such a great thing for his future.

Kelsi realized she could miss Bennett and wish she saw more of him even while totally supporting him. Or, anyway, she felt like she could.

When Kelsi finally reached the gallery, she paused for a moment outside and tried to collect herself. The last time she'd come down, she'd been so excited to see Bennett that she'd burst into the gallery, all sweaty-faced and out of breath. And while no one had made fun of her or anything — at least not to her face — she'd gotten the distinct impression that it *wasn't how they did things in Chelsea.* Bennett liked to joke that all that artistic flair meant a humor deficit.

Kelsi pushed through the big glass doors, careful not to leave any fingerprints because that also *wasn't how they did things,* and wandered into the vast, open space. The gallery spread out in front of her like a labyrinth: white brick walls snaked this way and that, and up above was the balcony where the offices sat.

Bennett had told Kelsi that Carlos was currently showing art and installations related to his concept of summer. That sounded so simple, and yet the art in front of Kelsi was arresting and bold. The canvas nearest her, all cream lines and splashes of blue, made Kelsi gasp a little bit. It was like a perfect depiction of how Kelsi thought a summer afternoon should feel. It was beautiful.

Carlos was amazing. Kelsi knew that. She knew that the art magazines hailed him as the most exciting modern artist of his day. But in that moment, nothing was more exciting to Kelsi than the sound of a voice she knew so well. She wandered past one of the larger installations and watched as Bennett led customers through the labyrinth.

Her heart still somersaulted when she saw him, and she could feel the goofy smile transform her face. It was fun to watch him when he didn't know she was there yet. She could congratulate herself on having such a fine-looking boyfriend, who was dressed all in black today — a tight T-shirt and what looked like new, probably expensive jeans. Even his auburn hair looked different, less emo and more slick. Kelsi remembered Bennett telling her that Carlos had insisted on what he called a "visible upgrade" for his intern. Kelsi couldn't deny that the changes suited Bennett. If it weren't for his trademark hipster glasses, she might have mistaken him for a hot New Yorker.

Until he saw her, that is, and his dark eyes blazed with joy.

Kelsi smiled back, and the nervous tension within her eased. She hadn't even known it was there until she felt it dissolve.

Things were different than she'd expected them to be

this summer, but who cared? The important thing was the look in Bennett's eyes as he walked toward her.

As long as she had that, nothing else mattered.

Bennett's new world was glitzy and wild, and Kelsi loved every moment of it. They'd left Carlos's gallery by taxi, and Bennett informed her that he'd be taking her on an art tour of New York.

"I don't even know what that means," Kelsi confessed.

"No one knows what that means," Bennett replied, holding her close in the backseat of the cab. "But it sounds good, right? You're excited without even knowing why, aren't you?"

"I'm excited." Kelsi nestled close and gave him a long, sweet kiss. "But I know exactly why."

Bennett kissed her back, deeply, and Kelsi had almost forgotten how the sweet pressure of his lips and the familiar touch of his tongue could make her feel. Their arms went around each other, and Kelsi fell back against the cracked vinyl as Bennett trailed kisses down her neck to her collarbone. She let out a sigh of pleasure, burying her fingers in his hair. She'd never made out in a cab before, and there was something naughty about that thrill, about feeling Bennett's fingers tiptoe up her thigh as the bright lights of New York City flashed by them in a blur.

She and Bennett got so carried away that Kelsi was out of breath and barely noticed that the cab had stopped.

"Crap," Bennett muttered. He handed the driver some bills through the plastic window separating the seats, and then pulled Kelsi out after him.

They were standing in SoHo. Trendy girls in pencil heels wove past them. The front door to a warehouse-like building was thrown open and flashily dressed people milled around within.

"Are you ready?" Bennett asked, looking down at Kelsi with mischief in his dark eyes.

"Of course," she said, fixing her twisted hair.

"Because you're about to see something kind of scary. I call it, the Art Snob." He grinned. "A breed not specific to Manhattan, though this is a major breeding ground. And the one you're about to meet is *particularly* egregious."

Kelsi peered around Bennett, trying to look inside the building.

"Which one?" she asked.

"Me, silly," Bennett chided her. Then he flipped open his cell phone. "This is the most important part of my job. And the most ridiculous."

He pressed a speed-dial button to get Carlos on the line, and led Kelsi into the gallery at the same time.

"It's me," he said into his phone, in a blasé voice Kelsi had never heard before. Then he winked at Kelsi. "No, there's not much of a turnout. Adequate at best."

Kelsi looked around at the crowded space. People were

literally cheek-by-jowl at the bar. Then she looked back at Bennett. Obviously he was speaking in code.

"I mean, sure, there are some people here," Bennett continued. "But we get more foot traffic on a Monday morning at the gallery."

Bennett marched his way through the show, his cell phone planted on his ear, giving Carlos a play-by-play of each piece of art. Kelsi trailed behind, listening.

A beautiful still life?

"Pedestrian," Bennett said into the phone. When Kelsi gaped at him, he pointed at the phone and mouthed, *I love it!*

A painting of a church, with what Kelsi thought was glorious use of light and shadow?

"First-year M.F.A.," Bennett pronounced, while shaking his head at Kelsi, and pointing right at the very shadows that Kelsi had felt drawn to.

And so on, throughout the show.

"Basically, this show is an insult to the rest of the art students," Bennett told his boss as they completed their circuit, despite the fact Kelsi had read in the literature that the artist was self-taught, not an art student at all. "It's everything you complain about," he added. He listened for a few moments and then hung up.

"Wow," Kelsi said, looking at him. "That was quite a performance."

Bennett rolled his eyes. "Did you like it? I hope so,

because we have two other shows to hit tonight, and they'll be exactly the same."

"I loved that church!" Kelsi protested.

"So did I," Bennett said with a shrug. "But it's not about what *we* like. It's about what Carlos would like, and he definitely would *not* like that painting. I have to be his eyes at these shows, not mine. This is what he's paying me for." His eyes twinkled. "Glamorous, huh?"

"That's one word for it," Kelsi replied thoughtfully. "Another one is *weird*."

"Reporting to Carlos is the annoying part," Bennett confided, taking her hand and kissing it quickly, then tugging her along with him to the bar. "But there are compensations."

"Like what?" Kelsi asked.

"Free wine and appetizers, for one," Bennett said, snagging two spring rolls from a passing waiter and offering one to her with flourish. "Or as it's known around here, Friday night dinner."

By the time they finished the report from the third show of the evening, Kelsi was feeling a little bit tipsy from all the free wine — or maybe it was just being with Bennett again. Or being in New York. Whatever it was, when they made their way out of the final gallery onto the busy sidewalk, Kelsi felt a giddy rush all through her body.

"I love you," she told Bennett — and half of Manhattan — grabbing his face between her hands to kiss him.

Kelsi felt as if the kiss could go on forever. Bennett slipped his hands around her waist and lifted her closer to his mouth. They practically breathed each other in.

"I have an amazing idea for our first night in New York," Bennett said, resting his forehead against Kelsi's when they finally pulled apart.

"I think this is an amazing idea already," Kelsi said, kissing him again.

"Trust me," Bennett said softly.

And that was how Kelsi found herself — after a hazardous cab ride through Manhattan that gave her a new appreciation for what a pinball must feel like — in a horse-drawn carriage, being pulled through Central Park at night.

Above, the city lights gleamed like the stars did in Maine, and Kelsi snuggled next to Bennett as the horse clip-clopped through the dark paths of one of the world's most famous parks.

"This is the most beautiful thing in the world," she told him, feeling like she couldn't get close enough.

"No," he said, running his fingers along her face, "you are."

They kissed again and again. Kelsi felt her heart swell, and her skin tingle like she might die if Bennett stopped kissing her. She felt like a goddess. She wanted to collapse into him and never get up again.

Once again, they lost track of where they were and what

they were doing, and only came back to reality when the carriage driver cleared his throat.

From the look on his face as he turned his head, it was not for the first time.

Kelsi giggled, embarrassed, but also secretly excited that she and Bennett could get so involved with each other that even New York City faded away. Bennett had to set his glasses straight on his face, and pretend to be solemn while he paid the driver. They both laughed as they walked away.

Bennett stopped walking, and pulled Kelsi in to kiss her.

"God," he said, "this is crazy. I have to get you home. Like, *now*."

It felt good to be wanted so much, and to want him in the same way. Kelsi moved closer and kissed her way down his neck.

"I'm ready whenever you are," she murmured into his skin.

"That would be immediately," Bennett said, his voice a little bit strained. He stepped into the street and hailed a cab, never looking away from Kelsi or letting go of her hand.

"I'm so glad I'm here." Kelsi looked at him, and the city all around them. "This is all so wonderful."

A cab careened to a screeching halt beside them, and Bennett pulled her close to kiss her one more time.

"It is now," he whispered.

Ella adjusted the top of her black bikini and arranged herself across her towel, making sure her legs appeared to their best advantage. Jeremy was high up in his lifeguard chair, and she knew he'd be watching.

Jeremy had mentioned that he enjoyed glancing down from his ocean-scanning duties to see her there, looking hot. Who was Ella to deny her boyfriend something that required so little effort on her part?

And if the cute-boy parade along the water's edge also happened to notice her as she lounged? Well, that was life. She'd just have to suffer through it.

A wide-shouldered hottie wandered up just then, all square-jawed and curly-haired, and Ella smiled at him, but then saw that his attention was focused on Jamie, who was sitting beside her. As she was very much taken, Ella decided she didn't feel slighted. Jamie had broken up with Dex from her private school way back in, like, February, if Ella remembered right — and she always remembered boys right. Ella had high hopes for Jamie and Mr. Broad Shoulders.

"Hi," he said to Jamie, with a sparkling smile. Ella liked the look of it. "You kind of remind me of Enid from *Ghost World*, which is, like, my favorite movie of all time."

"Hi," was Jamie's response, and she didn't really smile. Ella couldn't believe this was her own flesh and blood, dropping the ball like that. Had she taught Jamie *nothing*?

"I just wanted to tell you that if you feel like playing volleyball, my friends and I are starting a game," the guy continued, still working overtime on the smile. "I mean, volleyball on the beach is definitely more *Baywatch* than *Ghost World*, but I hope you'll give me the benefit of the doubt."

He was adorable. Ella was tempted to go play a little volleyball herself, and she only knew what *Ghost World* was because Jamie had once been obsessed with the movie herself.

Jamie, on the other hand, who had just been told she looked like Thora Birch by a delectable guy, was having none of it.

"Thanks. That's really nice of you," was what Jamie said. She smiled then, but not in any kind of come-hither way. Ella was appalled. "But I'm not really into volleyball. Sorry."

"Um, *hello!*" Ella hissed when the poor guy had taken his glorious shoulders out of earshot. "What just happened?"

"Eh." Jamie shrugged, and dug into her big straw bag for a thick paperback. *Atlas Shrugged*, the cover read. Ella was bored by the very sight of it.

"Not my type," Jamie explained.

"Since when has hot and smart not been your type?" Ella demanded. "Have you gone blind?"

"I don't know, he seemed so *jocky*." Jamie made a face.

"I don't think he was born with that body. He's like Toby Maguire in *Spider-Man*," Ella pointed out. "He may have worked on it a little bit. But then, neither one of us woke up this morning with this hair, did we?"

"I don't know," Jamie murmured.

"Here's what *I* know," Ella said. "The only reason I ever even saw that *Ghost World* movie is because you thought you looked like Enid yourself. Don't think I've forgotten that!"

"Let's just enjoy the beach, okay?" Jamie asked, reaching up to touch her artfully arranged curls as they exploded from her bun. She wrinkled her nose at Ella. "I just kind of want to sit and read my book."

Not an urge Ella shared, but then, she wouldn't have worn the 1950s-looking bathing-suit thing Jamie was wearing, either. It had a *skirt*. *Different strokes*, she thought.

She closed her eyes and luxuriated in the feel of the Maine sun. It caressed her face and body, and the slight breeze ruffled the hair she'd twisted up in a sleek ponytail. It was a perfect morning, and Ella had the intention of wasting every single moment of it.

"Hello, ladies!" singsonged a familiar voice.

Even before she opened her eyes, Ella knew it was Taryn.

Taryn, sashaying her way through the colorful spread of beach towels, swinging her hips in hope that every single guy in a five-mile radius would sit up and take notice.

Which they all did, because Taryn was sporting a tiny black bikini and nothing else.

The same black bikini that Ella herself was wearing, in fact.

At first Ella thought maybe the bikinis were just similar — after all, a lot of them looked the same. But no. She could see the logo on the hip as Taryn swayed closer, and there was no mistaking it.

It was the exact same bikini.

Ella narrowed her eyes and said nothing as Jamie cheerily welcomed this Single White Interloper into Ella's no-longer-quite-so-perfect morning.

Ella had felt pretty neutral about Taryn's presence up until this moment. Sure, she would have preferred to be sleeping in her traditional place in the bedroom she usually shared with her sister. And yes, it was the teensiest bit annoying that Kelsi always made plans with Taryn and invited Ella only as an afterthought.

But Ella had been handling all that. What she found she was less inclined to handle was someone rolling up in *her* bikini.

Taryn had been lounging around soaking up Ella's dad's attention at breakfast when Ella had announced her plans for the day, and so the other girl had clearly seen what Ella was wearing. Why would she go out of her way to wear the same thing? Ella knew for a fact that Taryn had brought about *seven* other swimsuit combinations to the cottage.

It was outrageous, and, possibly, a deliberate challenge. Ella already had to share her sister's time with this girl. Now she had to share her fashion choices?

The truth was that Ella had never had this issue in Pebble Beach before. Back at school, sure, she and her friend Marilee had been known to tussle a time or two over certain shades of Chanel Glossimer and the odd H&M halter top, but this was Maine. The only other hot girls around, in Ella's opinion, were her family members, and none of them would ever appear in Ella's exact outfits, because they all had such different styles.

Not Taryn, Ella thought then. She took a moment to size the older girl up. She'd kind of avoided doing so previously, in the hopes she could just ignore Taryn's presence in her world. Well, no more.

Taryn was little, like Ella. She didn't have Ella's curves — or her Prada sunglasses, thank you — but she did have the sort of body that called to mind Keira Knightley, the bitch. In fact, she was sort of Keira-d out — from short dark hair to small, cute feet, now that Ella thought of it. Ella, on the other hand, was far more Jessica Simpson.

Taryn plopped herself into the hot sand, and smiled broadly. Jamie smiled back.

"Where's Beth?" Taryn asked.

"She said she wanted to run ten miles today," Jamie replied.

Taryn shuddered. "That sounds incredibly unappealing to me," she said.

Ella could relate, but she hated thinking she had a single thing in common with Taryn.

"That's our Beth," Jamie said with a laugh. "The more exhausting and physical something is, the more she wants to be a pro at it."

"She's the only one in the family who runs," Ella chimed in, clearing her throat. "She has mutant genes, obviously."

"Kelsi runs sometimes," Taryn said. "Never ten miles, though. Kelsi says a couple of miles here and there are good enough."

Ella couldn't believe what she was hearing. As far as she knew, her sister didn't own any shoes that didn't run the risk of being stolen by hippies in a VW van headed for Burning Man. There were no running shoes in Kelsi's closet.

"What are you talking about?" she asked Taryn,

laughing. "The only way Kelsi Tuttle would run anywhere was if someone chased her. With meat, or something. Her vegetarian principles would force her to flee."

Taryn's eyebrows rose over her designer knockoff sunglasses.

"I don't know what her vegetarian principles have to do with anything," she said. "But I do know that Kelsi runs a couple of times a week, usually."

Ella gritted her teeth. It was one thing if Kelsi wanted to take her college roommate everywhere with her like a tote bag. But Kelsi was currently driving back up to Maine from another New York City trip, and Ella didn't see why *she* had to hang out with Taryn in the meantime. *She* didn't need a tote bag.

"So Kelsi should be back soon," Ella said, as if Taryn had asked. But mostly to point out that soon they could get to the bottom of her running habits — assuming she really had any.

"Around three or four this afternoon," Taryn said. Because she knew everything, apparently. "I just got off the phone with her."

"How was her trip?" Jamie asked immediately.

Taryn began to tell Jamie all about Kelsi, because she was clearly an expert on that subject after knowing her for — what? Ten months? Ella had known Kelsi her entire seventeen years. But whatever, that didn't seem to matter much anymore, since Kelsi was now *a runner like Beth*, and who knew what else?

Ella didn't have to check her messages to know perfectly well that Kelsi hadn't called *her only sister*, because Ella's cell phone was located six centimeters from her elbow and it hadn't so much as beeped in the past hour.

It took all the strength in her body not to look at the phone, anyway, of course, and then about twice that strength to keep from biting Taryn's head off. She knew it would only make her look like a gigantic baby.

It was good that Kelsi had a close friend, Ella told herself sternly, even if that friend was a slinky little know-it-all like this Taryn. No, really, Ella knew it was good, and that Kelsi was happier than she'd ever been before.

Ella remembered all the other summers when Kelsi just sort of wafted around in Indian-print batik shirts and claimed to be really interested in the undergrowth out in the forest or butterflies or something, when anyone could see she was actually just sort of lonely. It was *terrific* that she'd found this fun new girl to confide in, and this fun new girl's sort of nerdy brother, for whom Kelsi had unaccountably dumped that hottie Tim, and Ella felt so freaking supportive she practically threw up from it.

"Are you okay, El?" Jamie asked, frowning, and Ella guessed that her "supportive" face needed some work.

"I think Jeremy's shift in the chair is almost up," she said instead of answering. She had to escape. "I'm going to go over there for a while."

"We'll have to hang later, okay?" Taryn said, as if news of Ella's departure distressed her, which Ella very much doubted.

"Absolutely," Ella agreed in the same tone, while getting to her feet.

"Do you mind if I use your towel?" Taryn asked, moving over even as she asked. "I think I forgot mine."

How someone set off for the beach clad in *somebody else's* black bikini, yet somehow neglected to bring anything else along with them, was a mystery to Ella.

"Of course," she said icily, waving at the towel Taryn had already completely taken over. "Be my guest."

"You're a sweetheart," Taryn said in such a way that Ella knew she'd been dismissed.

The *nerve!*

Was this what Kelsi had meant when she'd told Ella that *Taryn and you are so much alike, it's crazy?* Did Kelsi think Ella was a rude bi-atch? That was impossible, of course, since Kelsi obviously didn't think *Taryn* was anything of the sort.

What could Kelsi possibly see in this girl? And what made her think this girl was like Ella? Or — and Ella didn't like this thought at all — did Kelsi prefer Taryn to her own sister? Because Kelsi sure spent a whole lot more time with this person she claimed reminded her so much of her sister than she did with her *actual* sister. Ella's stomach hurt just thinking about it.

But there also wasn't any room left on her towel, so she had no choice but to suck it up and go complain to her boyfriend about Taryn, the Interloping Tote Bag.

7

"I don't know if you know this about me," George said in an overly loud, dramatic voice that attracted the attention of the nicely dressed family of four ahead of them. They were taking, in Beth's opinion, far too much time trying to sink their golf balls into the concrete clown face.

"Why are you yelling?" Beth asked mildly, swinging her mini golf club. She smiled sweetly at the family of four, as if she, too, was baffled by George and his volume.

"I don't know if you know this," George repeated in a fractionally lower voice, "but this past year has stripped me of my charming veneer."

"Yeah?" She started to say *what charming veneer?* but thought better of it. They were trying to be friends, after all.

"At any second, I might unleash the inner demon on that family. I'm just letting you know."

Beth eyed him. "Thanks for the heads-up."

"My pleasure."

Idiot, Beth thought. But it was a fond sort of thought. So far the whole *friends* thing was going okay. It was almost like old, old times.

It was a sunny, breezy summer day — far too beautiful to waste back in the cabins. Beth turned her head so she could see across the mini golf course to the stretch of ocean on the other side of the street.

Beth sometimes wondered what the ridiculous Circus-themed golf course must look like from out in the water, particularly at night when she knew the clown's face, for example, was so hideously lit that it looked creepy and alive. She didn't think she'd ever taken a trip this far up the coast at night. Or maybe she had and had forgotten to look when she was out there enjoying the crisp sea air and the roll of the waves. She wondered if it was possible to see the dancing bears or the truly disturbing clown from out there. The fact that she had no memory of even noticing the mini golf course from the water indicated that probably there was nothing to see. For some reason, Beth found that a little bit depressing.

The family finally vacated the hole, and George stepped into place.

"I'm glad we're not together anymore, Beth," George

announced, smacking his golf ball with a clean, neat stroke and sending it directly into the clown's horrible grinning mouth. It looked like something out of Stephen King. Beth shuddered.

"Because you completely choked on that last hole," George continued with unmistakable glee in his voice, "and as your friend, I can be delighted about it."

"I'm glad we're broken up, too," Beth retorted. "Since we're no longer dating, I don't have to let you win."

George gasped in fake shock, and Beth hid her answering smile. Then she concentrated on making her shot, because she knew she'd never hear the end of it if she didn't.

And also because she was Beth Tuttle and — she could admit it — she hated to lose. She had the usual athlete's approach to any and all competitions. And admitting she had a problem was the first step, she thought with a smirk.

"You have never in your life *let* me do anything!" George was protesting.

Beth tuned him out, a skill she hadn't lost in the months since they'd last spent time together.

And then she made her shot. One stroke. Clean and neat. Perfect.

She whooped with joy and jumped into the air.

"In your face!" she cried at him. "So much for being the Tiger Woods of mini golf!"

"That was luck," George complained. "Total luck. I am way better than you at mini golf. Our entire history proves it. This was luck!"

"Call it whatever you want," Beth said, and let herself swagger a little bit as she headed off the mini golf course toward the new, improved complex, which now included a bowling alley and arcade. For all your Pebble Beach recreational needs.

She was glad George had called a few days ago, and suggested this outing, she thought as she made her way out of the complex. It felt ridiculously easy to be around him. Without consciously meaning to, she felt as if they'd rewound somehow. As if they were good friends again, before all that romantic stuff had come between them and ruined everything.

They wandered out into the parking lot, where the afternoon was lengthening into shadows.

"That was fun," George said. His dark eyes met hers, and he smiled. "You're still fun."

"You, too," Beth said.

By prior arrangement, they'd met at the mini golf course, so there was a small moment of awkwardness as they said good-bye, but then they each headed their separate ways. George took off in his car, and Beth headed through the woods on foot.

Beth stretched her legs as she walked, breathing in the

piney scent of the path in front of her and feeling light, happy. She zipped up her hoodie against the coolness of the shaded woods, shoved her hands into her jean pockets, and smiled to herself.

Her cousins had all counseled her against hanging out with George. They'd warned her that it was a big fantasy to think they could be friends again when they'd once been so much more. Beth had worried they were right, but she'd gone to mini golf, anyway, because she'd wanted to test out their theories for herself. She'd expected it to be a little bit upsetting, and maybe tense, too.

But it had been really good, Beth thought. Who said you couldn't hang out with your first love?

What did her cousins know?

Apparently, more than she did, Beth thought a few days later as she arranged her towel in the sand. Because she'd forgotten that first loves tended to be annoying. Supremely annoying.

Or, anyway, the George variety did.

Had he always been so demanding and weird about where he wanted to sit on the beach? Beth racked her brain, and couldn't come up with a single instance during which he'd ever cared in the slightest.

Which made his theatrics on the beach today all the more irritating.

Possibly he'd done it to impress his friend Dean, whom he'd brought with him today, although Beth couldn't imagine why Dean would find childish tantrums impressive in the least. She threw a dirty look at George.

"Stop giving me that look," George ordered from his sprawled position on the towel next to Beth's, with his huge sunglasses wrapped around the entire upper half of his narrow face.

"You can't see where I'm looking," Beth told him, and snorted. He looked ridiculous and, as far as she could tell, he probably couldn't see at all.

"I can feel it," George retorted. "Like a laser beam to the brain, in fact."

"I just want to make sure you're okay with this spot," Beth shot back. "Are we close enough to the water? Far enough from the trees? Near enough to the lifeguard stand? Far enough from all possible beach irritants, like horseflies and ten-year-old girls?"

"Because you love to sit next to screaming ten-year-old girls yourself?" George argued. "I guess I forgot."

"You're a beach snob," Beth pronounced, almost as if it made her sad. "Have you looked around? Every inch of this beach is gorgeous. You might try appreciating it, instead of freaking out and making us move seventy-five times."

"We moved exactly *one* time," George protested.

"Oh, right, my mistake." Beth looked at him over the

top of her own sunglasses. "The forty minutes we trudged up and down the beach, practically from Portland to Bar Harbor and back again, must have shorted out my brain."

"It would have taken a lot less time if you'd *helped*," George shot back at her. "But no, you thought it would be better to stomp along behind, making snide remarks."

"It's not a snide remark if it's *true*," Beth pointed out. "You were being ridiculous." She paused and cocked her head to one side. "See? Still not snide!"

George's jaw tightened and Beth felt a sudden surge of anger herself. She *wanted* to fight with him, she realized. She *wanted* to be mean.

Which made her wonder if maybe neither one of them was actually mad about the beach.

"Wow," commented Dean, raising himself up from George's other side and looking from Beth to George and then back. It broke the spell, and Beth looked at Dean instead of George, feeling the heat of embarrassment on her cheeks. "Are you sure you're broken up?" Dean added with a grin.

"Yes," Beth snapped, and felt herself blush a little bit when she realized George had said it at exactly the same time, with exactly the same inflection.

We're like Tweedle-dee and Tweedle-dum, she thought sourly. *Even after all this time.*

"Why?" George asked his friend, scowling openly.

"Because you sound like an old married couple," Dean

said in disgust. "I'm going to go jump in the water. The possibility of being sucked out to sea by the undertow sounds way better than listening to the two of you. I feel like I'm hanging out with my parents."

"Great," George said as Dean ran toward the water's edge. "That's just great."

Beth said nothing. Pointedly.

"I don't feel like an old married couple," George continued, sounding aggrieved.

Without even meaning to, Beth snickered.

"I agree," she said when he looked at her. "That definitely had a family feel to it, but more in a sibling sort of way."

"Terrific," George said, sounding peeved. "My ex-girlfriend has become my irritating sister."

"You mean, *my* ex-boyfriend has become *my* annoying brother," Beth retorted.

They looked at each other, and while they weren't smiling, Beth could tell they were both finding the situation funny.

"Ew," George said. "I'm going to swim, too."

"Whatever." Beth pulled her Tess Gerritsen thriller out of her beach bag and cracked it open. "Try not to drown."

"I'll do my best, thanks," George replied, taking off his sunglasses. "And by the way, that sounded like my mother."

Beth watched him walk toward the water, his long, pale

body and that lope of his she knew so well, and let out the laughter she'd been holding in.

Being friends might be tricky sometimes. But family? *That* she knew how to deal with.

This ex thing was going to be a snap.

"I'm really sorry, Kels," Bennett told her again. "I just can't leave town this weekend. Carlos is having this big party at the gallery and he's freaking out. I have to stay here and deal with him."

"It's okay," Kelsi said automatically, even though she felt like crying. She pressed the phone closer to her ear. "I just wish I'd known a few days ago. I wouldn't have loaned my car to Jamie."

Kelsi had taken her cell phone back into the bedroom for this call, expecting Bennett to tell her he was on his way. Instead, he'd announced that once again, he wouldn't be able to come up to Pebble Beach. Kelsi would have happily driven down to see him, but Jamie had left a few hours earlier in Kelsi's car to visit some friends down in Boston, and she wasn't coming back until Sunday.

So that meant another long week ahead without the boy she wanted to kiss nonstop.

"Don't be mad," Bennett said into the phone. Kelsi could hear the concern in his voice, and she told herself to get it together.

"I'm not mad," she told him. "Just disappointed."

That was a good word for it, Kelsi thought after they'd said good-bye and hung up. But the truth was, it felt much worse than just *disappointment*. It felt like the air had gone out of the room.

Why did she feel like this? It didn't make any sense. Kelsi knew that things were great with Bennett. She knew he loved her. She knew that he was just busy, and trying to do a good job for Carlos.

But why did her heart hurt?

"What's the matter?" Taryn asked, breezing into the room. She was undressing while moving — flinging her hoodie toward her pile of clothes and stripping her black bikini from her torso.

"Bennett's not coming up," Kelsi said. She didn't bother with trying to modify her tone. "Again."

Taryn gave her a sideways look, and then went and pulled on a T-shirt.

"What?" Kelsi asked.

"I didn't say anything," Taryn replied. "Does he have to work again?"

"Some party," Kelsi said. She could feel herself slumping on the bed. "It seems like Carlos's idea of an assistant is more like a personal slave. I mean, this is Bennett's summer vacation. You'd think he might get a weekend off every now and again."

Kelsi expected Taryn to agree, and thought they might rant about the unfairness of it all for a while. But Taryn was messing around with her hair in the mirror, and she didn't seem particularly inclined toward ranting.

"Well, that sucks for the two of you and your weekends," Taryn said philosophically, "but that's the job."

It felt a lot like a rebuke. Kelsi frowned at her friend, confused.

"I know it's the job," she said.

"Kels, every time I talk to him, he's, like, fully incapable of containing himself," Taryn continued, her eyes meeting Kelsi's in the mirror. "I'm talking full-on joy. He can't stop going on about what an amazing experience he's having. He gets to watch Carlos work — it's beyond Bennett's wildest dreams."

Kelsi looked down. Why was Taryn saying all this like Kelsi didn't know it?

"I understand how cool it is that he has the job," she

murmured, staring at the phone in her hand. She felt very young all of a sudden.

"I'm going out," Taryn said after a moment. When Kelsi looked up, she saw her roommate had pulled on a pair of skinny jeans. "Want to come?"

"Where are you going?" Kelsi asked, trying to pretend her feelings weren't hurt.

"I don't know," Taryn said with a shrug. "I met some guys on the beach earlier. They said there was a party out by some freshwater lake. Are you up for it?"

"Not today," Kelsi said, and summoned a smile. "I think I'm going to take a nap." And if she let herself cry a little bit into her pillow where no one would hear, who would be any the wiser?

"Okay," Taryn said. She walked toward the door, but stopped before walking out. "You know, he really does love this position, Kels. But it doesn't mean he doesn't love you."

"I know," Kelsi said. But she didn't look at Taryn. "I just wish he was coming up this weekend."

Taryn paused there for a moment, and it seemed like she might be about to say something, but then she set her mouth in a line and she walked away.

Leaving Kelsi to feel even worse.

Kelsi spent Friday night moping in her room, and then pretending to be asleep when Taryn staggered in just before dawn. After finally drifting off, Kelsi got up feeling slightly better and wandered into the kitchen. It was lunchtime, and she figured she should eat something. She was surprised to find her sister already there.

"I thought you'd be at the beach," Kelsi said, walking over to inspect the Brie and leftover filet mignon sandwich Ella was making.

"I was," Ella said, wrinkling her tanned little nose. "But then I decided that I needed a Philly cheesesteak for lunch."

Kelsi eyed Ella's plate.

"I think that's more Paris than Philly," she said.

"What can I say?" Ella asked lazily, waving a hand in the air. "I'm so *Vogue* I bring it to my food."

Kelsi smiled at that, and poured herself a glass from the pitcher of sun tea she and Taryn had made the day before. Then she settled herself across the table from Ella, and looked out the window. There were seashells and beach glass on the windowsill to catch the light, and out beyond the open screen, the fresh-cut grass and the woods. Everything was lush and green, with bees humming and the soothing sound of the surf in the distance.

Kelsi just wished she could love her surroundings as much as she had in previous, pre-Bennett summers. Now it was as if she could only see the world through the ache of missing him. It sucked.

"Are you okay?" Ella asked.

Kelsi blinked and turned her attention to her sister. Ella had her hair on the top of her head in a messy yet adorable ponytail, and her brown eyes were filled with concern. Kelsi realized that they hadn't spent as much time together this summer as they normally did — something she'd be surprised Ella even noticed, now that she had a boyfriend.

"I'm fine," Kelsi said.

"You don't look fine," Ella pointed out, licking cheese from her index finger. "You look like someone kicked your puppy."

Kelsi made a face. "I don't have a puppy."

Ella looked at her for a long moment, as if she expected Kelsi to say something.

"What?" Kelsi finally asked.

"You can tell me what's bothering you, you know," Ella said.

But Kelsi couldn't imagine telling Ella that she was this upset over something so incredibly minor. Because she knew it was minor. It was just a cancelled weekend — she and Bennett hadn't broken up or anything. And Kelsi knew that Ella certainly wouldn't mourn a cancelled weekend. In fact, she'd probably take the cancellation as an indication that she should head out and find a replacement.

So Kelsi shrugged.

"It's nothing," she said.

Ella looked down at her plate. "I thought Bennett was coming up this weekend."

"He had to work," Kelsi replied too quickly. She flushed when Ella glanced at her. "Seriously, it's fine."

"Is something going on with you guys?" Ella asked. Her eyes filled with sympathy. "Is it a sex issue, like with Tim?"

"What? No!" Kelsi cried, throwing a hand up as if to ward Ella off. "What are you talking about?"

"You don't have to yell at me," Ella continued, her chin up. "It just seems like the last couple of times you were this upset, it was because of the virgin thing, that's all."

Kelsi gaped at Ella. She hadn't realized until just that minute that she *hadn't* told Ella that she and Bennett had slept together. Her sister still thought she was a virgin. And now that Ella had brought it up, Kelsi wondered if maybe the reason why she was missing Bennett this much was because they'd taken that step, and she felt so much closer to him than she had to anyone else. It was definitely something she hadn't thought about before.

But how could she tell Ella any of this? First she would have to confess that, in fact, she'd lost her virginity. Then she would have to explain that she hadn't meant to keep it a secret. And then she would have to confess to her wild, experienced younger sister — who in her pre-Jeremy days, had gone through boys the same way she went through new ringtones — that Kelsi was all messed up because she'd finally had sex with her boyfriend. She knew exactly how many times she and Bennett had had sex, in fact (four). She was still counting. How could she tell Ella that? Didn't that make her completely lame by default?

So she just shook her head.

"Really," Kelsi said in a low voice, "everything's fine."

Ella's eyes flashed with hurt, and Kelsi reconsidered — but then they both heard the sound of a large vehicle chugging up the dirt road. It was a FedEx truck, which was unusual enough to get both sisters out of their chairs and to the front door.

"Kelsi Tuttle?" the delivery man asked when he climbed down from his high perch behind the wheel.

Kelsi ran across the lawn in her bare feet, flinching a little because the grass was still damp, and signed for the slim package.

"What is it?" Ella asked when Kelsi walked back into the cottage.

"I have no idea," Kelsi said.

She ripped open the package and pulled out a single sheet of eight by eleven paper. On it was a sketch of a girl with short brown hair, lying on her side, asleep.

"Hey," Ella said, delight in her voice. "That's you!"

Kelsi remembered waking up in Bennett's bed the morning after their magical moonlit horse-drawn carriage ride to find him sitting on the floor, sketching her.

You're just so beautiful, he'd told her.

Kelsi opened the card that came with the drawing. It was short and sweet:

I WISH YOU WERE HERE.

And suddenly Kelsi knew that everything really *was* fine. Distance was only miles. Everything else was in her head. She had to figure out how to be okay with what she knew to be true: They were in love. This was just temporary.

Deep in her heart, she believed it.

"Finish your lunch," she told Ella. "I want to go swimming."

The crowd at Ahoy Bar and Grill in town was jumping, as it was every single night of every single summer. Beth stopped on her way back from the bathroom to take a look around the place. She loved that no matter what else might be going on in her life, Ahoy would always have the same rowdy groups spilling out of their booths, shoved in around the bar, and eventually making their moves across the dance floor. It was frantic and loud, and made her feel right at home.

Beth smiled to herself. She'd dressed up a bit, having taken Ella's scathing remarks about her clothes to heart. Of course, her version of "dressed up" just meant a green tank top with tiny little spaghetti straps and a built-in bra.

She figured Ella, who liked to re-create outfits from *Lucky* spreads, still would not approve, but Beth liked the change.

Beth made her way through a cluster of dancing girls, and saw George's familiar head in the booth ahead of her.

Friends could be hard, it was true, but she'd decided a little while after the beach incident that no matter what, she still wanted to try. It didn't seem right that someone who'd meant so much to her could just disappear from her life. George wasn't just an ex, the way girls like Ella had exes in the dozens, interchangeable from one another. He was so much more than just that, for better or worse. He was Beth's childhood, in a lot of ways.

And so what if they occasionally behaved like an old married couple? They had a history.

This was what Beth told her cousins each time someone pointed out that the hang-out-with-the-ex thing sounded like a disaster in the making.

She was eighty-seven percent sure of it herself.

Beth went to slide into the booth across from George, but stopped short at the sight of the female figure already there.

Already there, and laughing merrily at something George had said. It was strange, but Beth could see how he sort of expanded under this other girl's laughter, like a plant under a stream of water. It made her feel sad for him, and for her, too, that they didn't laugh that freely anymore.

But then she shook the feeling off, because George was turning toward her.

"Hey!" he said. "This is Larissa. She fell into our booth."

"It's true," the girl said, grinning up at Beth. "There was a crowd situation and I fell right in."

"But that's not the cool part," George continued quickly. "The cool part is that Larissa's going to Carnegie Mellon in the fall!"

"That's great!" Beth said enthusiastically, although she wasn't sure why.

George rolled his eyes. "My friend Beth is slow on the uptake," he told Larissa. He looked back at Beth as she slid into the booth. "Carnegie Mellon is in Pittsburgh. Pitt is in Pittsburgh. We're going to be in the same city!"

"Have you ever been to Pittsburgh?" Larissa asked George.

"Only for the weekend when I took a tour," George said. "But I'm psyched to explore it. I've spent my entire life in suburban Massachusetts."

"How cool is that Cathedral of Learning?" Larissa asked.

"Pretty cool," George said, looking over at Beth. "It's this huge tower in Pittsburgh."

"Wow," Beth murmured. She was feeling somewhat less at home than she had a few moments before, because she knew absolutely nothing about Pittsburgh. Except the fact that George was going there. And now, Larissa.

"I'm really excited," Larissa continued happily. "I grew up in Rhode Island, and Providence just doesn't compare. Have you heard from your roommate yet?"

"He just e-mailed me the other day," George said. "He sounds cool. What about you?"

"She said she grew up in Pittsburgh, so she could totally give me like an insider's tour," Larissa said. "It should be great, even if we don't end up as good friends."

Beth considered the fact that she had yet to hear from anybody from Georgetown, and wondered if that should worry her. She hoped she wouldn't get stuck with any major partiers, since she had a full courseload and track to keep up with. Not that that was anything new.

Beth looked at George and his new friend, and noticed that they sort of looked alike. Larissa had black curly hair that spilled down her back and big dark eyes just like George. They even laughed alike. She imagined they would make a cute couple, and then waited to see if that thought upset her.

Strangely, it didn't. And *that* made Beth feel a little like crying.

"It's so crazy that we're going to spend a year of our life living with a person we haven't even met yet," George was saying, very animated.

Beth opened her mouth to respond, but then stopped, because it looked like Larissa was getting her first taste of George in his fully excited mode. George ranted about the possible horrors of freshman year, and it was like Beth could see Larissa getting more and more into him every time she laughed. After all, Beth knew the signs. She knew what it felt like to laugh your way into serious trouble with this boy.

And she began to feel all kinds of weird, because as friendly as she and George might be at the moment, and as much as it didn't upset her to *imagine* him with this girl, she wasn't at all sure she wanted to sit there and *watch* as it happened.

"I'm going to go get a soda," she said softly, and it didn't seem like either of them was listening. And why should they pay attention to her, anyway?

Beth pushed through the crowd again, and realized that she didn't feel *jealous*. She didn't necessarily want to hang around watching George hook up or anything, but she didn't want to prevent him from doing so, either.

Beth was dodging a group of people performing the Electric Slide — without benefit of the music — when the truth occurred to her. She'd been concentrating so hard on building a friendship with her ex-boyfriend that she'd somehow failed to notice that her summer was approaching the halfway point. Shouldn't she be meeting people, too? How much could she claim to be moving on when all she did was hang out with George?

"Careful there!" a warm voice cautioned, and Beth felt a strong hand wrap around her bicep and steady her moments before she would have plowed into one of those tiny bar tables.

Beth looked up into a pair of hazel-green eyes. They looked out of a face that was open and friendly, and belonged to a seriously cute guy. He was standing there in khakis and an old, fitted Bruce Lee T-shirt, and he looked thrilled to see her.

"It's you," said the baseball-playing drill sergeant.

Beth shook her head. "Hi. I was a million miles away," she told him.

"Come back to Pebble Beach," he suggested, his grin deepening. "We need you here."

"You don't even know me," Beth pointed out, but his grin was infectious. She couldn't help but grin back.

"That's true," he said. "Although I have a perfect memory of you telling me you had many talents. Besides running, throwing, and looking cute, that is."

Beth felt herself flush with pleasure. It was so girly, and thinking that made her laugh.

"I'm Beth," she said. "Are you a camp counselor?"

"There's a baseball camp just outside of town," he said as he nodded and gently led her a few steps away from the table. "I've been a counselor there for a few years, and went there myself as a camper." His eyes gleamed. "I'm Jimmy, by the way."

"You must really like baseball," Beth said. She remembered the flash of nostalgia she'd had when she'd first seen him at the track. "I used to love it. I played Little League, and on the freshman girls' softball team in high school."

"What position?"

"Shortstop," Beth said, remembering. "It was really fun, but I haven't played since then."

"Why'd you stop?" Jimmy asked. Beth shrugged.

"There were so many other sports I wanted to try," she said. "Swimming, tennis, basketball. Although, between you and me, I'm not as good at basketball as I'd like to be. I'm going to run track at Georgetown in the fall."

"I suck at tennis, but I still like playing, and I love soccer," Jimmy said, leaning closer. "And I play lacrosse on the weekends, but baseball's my first love. My dream is to go out for the majors."

"That would be amazing!" Beth was genuinely impressed.

"We should go for a run sometime," Jimmy said. "There's this cool trail out by my camp. It takes you down so you can see out into the bay from high on the cliffs. It's a great morning run."

Beth grinned at him, and felt her skin tingle. This was the first guy she'd noticed in ages, and here he was, in Ahoy. *And* he was a sports fanatic, just like her. It was crazy.

"I usually go on that inland trail past the swamp," she said, trying to keep the pleasure from showing on her face. "I like the woods a lot."

"We should change it up," Jimmy said with a slow, long look that made Beth feel a little breathless. She loved his confidence. There was no doubt in Jimmy's mind that she was going to go for a run with him.

For a second, Beth wondered if she was ready.

"How about tomorrow morning?" Jimmy offered.

She looked up then, and saw George standing just behind Jimmy, a strange expression on his face.

When Beth caught his eye, he smiled, a little ruefully she thought, and then pointed back toward the table with his eyebrows raised. Larissa was still there, demurely sipping a Coke.

Beth waved him away.

And then felt a little twinge when he went.

This was it. They were both moving on. Right there in Ahoy, on a typical summer evening.

"You know what?" Beth said to Jimmy. "I think I might be in exactly the right mood to change it up. Tomorrow morning sounds great."

George was moving on.

She could, too. Starting right there and then.

Ella hadn't exactly recovered from Kelsi's blowing her off last week. (Her sister had *freaked* when Ella had dared bring up the virginity issue.) Nor was she at all okay about Taryn's continued flaunting of the little black bikini. But after consideration she'd decided to be gracious about all of it. Partly because Ella had decided that Kelsi's refusal to confide in her was just a momentary lapse in sisterly closeness — one that would be fixed the moment they hung out again. But mostly because Kelsi was back from another weekend in New York with her boyfriend and if Ella wanted to hang out with Kelsi, that meant putting up with Taryn the Tote Bag, too.

Easier said than done, of course, but Ella was making the effort.

More effort than she would have thought necessary, since apparently all Kelsi wanted to do with her day was hike to some remote beach (apparently, the one right through the clearing was not good enough) and eat a picnic lunch. Ella didn't understand why a lunch had to be transported across such a distance — it seemed like a whole lot of unnecessary hauling and carrying when the sandwich could be eaten in the comfort of the kitchen in their cottage. But no one had asked for Ella's opinion on the matter.

Naturally, Taryn had been absolutely thrilled with Kelsi's long-distance picnic prospect, and the two of them had been busy making their lunches when Ella discovered them in the kitchen that morning.

It did not escape Ella's notice that the two girls were not planning to invite her along.

It seemed that now she had to wait to be *invited* to spend time with her *only sister*.

"Cool," she'd said when they'd explained what they were doing. "I think I'll come, too."

The looks Taryn and Kelsi exchanged at that point were just plain obnoxious, but Ella had ignored them. There was no point getting mad if she wanted to be included in their plans.

She would just have to ignore the part of her that was pissed that Kelsi would try to exclude her in the first place.

"I don't think hiking's really your thing, El," Kelsi had said gently, which was worse than if she'd just said no.

Meanwhile, Taryn made herself look very busy with the sandwiches. Overly busy. Ella actually hated her for a moment. Because there was no question about whether *Taryn* would be invited along. After all, Kelsi loved Taryn so much that Ella had been relegated to the pullout couch on the sunporch for the summer, instead of the bedroom she'd shared with Kelsi for their entire lives. Ella hadn't even complained about it, and now this? It was so unfair.

"Don't be ridiculous," Ella had announced breezily. "I *love* hiking!"

There was no mistaking the expression on Kelsi's face. Ella had seen it many times before. It was the face Kelsi wore when their smaller cousins demanded she take them somewhere she would have preferred to go alone. It was half-suffering, half-patronizing, and Taryn's answering shrug was just as bad.

They were *tolerating* her.

It was hideous.

Which was how she'd come to find herself scrabbling her way down a rocky cliff while Taryn bounded alongside Kelsi like some kind of freakish mountain goat. But if this was what it took to reclaim Kelsi, then Ella would do it.

Assuming she didn't fall to a bloody death on the rocks below, that was.

Down at the bottom of the cliff, there was a perfect, pristine little cove that Ella had never seen before. It was like something out of a movie. One involving Leonardo DiCaprio back when he was young and cute. Ella missed those days.

"This is just beautiful," Ella said with an appreciative sigh, smiling at her sister. She was tempted to reconsider her lifelong position on hiking, that's how gorgeous the little cove was.

"I know," Kelsi said, smiling back, and for a moment everything seemed normal and okay. "Tim brought me here last summer."

Ella breathed a little sigh of remembrance for Hot Frat Boy Tim (as she always thought of him), Kelsi's ex, whom Ella had found very amusing on an otherwise not at all fun road trip last summer. As she stared at the rocks and the clear water breaking over them, she also remembered the awful fight she'd had with Kelsi by the side of the highway later, during that same road trip. She thought about how angry Kelsi had been, but how she'd chosen to forgive Ella for sleeping with her boyfriend Peter the summer before.

Well. Technically, Kelsi and Peter had been broken up when Ella had slept with him. Yes, only for a few hours. But still, broken up.

Anyway, Ella still felt awfully guilty about the Peter betrayal, and forever grateful that Kelsi understood how badly Ella felt. Thinking about all of that history reminded Ella of how much she loved her sister, who had decided to overlook something most people wouldn't.

"The cove was like this magical escape then, too, right when I needed it," Kelsi was saying, still gazing around.

"Ah," Taryn said significantly, and then looked over at Ella.

Which was when Ella realized that Kelsi had told this total stranger about the sisters' big fight the summer before, in all its detail. It made her feel like throwing up. Fury shot through Ella.

But she didn't know what to do about it.

"I'm hungry," she announced carelessly, like she hadn't gotten Taryn's point. There was another shared look between Taryn and Kelsi, but Ella figured that was better than exploring the previous subject.

Ella searched around in her knapsack, blinking back the heat that surged behind her eyes, and pulled out the turkey sandwich she'd thrown together in the fifty seconds she'd had to get ready. She took a huge, angry bite and pretended it was Taryn's head.

"Oh," Taryn said, looking at Ella. "Do you still eat meat? I don't know why I thought you were a vegetarian."

Ella didn't know why, either. The Tote Bag had, by this point in the summer, had so many meals with Ella during which Ella indulged her inner carnivore that Taryn would have had to *deliberately* not notice it.

"Kelsi's the vegetarian, not me," Ella replied, forcing a smile. *Duh*, she thought. *I'm eating turkey, aren't I?*

"Kelsi's actually vegan," Taryn said, because, of course, she knew everything about Kelsi. "We all went to this PETA rally up at school this winter, and it changed us. Probably for good."

"You're vegan?" Ella demanded of her sister, ignoring the whole PETA aside, because she was tired of all of Taryn's little stories about how she and Kelsi were so much like sisters, or maybe identical twins.

"I'm trying," Kelsi said, smiling back at her, but kind of quizzically. "Why? Since when do you care what I eat?"

"I really don't," Ella said, and took another bite. Which was true. She didn't care what Kelsi ate. What she cared about was the fact Kelsi no longer shared anything with her.

Kelsi and Taryn launched into a discussion of their mutual friends, none of whom Ella knew, and so she just ate her sandwich and felt like a bratty little kid. An *unwanted* bratty little kid, which was even worse.

She was stuck at the bottom of a cliff, she was miserable, and it was perfectly clear to Ella that Taryn had completely usurped her position in her sister's life.

"I just don't know what to do about it," she complained to Jeremy a few nights later.

Ella's legs were still protesting from hiking the other day, or possibly from her selection of extremely precarious cork wedges. She wished they didn't have to walk all the way back from the old movie theater that was Jeremy's second home in Pebble Beach. But there had been a John Hughes eighties movie marathon, and they'd obviously had to go. Eighties movies remained Jeremy's greatest passion. Other than Ella, that is.

"Why do you have to do anything?" Jeremy asked in his reasonable voice. "Sometimes you don't feel all that close to Kelsi, either. So who cares if she feels closer to Taryn right now?"

It was his *overly* reasonable voice, actually. It was the one he used when he thought Ella was being *un*reasonable.

"She's essentially stolen my sister!" Ella cried. "I have to do *something!*"

"She's your sister," Jeremy pointed out calmly. "She's always going to be your sister. It doesn't matter if she has other friends."

But it mattered to Ella. It mattered that Kelsi thought Taryn was so wild and untamed and fun, which were the ways she *used* to describe Ella. It mattered that the other friend in question was basically a different version of Ella, but one — and this hurt to admit even to herself — that Kelsi clearly liked better.

Ella curled her hand tighter into Jeremy's, and leaned into him as they walked back into town.

It was another beautiful summer night, with a great mess of stars above, and people milling around in the quiet village streets. Music echoed off the water out in the bay, and laughter hung in the air like fog. The night felt thick and secret all around them, and Ella loved that the temperature had dropped enough so that she could feel cozy in her hoodie, with Jeremy right next to her, giving off heat like a furnace.

If there was a better place than Pebble Beach, Ella didn't know what it was. She reached up and pulled Jeremy's head closer to hers, so she could kiss him with all the sweetness she felt in the summer air around them.

He held her close, and the kiss changed. It got hotter, and Ella moved closer, pressing herself against him to hear his sexy little groan, until they remembered where they were.

"Oops," Jeremy said with that lopsided grin Ella adored. He swiftly kissed her once more, then took her hand and kept walking.

Together, they wandered down Main Street, skirting the lines outside Ahoy and the Lighthouse. Ella had wanted to go out, but now, after that kiss, she was far more interested in returning to Jeremy's place, where he basically had the house to himself. She could tell from the longing look in Jeremy's eyes that he felt the same.

They were walking past the big group of bars and shops when Ella happened to glance over at a couple sitting on a bench near the little Chamber of Commerce shack. She didn't know what caught her eye. Maybe it was the way the guy held himself with easy confidence that made him seem like a better person than she knew him to be.

But Ella thought that really, she'd noticed the girl. She was wearing a beat-up pair of Bermudas and a breathtakingly daring halter top, and she looked even more like Keira Knightley than usual.

Taryn. The Tote Bag.

And the guy she was making time with was none other than Peter.

Peter, who had broken Kelsi's heart by sleeping with another girl three seconds after she'd dumped him.

That other girl being Ella herself.

All that pain and upset because of one midnight-eyed guy with smooth shoulders and a wicked grin, and Taryn was touching his arm and leaning in close like she didn't know anything about it.

Except she did. Ella knew she did.

Ella felt a surge of rage, and something like triumph, too. It was dizzying and made her breathless.

If Kelsi had been upset about Ella getting with Peter, *this* was going to kill her.

Ella didn't know if she wanted to race home and expose Taryn's behavior to Kelsi immediately, or just run over to the bench right now and have it out with Taryn on Kelsi's behalf.

Not to mention that she could think of a few things to say

to Peter, too. Like, why had he texted her all last summer? After completely failing to call her the summer before?

Her stomach churned. Her head spun.

"What is it?" Jeremy asked, and Ella realized they'd stopped walking. Ella tugged his arm, and led him away from the scene of the crime before she knew what she wanted to do. "Is something wrong?" he asked, frowning down at her.

"Everything's fine," Ella lied, because she needed time to think. To plan out what she should do.

"Are you sure?" Jeremy asked. "You look kind of weird all of a sudden."

"I'm fine," Ella said.

She forced a smile, and eased her body against his to remind her of all that heat she'd been so excited to play with just a few moments before. It worked, too. Touching Jeremy always made everything better, and it gave her time to think.

"Come on," Jeremy said then, holding her face with his hand. "I can think of better things to do than stand out here in the street."

"That depends on what you're doing while you're standing in the street," Ella teased him.

She would think about Taryn and Peter tomorrow, she thought as her boyfriend gave her a wicked grin, and led her toward his house.

Tomorrow she'd form a plan.

It was hard, Kelsi thought, stripping off her bathing suit and rummaging around for something dry to throw on. Her family was gearing up for one of their trademark barbecues, and all she felt like doing was curling up in a ball, missing Bennett, and sulking.

She missed him all the time. She missed his warm, easy presence when she woke up in the morning, and she missed the warmth of his hands on her skin. She missed him every time Taryn told her she was moping, which was about seven times a day. She missed him every time she wanted to tell him something, and had to decide whether it was worth bothering him at work to do so.

Kelsi had never been the clingy type. It was just that during the school year, she and Bennett had spent every possible second together. It felt so bizarre to be cut off from him now. At least it was just for the summer. Kelsi was practically counting the days until school started again, and things returned to the way they were supposed to be.

Checking the clock on the table between the two twin beds, Kelsi saw that it was six thirty P.M., and Bennett should be wrapping things up at the gallery. He usually had an hour or so to himself before Carlos's various nighttime activities began. Quickly, she pulled out her phone and pressed his number.

"I'm so glad you called," he said instead of a hello. His voice was warm and brimming with laughter. "You won't believe what just happened."

"Tell me," Kelsi said, smiling. She lay down on her bed and let his voice flow over her.

"This horrible old woman came in, and was going on about the art she wanted to put on her wall. She wandered all over the gallery, and complained because — and I'm not exaggerating — she didn't understand why Carlos couldn't paint something *pretty*." Bennett laughed. "Can you imagine?"

"That blue-and-cream piece in the entryway is pretty," Kelsi said, trying to catalog in her head the different canvasses Bennett had shown her. They weren't all experimental or particularly daring. Some of them really *were* pretty.

"Carlos's work is a lot of things," Bennett replied

impatiently. "Important, maybe. Or evocative. But *pretty*? Please. She can go to Bed, Bath & Beyond and get a Monet water-lily print."

Kelsi let that comment sit there for a moment. She felt kind of hurt, and she wasn't sure why. It had something to do with that tone Bennett had used. Like she was as *pedestrian* as the still life he had described to Carlos over the phone.

"I just called to say hi," she said eventually. "I was missing you."

"I miss you, too," Bennett said, back to his normal, sweet tone, but Kelsi still felt off-balance.

When she hung up a few minutes later — Bennett had a dinner party to attend and had to run — she felt a good deal more unsettled than she wanted to admit. She wondered if Bennett's Art Snob persona maybe wasn't such a joke to him anymore.

Shaking it off — because she could smell the grill firing up — she pulled on a pair of jeans and a high school sweatshirt, and headed outside into the cool evening.

Various Tuttles roamed around the grassy area in the center of the cottages as dusk fell all around them. The littler cousins chased lightning bugs in and out of the darkening woods, the aunts sat and sipped wine and ate cheese from a round wooden platter, while Kelsi's dad was busily flipping burgers and telling lies to Kelsi's uncles about his latest deep-sea fishing trip.

It was a perfect family scene, and Kelsi knew that she should enjoy being a part of it, but instead, she found herself feeling sort of empty. She wondered if it was the phone conversation — as if maybe she knew, deep down, that things with Bennett were changing.

Or maybe, she thought with a rueful smile at her own drama, she was just having a blood-sugar crash, and should get some dinner.

After coaxing her father to grill her a veggie burger, Kelsi headed toward the picnic tables. At one, Ella and Jeremy were talking animatedly with Beth, George, and a freckled, athletic-looking boy whom Kelsi didn't recognize. Kelsi smiled at them as she passed, and then sat down at the next table with Jamie and Taryn.

"I know I've been in my own world since I got back from my last New York trip," she said by way of a greeting, "but I'm pretty sure I've never seen that guy before. Have I?"

"His name is Jimmy, and he's Beth's new person," Jamie explained, her green eyes dancing. "Apparently, they've been running in the mornings, which is like flowers and dinner dates in *Beth's* world." She leaned in close. "And George is here as an honorary Tuttle, thanks to Beth's dad, who ran into him yesterday. Except Beth said that he's not pining or anything because he met some chick who's also going to school in Pittsburgh this fall, who seems nice, who she thinks he might be dating. Beth and George are moving on *together*, it seems."

Finished with that involved summary, Jamie proudly sat back and popped a carrot into her mouth. Kelsi looked over to the other table.

Ella and Jeremy looked to be in high spirits, as Ella told some tale to Beth's new guy, one that involved lots of hand gestures. But the new guy kept glancing over at Beth and George. They were talking to each other, with George tapping out points on the wooden table, like he was either drumming or giving a presentation.

"Yikes," Kelsi murmured.

"Exactly," Taryn agreed, snorting with laughter. The only other person who snorted when she laughed was Ella, Kelsi thought, which made her love the both of them even more.

"Maybe not *yikes*, exactly," Jamie said, frowning slightly. She shrugged. "I've always loved George. I think it's really cool that they're trying so hard to be friends."

"Has that ever worked, though?" Kelsi asked. She remembered how insanely in love George and Beth had been, and how badly they'd hurt each other. "In, like, all of human history?"

"I can't even watch," Taryn told Kelsi. "It makes my head hurt."

Kelsi tore her gaze away from what she was certain was the impending catastrophe at the next table, and focused on Jamie instead.

"I'm so excited that you're going to Amherst!" Kelsi told

her cousin. "Bennett's already promised to give you the full rundown on campus life. Taryn and I are always there, and we'll get to hang out all the time. Next year is going to be amazing!"

"I love Northampton," Taryn chimed in. "It's this totally crunchy but hip little town, with zillions of bookstores and thrift shops and cafés. It's such a great place to live. You'll definitely love it."

But Kelsi noticed Jamie didn't respond. "I'm so hungry," she said eventually. "I'm going to go grab some more of my mom's Caesar salad. Do either of you want anything?"

Neither one of them did, because they were both stunned and staring at her, so Jamie got up and hurried away.

"Um, that was weird, right?" Taryn asked when Jamie was out of earshot. "She totally didn't want to talk about school. I figured she'd be so excited about Northampton that she'd consider transferring to Smith, to be honest."

"Yeah . . ." Kelsi frowned after her cousin. "I don't know what's up with her. She's the most driven one of all of the cousins. She usually can't shut up about how great Amherst is and how psyched she is to be going there."

"Maybe she's freaking out," Taryn said with a shrug. "Remember how scared we were at the beginning of the year?" What Kelsi remembered was that *she* had felt terrified, while Taryn had seemed in her element, but she opted not to say anything.

"Yeah, but Jamie spent all last summer there," Kelsi said instead. "There's no fear of the unknown — she's already done it!"

"Then, clearly, she's just weird," Taryn concluded with a wink, making them both crack up.

The night darkened around them, and they lit citronella candles in the center of the picnic table to keep the mosquitoes at bay. Kelsi loved the tangy smell of the candles, and she stared into the center of the flame, while above them the night sky was a dark blue fading to black.

"Did you talk to Bennett today?" Kelsi asked Taryn when they were picking at fresh berries and debating about making vegan s'mores over the fire.

Taryn shook her head. "He's always so busy," she said. "Running around for that guy. Why, what's up?"

"Nothing." Kelsi sighed. "I don't know. Sometimes I feel like maybe New York isn't the best thing that ever happened to him, after all."

Taryn frowned. She looked impatient for a moment or maybe Kelsi just imagined it, because her face cleared.

"Are you kidding?" she asked. "Maybe he didn't tell you this, but he's been obsessed with Carlos Delgado since he was, like, nine. I mean, total hero worship. This is a fantasy come true for him."

"I know, and I think it's amazing for his career *and* his art," Kelsi said quickly.

"This is his dream, Kelsi," Taryn said. She looked confused, and taken aback. "I thought you understood that."

"I do," Kelsi said, feeling like the conversation had completely gotten away from her. "That's not what I meant at all."

But she didn't know how to explain what she meant. She didn't know how to talk about her boyfriend to her best friend, when the boyfriend in question was her best friend's brother, and Taryn was clearly feeling protective. And Kelsi knew why: Taryn had confided that she had spent years running interference with high school girlfriends of Bennett's who had tried to get to him through her. Kelsi understood.

But it made her feel so alone.

Taryn decided to get the stuff to make s'mores then, and Kelsi sat solo at the picnic table, inhaling citronella fumes and mentally kicking herself.

How was Taryn supposed to respond? Bennett was her brother. The fact that she and Kelsi were best friends just made moments like this incredibly awkward.

Because while Kelsi knew what a huge opportunity working with Carlos was for Bennett, she wasn't sure it was the best thing for *him*. Like, for his *character*. Tonight wasn't the first time she'd thought he was becoming kind of snobbish about art. She would have thought that the generous, enthusiastic guy she knew so well would have welcomed the opportunity to find *something pretty* for a nice old lady, instead of mocking her.

Her phone vibrated in her pocket, and she pulled it out. It was a text message from Bennett:

SORRY, BAD DAY, LOVE U.

And just like that, Kelsi's entire mood lifted.

How pathetic, she thought. She should be ashamed of herself for being such a *girl.* But she couldn't deny the flush of happiness that washed through her, altering the whole night around her. She couldn't deny that just hearing from him when she didn't expect to made everything seem better. So what if it was pathetic — it was also true.

She vowed to be more supportive and less judgmental.

It was only a summer, after all.

Only a summer, Kelsi thought, *and it's halfway over already.*

"You better save me some marshmallows!" she called across the clearing to Taryn, and found she was all but skipping as she got up and headed toward her friend.

The first step was to make sure that what she thought was happening was really happening, Ella told herself. There was no point doing anything until she was sure.

After all, Peter was beautiful and smoldering, and he could lure any unsuspecting girl into his little web. Ella knew this better than anyone. It wasn't so hard to imagine a scenario in which Taryn accidentally got involved with a hot guy one evening, only to discover later that it was *the* hot guy who'd treated Kelsi so badly way back when. In this imagined scenario, Ella found she could give Taryn the benefit of the doubt.

But she knew that was only because she didn't believe it.

Taryn knew exactly who and what Peter was. Ella was certain of that.

And because Ella was certain, she wanted to be extra careful in proving it. Because she could tell that Kelsi wasn't going to accept the ugly truth about her supposed best friend without a boatload of evidence.

This was how Ella convinced herself that her only option that Friday night was to follow Taryn.

Kelsi had gone down to New York again, a last-minute trip brought on because Bennett had to cancel coming up once again. Ella didn't think it was too cool that he kept doing that to Kelsi. She happened to be an expert on the long-distance thing, having first failed at it, and then succeeded at it, all during this past year. With the same person, in fact. One thing she knew: You had to make time for the other person or you could forget about it.

But Kelsi's long-distance relationship wasn't really what was occupying her thoughts tonight.

She was determined that tonight she'd figure out what was really going on between Taryn and Peter.

Ella lounged around in the living room in her old Juicy sweats, yawning and reading *Allure*, looking like she planned to spend the night in. She waited until Taryn got the inevitable call on her cell phone. When Taryn started whispering and giggling, and then took the call to the bedroom, Ella moved herself to the sunporch and changed into something more appropriate for going out — in this case, a denim miniskirt, layered tank tops, and ropes of long beads.

It wasn't that hard to slip out of the cottage and wait in the shadows by the side of the dirt road. By this point in the summer, Ella knew the whole stretch of that road like the contents of her closet. She could walk it with her eyes closed, which was a good thing, as it was usually far too dark to see anything, anyway.

Soon enough, Ella's eyes adjusted enough so that when Taryn walked past, she could see her — or enough of her, anyway. Ella would know that saucy little walk anywhere, it annoyed her so much. It was easy enough to follow Taryn, keeping to the shadows and trailing her all the way into town. Ella was grateful her cork-soled wedges were silent on the pebbles.

Once in the village, there were other people around and Ella was able to draw closer to her prey. Taryn was dressed for a party. Her jeans were supertight and low, and her black tube top bared most of her abdomen and all of her shoulders. It was the sort of outfit that *should* have looked cheap and, Ella noted sourly, didn't look anything but hot on Taryn.

It just made Ella all the more determined to bring her down.

Taryn walked with confidence up to the Lighthouse, the new-ish bar in town that Ella had so far been completely unable to do more than peer into.

Ella waited for the gigantic bouncers to do their job, and deny entry to underage Taryn, but she just flashed an ID and sauntered right in.

Ella gritted her teeth. *Ugh.* It had never occurred to her to get a fake ID. She'd always relied on her charm and the kindness of well-positioned boys.

Ella knew the bouncers were a lost cause, having tried to talk her way past them last summer, so she looked around for other possibilities. It didn't take long. Around the back of the bar, a guy who looked like a bartender stood next to the propped-open back door, smoking a cigarette. It helped that he was cute, but it didn't actually matter.

Ella smiled, and made her move.

"Hey there," she singsonged, swaying her hips as she walked over to him. "What's going on?"

"Smoke break," the guy said, and then looked surprised, like he hadn't meant to say something so obvious.

Ella smiled wider.

"What do you want?" he asked in a gruffer tone, clearly trying to be all tough.

"I want to go inside," she said, cocking her head to the side. "I want you to let me in."

He smiled back, as if against his will.

"Now why would I do that?" he asked.

"Because you like me," Ella suggested, encouraging him to agree with the jut of one hip.

"And what's in it for me?" he asked after a long moment. But Ella knew she already had him. It was right there in the smile he was trying to hide.

She let her hips roll as she sauntered to the open door, and pulled it open. She stepped close to him, but not too close, and looked up at him through her lashes.

"If you're nice," she told him in a low voice, "I'll let you buy me a drink."

And then, before he could react, she stepped inside.

Ella was feeling pretty good about herself as she navigated the forbidden zone of the Lighthouse. She figured she probably wouldn't be back any time soon, so she took a small detour from her Taryn surveillance to check the place out. It was all plush red booths and dark decor, and it made Ella feel like an adult just to be inside. She liked the big, modernist paintings on the walls and the funky music from a DJ spinning in the corner that filled the place with a sexy, underground vibe.

But she could only revel for so long before her mind returned to the purpose of her visit: the treacherous Taryn.

Carefully, Ella made her way through the maze of booths,

making sure that her face stayed largely obscured behind a group of girls here or a big guy there. It helped that the bar was so dark and smoky. Eventually, she found what she was looking for.

Taryn and the horrible — though, tragically, still freaking hot — Peter were sitting entirely too close together in one of the booths near the door. As she glared at them, Ella realized that her stealth was unnecessary, since Taryn hadn't once looked away from Peter's face.

Ella remembered exactly how mesmerizing he could be. Those dark, dark eyes and that cocky smile.

Ella couldn't believe that Taryn would do this to Kelsi. Ella's outrage simmered near a boil, but she held it in, and simply watched from behind a pillar.

They had a drink. They kept touching each other. They laughed and laughed. Eventually, Peter's hand disappeared beneath the table, and it didn't take a lot of imagination to work out where it went. Ella knew exactly what that felt like. She could see those feelings she remembered on Taryn's face. It was crazy that she was standing here, watching this happen.

Soon after, the happy couple threw some money on the table and headed for the door, with Ella not far behind. They never glanced around. Once outside, they started down the street. Ella danced around the bouncers — hoping they didn't get too close a look at her — and followed.

About halfway down the street, Peter stopped walking, and pulled Taryn up against the side of a building, at the mouth of an alley. They started kissing, fiercely. They were plastered together. It was hot, and it should have been private. Ella didn't know whether to stare, scream, or run away.

Taryn's hands were all over him. His hands were all over her skin, everywhere the flimsy tube top wasn't. He yanked her up against him and she wrapped her legs around his waist, and still, they didn't stop kissing.

It was only when they retreated farther into the shadows of the alley that Ella forced herself to turn and run away.

The next day, Ella spent the morning with her cousins on the beach, sunning herself, reading *Vogue*, and fuming.

Taryn joined the group just before lunch, looking sleepy and not at all guilty or ashamed.

Ella had to work overtime not to throw her magazine at Taryn's head. It was the extra-heavy fall issue, after all, and it might have knocked her out.

"Okay," Jeremy said, appearing in front of them. "Who's up for lunch?"

Ella smiled up at him, and let him pull her to her feet. She also let him kiss her a little bit — but not much; she had important things on her mind.

"Let's go to the Snack Shack," Beth said, naming the

deliciously greasy snack bar steps from the beach. "I want a big cheeseburger."

The group headed off to lunch together. Ella laced her fingers with Jeremy's, and liked the way he squeezed her hand.

"Are you having fun even though Kelsi's not here?" Beth asked Taryn as they walked.

Ella wondered how concerned Beth would be about Taryn if Beth knew what Taryn was really like. She remembered how cruelly Beth had treated Ella herself in similar circumstances, and pursed her lips.

"Oh, sure," Taryn said easily. "I'm pretty good at entertaining myself."

"Like last night," Ella said, as if agreeing.

Taryn looked at her. Always interested in something gossipy, Ella's cousins all but perked their ears.

"What happened last night?" Jamie asked, clearly thrilled at the possibility that something scandalous might have occurred. It was the writer in her, Ella knew. She always wanted the story.

"Oh, *I* don't know," Ella said casually. She looked at Taryn. "Didn't you go out?"

"Yeah," Taryn said, blinking. "I did. This place called the Lighthouse?"

"That new place," Beth said, nodding. "They have a

tough door policy. I can't get anywhere near it, unless I want to go there for lunch. And I think all they have then is clam chowder."

The conversation looked as if it was going to turn into a debate on door policies and New England clam chowder. Ella couldn't have that.

"Did you go by yourself?" she asked Taryn, with all the feigned innocence in the world.

Taryn looked at Ella again, like she could sense that Ella was after something but wasn't sure what.

But Ella knew that Taryn knew perfectly well what Ella was after.

"Actually, no," Taryn said slowly. "I kind of met this guy the other day."

"Met" was one way to put it, Ella thought.

"Tell us everything!" Jamie demanded, her green eyes sparkling.

"Not much to tell," Taryn said, and Ella had to suppress a snort. "Just a guy. He's cute, and kind of funny . . ."

So, Ella thought darkly. *That makes it okay to screw over Kelsi, is that it?*

"Do we know him?" Ella asked pointedly, trying to sound as if she was just casually interested. "Is he a summer guy or a townie?"

"He's just a guy," Taryn said again, her eyes meeting

Ella's, hard. Then she shook her head. "I'm going to run to the bathroom. I'll meet you guys over in the food line."

Because they didn't know enough to dig deeper, Beth and Jamie easily turned their attention to what they planned to order for lunch.

Jeremy, however, was just frowning at Ella.

"What?" she asked when her cousins had drifted into their preferred line — Jamie went for ice cream, Beth for her burger. "What's going on?" he asked quietly. "What do you care what that girl is doing?"

"It's *who* she's *doing*," Ella snapped. "We saw them together the other night, remember?"

"I know. I'm not an idiot." But he smiled at her, and shook his head. "So why do you care that your sister's roommate is another notch on Peter the Waiter's bedpost?"

Ella felt her heart catch.

"You know him?"

"Of course I know *of* him," Jeremy said. He shrugged. "Pebble Beach isn't that big."

Jeremy knew Peter.

That was so weird, to think about the possibility of Jeremy knowing things about her before he'd met her, but Ella brushed it away. There were more important things to worry about. Besides, Jeremy couldn't have known too much about her or he wouldn't still be here. She was sure of that.

"Well, Kelsi used to date him," she said. "I just think it's really trashy and gross that Taryn would do this to Kelsi."

"Does Kelsi know about it?"

"Not yet," Ella said. She made a face. "She'll be devastated."

Lowering her voice to a whisper, Ella told him about how she'd followed Taryn the night before, what she'd seen, and how there was no way to pretend it wasn't happening. Taryn really was doing this to Kelsi.

"Okay." He cocked his head as his brown eyes searched her face. "But you seem really invested, El. And a little bit insane. I mean, you actually *followed* her? And then *spied* on her?"

It did make her sound like a raving lunatic, actually, when he put it like that.

"I don't like it when people hurt my sister!" Ella exclaimed, knowing that she was coming off defensively.

"I don't know. It seems more personal," Jeremy countered, looking at her quizzically.

"No, it's just that I . . ." Ella started, but then she stopped. She couldn't bring herself to tell him that she had hooked up with Peter after he had just barely broken things off with Kelsi. "It's nothing," Ella finished. "I just don't want

126

to see Kelsi get hurt, that's all. Especially by her boyfriend's sister."

Jeremy smiled at her for a moment, and then sweetly touched her hand as he got up to get their lunches.

Ella hated lying to Jeremy, but looking at him, she just couldn't bear to tell him the truth. And between choosing the truth and having Jeremy leave her in disgust or hiding it and dealing with her own angst, Ella chose the latter.

And it nearly broke her heart.

Beth loved the cold, wet snap of the early morning in Pebble Beach. She got up when the light was just sneaking in through the pine trees. She liked to imagine the sun hitting Cadillac Mountain up north in Acadia National Park, then slipping down the coast to heat up the gray air just as she stretched outside her cabin and began her run.

This morning, Beth headed down the dirt road, then swung away from the main village of Pebble Beach. Once she passed the mile marker, she turned toward the forest trail.

That was where she met up with Jimmy each day.

Beth grinned widely when she entered the forest, because it was always so much fun to see him there. Waiting for her, his eyes bright, equally pleased to see her.

So far, everything with Jimmy was going great, which Beth almost didn't want to let herself think about for fear of jinxing it. They'd had a bunch of very casual, friendly activities. Not dates, Beth thought, because there had been no kissing, or even a hint of kissing. Just a lot of hanging out, doing the healthy, sporty things Beth loved.

Jimmy could swim for ages in the chilly ocean without getting winded. He knew some cool hiking trails that led to secret lakes Beth had never seen before. And he still wanted to meet in the woods every morning and start the day with a few miles.

"Looking good," was all he said this morning, as he fell into place beside Beth.

"You, too," she replied, and then they just ran, letting the woods wake up all around them.

They were almost finished with their loop when Jimmy turned to look at her, his eyes glinting with mischief.

"I'll race you back into town," he said. "Loser buys coffee."

"I don't feel like racing," Beth lied casually, and then took off with a burst of speed, laughing when she heard Jimmy's shouted protest behind her.

"That was unfair!" he yelled.

"You only think so because you can't catch me," Beth threw over her shoulder.

But those were words she was forced to eat two miles

and a defeat later. When she finally caught up with him outside the Wharf Café, Jimmy was looking especially smug. He handed her an iced latte.

"I thought *I* had to buy the coffee," she said. Or tried to say, as she was still out of breath.

"Nah." Jimmy tilted his head to one side. "I think it's cute that you thought you could beat me."

He smiled before she could protest, and Beth's annoyance died a quick death. He had such a great smile.

"Well, thanks," she replied with an eye roll, reaching for the latte.

"And in general," Jimmy added softly, "I just think you're cute."

Beth smiled back at him, sipping her latte and feeling her heart give a kick.

And with a perfect summer day all around them and the smell of the sea on her skin, Beth almost forgot that she'd lost the race.

"Where's Jimmy Neutron?" George asked later that day, while the two of them sat on the edge of the pier. They had stolen Beth's uncle's fishing poles and were casting lines off the end of the wooden walkway. George called it "Making like Huck Finn," which Beth thought was funny, even though she now sort of wanted to push him into the water.

"Excuse me?" she questioned, raising her eyebrows.

"Your new pal," George replied. "Isn't he surgically attached to you throughout the day?"

"Unlike some people," Beth said pointedly, "Jimmy actually works. He's a camp counselor at that baseball camp out on the coast road." She flicked some hair out of her eyes. "And your new girlfriend? What does she do again?"

"Well, she tans," George replied. "She applies enough sunscreen to block out the sun entirely, and then she lies on the beach. I don't actually see the point."

Beth kept her gaze on her fishing line, and the dappled water below. She'd hung out with Larissa a few more times, and thought she was okay — in a hyper, giggly sort of way. Beth didn't see any particular spark between George and Larissa — she just saw that Larissa thought George was funny. And George *was* funny, so she guessed that worked out.

"It makes perfect sense to me," Beth told George with a shrug, even though she secretly agreed with him.

George rolled his eyes and wiggled his fishing pole between his palms.

"Girls are weird," he said.

"Hey, guys," came a voice from behind them.

Beth turned to smile up at Jimmy, who was freshly showered after his long day of summer camp, and looking extra cute in his long-sleeved T-shirt, cargo shorts, and flip-flops.

Jimmy smiled at George.

George smiled back, but it didn't make it to his eyes.

"Catch anything?" Jimmy asked George, sitting down between the two of them.

"Not yet," George said. "But I'm working on my lies. You know, to tell my family. You can't fish if you don't lie."

Beth laughed. Jimmy looked at George for a moment, then turned his head and looked at Beth.

"What are you doing tonight?" he asked.

"I'm up for anything," Beth replied happily. "George said there's this outdoor concert out by —"

"Because I have two tickets to the Portland Sea Dogs game," Jimmy said, his excitement coloring his voice. "Want to go with me?"

Later, it occurred to Beth that George might not have completely enjoyed watching some other guy ask out his ex-girlfriend. Not because he still had feelings for Beth, of course, since he was with Larissa, but because . . . well, it was weird. But by the time Beth thought of that, she was sitting in Hadlock Field in Portland, staring at a replica of Fenway's Green Monster from across the baseball diamond.

And the truth was, she was having a great time.

There were warm hot dogs covered in yellow mustard and occasional sips from Jimmy's cold beer. Jimmy knew the complete stats of every single player on the field, and managed to share all that information without sounding like

SportsCenter. It was a beautiful summer evening, the home team was kicking butt, and she was out with a boy who looked at her like she was the only girl in existence. When he wasn't shouting along with the crowd, that is.

It seemed like every time their eyes met, they held on to each other for a few extra moments. Like it was hard to look away. Beth had to remind herself to keep breathing, and she couldn't get the smile off her face.

The Sea Dogs were ahead at the seventh inning stretch. Beth jumped to her feet and threw her arms over her head.

"Come on!" she cried, tugging at Jimmy's arm. "You have to sing!"

"I have a terrible voice," he protested.

"That's the whole point!" Beth tipped her head back and shouted out the words to "Take Me Out to the Ball Game," which she thought must have been imprinted on her brain when she was very little, because she might not have been to a baseball game in a long time, but she could remember every single word. Not only that, she *loved* singing it.

Jimmy stood next to her, adding his voice to the crowd's, and Beth loved the feel of his strong arm around her shoulders. It made everything seem magical.

As the last notes of the organ died away, Beth leaned over to watch a commotion near the dugout. The Portland players had released a pig onto the baseball diamond. Which would have been strange and silly enough, but this particular pig had a rake attached to its back, so it could rake the dirt of the infield.

Beth laughed so hard she felt tears well up in the corners of her eyes, and had to sag against Jimmy for support.

"How could you not tell me this was coming?" she asked when she could finally speak again. "What *is* this? Is it, like, a Portland tradition?"

But when she wiped at her eyes to clear them, she saw that Jimmy wasn't laughing. He looked serious and had a weird look in his eyes.

"What's wrong?" she asked, sobering.

"Nothing," he replied, and smirked. "I just don't think it's very funny, that's all. But you look pretty when you laugh that hard." He smiled and turned back to the game, but Beth winced. She didn't know how someone couldn't find the humor in something so inherently ridiculous. She smiled briefly, thinking that George would have thought the pig was hilarious. Then Beth looked over at Jimmy, sighed, and finished watching the game.

"I'm so glad we won!" Beth rejoiced, walking out of the stadium and into the heat of the packed parking lot to Jimmy's car. She had a good time at the game and had mostly forgotten the earlier incident about the pig.

Beth looked over at Jimmy who was, once again, strangely silent. "Wasn't it a great game?"

Jimmy grinned. "I can't believe that you want to talk about the game. Right now, I don't care about baseball at all."

"What do you —" Beth started, confused. But then he slid his palm around to the nape of her neck, pulled her close, and kissed her, hard.

Beth gasped. And then she kissed him back. Electric heat shot over and through her like she'd been hit by lightning, and she moved closer, angling her head for a better fit.

As people swarmed around them on the way back to their cars, Beth and Jimmy stumbled and he gently pinned her against the car for support. Jimmy kissed her lips again, gently this time. Then he followed the line of her chin down to her neck, which he kissed very softly, taking Beth's breath away. When he pulled back, he was smiling.

"We should go . . . somewhere else," Beth said. She shivered from the kisses and the sudden lack of body heat.

Jimmy grinned and kissed her again, knowingly. "Sure. Only if you promise not to talk about baseball."

Kelsi was pretty sure that she knew every single inch of I-95 that stretched between New York City and Maine, and could, if asked, draw the route in extensive detail from memory.

Which, she realized as she sat in Bennett's apartment, did not make the prospect of making the trip again appealing in any way.

When Bennett came out of the kitchen, Kelsi was sitting on his bed in the direct path of the air conditioner in the window, staring glumly at her backpack.

"I know," he said at once, coming over and climbing onto the bed next to her. "I don't want you to go, either."

Kelsi smiled at him, but she wasn't sure she managed to hide the weariness she felt. She didn't want to make the long drive back to Maine. She didn't want to wake up tomorrow morning and start missing him all over again. It seemed like everything was way harder than it should have been this summer.

But she knew that getting upset about it would only make their good-byes worse than they had to be. Kelsi took a deep breath and forced herself to smile.

"It's okay," she said. She reached over to touch his cheek, and then lay her head on his shoulder. "I'll see you next weekend."

But before he said anything, she knew, because he went silent and still.

Slowly, she sat back up, and searched his face.

"What is it?" she asked. She didn't get hysterical. She didn't even really change her expression. If anything, she just felt kind of numb.

"I don't think I'll be able to come up to Maine this weekend," Bennett said. He looked at her, then down at the floor. "Carlos is freaking out over this exhibit we're putting together. He thinks everything we have so far looks totally collegiate. I don't see me getting away for at least a few weeks."

"A few *weeks*," Kelsi repeated. As if repeating the words would help her make sense of them.

"The exhibit is coming up fast, and Carlos is determined to get that prima donna from Artspace to write him a good review," Bennett explained, his brow slightly furrowed.

Kelsi didn't necessarily know exactly what he was talking about, but she recognized that scornful tone of voice. It seemed like she was hearing it more and more these days. When had Bennett become so judgmental?

"Okay," Kelsi said, feeling as if she might just break down and sob. "You have to concentrate on work stuff. I guess I'll just see you when I see you."

"Don't worry," Bennett said then, kissing her. "It's all going to be okay."

And for a while, sitting on his bed and kissing him, wrapping herself around him, it was.

But then, inevitably, Kelsi found herself behind the wheel of her car, inching up I-95.

Don't worry, he'd said. The fact was, Kelsi worried over everything these days. What Bennett was thinking when he made his snide art observations, for example. Somehow it made Kelsi wonder if he'd started seeing her differently, too. At some point, he was bound to think she was *collegiate*, too, wasn't he?

Or maybe he just wished she were around more.

Kelsi felt completely torn. On the one hand, she loved her lazy summers in Maine with her cousins and wouldn't want to trade them. But on the other hand, there was no particular *reason* for her to be there. She could just as easily be spending her summer in Manhattan with Bennett — and for all intents and purposes, she was. She just seemed to go back up to Pebble Beach to do her laundry.

A twelve-hour drive to do laundry and look at the bay? Ridiculous. Not to mention, it was getting harder and harder to leave Bennett. It actually hurt physically. Especially when she had no idea when she'd get to see him again.

Kelsi plugged in her iPod, cranked up Joan Baez for some old-school angst, and tried to concentrate on the drive.

Many hours later, Kelsi tried to shake off her blue mood as she turned onto the coast road that led into Pebble Beach. She still felt exhilarated when she rolled down her windows and let the salt air rush into the car. The Maine night was inky. As she turned the car away from the water and headed toward the Tuttle cottages, she could hear the lonely spooky sounds of the loons calling to one another from the inland lake, and it made her sigh.

It was so beautiful, and yet she wished she were back in New York City.

She pulled her car in behind the cottage, got out, and stretched.

When Kelsi went inside, the cottage was hushed and empty. It was late, so Kelsi supposed her dad was sleeping. There was no sign of Ella, which wasn't surprising. Taryn had told Kelsi that when Kelsi was away, Ella practically lived at her boyfriend's house. It still surprised Kelsi that Ella had managed to hold on to one boyfriend for so long, but she was happy for her sister. She liked Jeremy.

Kelsi walked back into the bedroom, and was surprised to find Taryn there, just sitting on the bed.

"Are you meditating?" Kelsi asked, laughing. "I don't think I've ever seen you sit so still."

Taryn looked up at Kelsi with a strange expression on her face, but almost immediately she wiped it clean and went blank instead.

"I'm running out," she said quickly, tucking her cell phone into the pocket of her cargo pants. "I'm already late." She jumped to her feet.

Confused, Kelsi put out a hand as Taryn charged past her. Taryn stopped, and looked at Kelsi with that same blank expression.

"Are you okay?" Kelsi asked. "Did something happen?"

"I'm late," Taryn repeated, and there was no mistaking the coldness in her voice.

Bewildered and still wound up from the drive, words failed Kelsi.

So she just moved aside and let Taryn go.

Kelsi slept for almost fourteen hours, and when she woke up, she felt like a different person.

Puttering around in the kitchen, she decided to make breakfast while she mulled over Taryn's weirdness the night before.

Probably nothing, she concluded. Everyone got a little weird sometimes, and Kelsi had discovered that when Taryn got stressed, she often got a little crazy.

That was what she told herself right up until her best friend walked into the kitchen, visibly flinched when she saw Kelsi standing there, turned on her heel, and walked right out.

"Taryn!" Kelsi called out in disbelief, leaving her tofu scramble to burn on the stove.

She ran over to the door and saw that the other girl had stopped walking, though she didn't turn around.

"What's going on?" Kelsi asked Taryn's back. "Did I do something to piss you off?" But that was ridiculous — they hadn't even been in the same state for days.

"I forgot that I have to meet someone," Taryn said, still without turning. "I have to go."

And, again, she did.

Kelsi barely registered the fact that Ella had appeared from the sunporch, looking rumpled and sleepy-eyed. She watched Taryn walk away, and then she looked at Kelsi.

"What's up with her?" Ella asked with a frown, slipping into the kitchen.

"I have no idea," Kelsi murmured.

The late afternoon sun poured golden across the traffic on Route 1, making it seem beautiful instead of annoying — which traffic usually was. Ella leaned back in the passenger seat of Jeremy's car, and curled her long, bare legs up beneath her.

"This was a good idea," she told Jeremy, reaching over to put her hand on his knee as he drove.

"I can't believe it's August and we haven't had lobster rolls yet," Jeremy said. "*What* have we been thinking?"

Ella knew what she'd been thinking: that things were strange and upsetting with Kelsi, and that Kelsi's best friend was betraying her. Possibly she was doing so *at this very moment*. And that she had lied to Jeremy and was keeping a huge secret from him.

But Jeremy had probably been thinking about his job.

And Ella. That was one of the reasons she loved him so much, the fact that he was always thinking of her. Ella was used to guys obsessing over her, but Jeremy wasn't like that. He worried for her.

He'd gotten off work at noon today, and had told her to go home and shower off the salt and sand of the beach, because they were going on a date that required a road trip.

Ella had complied happily. She'd found her favorite pair of Bermudas — cut to emphasize the curve of her hips — and paired them with wickedly high espadrilles and a deep purple tank top. She looked like L. L. Bean gone naughty.

Which Jeremy had fully appreciated, of course.

"I don't know what you're wearing," he said the moment the screen door slapped shut behind them on their way out of Ella's house, "but it's already driving me crazy."

He'd grabbed her hips with his hands and pulled her to him, covering her mouth with his.

Ella poured herself into the kiss, wiggling closer to him and arching her back so she could feel him press tighter into her.

God, she loved touching him.

They'd barely made it into his car — only breaking apart from a blistering hot kiss when Beth and Jimmy interrupted them by walking around the side of Beth's cottage, dressed in whites and holding tennis rackets.

"You might want to get a room," Beth had suggested, swinging her racket for emphasis. "Maybe one a little farther away from your entire extended family."

Jimmy had just watched them, swinging his racket as if he was hitting a tennis ball. If he was offended by the PDA he'd just witnessed, he didn't mention it.

Ella and Jeremy looked at each other and laughed, and then kissed once more. But then they'd jumped in the car. The next person to come around the side of the building might very well be Ella's dad, and no one wanted *that*.

The moment Jeremy had started heading south out of town on Route 1, Ella had known where they were going. And she was thrilled. Lobster rolls at Red's were becoming a Jeremy and Ella tradition.

"What made you think of this today?" she asked him now, as they entered the town of Wiscasset.

"You've seemed sad lately," Jeremy said, smiling at her. "And you know I hate that. It's, like, my duty to make you smile, and I like that." Ella knew that she had been a little distracted recently, feeling guilty about not telling him the truth about Peter. Part of her knew that it was the right decision, but keeping something from Jeremy was tearing her apart.

Ella looked over at him, and then reached across the space between them to trace his lips with her fingers.

"And you're good at making me smile," she told him.

"I love you," Jeremy said simply, his smile crooked and perfect.

Ella let out a sigh of contentment, and looked around at the pretty town, where traffic was always at a crawl, and tourists browsed through antique shops while walking up and down Main Street's brick sidewalk. Here it was easy to forget about the whole Kelsi-Taryn-Peter drama, but every time she looked over at Jeremy, so perfect and so in love with her, she felt those little pangs of guilt again.

Jeremy parked, and then they walked hand in hand toward the little roadside shack that was Red's — easily identifiable from far away, thanks to the long line in front of it.

As a rule, Ella was opposed to waiting in line. But this afternoon was different. Jeremy was there with her, tickling her when she got impatient and making her giggle before she swatted at him.

"I will beat you down," she warned him at one point through more giggles. "Stop tickling me!"

"It's that snort that kills me," Jeremy said, completely ignoring Ella and tickling her again.

And then it was finally their turn at the window, which was just as well, because Ella could tell that the old couple behind them were growing a little impatient with their wrestling.

Luckily, Ella didn't care what they thought.

Jeremy ordered two lobster rolls, and Ella watched through the window as the woman picked out the best meat and threw rolls onto the grill. Red's lobster rolls weren't salad-y (which Ella found revolting), they were just overstuffed with lobster meat. Butter and mayo came on the side.

When their rolls were ready, Jeremy held the plates and they snagged prime seats on the deck, sandwiched between the Sheepscot River and the traffic on Route 1.

They sat side by side and looked out over the water. Jeremy fed Ella succulent bites of sweet lobster drenched in butter, and kissed her fingers when she did the same for him.

"This is perfect," Ella whispered. "Just what I needed. Thank you."

"You know I would do anything for you," Jeremy said, his dark eyes crinkling a little bit at the corners.

Ella looked at him and saw all of that love in his eyes. She felt something swell in her, something so intense she almost wanted to cry. Ella knew in that moment that she had to tell Jeremy everything. She loved him too much to have something this big between them. "Jeremy . . ." she began, not really knowing how to begin.

Jeremy looked at her expectantly. Suddenly she blurted it out, unable to stop the mess spewing from her lips. "I kind of had a thing with Peter, too. Right after he and Kelsi broke up. Like, within hours. She stopped talking to me when she found out last summer."

Jeremy blinked, and shook his head. Some emotion passed across his face, and he shook his head again, silently looking out over the harbor.

"Please say something," Ella begged, after a moment of terrible silence. Part of her wanted him to say something horrible, so she could yell or scream or *something*.

"I don't know . . ." he said, looking disgusted. "I mean, what do you want me to say?"

"I don't know!" Ella retorted, suddenly feeling exhausted by the stress of the whole thing. "I wanted you to know because I love you. But I can't apologize to you for my past. And I shouldn't have to." Even if the past repulsed her, too.

"Hey," he said, angrily. "Don't get mad at me. I'm not the one who hooked up with Peter the Tool."

Ella knew that she had messed up. She had selfishly blurted it out and now she was going to lose him. She had to look away as small tears began to fall down her cheeks.

"Ella, I'm sorry. Please look at me."

"I don't want to," she whispered.

"Look, Ella. I love you," Jeremy said, and he took her hand again, so she looked at him. His eyes were serious and he started speaking, slowly. "It kills me to think of you with another guy. And I especially hate thinking about you with Peter."

Ella gulped, trying to force down the sobs that were in her throat.

Jeremy continued. "But I know that it was all in the past. Honestly, I don't care what happened before me, okay? I really don't."

"Really?" Ella asked, quietly. "Because nothing before you matters."

"I know. It's hard for me to hear, but I know."

Ella sighed in relief and leaned in against him. Jeremy moved closer to her and put his arm around her shoulders. They looked over the water as the sun began to go down. "But, El," he said. "I think this thing about Taryn and Peter has to stop," he said gently. "It's like you're jealous or something."

"I am *not* jealous," Ella replied immediately.

"Not about Peter. About Taryn and Kelsi," Jeremy said in the same easy tone. "I know you feel like she's taking your sister away from you. Maybe you want to make up for what you did, but Taryn isn't you. This isn't your business."

He didn't understand, Ella thought, looking away. He couldn't possibly, but she also didn't know how to explain it to him, either. She didn't say anything, but luckily, neither did he. They just sat in silence, Ella in Jeremy's arms. They looked out over the water and the old, decaying fishing boats, breathing in the cool sea air, and Ella felt lucky and confused all at once.

It had been raining for almost a week, and Beth decided everyone had gone completely stir-crazy.

She stood at the screen door of her cottage, staring out at the grassy picnic area, which was now reduced to mud and rivulets. Sheets of rain obscured the view and made it all a little bit blurry.

Okay, *she* had gone stir-crazy, anyway.

The first day it poured had been fun. The little cousins jumped in the puddles, and the adults played card games while Beth, Kelsi, Jamie, and Ella had lounged around reading, watching movies, or catching up on sleep.

By the third day of unrelenting rain, however, Beth had suffered a severe sense of humor failure. She missed her morning runs with Jimmy. Because he worked rain or shine, Beth still had to sit around all day waiting for him.

Not, of course, that there weren't a million things to do around the Tuttle compound, Beth thought ruefully. Jamie had been knitting what seemed like entire sweaters, but then had randomly ditched Beth yesterday when they were supposed to go to Bed, Bath & Beyond for a dorm shopping spree.

Like it wasn't weird enough to be off buying things like hot plates and coffeemakers, all in preparation for some big new life Beth couldn't entirely picture in her head. She had been excited to pick out shower supplies, but at the same time, nervous. Change was hard. Especially when it involved things Beth had always taken for granted, like having her own bathroom and her mom doing her laundry.

Kelsi and Taryn, meanwhile, had been holed up in their bedroom with the entire seventh season DVD set of *Buffy the Vampire Slayer*. When Beth had peeked in yesterday — looking for Jamie — they'd both been weeping.

And Ella, alarmingly, claimed that she was *reading* in bed, and had barricaded herself on the sunporch.

Which meant that Beth had nothing to do but sit around all day, and Beth wasn't the kind of person who *liked* to sit around for days on end. She liked to *do* things. Normally, she loved her family's summer cottage, but today she felt trapped in it. Forced inactivity made her feel like screaming.

Which was very nearly what she did when George slammed in through the front door, like Kramer from *Seinfeld*, which Beth assumed George still watched in nightly reruns.

"The thing is," she said, hearing the crankiness in her own voice and not really caring since it was just George, "I'm not Jerry Seinfeld and you actually don't live next door."

"Really? This shocks me," George said.

"My point is, you could call ahead. Or, you know, knock?"

"Because you're so busy," George mocked her.

He stripped off the neon-yellow rain slicker he was wearing and they both watched as water cascaded from it across the floor. Underneath, he was wearing a long-sleeved T-shirt and cargo pants. And extremely muddy boots, which he left next to the puddle he'd just made.

Beth sighed as if she found him unbearably annoying, which made George laugh. In truth, she was happy to see him. He'd been sort of MIA lately.

"What have you been up to?" Beth asked, getting to her feet. "Please tell me it's been something fun, because I've hit complete cabin fever here," she continued gloomily, aiming her words over her shoulder as she headed into the kitchen to grab the roll of paper towels. Heading back out to the living room, she tossed the roll at George.

Predictably, he bobbled the roll of towels in the air and ended up batting it to the ground.

He was such an idiot. Beth felt a mix of affection and exasperation snake through her.

"Your problem is that you view the rain as your enemy," George announced. He tore off a paper towel square and ran it over his damp head, instead of at the huge puddle at his feet.

"The rain is fine," Beth contradicted him, just because she felt like being difficult. "You, however, I'm not so sure about."

"You manage to find things to do all winter long," George pointed out. "You don't have to sit here, being gloomy."

"If you're not going to be entertaining, you can leave," Beth told him, flopping back down on the couch.

George rolled his eyes and flopped into the armchair.

They sat there for a long moment in silence, listening to the rain batter the roof of Beth's cottage. Beth turned her gaze up toward the ceiling, knowing without having to go look that there would be a pool forming in the cellar and an inevitable leak in her parents' bathroom. Everything was damp, as if the cottage was a sponge and just soaked in the weather.

"You still seeing Jimmy Neutron, Boy Genius?" George asked after a minute.

Beth eyed him.

"We've been on a few dates, yeah," she said, pretending to be indifferent. The dates had actually all been great, and kissing Jimmy was amazing, but she didn't think George really wanted that information.

"That's cool," George said, his knee jerking in a staccato rhythm. Beth realized she still thought it was kind of cute that he was such a fidgeter. So she figured his new girlfriend probably thought so, too.

"How are things with Larissa?" she asked. "She seems really nice. You guys will have so much fun in Pittsburgh."

George shrugged.

"I don't know," he said.

"What do you mean?" Beth had to wonder if she sounded too interested when George looked at her. But she didn't know how else to sound. She didn't know what the rules were when it came to talking to her ex about his new relationship.

"She's definitely a nice girl," George said slowly. "Don't get me wrong. But I don't know if I really . . ." He shrugged again. "I just don't think she's right for me, you know?"

"Why not?" Beth asked.

"I'm not sure I can offer, like, a full analysis here, Beth," George said. "You either feel it or you don't, right?" Then he grinned. "The G-Man has high standards."

Beth rolled her eyes, but couldn't hold back her laughter.

"Spare me," she said.

"You know it's true," he retorted.

"I know you're a dork," she threw right back at him, and then tossed a pillow at him, too, as punctuation.

"Does George come around a lot?" Jimmy asked the next night when the rain had stopped. It was still gray, cold, and overcast, but at least it wasn't raining. When Jimmy had shown up after camp let out, Beth had practically tackled him with joy. His cheeks were a little bit flushed, his eyes sparkled green against the gray evening, and Beth wanted to rub his close-cut auburn hair against her palms.

Now they were walking along the coast road, where the water crashed against the beach and the wind kicked through the houses and cut to the bone. No one else was out, so it was like they were the only two people alive in the world.

Jimmy had not been too excited to find George hanging out in the cottage with Beth again.

"I think he's just bored," Beth said now, leaning forward into the wind. "He used to spend his summers with my family, so there used to be a lot more going on."

"Your family," Jimmy repeated.

"Yeah, he was like the unofficial boy cousin," Beth said. "Because we don't have one of those. Not our age, anyway."

"Give me a break, Beth," Jimmy said with a sigh.

"What?"

"You think your family is the big attraction?" He shook his head. "The guy isn't hanging out with your family. He's there to see you. What happened to that other girl he was hanging out with?"

As far as Beth knew, Jimmy had never actually met Larissa. He'd just heard Beth mention her.

"George just said she wasn't girlfriend material," Beth said with a shrug. "Whatever that means."

"I know what that means when a guy says it to another guy," Jimmy said, shooting Beth a look. "I also know what it means when a guy says it to the ex-girlfriend he can't seem to stop hanging out with."

Beth let her breath out, and tucked her hands into her jeans.

"Jimmy, we're just —"

"— friends, I know," Jimmy finished. He shook his head. "But does he know that? Seriously? Because it seems to me that he's just waiting."

"Waiting for what?" Beth asked.

"For you," Jimmy said impatiently. "Don't be *naive*, Beth."

Beth didn't know how to answer. She looked down at her muddy boots, and wished she could think of what to say.

Was George waiting? She certainly wasn't. But if she was honest, she knew that part of her had kind of liked the idea that Larissa hadn't been up to George's high standards. Because that meant that only Beth was. Surely, though, that was just normal, residual ex stuff that didn't mean anything.

She thought of how easy it was to talk to and banter with

George, to slip back into their old patterns. But she didn't still have romantic feelings for him.

Jimmy was so different from the other guys she'd known. Those guys being George, and last summer, Adam, who was a lot like George when all was said and done. Jimmy was something else entirely.

"Listen," Jimmy said. He stood there until Beth looked up, and she relaxed a little bit because he didn't seem mad or upset.

"I'm listening," she said.

"I like you," he told her, his eyes clear and, she could tell, completely sincere. "I think you like me, too, and we have a good time together."

"I think so, too," Beth said. There was something kind of amazing about having such a direct conversation. She felt electricity shoot through her.

"But I can't handle George," Jimmy said. "I tried to just roll with it, but he's always around. And he's all over you."

"He's not all over me!" Beth protested, feeling her cheeks heat up.

"He makes up excuses to touch you," Jimmy said very patiently, and Beth knew he was right.

"Okay," she conceded. "But I don't think he means anything by it. I think it's just habit."

"Tell me how I'm supposed to deal with this." Jimmy's

eyes searched hers. "Summer's almost over. Do I fight him for you? That seems pretty lame."

"There's nothing to fight about!" Beth exclaimed. She frowned, and tucked a stray golden hair behind her ear before the wind snatched it across her face.

"I'm friends with my exes, too," Jimmy said patiently. "But they don't hang out at my house, or . . ."

"George is just . . ." But Beth didn't know how to describe him anymore. She wasn't even sure why she was defending him.

"I kind of like him, to tell you the truth," Jimmy said. But he shrugged then, and let his hands fall at his sides. "But I don't want to compete with him."

Beth's head was reeling. "You're not competing with him." She took Jimmy's hands and squeezed them until he looked at her, straight in the eye. "You're not," she said again. "I don't know what's going on with George, but I do know that he and I are over. We broke up almost a year ago, and I've never regretted it."

"You're saying you're totally over this guy," Jimmy said very carefully, as if he expected her to deny it.

But Beth met his eyes. Because she knew this was right.

"Believe me," she said in the same tone, "I am completely over George."

Because she had to be.

17

On another gorgeous Pebble Beach day, Kelsi decided not to mope around the house, and took her frustrations out to the yard and focused them on the tetherball set. It was surprisingly therapeutic to hit the ball, sending it spinning and spinning on the end of its rope.

Kelsi was seriously considering installing a tetherball set in her dorm room next year. She had a feeling it would come in handy during finals.

She gave the ball a *whack* because she missed Bennett.

Then another, more vicious *whack* for his new Art Snob persona, which Kelsi now fully admitted to herself that she hated.

Whack for Taryn, and whatever *her* problem was these days.

Whack because Kelsi didn't know what to do with a best friend who was cold, distant, and seemed to be avoiding her.

Whack and then another, harder *whack* because when Kelsi asked, Taryn totally lied and said she didn't know what Kelsi was talking about, and that everything was fine.

Kelsi hit the ball back and forth, harder and harder, with escalating force, and then, finally, put everything she had into one last *whack*.

It was pretty satisfying to watch the cord wrap itself around the pole. She *almost* felt better about the fact that it was yet another Saturday and she wasn't with her boyfriend.

Almost.

Kelsi turned back toward the cottages.

"I wouldn't want to be that tetherball," a deep, familiar voice said. Kelsi turned and saw Bennett sitting on the nearest picnic table.

Kelsi felt herself gape at him.

She couldn't believe it.

There he was, stretched out across the bench, looking rumpled and adorable in his jeans and a Ramones T-shirt. He had stubble on his jaw, and his eyes were bloodshot behind his black glasses, but he was sitting there in all the glory of the Maine sunshine.

"I can't believe you're here!" she cried, and ran, hurling herself into his arms. She held him so close, she could actually feel his skin, and convinced herself that she wasn't dreaming. She shut her eyes and leaned into him.

"I knew I was coming up since yesterday," he whispered into her ear, pulling her down onto the bench and nuzzling her neck, "but I wanted to surprise you."

"This is the best thing that's happened all summer," she whispered back, letting him rock them both.

"Plus, I've bailed so many times, I thought you might not believe me, anyway," he admitted.

Kelsi pulled back so she could look him in the eye, and smiled. Then she kissed him.

"I'll always believe you," she promised.

Then she fell back into his arms, and felt like she could stay there forever.

It was the most perfect Saturday of the summer. Kelsi showed Bennett *everything*. She introduced him to all her relatives, and took him on a tour of Pebble Beach, from her favorite schooner spot on the rocky bluff to the pier. She pointed out the sand pits where the town held their Fourth of July clambakes, and the farmer's market where all the fresh produce was sold. They had coffee and shared a vegan cupcake at a little café Kelsi had always loved, and then walked up and down Main Street as night began to creep in.

"It's beautiful here," Bennett said. "New York feels like another lifetime."

Which Kelsi liked hearing. Because maybe realizing that there were things beyond Carlos's art world would be good for Bennett. Maybe it would remind him that he didn't have to be as pretentious and work-obsessed as it seemed everyone else in Manhattan was.

But Kelsi didn't say any of that. She didn't want to ruin the moment. So instead she just took his hand.

Later, they stood together on the edge of the pier, looking out over the water at the small, rocky islands that cluttered the bay. They were all pines and boulders, and they created fascinating shadows across the calm water, which Kelsi and Bennett took turns pointing out to each other. They stood there until the sun was completely gone, the last streaks of red and pink faded into the inky blue of the oncoming night.

Bennett sighed a little bit, and pulled Kelsi into the crook of his arm.

"This has been an amazing day. It's going to be tough to go back to New York tomorrow."

Kelsi let out a sigh of protest. "I don't want to talk about it yet," she told him. "We'll have to deal with it tomorrow."

Bennett kissed her, hard and long, and then kissed her again on her forehead.

"I love you," he said. "This summer has been so tough, but everything's going to be fine in a few weeks."

Kelsi smiled into his eyes. "I know. I'm glad," she said.

They held hands and walked back into town. They were standing on Main Street, debating whether to have dinner out or at home, when Kelsi saw a familiar figure detach from the jostling crowd outside Ahoy.

It was Taryn, who Kelsi had been expecting to run into all day. Somehow, they never had.

"She's going to freak when she sees me," Bennett predicted, laughter in his voice.

Kelsi hadn't told Bennett about the cold shoulder Taryn had been giving her. She thought that would only put him in an awkward position, and she didn't see the point in that. So she put on as big a smile as she could, fully prepared to pretend that everything was fine between her and Taryn.

"Hey there," Bennett said when Taryn drew close, her head down.

She obviously recognized his voice because she jumped, and her mouth fell open when she looked up and saw him standing there.

"Surprise," Bennett said softly.

His tone was strange, Kelsi thought — almost careful. But then she quickly forgot about that, because Taryn stiffened and looked from Bennett to Kelsi, and then back again.

"You've got to be kidding me," she said fiercely. "What are you doing here?"

"Surprising me," Kelsi said, feeling her stomach tense.

"Ease up, Taryn," Bennett suggested quietly, sounding tense.

"Whatever," Taryn snapped. She wrapped her arms around her middle. "I can't deal with this."

"Taryn —" Kelsi started, but Taryn threw up a hand and Kelsi's words died in her throat.

"Have fun," Taryn said bitterly, and then she turned on her heel and took off in the opposite direction.

For a moment, Kelsi and Bennett just stood there in the dark.

"What was *that*?" Kelsi asked, bewildered. She shook her head. "She's been acting like a weirdo for a while, you know. It's like she's mad at me about something."

"I wouldn't worry about it," Bennett said. He settled his arm around Kelsi's shoulders and kissed her ear. "In a few weeks, we'll be back in Massachusetts and everything will be back to normal."

"I don't know," Kelsi said, but Bennett kissed her again, this time on her mouth.

"Trust me," he urged her. "It's been a hard summer, but everything's going to be okay."

Kelsi wanted to believe him more than anything, so she kissed him back, and then gazed at him. He was more beautiful to her than the stars that crowded the sky above them.

"Come on," she whispered, and gave him a sexy smile. "Let's not waste our one night together in Pebble Beach."

The next morning was hard, as Bennett had to leave very early, and Kelsi got up to see him drive south, down the dirt road toward town. It was so early that she waved a hello to Beth, who emerged from her cottage already in her running gear, and looked surprised to see anyone else up and about.

Kelsi watched her cousin take off at a good speed, and then went back inside to crawl into her bed.

Much later that afternoon, she was awake again — but just barely. She was sitting sideways out in the hammock in the backyard, talking to Bennett on the phone and contemplating the sunshine that made it through the pines to warm the grass beneath her feet.

"I'm sitting in traffic outside Danbury," he told her. "But it was worth it. Are you okay? You sound strange."

"I'm just mellow," Kelsi assured him. "Yesterday was wonderful. I'm so glad you came."

"Me, too," he agreed. Then he laughed a little bit. "Don't get so relaxed you forget to miss me," Bennett teased her. "That's unacceptable."

Kelsi laughed, and enjoyed some highly satisfying mushy talk with him. So it was particularly embarrassing when she hung up to find Taryn standing there.

"How's Bennett?" Taryn asked, giving Kelsi an icy stare.

"He's fine," Kelsi replied uneasily. "Just stuck in traffic. Why?"

"He didn't tell you, did he?" Taryn blurted out. Her cheeks were very pink.

"I don't know what you're talking about!" Kelsi felt helpless. "What's going on with you?! What was last night all about?"

"I get that this isn't my business, but I can't believe you would want him to throw his life away," Taryn said in the same hard tone — which, Kelsi realized belatedly, was masking the fact that Taryn was very upset.

"You have to tell me what's going on, Taryn," Kelsi finally said firmly. "Or I can't contribute to this conversation."

Taryn took a deep breath, and then met Kelsi's eyes.

"Carlos offered Bennett a residency in his gallery, for next year. It's an unheard-of honor."

"That's *amazing!*" Kelsi agreed. She frowned at the phone in her hand. "I don't understand why he hasn't told me —"

"Because he turned it down," Taryn snapped. She took a ragged breath. "He turned it down, Kelsi, even though Carlos hasn't offered anyone a residency in years! He turned it down because he wants to stay in Massachusetts. With you."

Kelsi just stared at Taryn, uncomprehending.

"But that's . . ." She couldn't finish.

"Career suicide," Taryn finished for her. Her mouth tightened. "He won't listen to me. So it's up to you. What do you think he should choose? His entire future? Or you?"

Ella watched Taryn storm away from the hammock, headed in the direction of the beach.

She realized she was holding her breath, waiting to see Kelsi's reaction to the news.

Because she'd engineered the confrontation and because she was just hoping Kelsi would take it better than she had last summer when the person who'd betrayed her was Ella.

Ella had been watching the cold war between Taryn and Kelsi develop ever since she'd stumbled into it the morning Kelsi returned from New York. The last few weeks had been excruciating — Taryn had been avoiding Kelsi, who, in turn, just looked confused. And worse, hurt. Things had been better briefly when Bennett had shown up yesterday, but Ella suspected that Kelsi's good mood probably left with him in his rented Impala.

Ella hadn't been able to bear it another second, so when Taryn wafted into the living room earlier that afternoon, Ella had taken matters into her own hands.

"You need to tell her," she had announced.

Taryn had looked startled. As well she might. As far as Ella knew, Taryn had no idea that Ella was onto her.

"Um, okay," she'd said, acting as if she hadn't known what Ella was talking about.

"Kelsi deserves to know what's going on," Ella had told her. She couldn't remember ever having been more serious.

Taryn had stared at her for a long while. Ella had been afraid for a moment that she would demand to know how Ella had figured everything out, but she didn't. She just shook her head.

"You're a little bit spooky," she said, which Ella might have taken offense to, until Taryn continued, "but you're absolutely right."

Maybe she *was* right, Ella thought now, but that didn't make her feel any better if Kelsi's heart was shattered *all over* again.

Finally, Kelsi rose from the hammock, and turned so Ella could see her face. She looked dazed more than anything else. But not, Ella was relieved to see, in pieces.

Kelsi walked in the cottage door and didn't seem to notice that her sister was sitting right there until Ella shifted position on the couch.

"Oh," she said, distracted. "I didn't see you."

"It's better that you know," Ella said hurriedly.

Kelsi focused on her and shook her head.

"Are you kidding me?" she cried, color flooding her cheeks. "Did Bennett tell everyone on the planet except me?"

Ella frowned. "What does Bennett have to do with anything? I'm talking about Peter."

"Peter?" Kelsi's brow furrowed. It was like she didn't know who Peter was. Like she'd forgotten him. Ella rushed on.

"Your roommate is seeing him. In alleys, apparently." It was maybe a little bitchier than necessary, but Ella was off-balance. If Taryn hadn't told Kelsi about Peter, what *had* they been talking about out by the hammock?

"Oh," Kelsi said, her forehead creasing in confusion. "*That* Peter." She blinked as if to clear her head. "I can't imagine why you'd want to talk about that guy, El, but I can't do it right now. I have to lie down."

Ella was at a loss.

"Did you hear me?" she demanded. "Taryn is, like, *actively* dating him! They were all over each other in the Lighthouse!"

"I don't need details, Ella," Kelsi said impatiently. She

pushed her hair back from her forehead. "And what do you care what Peter does?"

Ella gaped at her. She actually felt her mouth drop open. "Why don't *you* care?" she threw back at Kelsi.

"I told her he was a player," Kelsi said dismissively, and waved one hand in the air to underscore her disinterest. "Taryn can handle herself."

She knew.

Ella literally couldn't take that in. Her body shook a little bit, and her ears popped, like she'd just gotten off an airplane.

But her voice still sounded kind of normal.

"You knew?" she asked, with a little squeak at the end.

"What?" Kelsi's eyes narrowed as she searched Ella's face. "Of course I knew. Why are we talking about this, anyway?"

"Because I don't get it!" Ella cried. The fact that she was upset seemed to finally dawn on Kelsi, who frowned. But Ella just kept going. "Why don't you care? Why aren't you outraged that Taryn would do this to you?"

Now Kelsi looked like she was at a loss.

"Do *what* to me?" she sputtered, and Ella could see that her sister had no idea what was happening.

"Let me be sure I understand this," Ella said shakily. "So when you found out what happened with Peter and me a whole *year* after the fact, that was so awful that it completely ripped us apart. But when *Taryn* has a full-on *fling* with the same guy, it's all good. Because *Taryn* is so wonderful that no matter what she does, you adore her. Is that it?"

Kelsi sighed. "Okay, you're kind of jealous of her," she began in that long-suffering tone that Ella hated. The one that meant that Kelsi thought she was a complete pain in the ass.

"I am not *jealous* of her!" Ella cried, completely losing her cool. "I just don't see why when I do something, it's the end of the world, but when she does the *exact same thing*, except even *worse*, you don't give a shit!"

"It is not the same thing!" Kelsi snapped. Then she closed her eyes. "I'm not going to fight with you about this. I don't even understand why you care! It's none of your business, Ella."

"Yeah, I can see that," Ella said bitterly. Her hurt feelings from the whole summer rose up in her like nausea. "Nothing you do is my business anymore. Now that you have the great and wonderful Taryn, why should you care about anyone else? You've barely even been here this summer, Kelsi. And you spend every one of the five minutes a week you actually are here with your college roommate — you know, the one you *lived with all year* — instead of even *pretending* to hang out with your family. Why did you even bother to come to Pebble Beach at all?!"

"You are unbelievable," Kelsi replied slowly, her eyes wide. "I don't even know what to say!"

"You don't know what to say or do about anything!" Ella yelled at her. "When you're here it's like you're on a different planet! Did I miss the part where we suddenly don't even talk? You look right through me! Have you even noticed the fact that I'm sleeping on a pullout couch this summer like a loser so that you can install your stupid friend in *my* bedroom?"

Kelsi put out both her hands, as if to ward Ella off. "I can't deal with this right now!" she said, her voice rising. "You don't understand. Bennett has made this incredibly —"

"Oh, right, *Bennett*," Ella interrupted with a roll of her eyes. "Because *he's* a winner."

"What did Bennett ever do to you?" Kelsi demanded.

"I, personally, couldn't care less about Bennett," Ella informed Kelsi angrily. "But he's spent the whole summer breaking plans with you, and every time you come back from New York you're more and more miserable. What's there for me to like?"

"Maybe you didn't notice that he was *here*, like, five hours ago?"

"For the first time all summer," Ella snapped back. "And I bet you'll be miserable all over again before nightfall!"

"I'm miserable because I want to be with him, Ella," Kelsi threw at her, furious. "I'm *in love* with him! I think about him all the time, I feel like I won't make it until the next time we have sex again, I feel like I can't breathe —"

"Wait — *what* did you say?"

Because Ella could not possibly have heard that right.

"Forget it," Kelsi said angrily. "You wouldn't understand."

She clearly didn't understand what *she'd* said. Or Ella had misheard her. Nothing else made sense.

But Ella had to be sure.

"Did you say until you have sex? *Again?*"

Kelsi looked flushed. "I don't know what I said."

But Ella wasn't going to let it go.

"So, you've slept together," she said softly, feeling young and small, and hating it.

They stared at each other across the living room and, it seemed to Ella, the entire span of their childhood.

"Yes," Kelsi said finally. "I have had sex with Bennett."

Ella nodded. She ran her tongue over her teeth and then nodded again. "When?" she asked.

"The first time was a couple of months ago," Kelsi said. "But I don't —"

"A couple of months ago," Ella repeated, "and you didn't tell me. Your virginity was this *huge* thing to you for *years*, and you didn't even tell me that you lost it."

She felt like such an idiot. She remembered sitting in the kitchen earlier this summer, trying to get Kelsi to open up about boys and sex. She'd thought it was Kelsi's same old problem of being pressured. She couldn't believe how stupid she'd been or that Kelsi had let her blunder around like that. Ella felt hot tears sting her throat. She wanted to curl up in a ball and cry.

Kelsi groaned. "I know this seems like a big deal, but really, I didn't mean to not tell you. I just didn't have time."

"But there was enough time to fill Taryn in on the details of what went down with me and Peter," Ella snapped. "Summer's almost over, Kelsi. You were *never* going to tell me."

That just hung there.

And the longer it hung there, the more Ella knew that she was right.

It was awful.

"You're making this into a much bigger thing than it is, El," Kelsi finally said, taking a step closer.

What she didn't say was that Ella was wrong.

And it was like Ella finally saw everything for the first time.

Kelsi liked Taryn better. There was no competition. Taryn had already won. Ella was just the foolish little sister, the one who didn't get the in-jokes. The one who tagged along, unwanted.

The little tramp who Kelsi didn't even include in her life anymore.

And that was how Kelsi wanted it.

"You're right. I was making it into a bigger deal than it was," Ella said finally, her tone as cold and hard as ice.

"Come on, Ella," Kelsi murmured, not quite looking at her.

"Don't worry," Ella said stiffly. "I won't make that mistake again."

And then she turned around and headed outside, as fast as she could walk with the tears blurring her eyes.

Beth had spent days planning out what she was going to say, but when she saw George waiting for her at the sandwich place behind Main Street, the whole plan just sort of disappeared.

She stopped walking and looked at him for a moment. The sandwich shop took over most of the airy little court-yard that sat between the Pebble Beach Inn and the Lighthouse. Before turning into a sandwich shop this year, it had been a private home. The building was an adorable white cottage with a picket fence, and it felt like the perfect place to while away a pretty Maine afternoon.

She had asked George to meet her here, at this brand-new place that they had never been to together and which, she thought, would be completely free of any George-and-

Beth residue. He was early, which made Beth chuckle. Normally, the concept of time was completely foreign to George. He sat under the red-and-blue-striped umbrella, which was wedged in the tabletop at a lopsided angle, and was drawing shapes with his finger against the wood.

When he saw her, his narrow face broke into a wide smile.

"Bethy!" he cried. "Finally! Did you know the sandwiches at this place are, like, epic?"

"Epic?" she echoed, with an amused smirk on her face. She was unwilling to launch so quickly into what she was afraid would be a tense, horrible conversation.

"We are talking a complete and dazzling array of condiments," George was saying excitedly. "Different varieties of pickles, like, seventeen different mustards including the vile Dijonnaise that will never again pass these lips —"

"You're insane." Beth interrupted his rant by swinging her leg over the bench across from him.

"I like my mustard to be mustard and my mayo to be mayo," George retorted. "Is that so wrong?"

Beth laughed. He was so funny. He would never stop making her laugh.

But he was also her ex-boyfriend. The first guy she'd ever loved. The only one she'd slept with so far. Their relationship had gone to some dark places and sometimes that darkness still stirred in her when she looked at him. Being here in Pebble Beach should have reminded her of better times with him. Instead, she shivered, remembering their awful breakup in the freezing-cold November morning with perfect, stomach-lurching clarity.

Beth wondered if maybe they shouldn't have even tried this friend thing out in the first place. Maybe it would have been better for everyone if they'd just said good-bye and then gone their separate ways. School was starting soon, anyway. They wouldn't see each other anymore, so what did it matter if they were friends or not?

It was all so complicated.

"Earth to Bethy," George said quietly, making Beth realize she hadn't answered him. "Why are you looking at me like that?"

The fact was, Beth didn't want complicated. Her new life was set to begin in a few short weeks, and she didn't want it to be threaded through with this same regret and history. She wanted to enjoy her last summer and pretend there had never been anything before. She wanted to move on. She really, truly did.

Was that *so* wrong?

"I don't know how to say this," she began.

"Already I love this conversation," he replied. His tone was light but his brown eyes darkened.

"I just don't think this friends thing is working," she blurted, throwing it out there. "Jimmy pointed out that maybe we're kind of kidding ourselves." Or *she* was, anyway.

"Why?" George demanded. "We're terrific friends! We're exactly the way we've always been!"

"That's the problem. You and I don't know how to *just* be friends anymore," Beth said gently. "And if you think about it, we never really were."

George seemed to deflate at that, and looking away, poked at the table.

Beth was aware of how the sun beat down on the pavement beyond their table, and the laughter from a group of people to their left. But all she could see was George.

His eyes were still too dark when he looked back at her, but there was nothing angry in his face.

Beth felt her heart clutch a little bit, because she could see that he understood. He wasn't going to fight. She felt a swell of something close to disappointment in her chest, but ignored it.

"I guess you're right," he said quietly. "If I was Jimmy, I wouldn't be a big fan of me, either."

"George, it's not really that —"

"Bethy. Please."

"Well, okay. It's partly that," she said with a sigh. "He thinks you want me back."

George just smiled and didn't answer.

Beth looked down and tried to focus.

"So," she said.

"How does this work?" he asked. "Are we enemies again?"

"We were enemies?" she asked, startled.

"I wasn't your biggest fan right after we broke up," George admitted. "I might have cast you as a Public Enemy of George. Number One, even."

Beth frowned. "We weren't enemies, we were broken up," she told him. "And we're not enemies now. I think we need some space, that's all. It's like we only have two speeds: be together the way we always were, or don't speak at all. And we can't be together like we always were, so maybe we should take a step back."

"A non-talking, non-hanging-out step back," George said. He shrugged when she glared at him. "I'm just clarifying things."

"I don't think it's good for us to hold on," Beth said firmly. "I think you should date Larissa. You guys have so much in common, and you'll both be in Pittsburgh next year."

George blinked. "What?"

"I'm not saying you stopped dating her because of me, I'm just saying that it seems like maybe you did and if you did, maybe you should —"

"Beth." He interrupted her and then paused for a

moment, as if trying to calm down. "I get that you're over me, but you don't have to give me dating advice," he said.

And then the problem was what to say next. Beth knew there was nothing else to say, but she couldn't quite bring herself to just get up and walk away from him.

Not yet.

"Okay," she said eventually. "I guess I'm surprised that you're so understanding."

"Always," he replied with the ghost of his smile near his mouth. "Or almost always."

Beth looked at him then and it was like she fell into his eyes the way she used to, and could see their whole history spread out there. She remembered meeting him at that party when they were both freshmen. How he'd started talking to her and never once looked at her boobs, and that was back when Beth thought her boobs had taken over her life. Their marathon television-watching weekends, and numerous debates on who kicked more ass: Buffy or Aeryn Sun. Mini golf tournaments, George's birthday bonfires on the beach, their Halloween costumes . . . Even last year's hooker attire seemed almost funny now that she looked back on it. He was her entire high school experience, all wrapped up in one goofy, maddening, adorable guy.

She loved him, she knew in her heart. But she didn't want to be *in* love with him again. She didn't want the history and emotion that swirled all around them.

"Good-bye," Beth whispered.

"Take care, Bethy," George replied in a low voice, and he didn't look away.

She wanted to reach over and touch him, but she didn't.

Instead, she rose to her feet and tried not to cry as she turned away and marched toward her new life.

Kelsi sat on the front stoop of Bennett's building and let the hot city night settle all around her.

She wished she hadn't worn her favorite pair of jeans, because the August night was way too muggy for them. But when she'd made up her mind to head for New York City, it had been the middle of the night. The next morning, the alarm had gone off way too early, and Kelsi knew she should be grateful she'd managed to put her shirt on right side out.

It had been a long, stuffy car ride, and she'd rushed to Bennett's building filled to the brim with all the things she needed to say. It was a little bit of a letdown to have to wait.

Or maybe it was for the best, because the truth was, she wasn't sure what she had to say was even coherent.

Either way, she had nothing to do but sit and watch New Yorkers pass back and forth in front of her.

Skinny jeans were still in, if the girls sauntering by were any indication, which made Kelsi smile wryly. She would *never* wear skinny jeans. Her thighs were reasonably sized, which was why she didn't need to put them in jeans that would make a giraffe look fat.

She was giggling at that mental image when she saw Bennett come around the corner.

Her heart skipped a beat.

She was beginning to realize it always would, no matter what happened.

He looked simultaneously tired and keyed up, walking fast with his head down, his iPod in his ears. She knew the only exercise he got was walking, and he liked to do it to musical accompaniment. Kelsi was secretly glad, because she got to study him as he moved closer.

He was nearly on top of her before he noticed that there was someone sitting on his stoop, and it took a few moments for it to register that the person sitting there was Kelsi.

Bennett's entire face lit up.

On cue, Kelsi's heart melted.

"What are you doing? Where did you come from?" He was asking questions and chanting nonsense as he took her into his arms, rocking her back and forth and pressing kisses to her neck and the side of her face.

"Surprise!" She couldn't help but kiss him back. It was like she could never get enough of him. Kelsi tried to steel herself.

"This is fantastic!" Bennett continued happily, stepping back to look at her. "What's going on? I can't believe you didn't tell me you were coming down!"

Kelsi's smile faltered, and she reached over to stroke his jaw. Then she dropped her hand.

"We have to talk," she said.

Bennett frowned. He eased back a little bit, so he could search her face.

"No conversation that begins with that sentence leads anywhere I want to go," he said. "What do we have to talk about?"

Kelsi sucked in a breath, and then dove in.

"Your residency," she said.

Bennett looked at her, and then dropped his eyes.

"Taryn is dead," he muttered.

Kelsi shook her head. Her hurt feelings threatened to swamp her.

"Why are you keeping secrets from me?" she demanded. "First you didn't tell me you applied for the internship and now *this*? What's going on with you?"

Bennett sighed. "I guess I just didn't know what to say, so I didn't say anything."

"What relationship are *you* in?" Kelsi asked, suddenly

furious with him. "I thought we talked about everything! I thought that was the *point*."

"Everyone is so excited for me to be here," Bennett said after a moment, not meeting Kelsi's gaze. "But what if I'm not sure that this is the place for me? What if I'm not so sure I like it? How could I tell you that, when I know you think this is the best thing that ever happened to me?"

Kelsi processed that for a minute.

"You've changed here," she said, and it was such a relief to say it that she felt a warmth flood through her. She'd been waiting to say it for far too long.

"What do you mean?" he asked, frowning at her.

"I mean that you're different," Kelsi said. She laced her fingers together in front of her and concentrated on them fiercely. "When you started this job, you only pretended to be all snotty about art because that's what Carlos wanted to hear. But I don't think you're pretending anymore — I think part of you really is that New York hipster guy, full of himself and mean to other people." She looked at him then. "What happened to just loving art? Why do you have to judge everything?"

"I don't . . ." But whatever he'd been about to say, he didn't finish. "This is exactly what I'm talking about," he said instead. "I'm not so sure I like it here."

They sat quietly for a moment. Kelsi concentrated on the sound of traffic along the avenues.

"None of this even matters," Bennett said finally, taking Kelsi's hand. "I'm sorry I didn't tell you before, but it's irrelevant, anyway. I'm not taking the residency. I don't want to miss you this much."

"Missing me has nothing to do with it," Kelsi began.

"It has everything to do with it!" Bennett cried. "I mean, I don't know about becoming a New York hipster or whatever, but I know I want to be with you. This summer has sucked, Kels."

"I know," she said.

"See?" He slid his arms around her. "Settled." He rested his forehead against hers and breathed in. "How could I give this up, Kelsi? I'd have to be crazy."

"Bennett," she said, feeling brave and scared all at once. She took a breath and then let it out. "You have to take the residency. You know you do."

"It's too late," he said stubbornly.

Kelsi gently removed herself from his arms, and stood.

"It's not too late," she told him. "You have to think about what's best for you, Bennett. Take me out of the equation."

"You're what's best for me," he told her.

Kelsi looked at him, and she knew that she loved him more than she ever thought possible. She wanted nothing more than for the two of them to return to their schools and be together the way they been had last year.

But she also knew that wasn't the right thing for Bennett.

It was so strange to see things that way. To love him so much that she would prefer to see him doing what he was supposed to do — even if it meant losing him — rather than staying where they were just to hold on to him when it was clearly wrong.

"Kelsi?"

He looked so scared. Kelsi realized he thought she was going to end things, which was almost funny. She smiled at him instead.

"I love you," she told him. She felt strong and sad all at once.

"I love you, too," he said, still frozen in place.

"But you have to think about what's best for you, Bennett," Kelsi whispered. "We both do."

21

Ella let herself out the back door, letting it slap shut behind her. She had a bottle of Jägermeister she'd just liberated from her father's freezer and no clear idea about the best way to enjoy it.

It was coming up on six P.M. and she was bored. She went over the list of everyone who was off having fun without her: Jeremy was having an Almost End of the Summer event with his lifeguard buddies. Kelsi was still in New York, which was just as well, as thinking about her made Ella's stomach hurt. Taryn was nowhere to be found, which Ella assumed meant she was off with Peter, which also made Ella feel ill. Ella hadn't seen Beth all day. A large Tuttle contingent had taken a field trip to Bar Harbor, but Ella hadn't been able to force herself out of bed early enough to go with them.

That left Ella — and, apparently, one other cousin.

"It's you and me," Ella called to Jamie, who she could see lying down on one of the tabletops at the far end of the clearing. "Get ready to have fun, because I need you to amuse me."

As Ella drew closer, she saw that Jamie was on her cell phone. And that she was acting seventeen kinds of shady, too, whispering and muttering and hanging up before Ella could venture too close.

"Hi!" she cried, scrambling off the table and standing beside it. "I didn't know you were here!"

"Obviously," Ella said. She took in Jamie's flushed cheeks and the crazed look in her green eyes. "What's going on?"

"Oh, nothing," Jamie began in a completely over-the-top innocent voice.

"You're lying to me!" Ella cried, pretending to be shocked. Actually, she was thrilled. Intrigue! Her boredom disappeared at once. She shook her head at Jamie. "I definitely do not approve."

Ella flounced over and took a seat as if Jamie weren't behaving like a freak at all. She placed the bottle of Jäger in the middle of the table and waved at it.

"What?" Jamie looked at the bottle. "Oh. No, I don't want any."

"You need some," Ella told her firmly. "And then you

need to sit down and tell me why you've been acting so bizarre all summer."

"I've been acting bizarre?" Jamie asked. But she sat down. "You think so?"

"I think I saw more of you last summer when you were in a summer program a zillion miles away," Ella said mildly, reaching over and taking a swig. She shuddered. "I think you're hiding something, and you know how I get when I want to know a secret."

Jamie laughed. "I remember that time you forced me to tell you all about how I had a crush on Jon Tenenbaum, who was on my swim team at day camp," she said, her eyes lighting up with the memory. "I don't even know how you did it."

"I have magic powers," Ella drawled, pretending to wave an imaginary wand in the air.

"That's one way of looking at it," Jamie said with a snort.

"Don't think you're going to distract me," Ella warned Jamie. "All this memory lane stuff is fine, but I have a one-track mind."

"You used to," Jamie agreed. "Now instead of 'boys, boys, boys' it's 'Jeremy, Jeremy, Jeremy.'"

"That was a lame line," Ella told her sadly. "I'm not even a little bit distracted by that. I don't even think you could call that *trying* to distract me."

Jamie laughed again, and then reached over to help herself to the bottle of Jäger. Ella waited as Jamie took a healthy pull, and then laughed when Jamie made a disgusted face.

"Good for what ails you," Ella told her.

"It's disgusting," Jamie sputtered. "It tastes like medicine!"

"You stop tasting it after a while," Ella assured her. "Now stop talking about Jäger and tell me why, for the first time in your entire life, college is like this taboo subject for you."

Jamie tipped her head back toward the sky for a moment, and then looked over at Ella.

"I could," she said, "but I'm much more interested in what's going on with you."

"With me?" Ella shook her head. "Another pathetic attempt to divert attention away from yourself. *Nothing's* going on with me."

"Oh, yeah?" Her cousin's eyebrows rose. "So you don't have any issues with Taryn?"

"What?" Ella didn't like this turn of the conversation at all. "She's fine," she said carelessly. "If you like that sort of thing."

"Uh-huh." Jamie gave her a knowing look. "And you and Kelsi didn't have a big fight or anything, right?"

That was when Ella realized that Jamie had no intention of answering any of her questions.

She considered that for a moment, and thought that

really, she wasn't all that interested in answering Jamie's questions herself.

The cousins stared at each other for a long moment, with only the sounds of the distant waves between them, and then they both started giggling.

Ella raised the bottle between them in celebration of secrets left untold, and they both took another swig. Then they lay down on their respective sides of the table and waited for the stars to come out.

Looking at the sky, it took a while for them to notice a strange smell in the air.

"Hey," Jamie said, frowning. "Is that smoke?"

Ella sat up too quickly, and turned around. Smoke was pouring out of Beth's family's cottage in thick plumes, dark against the evening sky.

"Oh, my God," Ella cried, scrambling to her feet. "Is anyone in there?"

Beth leaned in to give Jimmy one last kiss and then smiled at him. They'd finished an early dinner and were drawing out their good-byes on the corner of Main Street.

Beth couldn't believe it, but summer was officially over. Baseball camp was finished for the season, and Jimmy was leaving Pebble Beach to head home for a week or so. He said that his parents had a place on the Jersey Shore where he'd stay before heading back to Bucknell for the fall semester.

What a strange summer, Beth thought, pulling away from Jimmy to look into his eyes.

"I'll call you as soon as I get home," Jimmy said. "And we'll e-mail."

"I know," Beth said, grinning. Beth thought that sounded

like fun, and imagined herself writing e-mails to Jimmy from her dorm room in Washington, DC.

"You're going to have an awesome time at Georgetown," Jimmy told her, as if reading her mind. "College sports are on a whole different plane than high school. Your level of competition is going to skyrocket."

"I'm really excited," Beth said. Then she couldn't contain herself any longer, and let her smile break loose. "Oh, and I got you something to remember the summer by!"

"You did?" Jimmy cocked his head a little bit to the side.

Beth laughed in delighted anticipation. "I saw it in a gift shop on Main Street the other day and I knew you had to have it," she told him. "It was obviously fate."

She reached into her bag and pulled out a plush stuffed pig. It looked like an exact replica of the one they'd seen at the baseball game, right down to the spots on its side.

With great flourish, Beth presented the pig to Jimmy. And then totally cracked up laughing, as the image of the real pig at the Portland Sea Dogs game raced through her mind.

"I was going to try to put a rake on its back," she told him through her giggles, "but it's really hard to find miniature rakes in Pebble Beach. Who knew?"

She laughed even harder and then wiped her eyes, and that's when she noticed that Jimmy wasn't laughing.

"What's wrong?" she asked.

Jimmy held the pig in his hands and looked at it like it was some kind of alien life-form. Like he'd never seen a stuffed animal before.

"Nothing's wrong," he said, staring down at it. He looked up at Beth. He was frowning slightly. "I just don't get it."

Beth blinked.

"It's supposed to be, like, the pig from the Sea Dogs game," she said. Jimmy looked at her, wearing a quizzical smile. "You know, the one that raked the infield during the seventh inning stretch?"

Did he really not remember?

"Okay," he said, sounding confused. "But what am I supposed to do with it?"

By this point, Beth just felt kind of embarrassed about the whole thing.

"You're not supposed to *do* anything with it, Jimmy," she said. She gestured at the pig sort of helplessly. "I mean . . . it's a *pig*."

Jimmy looked at the pig, and then he looked at Beth.

"Thanks," he said, but Beth could tell that he was just saying it out of politeness. He really didn't understand why she'd given it to him.

"It's just funny," Beth tried again.

And as Jimmy looked at the pig again, as if he was waiting for it to explain Beth's behavior to him, Beth had the most unsettling thought.

Didn't Jimmy have a sense of humor?

Because as they stood there both staring at the stupid stuffed pig, Beth couldn't remember a single time when Jimmy had actually laughed about anything. Smiled, sure, but laughed?

And had he ever made *her* laugh?

She racked her brain. When they'd been at the baseball game, Beth had laughed so hard when the pig came out but Jimmy hadn't, now that she thought of it. At the time, she'd figured that he had just been really into the game, so he'd ignored the hysterical thing happening. And then later, it hadn't been an issue because he'd wanted to kiss her so badly.

But what if that wasn't it at all? What if he just didn't get why a pig with rake on its back was funny? Because Beth thought that something so over-the-top was something you either found hysterical or you didn't, and no amount of explaining would make any difference.

She and Jimmy said their good-byes, promised to keep in touch, and kissed again.

It was a long, sweet kiss, and Beth definitely enjoyed the touch of his mouth on hers, but something had changed. Her heart didn't pound the way it had before.

"I'm going to miss you," Jimmy told her.

"Same," Beth whispered, but she felt like she was lying somehow.

She watched him walk away from her, down Main Street and past the pier toward the car he'd loaded up with all his stuff from the summer. Then she tucked her hands into the pockets of her new American Eagle jeans and started her walk toward home.

She couldn't believe what had just happened. More than that, she couldn't believe she'd hung out with this guy all summer and hadn't noticed his humor deficit. How was that possible?

The thing was, Jimmy was so athletic, and that made him so different from the other guys she'd known. Now that she thought about it, that was pretty much all that they'd talked about: sports. It had been a lot of fun for Beth to talk so much about that part of her life, but there was more to her than just athletics.

As she headed inland toward the road that led back toward her family's cottages, Beth wondered if maybe she'd been paying too much attention to the *idea* of moving on. Because Jimmy was the first guy she'd noticed at all since she and George had broken up.

Maybe noticing him had just been a way for her to figure out that she *could* notice a guy. It didn't necessarily mean that she was destined to fall in love with him or anything.

And maybe she didn't want to be with a guy who didn't get why that pig was funny, after all. Maybe Jimmy was that other kind of summer boy — the kind you stopped thinking about as soon as the weather turned colder.

Beth was so lost in thought that she didn't notice the first fire truck that zoomed past.

It was the second one, or maybe the third, that caught her attention.

She looked up, and that was when she saw the smoke. It billowed up from the trees in front of her — the trees that, she knew, surrounded her family's little compound. The smoke was so dark that it was almost black against the sky, and it made absolutely no sense.

Beth knew what smoke meant. Everyone knew what smoke meant.

It was like her brain completely froze, and then reset.

Beth didn't even think. She just broke into a run.

Beth had run that same stretch a thousand times.

During the school year, she sometimes even imagined running it while she was inside on the treadmill, because it was so beautiful, the way the dirt road curved into the dark woods, like it was curving into someplace magical. The mossy smells and deep pine usually embraced her, soothed her.

Not tonight.

Beth pumped her legs and her arms, her throat burning. Burning. She wasn't aware of breathing and when she made it around that last, final bend, she skidded to a stop.

The fire trucks were pulled up into the clearing, and firefighters in their yellow coveralls marched here and there with their hats pulled tight on their foreheads. Smoke still rose behind them. A hose poured water, and men shouted to each other in thick Maine accents. Beth could see all that.

But it was what was behind them that Beth couldn't make sense of.

Her house was gone.

The walls still stood, but they were blackened, and bits of roof were clinging to the charred remains. Everything else was just . . . rubble.

She bent over to put her hands on her knees, gasping for air, as frantic, panicked thoughts of her family filled her mind.

"Beth!"

She heard her name, but couldn't move. Suddenly, her mother was crying at her side, and she folded Beth into her arms.

"Oh, thank God!" she cried.

Next to her, Beth's father looked ghostly pale. "We didn't know where you were, kiddo," he said gruffly, and pulled her into a hug of his own.

Beth was just thankful they were okay. Her mind reeled away from thinking that through. From picturing what them *not* being okay might have been like. It was paralyzing.

"Is everyone . . . ?" She was afraid to ask.

And then she didn't have to.

She found herself swept up by all of her cousins at once. Ella grabbed her around the neck and Jamie bear-hugged the both of them. The rest of the Tuttles came to stand around them in a small, quiet circle, as if they were trying to figure out together what was happening.

For a long time, Beth just stood and watched, dazed on such a deep level that she didn't notice the tears pouring down her face until they tickled her neck.

Behind them, a car pulled into the driveway, sweeping everything with its headlights. In the twin beams, Beth saw that there was nothing identifiable in the mess of blackened rubble. Everything was just . . . gone.

Kelsi came racing over, her eyes wide with panic, and when she saw Beth and her parents standing there, whole and sound, she burst into tears.

"What happened?" Kelsi demanded through her sobs.

But all Beth could think was: *Everything is gone.*

Her whole childhood. All those summers. She had known every single floorboard in that back bedroom she'd slept in. She knew every settling sound the little cottage made during the night. She could walk through the entire place blindfolded and barefoot. Sometimes during the cold, bleak Massachusetts winters, she would dream that she was back in her Maine bedroom, and would dream of waking up and fixing breakfast, then settling in the front room that caught the morning light. She couldn't believe that she would never sit on that couch again, or look out the tiny porthole window in the bathroom.

She had so many memories of the cottage that she couldn't accept that it had just disappeared while she was off having dinner. How could that be?

"It was the lint trap," Beth's mother was telling Kelsi. "In the dryer. The fireman told me it's fairly common. We're just lucky no one was hurt, and that the fire was contained in the one cottage. When you think what might have happened . . ." But she didn't finish.

Beth watched her father wrap his arm around her mother's shoulders.

Beth had never really thought about the fact that fire trucks were always racing to specific fires. Or the fact that fires could do this — reduce a whole lifetime of memories to ash.

She'd lost her virginity in that cottage just last summer. It had seemed so perfect because the summer before, also right here, she'd realized how in love she was with George.

She'd become who she was here, and now she didn't know what that meant. If her childhood was gone in a flash like this . . . if everything could change so horribly, so suddenly . . .

"Beth."

She knew that voice, and turned, not at all surprised that he was there.

What *was* surprising was that George was covered in soot. His hair was even wilder than usual.

"What happened?" she demanded, not realizing it was the first she'd spoken until she heard her own cracked voice. "Are you hurt?"

"No," George said, his own voice scratchy. "I saw the smoke. No one knew where you were." His dark eyes locked on to hers.

"I was in town," Beth whispered. "I was having dinner with Jimmy."

"Thank God for Jimmy Neutron," George said brokenly, and he even smiled. Then he reached into his pocket. "Here."

"What is it?" she asked, because his hand was still a fist.

"I found it in the —" George stopped, and his throat worked, as if it hurt to swallow. "I don't know why it wasn't burned."

He opened his hand.

It was the cork fisherman figurine that had once sat on the shelf above the light switch in Beth's bedroom. It was slightly blackened at the edges, but still, unmistakably, it was the same silly knickknack that George had named Chauncey.

Beth had never been so glad to see Chauncey's silly little

shape in her life. She grabbed it and smiled before putting it in her pocket. She felt more tears fill her eyes.

"I'm glad you're okay," George said quietly, and he smiled.

Beth watched him start to walk away, but it was like she saw it from a distance. She saw the remains of her cottage, and wondered, suddenly, what she was supposed to take from this.

She'd been so afraid of the way that her life was changing that she'd clung to a friendship with George, as if that could stall it. But the moment she'd suspected that maybe they could work their way back to what they'd been, she'd recoiled. Because she didn't want to go backward, she'd told herself. She wanted to go forward into her new life. And whatever else George was, he wasn't new.

But he was so much else.

She didn't want to be in love with him because it was complicated. They'd broken up for a lot of valid reasons. Loving him hurt. Beth had wanted a fresh start because it was easier.

But she thought that maybe, while the firefighters were trudging through the remains of her house, *easy* wasn't exactly in the cards anymore.

Not after tonight.

She pulled the little cork figurine back out of her pocket.

And as she held the remains of Chauncey in her palms, she knew two things. That she could make all the plans she wanted, but those didn't much matter when fate stepped in.

And that memories were more precious than she ever could have imagined — and sometimes, it turned out they were all that anyone had left.

Ella scurried into the room with a huge mountain of clothes obscuring her face.

"Are we doing laundry?" Jamie asked from where she was lounging across the farthest of the twin beds. Next to her, Beth snickered. The fact that she could laugh made everyone else relax a little bit.

The whole family was still in a state of shock. Beth's parents were bunking down on Ella's pullout couch, while the cousins and Taryn were having an impromptu sleepover in Kelsi's room. It felt bizarre, Kelsi thought, to be having an all-cousin sleepover party under such terrible circumstances.

Without discussing it, Kelsi had pulled the shades down on the windows that looked out over the remains of Beth's cottage. They'd all stared at it enough tonight.

"I don't do laundry," Ella said then, tipping her pile forward so that all her clothes fell onto the edge of the other bed, where Kelsi and Taryn were sitting cross-legged. "These are for Beth."

Everyone stared at the clothes, a riot of color that spilled across the coverlet. They'd all contributed from their own wardrobes. Beth was wearing a pair of Kelsi's sweats with one of Jamie's huge, blanket-like sweaters. She'd taken a very long, very hot shower and Kelsi had heard her crying softly under the spray. Now her eyes were red, but her skin was scrubbed clean and her flaxen hair was in a damp ponytail high on her head.

Kelsi thought Beth looked older somehow. She felt that way herself. Like everything had changed, in ways she couldn't even imagine just yet. She shook the feeling off.

"At least it was just the summer cottage," Jamie said softly, patting Beth's leg. "If it had been your house in Martin . . ."

Beth scooted off the edge of the bed and picked up one of the items of clothing Ella had brought. It was a tiny little tank top with the words TEAM JOLIE emblazoned across the front. It looked like it would barely fit Ella, much less Beth.

"If I didn't know better," Beth said drily, "I would think you set the fire yourself, El, so that I'd be forced to wear your clothes. After so many years of trying to get me into them."

Ella stuck her tongue out at Beth and flopped down on the chair in the corner of the room.

"Not to mention," Beth continued with that same dry, sort of dark tone. "I am totally Team Aniston."

"Of course you are," Ella said with a dramatic eye roll. "Big surprise there."

There was no real laughter, not yet. But it felt good to be all together, safe and sound despite the fire.

"What a night," Kelsi sighed, leaning back against the headboard. Next to her, Taryn smiled at her for the first time in what felt like ages. Kelsi guessed the fire had scared everybody into being nicer.

"I have a confession to make," Jamie announced into the quiet.

"About time," Ella murmured. Jamie glanced at her.

"Ella told me earlier tonight that she thought I was acting weird this summer, and it's true." Jamie took a deep breath. "I know I've been strange."

"Yeah," Beth said, turning to look at Jamie. "Like when you abandoned me before we were supposed to go dorm room shopping."

"Or when you refused to talk about hanging out in Northampton with us," Kelsi agreed, exchanging a look with Taryn.

Jamie looked up at the painted white ceiling with the cracks running through it, and then back at her cousins.

"I don't know why I didn't tell anyone," she said in a small voice. "I kind of didn't want people to freak out or anything."

"You can tell us anything," Kelsi assured her. "Nobody's going to freak out." After the fire, any other kind of freak-out seemed minor.

"Seriously," Beth agreed. "We're family."

Jamie raised her shoulders up and then spit it out, like she was afraid of losing her nerve. "There was this guy last summer, at the writing program," she said. "We were buddies. It was great. And then we e-mailed all year."

"Is this a friends to more-than-friends thing?" Ella asked. "Because I think Beth could give you some pointers on that one." She considered. "Or, you know, maybe not."

"Shut up, Ella," Beth said mildly.

"Go on," Kelsi urged Jamie.

"There was this reunion thing we had over spring break," Jamie continued, a bit dreamily. "Dex and I had broken up, and there was just something about Mark. It was like I'd never seen him before. We totally got together."

"Define *together*," Ella suggested, with a wicked grin.

"None of your business, gutter brain," Jamie replied tartly.

"Everyone knows what it means when people say 'none of your business,'" Ella murmured, arching her brows at everyone except Jamie.

"Can she tell her story?" Kelsi asked Ella. The sisters looked at each other for a moment. Ella had grabbed on and hugged Kelsi tight when her sister had arrived at the scene of the fire, but Kelsi was all too aware that they still hadn't talked since their big fight. Things were still unresolved between them. She wasn't surprised when Ella looked away.

"Anyway, we ended up seeing a lot of each other since then," Jamie was saying, blushing.

"I don't get the need for secrecy," Beth said. "Since when have we *not* been excited about you getting together with a boy?"

"We already know you met him at voluntary summer school, so I think the dork factor is already out of the bag," Ella said as if she was agreeing with Beth. She gave Jamie a lazy smile. "No need to hide it."

"You're hilarious," Jamie told her. She wrinkled her nose. "The thing is, Mark is deferring Amherst for a year. He was supposed to start with me this fall, but he wants to backpack around Europe instead. See the world. Get a little perspective." Jamie looked down, focusing on the silver rings on her fingers. "Do you know that I've been so focused on getting into Amherst that it, like, took over my whole life?"

The others all looked at one another, amused. Ella tried to muffle her snorty laugh. Beth laughed without hiding it.

"Um, yes," Kelsi said when no one else spoke. "We know."

Jamie looked up, and her green eyes were filled with something Kelsi had never seen in them before. Jamie had always been driven. But this was a different kind of ambition altogether.

"I'm going with him," she whispered. "I'm postponing school for a year. I'm just going to see what happens. It's so unlike me that it's been keeping me up at night, but it's the exact right thing to do. I know it." Jamie let out a breath, and gave a small smile. "Surprise," she added softly.

There was a beat of silence.

"Wow!" Kelsi breathed. It was more than a surprise. For studious Jamie, it was like a revolution.

"That sounds amazing," Taryn said firmly.

Beth shook her head. "Did your parents freak?"

"They were surprisingly okay with it," Jamie said, looking still taken aback by that unexpected turn. "But I was much more worried about telling you guys." She looked at Kelsi specifically. "I thought you'd give me a hard time, for sure."

"Me? Why?" Kelsi asked. "Are you kidding? I'd love to go to Europe!"

"Kelsi's not *all* about academics the way she used to be," Ella said, and giggled. "That's what happens when you get a life." She still didn't look at Kelsi, but Kelsi thought that it sounded a lot more affectionate than it could have. She chose to take it as a good sign.

"I thought everyone would think I'm crazy," Jamie said softly. "I've been obsessed with Amherst since I was a kid. All I've ever wanted was to go there. And now I'm putting it off a year?"

"Well," Beth said philosophically, "you were there all last summer. Maybe that eased your obsession a little bit."

"You don't think I'm crazy?" Jamie asked.

"No!" everybody cried — everybody except Ella.

"I think you're completely crazy," Ella said when everyone else fell quiet, "for not telling me so we could plan the perfect European wardrobe. But other than that, no way. I think you're going to have the most incredible time!"

"Me, too!" Jamie whispered, her green eyes glowing. "I'm so excited!"

Kelsi's phone buzzed then, and she picked it up to see that it was Bennett.

"I have to take this," she told the girls, and jumped to her feet.

Out on the back steps, Kelsi sat with her knees pulled up, hunched over against the chill of the night air. It still smelled like fire, even though there was a fairly decent breeze. Fire and yet mixed with the normal smells of Maine: sea, pine, and the hint of moss and deep greens from the woods. Far above, the moon shone down as if nothing had happened.

Kelsi filled Bennett in on the whole story, wishing all the time that he was there to give her the hug she so desperately needed. Even with the tense way they'd left things, she still believed that everything was better when he was near. It felt good to know that.

"I'm so glad everyone's okay," Bennett said quietly. "I mean, it could have happened in the middle of the night. I can't even think about it."

"We're really lucky, I guess," Kelsi said. It sounded strange to say that out loud. Beth and her parents had lost so much. So much of what made summer summer. The entire Tuttle family was changed by what had happened that night. And yet, they were so very, very lucky.

"What about us, Kelsi?" Bennett asked softly. "Are we okay?"

"I don't know." Kelsi thought her voice sounded loud in the night. "I hope so." She closed her eyes. "Have you decided what you're going to do?"

Bennett sighed.

"It's hard," he said. "I mean, I know you're right. I know I should take it. I just can't get my head around not being with you."

"Then it sounds to me like you've decided," Kelsi said. She sort of wished someone was witnessing this. She was being so brave. Everyone talked about loving someone and setting them free, but who really did it?

"I know that this could be the best thing that ever happened to me," Bennett said, his voice thickening. "I know I'd have to be crazy not to do it."

"I think," Kelsi said, "that you would regret it for the rest of your life."

"We'll just make it work," Bennett said then. "I mean, we have to. I can't do this without you, Kels. It's like I can feel myself turning into an asshole and you're the only thing that keeps me grounded. You keep me *me*."

"I want us to work, too," Kelsi told him then. "I think we can do it. I really do."

"I bet every couple says that," Bennett pointed out. "And yet no one seems to know of a long-distance relationship that lasts."

"I know of a long-distance relationship that worked," Kelsi said after a minute. "That's working right now, in fact. My sister's. They had some rocky times, but they're fine now. Great, even." She smiled, thinking of Ella and how much she'd changed in the past two years. "And believe me, she would have once told you long distance was impossible — and that's when she thought the term meant a guy who didn't happen to be right in front of her that very second."

"Well, if Ella can do it," Bennett said, with a laugh in his voice, "then I think we should be able to."

Kelsi didn't know what would happen in the coming

year. But she did know one thing: She wouldn't have changed a single thing that brought her to this point.

"I have a good feeling," she told him then.

"Oh, yeah?" She could hear him smiling.

"Yeah," she said. She was smiling, too, as if he were in front of her. As if she could reach out and take his hand. "I waited my whole life for you. Now that I've found you, what's a little commute?"

The back door opened, and Ella jerked upright, whirling around from the open refrigerator door.

"My God," she said when her heart stopped pounding, "you scared me to death."

Kelsi stood there, looking cold in her pajama bottoms and a Smith sweatshirt, her cheeks flushed pink. She held her cell phone in her hand, and Ella didn't even know why she'd been so startled: She'd known Kelsi had gone off to take a phone call.

Staring at her sister in the pale fluorescent light in the kitchen, Ella marveled at how much had changed over the past two years. And in a weird way, Peter was to thank for a lot of it. He was why Ella had felt so guilty and had gone out of her way to be good to Kelsi two years ago. He was why Ella and Kelsi had had that huge blowup last summer, which had been awful at the time, but which Ella thought had brought them even closer.

And he was responsible once again for what Ella had learned most recently: that it didn't matter who Kelsi felt closer to — she and Ella were sisters, and that was just deeper. Ella had done some bad things to Kelsi over the years. If it were Kelsi's turn to be a little less loving, well, Ella would just have to suck it up.

The phrasing of that was vintage Jeremy, of course, but the sentiment was true either way.

She didn't realize that the moment had stretched out until Kelsi spoke into the silence between them.

"Okay," Kelsi said, nodding. "You're mad at me. I guess that's understandable. I should have realized how upset you were."

Ella stood up a little straighter, and found herself noticing random things, like the new wind chimes one of her aunts must have hung near the hammock, and the low tones the brass tubes sent spilling across the clearing outside and into the open windows, lulling them all into a false sense of security.

She also noticed that Kelsi wasn't exactly apologizing.

Part of her wanted an apology. She'd been hurt, and she wanted Kelsi to acknowledge that — to feel guilty about it.

But if how angry she'd been about Taryn and Peter was any indication of how she'd felt about *herself* and Peter (which was what Jeremy kept saying), then maybe the fact that Kelsi couldn't make her feel better was related to everything that had happened over the last few summers.

Ella still didn't know why Kelsi had forgiven her for sleeping with Peter.

But she could, in a small way, return the favor.

"I'm not upset," she said, looking at her older sister. "I was, but I'm fine. You, however, look kind of sad. I mean more than we all do tonight."

Kelsi sighed and shrugged.

"It's Bennett," she said, and then she walked past Ella to collapse onto one of the kitchen chairs and let the whole story spill out.

How Bennett hadn't even told her about his decision and just pretended everything was fine when they talked, no matter how much she'd pushed. How Taryn had been so furious with her, and had spent the week of rain only speaking to Kelsi if it related directly to the *Buffy* episode they were watching. How Kelsi had confronted Bennett, and how they'd decided that he would take the internship.

"Which means we won't be together," Kelsi said softly.

"Why can't you be together?" Ella demanded, readjusting herself in the chair across from Kelsi.

"We can be together long-distance," Kelsi said, "but that's not the same as being together every day. We'll have to adapt."

"True. It's all ticking clocks and having to leave," Ella said, thinking of the year ahead. She didn't really want to confront going back to that place with Jeremy. It was so much better when they could see each other all the time — when phone and e-mail weren't their major forms of interaction. But Ella couldn't let herself think too much about it tonight. She would get way too sad.

But it was kind of nice to share a knowing sort of smile with her sister, because now they both understood how hard long-distance love *was*.

"The worst part," Kelsi confessed after a moment, "is that there's a really big part of me that wishes Taryn hadn't told me what was happening. I kind of want to ignore it, so we can just all go back to school and be together again."

"It's okay to be a little mad at her," Ella said. "It really wasn't any of her business."

"I know you don't like her," Kelsi said, looking up at her sister. She shrugged. "I just don't know *why* you don't. I thought you guys would love each other."

Ella chose not to dig into that statement, which clearly indicated that Taryn didn't like Ella very much, either.

"It's not that I don't like her." Ella leaned forward so she could be direct. "It's that . . . she wears the same bikini I do, in, like, the same exact way."

Kelsi blinked. "What?"

Ella raised one shoulder. "You know. If *you* wore the same bikini as me, there would be a whole different vibe. I like being the only person who wears *my* black bikini in *my* way." She hoped she was explaining herself.

Kelsi actually laughed. "I kind of see your point," she said.

"And I think that you can grow to tolerate and even appreciate someone who wears the same bikini," Ella said, slowly, "but you're never going to be BFF. You know?"

"I do know," Kelsi said. Her brown eyes were warm when she looked over. "Just for the record, I only have one sister."

Ella made a face, to hide the fact that she was ridiculously touched by Kelsi's words. "I know how many sisters you have," she assured her. "Believe me."

"Okay, then," Kelsi said. "Just so we're clear."

Ella could sense a difference in the air — an easing. The summer was over, Ella thought, and somehow she and Kelsi had found their way back to each other. She would try to remember that they always did.

"So," she said casually. She smirked slightly and raised her eyebrows at Kelsi. "You've had sex."

Kelsi flushed, and then shrugged. "It's true," she said. "I have."

Ella could see the traces of wariness in her sister's gaze. She felt a surge of protectiveness and love. She propped her chin on her hand and raised her brows.

"I don't know what you're waiting for," she said lightly. "Tell me everything."

The next morning, Beth woke up very early, jolting awake at her normal running time. She blinked in surprise to find herself trapped in a too-small bright blue sleeping bag she recognized as her aunt's from, like, the seventies. She was also crammed into a corner of Kelsi's floor between a gently snoring Ella and the wall.

First, she remembered Jimmy and the stuffed pig incident, and wondered again if she should keep in touch with him. She didn't know how to go about processing that.

Then she thought about going for a run on her own this morning, since she was awake — and that was when she remembered the night before.

And next she remembered that she no longer had running shoes. Then everything else hit her. It was dizzying.

Beth crawled out of her little sleeping area, and shivered the moment her warm skin encountered the cold morning air. It was already getting chillier, and any day now there might even be frost on the ground despite the summer sun in the sky. Autumn came so much quicker in Maine.

Beth snuck over to the window shade that Kelsi had shut the night before, and pulled up a corner of it so she could let herself peek out. Part of her truly expected the fire to have been some kind of horrific nightmare. She would peel back the shade and see the cottage standing where it had always —

But no, the nightmare was real.

Beth inhaled a deep, shaky breath as she looked at the pile of charred rubble that stood where the cottage should have been. The first morning light was just sneaking into the clearing, illuminating the dew on the grass and the sickening wreck of Beth's summers, which were now just so much dark ash.

Beth decided to crawl back into her sleeping bag, and pull the covers over her head. She couldn't cry, exactly, but she let the heaviness weigh on her until she drifted back to sleep.

Later that morning, all the girls woke up together when Ella and Kelsi's dad appeared in the doorway.

"Time to get moving, ladies," he announced, making Ella groan from beneath her pillow.

And so the Tuttles set about packing up the summer a

whole week early. Beth didn't like the idea of summer ending, but there was no use arguing about it. Beth's family's cottage was gone, and all the Tuttles were leaving Maine so that the landlord could decide what to do with the property.

Beth spent the first part of the morning realizing, as she observed the beautiful sunlight that illuminated the blackened remains of her cottage, that unlike her cousins, she had nothing to pack up. Talk about traveling light. She pulled on the jeans she'd been wearing the night before, and a T-shirt of Kelsi's that had Janis Joplin on the front, and that was pretty much that.

At first she tried to make jokes about it, because she was getting in the way while her cousins wrestled clothes into duffel bags and gathered up towels and shampoo and the shoes they hadn't worn since they arrived in June.

But it became a whole lot less funny the longer it went on, and Beth wandered out to the clearing to look at what was left. Her Uncle Carr was making trip after trip to his Jetta, packing boxes and bags, and he stopped when he saw Beth standing there.

"Are you okay?" he asked.

"I think so," Beth said, and smiled so he'd believe it. But inside, she wasn't sure. She was fine, of course. But she didn't think she was the same.

And it made Beth's heart hurt.

So she walked down to the beach, where she could look at the ocean. She whispered her final good-bye to the water, the way she did every year, and hated that this time it felt so much more final.

Everything changes, she told herself. The trick was to concentrate on the good things. Like how lucky she was to even be here, looking at the ocean. It could all have been so much worse. She'd only lost *things*.

Things could be replaced. It was people Beth knew she couldn't do without. And she knew that to be true this morning in ways she couldn't have imagined the night before.

After standing with her feet in the sand for a long time, she slid her flip-flops back on and walked back to the cottages to find her cousins sitting together in the clearing.

"There you are," Ella said. "We were waiting for you."

Beth slid onto the picnic table next to her, and the four Tuttle girls sat there in the quiet of the late morning, listening to the chimes in the wind and looking at the great mess of Beth's cottage in front of them.

"What a weird summer," Jamie said after a while, in a small, almost wistful voice.

"I think it's going to be fine." Ella's voice was very sure. "I'm sure they'll build a new cottage, right?"

"Even if they rebuild it, it won't be the same," Beth said then, with a sigh. "They can't replace the board in the kitchen where my mom recorded our heights. Or the secret place in the headboard of the bed in my bedroom. They can't bring it back."

"But on the upside," Ella said with a wink, "they might install a shower with actual pressure, so you don't have to keep using ours."

"That's what I love about you," Beth replied with an eye roll. "Always practical."

There was a long, quiet moment then. Seagulls wheeled in lazy circles far overhead, and the sun seemed sharp. Beth felt an ache in her chest, like crying, although she wasn't. Not yet.

Next to her, Ella made a small noise. "You guys," she said, as if she was trying to convince herself along with everyone else, "there will always be other summers. This one is just ending a little soon. That's all."

There was another small silence. Beth flexed her toes against the soles of her flip-flops and kept her eyes on the burned-down cottage. This felt like a bigger ending to her than just the last day of summer.

"I don't know," Kelsi said after a moment. She looked quickly at Ella, then at the pine needles carpeting the ground below her. "I'm not sure I'll come up for the whole summer next year. Driving back and forth to the city wasn't fun at all. If things work out with Bennett, I think I'll probably just stay there with him."

"I don't think I'll be back by next summer, either," Jamie

chimed in with a guilty shrug of her shoulders. "Mark and I want to travel as long as possible. And then we'll have to deal with culture shock and stuff before we go to school."

"It's nuts," Beth said then, still staring at the burnt remains of her cottage. "I can't imagine coming here and *not* staying in that cottage. A replacement cottage might be too much for me. Too depressing."

"I've never heard such a load of crap in my life," Ella scolded them, her voice outraged now. "This is Pebble Beach. This is where we come in the summer. *I* will be here with a smile on my face just as soon as I get the hell out of high school next summer. And I fully expect you to be here, too. Every summer. *Hello!*"

Kelsi rolled her eyes at her little sister, but her smile was affectionate. "You say that now, but just you wait," she warned.

"I'm not talking about this anymore with any of you. You're officially in trouble." Ella glared at each of them in turn. "You can't just abandon Pebble Beach!"

"Your boyfriend is three minutes away," Kelsi pointed out. "If that changes, you might change your mind."

"Things do change, El," Jamie agreed, grinning. "Look at me. Look at you."

"We are Tuttles. We belong in Pebble Beach," Ella said very deliberately. When Beth opened her mouth to speak, she waved her hand at her. "I don't want to hear any more! This is blasphemy!"

Ella jumped off the table and, with another glare at everyone, turned on her heel and flounced toward her sunporch. Laughing, Kelsi and Jamie followed her.

But Beth stayed put.

She drew in a breath. The usual golden sunshine and pine smell was tainted with the smell of the fire, but she knew that wouldn't last forever. Next summer, the woods would smell the way they were supposed to. The sun would be bright, the sky would stretch blue and clear above the green trees, and the water would smack against the shore.

It made her feel better to think of it that way, no matter where she might be at this time next year.

Beth stood in the dirt driveway to wave everybody off, which felt strange. Normally, Uncle Carr's family was the last to go.

"We'll see you at Thanksgiving," Kelsi said, giving Beth a huge hug. Then she climbed into her car, where Taryn was already picking through CDs in the passenger seat.

"I'm going to have to do the college-visit thing this fall," Ella reminded Beth with a knowing sort of look. "So, obviously, I'll have to hit D.C. and we'll party."

"Anytime," Beth said.

Ella got into the backseat, and leaned over the seat divider to give Kelsi bossy directions to Jeremy's house.

"I know where he lives!" Kelsi snapped, and then the sisters made faces at each other.

Beth smiled and waved as they drove away.

She helped her aunts and uncles cram the last tennis rackets and wet bathing suits into their cars, and then hugged Jamie tight after she'd stowed away her backpack.

"You better keep in touch," Beth told her fiercely.

"I'm going to keep a blog," Jamie promised. "I swear. It'll be like I'm just away at school."

"I'll see you," Beth said softly.

And then her cousins were all gone and she was alone. The clearing felt empty without them, and so did Beth. And then she knew what she had to do.

While her parents sat down with the fire inspectors, Beth took her last walk of the summer.

She walked down the dirt road, and turned onto the coast road. She followed it all the way into town and stopped for a moment to watch the summer crowds on the pier. Out in the water, the rocky islands glittered in the sunlight, and far above, birds made lazy circles around and around before landing in the upper branches of the tall pines.

Taking a deep breath of the salty air, Beth turned away from the water and followed the street that wound a bit inland, passing the town library where Beth and her cousins had spent many a rainy afternoon when they were kids. She found her way past cottages with bright flower boxes at the windows and bright white picket fences. She stopped at the farthest one before the woods and went around the house to the back.

George was packing up his car in the driveway behind the little house. When Beth came down the drive, he turned, looking surprised.

"Are you all right?" he asked. He closed the distance between them, his hands going out automatically and catching her shoulders.

For a moment, she couldn't breathe.

And just like that, Beth knew.

A warmth of certainty rushed through her.

"I lost so much last night," she told him in a rush. "I can't lose you, too."

George stared at her for a long moment, and Beth thought she could see the fire reflected in his eyes. But that didn't make any sense. The fire had been out for a long time now.

It was her whole life hanging here, Beth thought, waiting for him to respond. Waiting for him, the way she thought she might always be. The way Jimmy thought George had been waiting himself.

He wasn't just a guy, an ex. He was George. He was part of her.

"You have me, Bethy," he said softly. "And you'll always have me."

A tidal wave of emotion swept over Beth, and she caved. She barely felt George's arms as they went around her, barely heard whatever soothing things he whispered in her ear.

But she knew he was there.

And it meant everything.

After a while, Beth realized that he was holding her close, and she tipped her head up to look him in the eye. She loved the way his arms fit so perfectly around her. How their mouths were so close, almost touching, at the perfect angle. She loved that spark deep in his eyes, and she loved that she didn't care what happened next. She just wanted to keep holding on to him.

Beth tilted her head up, and kissed him.

He felt new and wonderful, and like coming home.

The kiss was so sweet she felt tears crowd her eyes. She didn't know what it meant — she was going to Georgetown and he was going to Pitt. They couldn't really get back together now. She wasn't sure she even wanted to. But something was there that they couldn't deny. It would always be there. They both sighed, and then smiled at each other.

"I should go," she told him, her smile fading. "My parents are waiting, and I just wanted to say good-bye."

"It's not good-bye, Bethy. Not for good." He touched her face and for a moment, she held his hand and looked in his eyes. There was so much history there, so much warmth and friendship and hope. Beth knew that no matter what, George would always be a part of her life.

"Bye, George," Beth said, softly. She turned back up the drive, willing herself not to cry. As she walked through the shady pines, taking in her last deep breaths of the clean Maine air, Beth thought about George and about everything that had happened this summer.

In a way, Beth *had* lost everything. But as she took one last look at Dean packing up the car, she suddenly realized that there was a lot more to these summers in Maine than just, well, being in Maine.

For a few brief, glorious weeks, everyone important to her set aside the rest of their lives — work, stress, school — and just cared about one another. Beth realized that even if her family lost everything, they would still have one another and they would all still have that feeling of Maine. And she now knew that George was somehow included in that wonderful, unconditional pact.

Beth smiled as the sunlight broke through the trees and onto her face. She knew that she was moving on to her future. But that didn't mean that she had to leave anything — or anyone — behind.

To Do List: Read all the Point books!

By Aimee Friedman

❏ **South Beach**
0-439-70678-5

❏ **French Kiss**
0-439-79281-9

❏ **Hollywood Hills**
0-439-79282-7

By Hailey Abbott

❏ **Summer Boys**
0-439-54020-8

❏ **Next Summer: A Summer Boys Novel**
0-439-75540-9

❏ **After Summer: A Summer Boys Novel**
0-439-86367-8

❏ **Last Summer: A Summer Boys Novel**
0-439-86725-8

By Claudia Gabel

❏ **In or Out**
0-439-91853-7

By Nina Malkin

❏ **6X: The Uncensored Confessions**
0-439-72421-X

❏ **6X: Loud, Fast, & Out of Control**
0-439-72422-8

❏ **Orange Is the New Pink**
0-439-89965-6

POINTCKLT